James Patterson first took the bestseller lists by storm with his phenomenally successful international No 1 bestseller '*Along Came a Spider*' in 1993. It introduced homicide detective Alex Cross, his highly popular hero who has also appeared in *Kiss the Girls*, *Jack & Jill*, *Cat & Mouse*, *Pop Goes the Weasel*, *Roses are Red*, *Violets are Blue*, *Four Blind Mice* and *The Big Bad Wolf*. James Patterson lives in Palm Beach County, Florida, with his wife and their young son.

JAMES PATTERSON

JACK AND JILL

HarperCollins*Publishers*

HarperCollins*Publishers*
77–85 Fulham Palace Road,
Hammersmith, London W6 8JB

www.harpercollins.co.uk

First published in Great Britain by
HarperCollins*Publishers* 1997

Copyright © James Patterson 1996

The Author asserts the moral right to
be identified as the author of this work

ISBN 0 00 775509 0

Set in Berkeley

Printed and bound in Great Britain by
Clays Ltd, St Ives plc

All rights reserved. No part of this publication may be
reproduced, stored in a retrieval system, or transmitted,
in any form or by any means, electronic, mechanical,
photocopying, recording or otherwise, without the prior
permission of the publishers.

This book is sold subject to the condition that it shall not,
by way of trade or otherwise, be lent, re-sold, hired out or
otherwise circulated without the publisher's prior consent
in any form of binding or cover other than that in which it
is published and without a similar condition including this
condition being imposed on the subsequent purchaser.

For John Keresty

Thank you—Robin Schwarz, for the poesy, Irene Markocki, Barbara Groszewski, Maria Pugatch, Fern Galperin, Julie Goodyear, Diana Gaines, Mary Jordan, Tommy De Feo, Frank Nicolo, Michael Hart, Stephanie Apt, Liz Gruszkievicz, Nancy Temkin, Donald M.

And, Richard and Artie Pine, Larry Kirshbaum, Charlie Hayward, Mel Parker, Amy Rhodes, Malcolm Edwards. And, last and most of all, Fredrica Friedman.

We share the same nightmares. I try to get them down on paper and temporarily make them go away.

PROLOGUE
THE GAMES BEGIN

I

SAM HARRISON swung his agile body out of the silver blue Ford Aerostar, which he had parked on Q Street in the Georgetown section of Washington. *Horror stories and games are popular for a good reason,* he was thinking as he locked the vehicle and set its alarm. *Not the comfortable sit-around-the-campfire horror tales and games we used to cherish as kids, but the real-life horror stories that are around us everywhere these days.*

Now I'm living one myself. I'm about to become part of the horror. How easy it is. How terribly, terribly easy to move past the edge and into the darkness.

He had stalked and shadowed Daniel Fitzpatrick for two long weeks. He'd done his job in New York City, London, Boston, and finally, here in Washington, D.C. Tonight he was going to murder the United States senator. In cold blood, execution-style. No one would be able to figure out why. No one would have a clue that might matter later on.

That was the first and most important rule of the game called Jack and Jill.

In many ways this was a textbook celebrity-stalker pattern. He knew it to be true as he took up his post across from 211 Q Street.

And yet, if anyone bothered to look more closely, it was like no other stalking pattern before. What he was going to do now was more provocative than secretly observing Senator Fitzpatrick down obscene numbers of Glenlivet cocktails at The Monocle, his favorite bar in Washington. This was the truest form of madness, Sam Harrison knew. It was *pure* madness. *He didn't believe he was mad. He believed only in the validity of the game of chance.*

And then, less than thirty yards across the shiny-wet street — there was Daniel Fitzpatrick himself. Right on schedule. At least, close enough.

He watched the senator stiffly climb out of a gleaming, navy blue Jaguar coupe, a 1996 model. He wore a gray topcoat with a paisley silk scarf. A sleek, slender woman in a black dress was with him. A Burberrys raincoat was casually thrown over her arm. She was laughing at something Fitzpatrick had said. She threw her head back like a beautiful, spirited horse. A wisp of her warm breath met the cool of the night.

The woman was at least twenty years the senator's junior. She wasn't his wife, Sam knew. Dannyboy Fitzpatrick rarely if ever slept with his wife. The blond woman walked with a slight limp, which made the two of them even more intriguing. Memorable, actually.

Sam Harrison concentrated fiercely. *Measure twice, measure five times, if necessary.* He took stock of all the details one final time. He had arrived in Georgetown at eleven-fifteen. He looked as if he *belonged* in the chic, attractive, fashionable neighborhood around Q Street. He looked exactly right for the part he was going to play.

A very big part in a very big story, one of the biggest in America's history. Or some would say American theater.

A leading-man role, to be sure.

He wore professorial, tortoiseshell glasses for the part. *He never wore glasses. Didn't need them.*

His hair was light blond. *His hair wasn't really blond.*

He called himself Sam Harrison. *His name wasn't really Sam. Or Harrison.*

For that night's special occasion, he'd carefully selected a soft black cashmere turtleneck, charcoal gray trousers, which were pleated and cuffed, and light-brown walking boots. *He wasn't really such a dapper, self-absorbed dresser.* His thick hair was cut short, vaguely reminiscent of the actor Kevin Costner in *The Bodyguard,* one of his least-favorite movies. He carried a small black duffel bag, swinging it like a baton as he now walked briskly toward 211. A camcorder was tucked inside the bag.

He planned to capture as much of this as possible on film. This was history in the making. It really was history: America at the end of its century, America at the end of an era, America at the end.

At quarter to twelve, he entered 211 through a darkened service entryway that smelled strongly of ammonia and of dust and decay. He walked up to the fourth floor, where the senator had his flat, his study, his love nest in the capital.

He reached Daniel Fitzpatrick's door, 4J, at ten minutes to twelve. He was still pretty much on time. So far, so good. Everything was going exactly as planned.

The highly polished mahogany door opened right in his face.

He stared at an ash-blond woman who was slender and trim and well kept. She was actually somewhat plainer looking than she had appeared from a distance. It was the same woman who had gotten out of the blue Jag with Fitzpatrick. The woman with the limp.

Except for a gold barrette in her hair, *a lioness from a trip to the Museum of Modern Art in New York,* and a gold choker, she was gloriously naked.

"Jack," she whispered.

"Jill," he said, and smiled.

II

IN A DIFFERENT PART of Washington, in a different world, another would-be killer was playing an equally terrifying game. He had found an absolutely terrific hiding place among the thick pines and a few towering, elderly oaks at the center of Garfield Park. He made himself comfortable inside a kind of tent formed by the overhanging tree limbs and a few sturdy, overgrown shrubs.

"*Let's get busy,*" he whispered, though no one was in the hiding place with him. This was going to be a wonderful adventure, a great fantasy. He believed it with his whole heart, body, and what remained of his soul.

He sat cross-legged on the damp grass and began to work on his face and hair. A tune from the rock band Hole was blasting from the speakers inside his head. This was really good stuff. He loved it to death. Disguises and costumes were a rush. They were about the only thing that let you truly escape, and goddamn; *did he ever need to escape*.

When he eventually finished with the costume, he emerged from the shadows of the trees. He had to laugh. He was cracking himself up today. This was the best yet. It was so goofy that it was great. Reminded him of a good joke: *Roses are red/violets are blue/I'm schizophrenic/and so am I.*

Hardy-har!

He definitely looked like an old, homeless fuck-bum now. He really did look like a hopeless old fart. Like the mangy character in the rock song "Aqualung." He had put on a white fright wig and a salt-and-pepper beard from an actor's costume kit. Any slight failure of his imagination, or skill as a makeup artist, was covered by the floppy hood of his sweatshirt.

The sweatshirt had HAPPY, HAPPY. JOY, JOY printed on it.

What an incredible, mindblowing adventure this was going to be, he kept thinking. *Happy, happy. Joy, joy.* That was the ticket. That said it all. The irony just killed him.

The killer-to-be crossed the park, walking quickly now, almost breaking into a run. He was headed in the general direction of the Anacostia River.

He began to see people. Strollers, muggers, lovers, whatever the hell they were. Most of them were black, but that was okay. That was good, actually. Nobody gave a damn about the blacks in D.C. That was a fact of life.

"Aqualung, oh-oh-oh, Aqualung," he sang the old rock-and-roll tune as he walked. It was from a really great old band called Jethro Tull. He listened to rock music incessantly, even in his sleep. *Earphones on all the time.* He had just about memorized the entire history of rock and roll. If he could just force himself to listen to Hootie and the Blowfish, he'd have it all down cold.

Hardy-har, he laughed at his Hootie joke. He was in a really fine mood today. This was such a cool, fucked-up, freaky blast of a head trip. It was the best of times, it was the worst of times. Best and worst, worst and best, worst and worse?

He had already selected the spot for the murder. The thicket of spruce trees and evergreens up close to the Southeast Freeway. It was wild and overgrown and nearly perfect.

The spot was at a ninety-degree angle to a grouping of *delapo,* yellow-brick row houses and a popular bodega on Sixth Street in Southeast. He had already scouted there, scoped the area out, fallen in love with his spot. He could already see kids from the Sojourner Truth Elementary School traipsing in and out of the corner candy store. The little buggers were so cute at that age.

Man, I hate cute with a passion you wouldn't believe. Little fucking robots was what they really were. Mean little parasites, too. *Kidz!* Everything about them was so *kute.*

He scrunched down and climbed under the thick, scratchy bushes and got down to serious business. He began to blow up several latex balloons — red, orange, blue, yellow ones.

These were big, really colorful suckers that no kids in their wrong mind could resist. Personally, he had always hated balloons intensely. Hated the forced, phony gaiety they seemed to symbolize. But most kids were ya-ya about balloons. Figured, right?

He tied about a ten-foot length of twine around one balloon. Then he secured the string to a thick tree branch.

The balloon floated lazily above the old tree. It looked like a pretty, decapitated head.

He waited in his tree hut. *He hung out with himself,* which he liked to do anyway.

"Got to waste some-*body* to-day," he hummed a little non-song to a non-melody. "Got to, got to. Just gotta, gotta, gotta," he sang and kind of liked the riff.

He heard something move near his hiding place. Something *cracked.* A branch or something? Somebody come to visit?

He listened closely. Tree branches were definitely being moved, stepped on, broken. Everything sounded amplified — like *SNAPPP!*

His mind had slipped away and the noise startled the hell out of him, if anybody really wanted to know the truth. His adrenaline was kicking in like crazy. He almost swallowed his Adam's apple.

Suddenly, the top half of a face appeared, came into his view. Just the forehead and the whites of someone's eyes.

THE WHITES OF HER EYES!

Peeking through the tree branches at him.

He saw the face of a tiny black girl. Five or six years old, really cute. She saw him, too. *Fair and square.*

I SEE YOU, HONEYPIE. YES, I DO. I SEE YOU!

"Hi." He said it real nice and polite, which he could be when he wanted to. He smiled, and she *almost* smiled back.

He spoke softly. "You want a big balloon? I've got plenty of extra balloons, balloons-a-plenty, balloons galore. Here's a cherry red balloon with your name on it."

The little girl just stared at him. She didn't speak a syllable. Didn't move. She was afraid of him — imagine that. Probably confused because he'd said her name was on one of the balloons.

"Okay, no balloon then. Fine. Forget about the free balloon offer. No balloon for you, little girl. That's okey-dokey with me. No free balloon today! No sir!"

"Yesssss, please," she suddenly said. Her brown eyes widened like blossoming flowers. Beautiful little girl, right? Beautiful, chestnut brown eyes.

"Stop being so shy, girl. Come over here, I'll give you a big, beautiful balloon. Let's see, I've got stop-sign red, sky blue, Popsicle orange, mellow yellow. Every color in the rainbow and then some."

He mimicked *somebody* — maybe it was that nutcase Kevin Bacon in *The River Wild,* which he'd rented a week or so back. Two weeks back? Who knew? Who cared! As he was speaking, his hand tightened on the handle of a miniature baseball bat, which was reinforced with electrical tape. The bat was eighteen and a half inches long, the kind the local gangbangers used to keep law and order in the projects.

He continued to speak to the little girl in a happy singsong that was actually sarcastic and ironic as hell.

"Red one," the girl finally chirped. Of course. She had a *red* ribbon in her hair. Red is the color of my true love's love.

She lightly, very tentatively, stepped out into the clearing. He noticed her feet were so tiny. Like a size *minus* three. She reached toward the colorful balloons clutched tightly in his outstretched hand. She didn't seem to notice that his hand was shaking badly.

Behind his back, he gripped the short, powerful ballbat. Then he swung — real hard.

Happy, happy. Joy, joy.

III

COULD THEYactually get away with murder — especially a high-level, provocative murder like this? Jack was confident they could. It was easier than anyone knew to kill another human being, or several of them, and never get caught, never even be suspected. It happened all the time.

Jill was scared and visibly tense, though. He couldn't blame her. In "real life," she was a Washington careerist, well-bred, bright, certainly not the typical murderous kook you read about. Not a very likely *Jill*, and therefore perfect for her part in the game of games. Almost as perfect as he was for his.

"He's drunk, completely out," she whispered as they stood in the dark foyer of the apartment. "It helps that he's such an absolutely repellent snake."

"You know what they say about our Dannyboy. He's a very bad senator, but a much worse date."

A hint of a smile — a nervous smile — from her. "Bad joke, but I can vouch for that. Let's go. *Jack*."

Jill turned on her bare heels, and he followed close behind. He watched the slight hitch in her step. Bewitching in its way. He watched her slender figure retreat through a tiny sitting room that was dimly lit by the hallway lamp. This was the way to the flat's bedroom, he knew.

They walked silently through a small living room. An American flag proudly stood beside the stone fireplace. The sight of the flag turned his stomach. Color photographs on the wall of a sailing regatta somewhere, probably Cape Cod.

"Izzit *you*, my dear?" a gruff, whiskey-soaked voice thundered from behind the living room walls.

"Who else could it be?" Jill answered.

Jack and Jill entered the bedroom together. "Surprise party," Jack announced. He had a Beretta semiautomatic out. It was aimed at the senator's head.

His gun hand was steady, his head very clear now. *History in the making. No chance to go back now.*

Daniel Fitzpatrick bolted up in his bed, surprised and burning mad. "What the bloody hell? What the . . . who the frig are you? How the shit did you get in here?" he slurred his words. His face and neck were bright red.

Jack couldn't help it — he smiled in spite of everything that was going on. The senator looked like a beached whale, or perhaps an aging walrus, in his fancy bed.

"I guess you could say I'm your despicable past, finally catching up to you, Senator," he said. "Now shut up. Please. Let's make this as easy as we possibly can."

He stared at Daniel Fitzpatrick and was reminded of something he'd read somewhere recently. Upon seeing the senator at a speaking engagement, a spectator had remarked, "*My God, he's an old man now.*" Indeed he was. Fitzpatrick was a white-haired, jowly, graceless, sprawlingly fat, old white man.

He was also the enemy.

Jack opened the black duffel bag and handed Jill a pair of handcuffs. "One hand to each bedpost. Please and thank you."

"It will be my pleasure," she said. There was a simple elegance in the way she spoke, acted, even the way she moved.

"You're in on this?" Fitzpatrick gasped as he looked around at the blond woman he'd picked up at the bar in La Colline. He seemed to be actually seeing her for the first time.

Jill smiled. "No, no. I was attracted by your vast, bloated belly, your alcoholic breath."

Jack took out the camcorder and handed it over to Jill. She immediately aimed it at Senator Fitzpatrick, focused, and started to film. She was good with the camera.

"What in God's name are you doing?" Fitzpatrick asked. His washed-out blue eyes were wide with astonishment, and then with genuine fear. "What the hell do you want? What's going on here? Dammit, I'm a United States senator."

Jill began with the shocked and surprised and *hurt* look on the senator's face. She pulled out to a wider shot. *Oops, a little too wide*. Grabbed focus again.

Jack smiled at the inappropriate outburst of bravado. How very *Fitzpatrick*.

Then, *voilà!* It was as if the whiskey-dullness swirling in his brain suddenly stopped. Daniel Fitzpatrick finally understood. "I don't want to die," he whispered.

Tears unexpectedly rolled from his eyes. It was strangely affecting. "Please don't do this. You don't have to hurt me," he said. "It doesn't have to be like this. Please, I beg you. Listen to me. Will you just listen to what I have to say?"

This was incredibly important footage, Jill knew. Academy Award stuff. Perhaps the documentary film of the century. They needed this for the game of games, for one of the surprises later on.

Jack walked briskly across the bedroom. He placed the Beretta inches from the senator's forehead.

This was it. This was where the exquisite game truly began. Rule two: *This is history. What you're doing is important. Never forget that for a single moment.*

"I'm going to kill you, Senator Fitzpatrick. There's nothing for us to talk about. There's no way out of this. You were a Roman

Catholic, so if you believe in God, say a prayer. Please say one for me, too. Say a prayer for Jack and Jill."

This was gut-check time. He noticed that his hand was shaking a little now. Jill saw it, too.

He told himself, *This is an execution, and it's well deserved. And this is most definitely a horror story that I'm in.*

He fired once, from a distance of no more than a few inches. Daniel Fitzpatrick's head exploded. He fired a second time. *Measure twice; cut twice as well.*

History was made.

The game of games had begun.

Jack and Jill.

PART I
IT'S TOMORROW AGAIN

Chapter 1

OH NO, it's tomorrow again.

It seemed as if I had no sooner fallen asleep than I heard banging in the house. It was loud, as disturbing as a car alarm. Persistent. Trouble too close to home?

"Shit. Dammit," I whispered into the soft, deep folds of my pillow. "Leave me alone. Let me sleep through the night like a normal person. Go away from here."

I reached for the lamp and knocked over a couple of books on the table. *The General's Daughter* and *My American Journey* and *Snow Falling on Cedars*. The mishap jolted me fully awake.

I grabbed my service revolver from a drawer and hurried downstairs, passing the kids' room on the way. I heard, or thought that I could hear, the sound of their soft breathing inside. I had been reading them Beatrix Potter's *The Tale of Peter Rabbit* the night before. *Don't go into Mr. McGregor's garden: Your father had an accident there; he was put in a pie by Mrs. McGregor.*

I clutched the Glock even more tightly in my right hand. The banging stopped. Then started up again. *Downstairs.*

I glanced at my wristwatch. It was *three-thirty* in the morning. Jesus, mercy. The witching hour again. The hour I often woke up without any help from outside forces, from things that go BANG, BANG, BANG in the middle of the night.

I continued down the steep, treacherous stairs. *Cautious, suspicious.* Suddenly, it was quiet all around me.

I made no sound myself. My skin felt electrified in the darkness. This was not the recommended way to start the day, or even the middle of the night. *Don't go into Mr. McGregor's garden: Your father had an accident.* . . .

I continued into the kitchen — my gun drawn — where I suddenly saw the source of the banging. The day's first mystery was solved.

My friend and partner was lurking at the back door like some high-octane version of a neighborhood hugger-mugger.

John Sampson was the noisemaker; he was the trouble in my life; the day's first disturbance, anyway. All six foot nine, two hundred forty pounds of him. Two-John as he's sometimes called. Man Mountain.

"There's been a murder," he said as I unlocked, unchained, and opened up for him. "This one is a honey, Alex."

Chapter 2

"OH, JESUS, JOHN. You know what time it is? You have any concept of time? Please get the hell away from my house. Go home to your own house. Bang on your *own* door in the middle of the night."

I groaned and slowly shook my head back and forth, working nasty sleep-kinks out of my neck and shoulders. I wasn't quite awake yet. Maybe this was all a bad dream that I was having. *Maybe Sampson wasn't on the back porch. Maybe I was still in bed with my pillow-lover. And maybe not.*

"It can wait," I said. "Whatever the hell it is."

"Oh, but it can't," he answered, shaking his head. "Believe me, Sugar, it can't."

I heard a creaking noise behind me in the house. I swung around quickly, still a little spooked and jumpy.

My little girl was standing there in the kitchen. Jannie was in her electric-blue-butterfly pajamas, in her bare feet, with a frightened look on her face. The latest addition to our family, a beautiful Abyssinian cat named Rosie, trailed Jannie by a step or two. Rosie had heard the noise downstairs, too.

"What's the matter?" Jannie asked in a sleepy whisper, rubbing her eyes. "Why are you up so early? It's something bad, isn't it, Daddy?"

"Go back to sleep, sweetheart," I told Jannie in the softest voice I could manage. "It's nothing," I had to lie to my little girl. My work had followed me home again. "We'll go upstairs now, so you can get your beauty sleep."

I carried her up the stairs, softly nuzzling her cheek on the way, whispering sweet nonsense, dream talk. I tucked her in and checked on my son, Damon. Soon the two of them would be heading off to their respective schools — Damon at Sojourner Truth, Jannie at Union Street. Rosie the cat continually crisscrossed between my legs as I performed my ministrations.

Then I got dressed, and Sampson and I hurried to the early-morning crime scene in his car. We didn't have far to go.

This one is a honey, Alex.

Just four blocks from our house on Fifth Street.

"I'm awake now, whether I like it or not, and I *don't* like it. Tell me about it," I said to Sampson as I watched the glittering red and blue lights of police cars and EMS trucks come into focus up ahead.

Four blocks from our house.

A lot of blue-and-whites were clustered at the end of a tunnel of leafless oak trees and red-brick project buildings. The disturbance appeared to be at my son Damon's school. (Jannie's school is a dozen blocks in the opposite direction.) My body tensed all over. There was a roaring, wintry shitstorm inside my head.

"It's a little girl, Alex," Sampson said in an unusually soft voice for him. "Six years old. She was last seen at the Sojourner Truth School this afternoon."

It *was* Damon's school. We both sighed. Sampson is almost as close to Damon and Jannie as I am. They feel the same way about him.

A lot of people were already gathered outside the Federal-style two-story building that was the Sojourner Truth Elementary School. Half the neighborhood seemed to be up at four in the morning. I saw angry and shocked faces everywhere in the crowd. Some folks were in bathrobes, others wrapped in blankets. Their frosty breath poured out like car exhaust all over the schoolyard. The *Washington Post* had reported that more than five hundred children under the age of fourteen had died in D.C. during the past year alone. But the people here knew that. They didn't have to read it in the newspaper.

A little six-year-old girl. Murdered at or near Damon's school, the Truth School. I couldn't have imagined a worse nightmare to wake up to.

"Sorry about this, Sugar," Sampson said as we climbed out of his car. "I figured you had to see this, though, to be here yourself."

Chapter 3

MY HEART was hammering and felt as if it were suddenly too big for my chest. My wife, Maria, had been shot down and killed not far from this place. Memories of the neighborhood, memories of a lifetime. *I'll always love you, Maria.*

I saw a dented and rusting truck from the morgue in the schoolyard, and it was an unbelievably disturbing sight for me and everybody else. Rap music with a lot of bass was playing from somewhere on the edge of the bright police lights.

Sampson and I pushed and angled our way through the frightened and uneasy crowd. Some wiseass muttered, "What's up, Chief?" and risked finding out. There was yellow crime-scene tape everywhere on the school grounds.

At six three, I'm not as large as Man Mountain, but we are both big men. We make quite the pair when we arrive at a crime scene: Sampson with his huge shaved skull and black leather car coat; me usually in a gray warm-up jacket from Georgetown. Shoulder holster under the coat. Dressed for the game that I play, a game called *sudden death.*

"Dr. Cross is here," I heard a few low rumbles in the crowd. My name uttered in vain. I tried to ignore the voices as best I could. Block them out of my consciousness. Officially, I was a deputy chief of detectives, but I was mostly working as a street detective these days. It was the way I wanted it for now. The way it had to be. This was definitely an "interesting" time for me. I had seen enough homicide and violence for one lifetime. I was considering going into private practice as a shrink again. I was considering a lot of things.

Sampson lightly touched my shoulder. He sensed this was bad for me. He saw it was maybe too close to the bone. "You okay, Alex?"

"I'm fine," I lied for the second time that morning.

"Sure you are, Sugar. You're always fine, even when you're not. You're the dragonslayer, right?" Sampson said and shook his head.

Out of the corner of my eye, I saw a young woman wearing a black sweatshirt with I'LL ALWAYS LOVE YOU, TYSHEIKA in white letters. Another dead child. *Tysheika.* People in the neighborhood sometimes wore the dark shirts to funerals of murdered kids. My grandmother, Nana Mama, had quite a collection of them.

Something else caught my eye. A woman standing back from the crowd, under the spectral branches of a withering elm. She didn't seem to quite fit with the rest of the neighborhood group. She was tall and nice-looking. She wore a belted raincoat over jeans, and flat shoes. Behind her, I could see a blue sedan. A Mercedes.

She's the one. That's her. She's the one for you. The crazy thought just came out of nowhere. Filled my head with sudden, inappropriate joy.

I made a mental note to find out who she was.

I stopped to talk with a young, intense homicide detective wearing a red Kangol hat with a brown sport jacket and brown knitted tie. I was beginning to take control.

"Bad way to start the day, Alex," Rakeem Powell said as I came up to him. "Or to end one, in my case."

I nodded at Rakeem. "Can't imagine a worse way." I felt sick in the well of my stomach. "What do you know about this so far, Rakeem? Anything juicy for us to go on? I need to hear it all."

The detective glanced at his small black notepad. He flipped a few pages. "Little girl's name is Shanelle Green. Popular girl. A sweetheart, from what I hear so far. She was in the first grade here at the Truth School. Lives two blocks from school in the Northfield Village projects. Parents both work. They let her walk home by herself. Not too goddamn smart, but what can you do, you know? They came home tonight, Shanelle wasn't there. They reported her missing around eight. That's the parents over there."

I glanced around. They were just a couple of kids themselves. Looked completely devastated and heartbroken. I knew they would never be the same after this horrifying night. Nobody could be.

"Either of them suspects?" I had to ask.

Rakeem shook his head and said, "I don't think so, Alex. Shanelle was their life."

"Please check them, Rakeem. Check both parents. How did she get here in the schoolyard?" I asked him.

Powell sighed. "That's the *first* thing we don't know. *Where* she was killed is the second. *Who* did it is strike three for the Mod Squad."

It was obvious from looking at Shanelle that she had been dumped here, probably murdered someplace else. We were right at the beginning of this terrible case. Lots of work to do. My case now.

"You know how she was killed?" I asked Rakeem.

The homicide detective frowned. "Take a look for yourself. Tell me what you think."

I didn't want to look, but I had to. I bent down close to Shanelle. I could smell the little girl's blood: *copper, like a lot of pennies had been thrown on the ground.* I couldn't help thinking of Damon and Jannie, my own kids. I couldn't stop the overwhelming sadness I felt. It ate at me, like acid splashed all over my body.

I knelt on the cracked and broken concrete to examine the body of the six-year-old girl. Shanelle lay in a fetal position. All she had on was a pair of flowered pink-and-blue underpants. A red bow was impossibly tangled up in her braids, and she had tiny gold earrings in her ears.

The rest of her clothes were missing. The killer had apparently taken the little girl's school clothes with him.

She was such a little beauty, such a sweetheart, I could see. Even after what someone had done to her. I was looking at the *how*; the manner in which the six-year-old girl had been brutally murdered sometime earlier that night, her whole life silenced in an instant of madness and horror.

I gently turned the girl's body a few inches. Her head lolled to one side, the neck probably broken. She weighed next to nothing. Just a baby. The right side of her little face was partly gone. *Obliterated* was a better description. The murderer had struck Shanelle so many times, and so violently, that little on the right side of the face was recognizable.

"How could he do this to such a beautiful little girl?" I muttered under my breath. "Poor Shanelle. Poor baby," I whispered to no one but myself. A tear formed in my eye. I blinked it away. There was no place for that here.

One of Shanelle's eyes was missing. *Her face is like a two-sided, two-faced mask.* Two sides to a child? Two faces? What did that mean?

There was another fiend on the loose in Washington.

A child killer this time.

Chapter 4

A TALL, THIN MAN in a black raincoat and black floppy rain hat slowly, cautiously approached the door of Senator Daniel Fitzpatrick's apartment a little before six o'clock Tuesday morning. He examined the outer hallway for signs of a break-in, a struggle of some sort, but didn't find any.

He was thinking that he didn't want to be outside this apartment or anywhere near it. He wasn't sure what he expected to find inside, but he had the feeling it would be bad. Powerfully, overwhelmingly bad. *This was so unreal.*

It was so odd for him to be here, a mystery inside a mystery. But here he was.

The man noticed everything about the hallway. Sprinkles of fallen plaster on the rug. Eight other doorways in sight. He had once been reasonably good at this routine. Being an investigator was like riding a bicycle, right? Sure it was.

He jimmied open the door to 4J with a square of plastic very much like a credit card, only thinner, slicker to the touch. He guessed that breaking and entering was like riding a bike, too. You never forgot how.

"I'm inside 4J," he spoke softly into a compact hand radio.

Sweat had begun to form all over his body. His legs quivered slightly. He was disgusted and he was afraid and he was definitely someplace that he shouldn't be. *Unrealville*, he called it in his mind.

He quickly walked through the foyer and into the small living room with photos of Senator Fitzpatrick on every wall. Still no sign of a break-in or any trouble.

"This could be a very nasty hoax," he reported into the radio. "I hope that's what it is." He paused. "Uh-oh. We have a problem."

Everything had happened in the bedroom, and whoever had done *everything* had left a terrible mess. It was worse than anything he could have imagined it might be.

"This is real bad. Senator Fitzpatrick is dead. Daniel Fitzpatrick *has been* murdered. This is not a hoax. The body appears to be fully rigorous. Flesh has a waxy tone. There's a lot of blood. Jesus, there's a lot of blood."

He bent over the senator's corpse. He could smell cordite, almost taste it on his tongue. Most likely from the gun that killed Fitzpatrick. Unfortunately, there was much more to the brutal murder scene. Too much for him to handle. He fought to keep his cool. *Riding a bike, right?*

"Two shots to the head. Close-in. Execution-style," he said into the handset. "Entry wounds about an inch apart."

He sighed heavily. Waited a moment, then began again. They didn't need to know everything he was seeing and feeling right now.

"The senator is handcuffed to his bedposts. Look like police cuffs to me. His body is nude and not a pretty sight. Penis and scrotum appear to have been gouged out of the body. There's *a lot* of blood all over the bed, a humongous stain. Big stain on the rug, too, where it soaked through."

He forced his face even closer to the senator's silver-haired chest. He didn't like it, being this close to a dead man — or any man, for that matter. Fitzpatrick was wearing some kind of religious medal. Probably real silver. He smelled of a woman's perfume. The tall man, *the investigator,* was almost certain of it. "The D.C. police are going to be guessing jealous lover. Some kind of crime of high passion," he said. "Wait — there's something else here. Okay. Hold on. I've got to check this out."

He didn't know how he'd missed it at first, but he sure as hell saw the note now. It was right next to the cordless telephone on the bed stand. Impossible to miss, right? But he'd missed it. He picked it up in his gloved hand.

The note was typewritten on thick, expensive bond. He read it quickly. Then he read it again, just to be sure . . . that the note was for *real.*

> Ah Dannyboy, we knew ya all too well
> One useless, thieving, rich bastard down
> So many more to go.
> Jack and Jill came to The Hill
> To hose down all the slime
> Most imperiled
> Was poor Fitzpatrick
> Right schmuck, wrong place, wrong time.
> Truly,
> Jack and Jill

He read the note over the hand phone. He took one more look around, then left the senator's apartment as it was: *in a state of bedlam and horror and death.* When he was safely down on Q Street, he called in the homicide to the Washington police.

He made the call anonymously. No one could know that he'd been inside the senator's apartment, or especially, *how it came to happen, and who he was.* If anybody found out, all hell would really break loose — as if it hadn't started already.

Everything was unreal, and it promised to get much worse. Jack and Jill had promised it.

> One useless, thieving, rich bastard down
> So many more to go.

Chapter 5

AT EVERY HUMAN TRAGEDY like this one, there is always someone who points. A man stood outside the crime-scene tape and pointed at the murdered child and also at me. I was remembering Jannie's prophetic words to me earlier that morning: *It's something bad, isn't it, Daddy?*

Yes, it was. The baddest of the bad. The murder scene at the Sojourner Truth School was heartbreaking to me and, I was sure, to everyone else. The schoolyard was the saddest, most desolate place in the world.

The chatter of portable police radios violated the air and made it hard to breathe. I could still smell the little girl's blood. It was thick in my nostrils and my throat, but mostly inside my head.

Shanelle Green's parents were weeping nearby, but so were other people from the neighborhood, even complete strangers to the little girl. In most cities, in most civilized countries, a child murdered so young would be a catastrophe, but not in Washington, where hundreds of children die violent deaths every single year.

"I want as large a street canvass as we can manage on this one,"

I told Rakeem Powell. "Sampson and I will be part of the canvass ourselves."

"I hear you. We're on it in a big way. Sleep is overrated, anyway."

"Let's go, John. We've got to move on this now," I finally said to Sampson.

He didn't argue or object. A murder like this is usually solved in the first twenty-four hours, or it isn't solved. We both knew that.

From 6:00 A.M. on, Sampson and I canvassed the neighborhood with the other detectives and patrolmen that cold, miserable morning. We had to do it our way, house by house, street by street, mostly on foot. We needed to be involved in this case, to do something, to solve the heinous murder quickly.

About ten in the morning, we heard about another shocking homicide in Washington. Senator Daniel Fitzpatrick had been murdered the night before. It had been a real bad night, hadn't it?

"Not our job," Sampson said with cold, flat eyes. "Not our problem. Somebody else's."

I didn't disagree.

No one Sampson or I spoke to that morning had seen anything out of the ordinary around the Sojourner Truth School. We heard the usual complaints about the drug pushers, the zombielike crackheads, the prossies who work on Eighth Street, the growing number of gangbangers.

But nothing out of the usual.

"People loved that little sweetheart Shanelle," the ageless Hispanic lady who seemed to have run the corner grocery near the school forever told Sampson and me. "She always buy her Gummi Bears. She have such a pretty smile, you know?"

No, I had never seen Shanelle Green smile, but I found that I could almost picture it. I also had a fixed image of the battered right side of the little girl's face. I carried it around like a bizarre wallet photo inside my head.

Uncle Jimmie Kee, a successful and influential Korean-

American who owned several neighborhood businesses, was glad to talk with us. Jimmie is a good friend of ours. Occasionally, he comes along with us to a Redskins or Bullets game. He supplied a name that we already had on our shortlist of suspects.

"What about this bad actor, Chop-It-Off-Chucky?" Uncle Jimmie volunteered as we spoke in the back of Ho-Woo-Jung, his popular restaurant on Eighth Street. I read the sign behind Jimmie: IMMIGRATION IS THE SINCEREST FORM OF FLATTERY.

"Nobody catch that motherfucker yet. He kill other children before. He the worst man in Washington, D.C. Next to the president," Jimmie said and chuckled wickedly.

"No bodies, though. No proof of it," Sampson said to Jimmie. "We don't even know if there really is a Chucky."

That was true enough. For years there had been rumors about a horrifying child molester who worked the Northfield Village neighborhood, but there was nothing concrete. Nothing had ever been proved.

"Chucky real," Uncle Jimmie insisted. His dark eyes narrowed to even thinner slits. "Chucky real as the devil. I see Chop-It-Off-Chucky in my dreams sometimes, Alex. So do the children who live around here."

"You ever hear anything more specific about Chucky? Where he's been seen? Who saw him?" I asked. "Help us out if you can, Jimmie."

"Oh, I gladly do that." He nodded his head and bunched his thick brown lips, his triple chin, his bulging throat. Jimmie habitually wore a chocolate brown suit with a tan fedora that bobbed as he spoke. "You meditating yet, Alex, getting in touch with chi energy?" he asked me.

"I'm thinking about it, thinking about my chi, Jimmie. Maybe my chi is running a little low right now. Tell us about Chucky."

"I know lots bad stories about Chop-It-Off-Chucky. Scare kids all the time. Even the gangbangers scared of him. Young mothers, grandmothers, put up handbills in playgrounds. In my stores, too. Sad stories of missing children. I always permit it, Detectives. Man who harms children is the worst. You agree, Alex? You see it differently?"

"No. I agree with you. That's why Sampson and I are out here today."

I knew a lot about the child molester who had been nick-named Chop-It-Off-Chucky. The unsubstantiated rumor was that he sliced off the genitalia of young kids who lived in the projects. Little boys and girls. No gender preference. Whether or not it was true, it seemed undeniable that someone had molested several children from the Northfield and Southview Terrace projects, not far from here. Other children had simply disappeared.

The police in the area didn't have the resources to create an effective crisis team to find Chucky, *if Chucky existed.* I had gone to the wall about it several times with the chief of detectives, but nothing had happened. Extra detectives never seemed available for duty in Southeast. The unfairness of the situation put me in a rage, made me as crazy as anything I can think of.

"Sounds like another Mission: Impossible," Sampson said as we walked up G Street, in the general direction of the Marine barracks. "We're on our own. We're supposed to catch a chimera."

"Nice image," I said, and had to smile at Man Mountain, his wild imagination, his *mind.*

"Thought you'd like it, man of culture and refinement that you are."

We were sipping steaming herb tea from Jimmie's restaurant. Patrolling the street. We *looked* like detectives, with our collars up and all. Big bad detectives. I wanted people to see us out working the neighborhood.

"No real leads, no clues, no support," I said, agreeing with Sampson's judgment of the current state of affairs. "We take the assignment, anyway?"

"We always do," he said. His eyes were suddenly hard and dull and almost scary to me. "Watch out, Chucky, watch your back. We're right on your sorry mythical ass."

"Your chimera ass."

"Exactly so, Sugar. Exactly so."

Chapter 6

IT WAS REAL GOOD to be working the streets of Southeast with Sampson again. It always is, even on a horror-show murder case that can make my blood boil over. Our last big case had taken place in North Carolina and California, but Sampson had been around only for the beginning and end of it. The two of us have been fast friends since we were nine or ten, and growing up in this same neighborhood. We get closer every year it seems. No, we *do* get closer.

"What's our primary goal here, Sugar?" Sampson asked as we walked along G Street. He had on the black leather car coat, nasty Wayfarer sunglasses, a slick black bandanna. It worked for him. "How do we know that we did good today?" he asked.

"We get the word out that we're personally looking for the Truth School killer," I said. "We show our pretty faces around. Make the families here feel as safe as we can."

"Yeah, and then we catch Chop-It-Off-Chucky and chop *his* off," Sampson said and grinned like the big bad wolf that he can be. "I'm not kidding."

I didn't doubt it for a minute.

When I finally got home that night, it was past ten. Nana Mama was waiting up for me. She had already put Damon and Jannie to bed. The concerned look on her face told me that she couldn't get to sleep, which is unusual for her. Nana could sleep in the eye of a hurricane. Sometimes, she is the eye of a hurricane.

"Hello, sweetheart," she said to me. "Bad day for you? I can see that it was." Sometimes she can be unbelievably sympathetic and kind and sweet, too. I like that she goes both ways equally well, and I can never predict which way is coming at me next.

As we sat together on the living room couch, my eighty-one-year-old grandmother held my hand in both of hers. I told her what I knew so far. She was shaking slightly and that wasn't like her, either. She is not a weak person, not in any way. She rarely shows her fear to anyone, even me. Nana Mama does not seem to be losing anything of herself; instead, she is becoming more luminous and concentrated.

"I feel so bad about this killing at the Sojourner Truth School," Nana said, and her head lowered.

"I know. It's all I've thought about today. I'm working every angle I can."

"You know much about Sojourner Truth, Alex?"

"I know she was a powerful abolitionist, an ex-slave."

"Sojourner Truth should be talked about when they mention Susan B. Anthony, Elizabeth Cady Stanton, Alex. She couldn't read, so she memorized most of the Bible for her teaching. She actually helped stop segregation of the transportation system here in Washington. And now we have this abomination at the school named in her honor.

"*Catch him, Alex,*" Nana suddenly whispered in a low, almost desperate voice. "Please catch this terrible man. I can't even say the name they call him — this *Chucky.* He's real, Alex. He's not a made-up bogeyman."

I would definitely try my damnedest. I was on the murder case. I was chasing down the chimera as best I could.

My mind was working overtime already. *A child molester? Boys and girls. Now a child killer? Chop-It-Off-Chucky? Was he real, or had he been made up by frightened children? Was he a chimera? Had he murdered Shanelle Green?*

I needed to pound the piano on our porch for a little while after Nana went up to bed. I played "Jazz Baby" and "The Man I Love," but the piano wasn't the ticket that night.

Just before I fell off to sleep, I remembered something. Senator Daniel Fitzpatrick had been murdered in Georgetown. What a day it had been. What a nightmare.

Two of them.

Chapter 7

JACK AND JILL.

   Sam and Sara.

   Whoever they really were, the two of them lay on their stomachs on a tasteful, knock-off Persian rug in the small living room of her Washington pied-à-terre. It was a kind of safe house. A fire blazed and crackled; fragrant apple logs were being crisped. They were playing a board game on the rug, which covered a hatched parquet floor. It was a special game. Unique in every way. *The game of life and death,* they called it.

   "I feel like a damn Washington, D.C., Georgetown University white liberal yuppie," Sam Harrison said and smiled at the unlikely image created in his mind.

   "Hey, I resemble that remark." Sara Rosen made a pouting face. She was kidding. She and Sam weren't yuppies. Sam certainly wasn't.

   And yet a guinea hen *was* roasting in the kitchen, the aroma sweetening the air. They *were* playing a parlor game on the living room rug.

   The game wasn't anything like Monopoly or Risk, though.

Actually, they were playing a game to choose their next murder target. In turn, they calmly rolled the dice, then moved a marker around a rectangle of photos. The photos were of very famous people.

The board game was important to Jack and Jill. It was a game of chance. It made it impossible for the police or FBI to predict their movements or their motive.

If there was a motive. But *of course* there was a motive.

Sam rolled the dice again. Then he moved the marker. Sara watched him in the warm, flickering glow of the fire. Her eyes glazed over slightly. She was remembering their very first meeting, the initial contact between them. The beginning of everything that was happening now.

This was how the complex and beautiful and very mysterious game had begun. They had agreed to meet at a coffee shop inside a bookstore in downtown D.C. Sara had arrived first, her heart trapped in her throat. Everything about the meeting was *insane*, maybe dangerously insane, and insanely irresistible to her. She couldn't pass up this chance, this opportunity, or especially this cause. The cause was everything to her.

At the time of their first meeting, she had no idea what Sam Harrison would look like, and she was surprised and delighted when he sat at her table. He excited her.

She had seen him enter the coffeehouse area, watched him order espresso and a scone. She hadn't imagined that the dreamy-looking man at the counter would turn out to be Harrison, though.

So this was *The Soldier.* This was her potential partner. He kind of fit in at the bookstore. He would fit in anywhere. He didn't look like a killer, but then again, neither did she. *He looks a little like an airline pilot,* Sara thought as she sized him up. *A successful Washington lawyer?* He was over six feet tall, trim and fit. He had a strong, confident face. And he also had the brightest, clearest blue eyes. He had a sensitive, gentle look about him.

Not at all what she had expected. She liked him immediately. She knew that they agreed on the important things in life, that they shared a vision.

"You're looking at me as if I'm supposed to be a bad person, and you're surprised that I'm not," he'd said as he sat across from her at the café. "I'm not a bad person, Sara. You can call me Sam, by the way. I'm a pretty good guy, actually."

No, Sam was much better than that. He was amazing — extremely smart, strong, and yet always considerate of her feelings, and committed to their cause. Sara Rosen had fallen in love with him within a week of their meeting. She knew that she shouldn't, but she had; and now here they were. Living this secret life.

Playing the game of life and death as a guinea hen slowly spun on the spit. Sitting before a cozy fire. Thinking about making love — at least, she was. She thought about being with Sam, *with Jack,* all the time. She loved it when he was inside her.

"This roll should do it," Sam said, and he handed her the dice. "Your turn. Six rolls for each of us. You do the honors, Sara."

"Here we go, huh?"

"Yes, here we go again."

Sara Rosen's heart began to thunder. She could feel it *thump, thump* under her blouse. She had the paralyzing thought that this single roll of the dice was like the murder itself. It was almost as if she were pulling the trigger right now.

Who was going to die next? It was all in her hand, wasn't it? Who would it be?

She squeezed the three dice incredibly tight. Then she shook them and let the dice go, watched them wobble and roll forward and then stop abruptly, as if someone had pulled an invisible string. She quickly added up the number of the roll — *nine.*

Sara picked up the marker and counted off nine places, nine photographs.

She stared down at the face of the next target, the next celebrity to die. It was a woman!

It's for the cause, she told herself, but Sara Rosen's heart continued to beat loudly all the same.

The next victim was a very famous woman.

Washington, the whole world, would be shocked and outraged for a second time.

Chapter 8

SAMPSON AND I walked into the fog-shrouded heart of Garfield Park, which borders the Anacostia River and the Eisenhower Freeway and isn't far from the Sojourner Truth School. *The color of truth is gray,* I was thinking as we entered the ground smog. *Always gray.* We weren't out for an early-morning run — we were hurrying to the place where Shanelle Green had actually been murdered, her skull crushed by some fiend.

Several uniforms, a captain, and another detective were already at the homicide scene. A dozen or so casual onlookers were on hand — looky-loos. Search dogs originally brought in from Georgia had led a search party to the murder site. I could see Sixth Street from the thicket of evergreens where the killer had brutally savaged the little girl. I could almost see the Sojourner Truth School.

"Think he carried the body out of here to the schoolyard?" Sampson asked. His tone of voice indicated he didn't believe it. Neither did I. So how did the little girl's body get to the schoolyard?

A bright red balloon floated a couple of feet above the over-grown bushes where the terrible murder had occurred.

"*O* marks the spot?" Sampson asked. "That balloon the marker?"

"I don't know. . . I wonder," I muttered as I pushed aside the thick evergreen branches and made my way into the hideaway. The smell of pine was heavy, even in the cold air. Reminded me that the Christmas season was here.

I could feel the presence of the killer inside the tree branches, challenging me. I sensed Shanelle's presence as well, as if she were trying to tell me something. I wanted to be alone in here for a moment or two.

It was a small clearing where the murder had actually taken place. Dried blood was on the ground and had even splashed across some of the branches. *He lured her in here. How did he do that? She'd be suspicious, or scared, unless she knew him from the neighborhood.* It suddenly struck me. *The balloon!* It was just a guess, but it seemed right to me. *The red balloon could have been the lure, the killer's bait for the little girl.*

I crouched down and was very still inside the tent of trees.

The killer liked it in here, hiding in the darkness. He doesn't like himself much, though. Prefers the dark. He likes his mind, his thoughts, but not what he looks like. There's probably something distinctive about him physically.

I didn't know any of that for sure, but it seemed right; it felt right as I crouched at the murder site.

He was hiding in here, probably because there's something about him people might remember. If so, it was a good clue.

I could see Shanelle Green's battered face again. Then an image of my dead wife, Maria, came to me. I could feel the rage climbing from my gut to my throat, blowing and billowing inside me. I thought of Jannie and Damon.

I had one more thought about the child killer: anger usually implies an awareness of self-worth. Strange, but true. The killer was angry because he believed in himself much more than the world did.

Finally, I rose up and pushed my way back out of the hideaway. I'd had enough.

"Haul down that balloon," I called to a patrolman. "Get that damn balloon out of the tree now. It's evidence."

Chapter 9

THERE WAS SOMETHING distinctive about him physically. I was almost certain of it. It was a place to start.

That afternoon Sampson and I were out on the street again, working near the Northfield Village projects. The Washington newspapers and TV hadn't bothered much about the murder of a little girl in Southeast. Instead, they were filled with stories about the killing of Senator Fitzpatrick by the so-called Jack and Jill stalkers. Shanelle Green didn't seem to matter very much.

Except to Sampson and me. We had seen Shanelle's broken body and met her heartbroken parents. Now we talked to our street sources, but also to our neighbors. We continued to let people see us working, walking the streets.

"I sure do love a good homicide. Love walking the mean streets in the dead cold of winter," Sampson opined as we went past a local dealer's black-on-black Jeep. It was blaring rap, lots of bass. "Love the suffering, the stench, the funky sounds." His face was flat. Beyond angry. Philosophical.

He was wearing a familiar sweatshirt under his open topcoat. The shirt had his message for the day:

I DON'T GIVE A SHIT
I DON'T TAKE ANY SHIT
I'M NOT IN THE SHIT BUSINESS

Concise. Accurate. Very much John Sampson.

Neither of us had felt much like talking for the past hour or so. It wasn't going all that well. That was The Job, though. It was like this more often than it wasn't.

Man Mountain and I arrived at the Capitol City Market about four in the afternoon. The Cap is a popular gyp joint on Eighth Street. It's just about the dingiest, most depressing bargain-basement store in Washington, D.C. — and that takes some doing.

The featured products are usually written in pink chalk on a gray blue cinder block wall in front. That day the specials were cold beer and soda pop, plantains, pork rinds, Tampax, and Lotto — your basic complete-and-balanced breakfast.

A young brother with tight wraparound Wayfarer sunglasses, a shaved head, and small goatee caught our immediate attention in front of the minimart. He was standing next to another man who had a chocolate bar hanging from his mouth like a cigar. The shaved head motioned to me that he wanted to talk to us, but not right there.

"You trust that rowdyass?" Sampson asked as we followed at a safe distance. "Alvin Jackson."

"I trust everybody." I winked. No wink came back from Sampson.

"You are badly fucked-up, Sugar," he said. His eyes were still seriously hooded.

"Just trying to do the right thing."

"Ah, yeah, you're trying too hard, then."

"That's why you love me."

"Yes, it is," Sampson said and finally grinned. "If lovin' you is wrong, I don't want to be right," he talk-sang a familiar lyric.

We met Roadrunner Alvin Jackson around the corner.

Sampson and I had occasionally used Alvin as a snitch. He wasn't a bad man, really, but he was living a dangerous life that could suddenly get much, much worse for him. He had been a decent high school track star who used to practice in the streets. Now he was running a little base and selling smoke as well. In many ways, Alvin Jackson was still a man-child. That was important to understand about a lot of these kids, even the most dangerous and powerful-looking ones.

"Thalilshanelle," Alvin said as if the three words were one, "you still lookin' for information on who ice her and alladat?"

Alvin's car coat was unbuttoned. He was sporting the current fashion look that's called jailin', or baggin'. His red-and-white pinstriped underwear was visible above the waistband. *The look* is inspired by the fact that a prisoner's belt is taken away in jail, tending to make the trousers droop and the underwear be accentuated. Role models for our neighborhood.

"Yeah. What have you heard about her, Alvin, but no Chipmunks?" Sampson said.

"Man, I'm tryin' to do you a solid," Alvin Jackson protested in my direction. His shaved head never stopped bobbing. His hoop earring jangled. His long, powerful arms twitched. He kept picking his Nike-sneakered feet up and putting them back down.

"We appreciate it," I told him. "Smoke?" I offered Alvin a Camel. Joe Cool, right?

He took it. I don't smoke, but I always carry. Alvin had smoked like a chimney when he was a high school road-and-track man. Things you notice.

"Lil' Shanelle, she live in my auntie's building. Over in Northfield? I think I know 'bout somebody maybe 'sponsible. You unnerstand what I'm sayin'?"

"So far." Sampson nodded. He was trying to be nice, actually. A head of lettuce could follow Alvin Jackson's patter.

"You want to show us what you got?" I asked him. "Help us out here?"

"I'll show you *Chucky* myself. *Howzat?*" He smiled and nodded at me. "But only cuz it's you and Sampson. I tried to tell some a them other detectives, *months back*. They wouldn't have none of it. Man, they wouldn't listen to jack shit. Didn't have the time of day for my airplay."

I felt like his father or uncle or older brother. I felt responsible. I didn't like it so much.

"Well, we're listening," I told him. "We've got the time for you."

Sampson and I went with Alvin Jackson to the Northfield Village projects. Northfield is one of the most dangerous crime areas in D.C. Nobody seems to care, though. The 1st District police have given up. You visit Northfield once, it's hard to blame them completely.

This didn't seem like a very promising lead to me. But Alvin Jackson was a man on a mission. I wondered why that was. What was I missing here?

He pointed a long, accusatory finger at one of the yellow-brick buildings. It was in the same shabby state of disrepair as most of the others. An electric-blue metal sign was over the double front doors: BUILDING 3. The front stairs were cracked and looked as if they'd been hit by lightning or somebody's sledgehammer.

"He lives in there. Ak-ak city. Leastways, he did. Name's Emmanuel Perez. Sometimes he works as a porter at Famous. You know, Famous Pizza? He goes after the little kids, man. Real freakazoid. He's a nasty fucker. Scary fucker, too. Don't like it none when you call him Manny. He's *Ee-man-uel*. Insists on it."

"How do you know *Emmanuel?*" Sampson asked.

Alvin Jackson's eyes suddenly clouded over and looked hard as rocks. He took a few seconds before he spoke. "I knew him. He was around when I was a little kid. Buggin' back then, too. Emmanuel always been around, you unnerstand?"

I got it. I understood now. Chop-It-Off-Chucky wasn't a chimera anymore.

There was an asphalt-topped playground across the quad. Young kids were playing hoops, but not very well. The basket had no net. The rim was bent this way and that. Nobody any good played on these particular courts. Suddenly, something in the playground caught Alvin Jackson's eye.

"That's him over there," he said in a high-pitched whine. Fearful. "That's him, man. That's Emmanuel Perez doggin' those kids."

He had no sooner said the words when Perez spotted us. It was as weird as a bad dream. I saw that he had a longish red beard that stuck out stiffly from his chin. *It was something distinctive about him physically. Something people would have remembered if he'd been seen in Garfield Park.* He leveled Alvin Jackson with a dark, scary look. Then he took off in a dead run.

Emmanuel Perez was a very fast runner. But so were we; at least, we were the last time I checked.

Chapter 10

SAMPSON AND I raced behind Perez, closing a little ground on him. We shot down a littered, twisting concrete alley that ran between the tall, depressing buildings. We could both still move pretty well.

"Stop! Police detectives!" I yelled loudly at the sorry excuse for a man running ahead of us. Bogeyman? Chimera? Innocent restaurant porter?

Perez, the suspected child murderer and child molester, was definitely trying to escape. We didn't know for sure if he was Chop-It-Off-Chucky, but he had some reason to run from Sampson and me, from the police.

Had we finally caught a break on the case? Something sure as hell was happening right now.

I had a very bad thought lodged in the front of my brain. *If we're this close to catching him, after two days on the streets, why wasn't he caught before?*

I thought I knew the answer, and I didn't like it much. *Because nobody cares what happens in these wretched neighborhoods around the projects. Nobody cares.*

"We're back!" Sampson suddenly shouted as we sprinted

between the cavernous buildings, stirring up street garbage in our wake, rousting pigeons.

"Remains to be seen," I yelled to him.

Nobody cares!

"Don't doubt it for a minute, Sugar. Think only positive thoughts."

"Emmanuel is fast, too. That's positively the truth."

Nobody cares!

"We're faster, stronger, tougher than Manny ever dreamed of being."

"Better trash talkers," I huffed. Just one huff, but a huff all the same.

"That, too, Sugar. Goes without saying."

We followed Perez/Chop-It-Off out onto Seventh Street, which is lined with four- and five-story row houses, bombed-out stores, a few tank bars.

Perez suddenly turned into a beaten-down Federal-style building near the middle of the block. The windows were mostly boarded with sheet metal, looking like silver teeth in a rotting mouth.

"He seems to know what the hell he's doing," Sampson yelled. "Knows where he's going."

"At least that makes one of us."

Sampson and I entered the sagging, ramshackle building several strides behind Perez. The strong smell of urine and decay was everywhere. As we climbed the steep, reinforced concrete stairs, I could feel a fire spreading into my chest.

"Had his escape route all figured out!" I huffed. A definite huff. "He's smart."

"He's trying to escape from *us*. That's not too smart. Never happen . . . WE GOT YOU, MANNY!" Sampson yelled up the stairs. His voice echoed like thunder in the narrow quarters. "HEY, MANNY! MANNY, MANNY, MANNY!"

"Stop! Police! *Manny* Perez, stop!" Sampson shouted at the fleeing suspect. He had his gun out, a nasty 9mm Glock.

We could hear Perez still running above us, his sneakers slapping stairs. He didn't yell back. Nobody else was on the stairs or in any of the stairwells. Nobody cared that there was a police chase going on inside the building.

"You think Perez really did it?" I yelled to Sampson.

"He did *something*. He's running like his ass is on fire. Spreading right up his spinal cord."

"Yeah. We lit the fuse."

We burst out a gray metal door onto a broad, uneven expanse of tar roof. Overhead the sky was a cool, hard blue. There were shiny surfaces and maximum glare everywhere. *There was nothing but bright blue sky above. I had the urge to take off — fly away from all of this. The urge, but not the means.*

Where the hell had he gone? He was nowhere in sight. Where was Emmanuel Perez? Where was the Sojourner Truth School killer?

Chimera.

Chapter 11

"FUCK YOU, peachfuzz," Perez suddenly yelled. "You hear me, peachfuzz?"

"Peachfuzz?" Sampson looked at me and made a face.

I saw a quick flash of Chop-It-Off-Chucky. He was off to our extreme right. He was sprinting across a connecting rooftop and was already about thirty yards away. I saw him grab a quick, worried look back over his shoulder.

His small eyes were hard black beads, evil-looking as they come. He had that weird red beard. Maybe he was a total psycho. Or maybe he really was just a pizza-store porter? *Forget it,* I told myself.

Four teenage boys and a girl were up there on the roof doing their sneaky business. Crack, probably. I hoped they weren't snorting heroin. They idly watched the wild, wild world go by. *The real city game was in progress here.* Cops and robbers. Child molester-killers. It made no difference to these kids.

Sampson and I covered three more narrow rooftops in a powerful hurry. We were gaining on him a little, but only by a step or two. Sweat was running down my forehead and cheeks, burning my eyes.

"*Stop! We'll shoot!*" I yelled. "*Stop, Emmanuel Perez!*"

Perez looked back again. He looked straight at me this time and grinned! *Then he seemed to disappear over the far side of the brick-walled building.*

"Fire escape!" Sampson yelled.

Seconds later, the two of us were rushing headlong down skinny, twisting, rusted metal stairs. Perez flew down the flimsy fire escape ahead of us. He was really moving. This was definitely his event, his home course.

Sampson and I were both too big for the tight-radius maneuvering. He gained a full flight on us, maybe a flight and a half.

Chucky definitely had an escape route figured out, I was thinking. *He'd practiced this. I was almost sure of it. He's a smart one. He's guilty. Those vicious eyes! Mad-dog eyes. What had Alvin Jackson said — that Emmanuel Perez had always been around?*

We saw him down on E Street. The red beard jutted out as if it were petrified wood. He was already a full block away. Lots of rush-hour traffic everywhere. He was getting into a gypsy cab, a dull red-and-orange hack that read, CAPPY'S. WE GO ANYWHERE.

"STOP, YOU FUCKING SQUIRREL!" Sampson screamed at the top of his voice. "GODDAMN YOU, MANNY!"

Perez gave us the finger in the crud-crusted rear window of the cab.

"PEACHFUZZ!" he leaned out and screamed back at us.

Chapter 12

SAMPSON AND I scrambled out onto E Street. Sweat was still streaming down my forehead and cheeks, my neck, back, legs. Sampson ran in front of a Yellow Cab and the driver screeched to a stop. Intelligent of the cabdriver to avoid hitting Man Mountain and totaling his car.

"Metro police! Detective Alex Cross!" my voice boomed as we simultaneously swung open the cab's back doors. "Follow that hack. Go! Go! Go! Dammit."

"Don't you lose him!" Sampson threatened the driver. "Don't you even think about it." The poor man was scared to death. He never even looked back. Never said a word. But he didn't lose visual contact with CAPPY'S. WE GO ANYWHERE.

We hit a bad snarl of traffic at Ninth Street where it approaches Pennsylvania Avenue. Cars and trucks were backed up for at least three blocks. Angry horns were honking everywhere. One tractor-trailer had a foghorn like an oceangoing vessel's.

"Maybe we better get out and run him down," I said to Sampson.

"I was thinking the same thing. Let's go for it."

It was one of those fifty-fifty calls. Either way, we could lose Chucky right here. My heart was pounding hard in my chest. I could see the crushed-in skull of little Shanelle Green. *Emmanuel had always been around! Those mad-dog eyes!* I wanted Chop-It-Off-Chucky real bad.

Sampson already had the creaking door on his side of the cab open. I was half a step behind. Maybe less.

Chucky must have felt us breathing fire on the back of his neck. He jumped out of his cab and started to run.

We followed him between the tight rows of barely moving traffic. Blaring car horns provided chaotic background noise for the foot chase along Ninth Street.

Chop-It-Off-Chucky burst forward. He'd gotten his second wind.

Suddenly, he veered right and into a gleaming, glass-and-steel office building. The building looked silver blue.

Madness, pure and simple.

I had my detective's shield already out as we entered the office building several strides behind Chucky. "Spanish guy, red beard. Which way?" I yelled at the dazed and confused-looking security guard standing around in the plush, paneled lobby.

He pointed to the middle car at a metal-on-metal elevator bank. The car had already left the ground floor. I watched the floor indicator: three — four — rising fast. Sampson and I jumped into the open door of the car nearest the front entrance.

I hit ROOFTOP with the palm of my hand. That was my best guess.

"Roadrunner said Perez was a porter at Famous Pizza," I told Sampson. "There was a Famous on the ground floor here."

"Think Chucky's a creature of habit? Likes roofs? Has his favorites all picked out?"

"I think he had a couple of escape routes figured out, just in case. And, yeah, I think he's a creature of habit."

"He's most definitely a creature."

The elevator bell rang, and Sampson and I scrambled out, guns first. We could see the Capitol in the distance. Also the

Statue of Freedom. Pretty sight under other circumstances. Weird, now. Kind of sad.

I couldn't stop thinking about Shanelle Green. I kept seeing her brutalized face. *What had he hit her with? How many times? Why?* I wanted to catch this bastard so bad, it hurt. Hurt my body; hurt my head even worse.

We moved away from the building, and I finally spotted Chucky outlined against the skyline. My heart sank.

Chucky *did* have an escape route in mind. He had thought about this before. *Somebody coming to get him. He sure was acting guilty. He had to be our killer.*

"Fuck you, peachfuzz!" he screeched, taunting us again.

Then he took off on a long, running start. He had a powerful stride — a long stride.

"No," I moaned. "No, no, no."

I knew what he was going to do.

Perez was going to jump from building to building.

"Stop, you son of a bitch," Sampson shouted, "or I *will* shoot!"

But he didn't stop. We watched him take a flying leap.

We ran to the edge of the roof, both of us screaming at the top of our lungs. There was a second office building catty-corner to our roof. The top of that building was a floor below where Sampson and I now stood.

Chop-It-Off-Chucky was airborne between the buildings, the glass-and-steel caverns.

"Jesus!" I gasped as I peered straight down over the side. The gap between the buildings was at least twenty feet wide, maybe more.

"Fall, you bastard. Hit a wall," Sampson yelled at the flying figure. "Go down, Chucky!"

He's done this before. He's practiced his escape, I thought as I watched. *No wonder he's never been caught. How many years on the loose? How many kids molested or murdered?*

We had our guns out, but neither of us fired. We had no

proof that he was the killer. He had only run from us, had never pointed a weapon. Now, this insane leap from one office building to another.

Chucky looked suspended in motion sixteen floors up. A long, long way down.

Something was wrong.

Chucky was pumping his legs furiously. It was as if he were trying to pedal a bike straight across the sky.

His long arms reached out, muscles hard and taut. His lead leg stretched until it was almost straight out from his body. Nike sneaker–poster stuff.

His frame was stiff, like a runner caught in a prizewinning photograph.

"Jesus Christ," Sampson whispered at my side. I felt his warm breath on my cheek.

Chucky's arm was outstretched, but his hand barely touched the restraining wall on the roof of the nearby office building, his legs still pumping in midair.

Then Chop-It-Off-Chucky screamed — bloodcurdling sounds, muffled only by the windows and walls of the two buildings.

He continued to shriek as he fell twenty stories. His arms and legs were flailing, stroking the air at a futile, furious pace.

As I watched, I saw his body suddenly twist in midair.

He looked up at me — still screaming in a hopeless, plaintive way, screaming with his mouth *and his eyes,* and that bushy red beard, *screaming.* Chucky was dying as I watched. The fall seemed to take forever. Four or five seconds that seemed like an eternity.

My stomach was falling with him. I experienced vertigo. The narrow alley below was a spinning gray band. The buildings, the *canyon,* seemed so steep and dark and faraway.

Then I heard Chucky hit the pavement. *Splat!* It was otherworldly to hear.

I stared at the crumpled body spread-eagled down below. I

could feel no joy in it, though. There was nothing even remotely human about it. It was crushed like the side of Shanelle Green's face. Chucky's unearthly screams still echoed inside my brain.

"Flameout," Sampson said at my side. "Case closed. Score one for the peachfuzz."

I holstered my semiautomatic. Emmanuel Perez had practiced his escape, but he hadn't practiced enough.

Chapter 13

MAJOR FAKEOUT. Faked you out something fierce, didn't I? I faked you all out.

The real Sojourner Truth School killer was alive and well. The killer couldn't have been any better, thank you very much. He had just committed the perfect crime, hadn't he? He had just gotten away with murder.

Yes, he sure as hell had. Scot-free. The crackerjack Washington police had caught and toasted the wrong twisted asshole. Somebody named Emmanuel Perez had paid for his sins, paid with his life, paid in full.

All he had to do now was cool it, he knew. That was what he had to concentrate on. He had already decided to hide out for a while — *inside his mind.*

He was cruising the Pentagon City mall in Arlington. He was getting absolutely rabid as he strolled through The Gap, and then Victoria's Secret. He was obsessing about how to get back at — *anybody and everybody. At* tout le monde — *pardon his French,* s'il vous plaît.

A song, an oldie he'd heard that morning on MTV, was stuck in his head. The lyrics had been bouncing around in his skull like Ping-Pong balls for the last couple of hours. He could hear the singer, Beck, a hopeless geek from Los Angeles: *I'm a loser, baby. So why don't you kill me?*

I'm a loser, baby. So why don't you kill me? he repeated the lyric in his head.

I'm a loser, baby. So why don't you kill me?

He loved the way the dumb-ass lyrics worked two ways for him. They were about him, and they were about his potential victims. Everything was an irritating circle, right? Life was beautiful in its screwy simplicity, right?

WRONG! Life was not beautiful. Not at all.

He was watching a little sucker now, a potential victim who looked way too good to pass up. The Truth School killer loitered inside the Toys "R" Us at the mall. Since it was the holiday season, the store was jam-packed with idiots.

The overhead speakers were playing the chain's irritating and moronic theme song: "I don't wanna grow up, I'm a Toys 'R' Us kid." Over and over and over, the kind of mindless repetition that kids loved. The sheer number of insane toys, the spoiled-rotten little kids, the smug-looking mothers and fathers, the whole raw deal made him feel hot, thickheaded, and almost physically sick.

I don't want to grow up, either, he said to himself. *I'm a Toys "R" Us kid killer.*

He watched his chosen little boy as the kid wandered alone down a wide aisle chock-full of action games. The boy was five or so, a very manageable age.

The anger button inside his head was going off like a powerful alarm. WOM! WOM! WOM! The terrible feeling quickly spread to his chest. WOM! WOM! It was tense and uncomfortable. Both his hands were clenched tight. So was his stomach. The back of his neck. His *brain* was clutching, too.

Be careful now, he cautioned himself. *Don't make any mistakes. Remember — you do perfect crimes.*

Chapter 14

THIS WAS GOING TO BE a mite tricky going, though, working in the crowded Toys "R" Us store. What if the boy's parents were close by? WHICH THEY DEFINITELY WERE! What if he were caught? WHICH HE WOULDN'T BE! COULDN'T BE!

That was incredibly important to him. Just watching the attractive, round-faced, sandy-haired boy, he could *feel* how badly this particular kid would be missed and, even better, mourned. He needed to imagine the stories that would bombard the television screens and the thrill of watching them, knowing he was responsible for so much pain and suffering and emergency activity.

The little boy was getting itchy in his woolens and starting to panic a little. He had big crocodile tears brimming in his eyes. There didn't seem to be anybody, any adult, anywhere around him. Poor Little Boy Lost. Poor Little Boy Blue.

The killer began to move in on his prey, slowly and carefully. He couldn't stop now. His heart was beating like a big tin drum, and he loved the powerful sensation. His legs and arms were a little wobbly. Jell-O city. His vision tunneled; he was dizzy with anticipation, fear, dread, exhilaration.

Do it.

Now!

He bent, picked up the boy, and immediately started smiling and talking the happiest, friendliest barf-babble he could come up with.

"Hi there, I'm Roger the Artful Dodger. I work here at Toys 'R' Us. What kind of fantastical toys do you like best, huh? We've got every kind of toy in the whole wide world, 'cause we're the world's biggest, *coolest* toy store. Yahoo! How 'bout that? Let's go find your superpathetic mom and dad!"

The boy actually smiled up at him. Kids could do weird mood changes like that. His beautiful blue eyes sparkled, glistened; *something* wet and wonderful happened. "I want Mighty Max," he proclaimed as if he were Richie Rich instead of Little Boy Lost.

"Okay, then come with me. One Mighty Max coming up! Why? 'Cause you're a Toys 'R' Us kid."

He cradled the boy in his arms and began to hurry up the wide shopping aisle toward the front of the store. Suddenly, he knew he could get away with it, even something this audacious and shocking, with almost a hundred eyewitnesses in the store. *Hey, he was the new Pied Piper. Kids loved him.*

"We'll get a Vac-Man. Then how about X-men? Or how about a Stretch Armstrong?"

"Mighty Max," the little boy repeated, stuck on his one track. "I only want Mighty Max."

The killer peeked out of aisle three. He was less than thirty feet from the store's front exit. The mall parking lot bordered on Columbia Park, which had been part of his escape package from the start.

He took a couple of fast steps, then stopped dead in his tracks at the front of the store.

Shit! A couple in their late twenties were walking toward him! The woman looked just like Little Boy Blue.

They had him . . . dead to rights. They had him nailed! They had him!

He knew what he had to do, so he never panicked for a nano-second. Except for the two or three major heart attacks he had on the inside. *Well, here goes everything. Time to bet the ranchero.*

"Hey, hi there." He smiled broadly and went into his best stand-up routine ever. "This little guy belong to you? He was lost in the action-figure section. Nobody came for him. I figured I better bring him up to the store manager. Little guy was crying his eyes out. You his mom?"

The mother reached out for her precious bundle of joy, while at the same time throwing her husband a dirty look.

Aha, *there* was our villain! Pop was obviously the one who had lost the boy in the first place. Pops couldn't get anything right these days, could they! His own pop sure hadn't been able to.

"Thank you, *so much,*" the mom said. She tossed another incredibly nasty look to pop. "That was very sweet of you," she told the killer.

He continued to hold his best smile. Man, he was acting his heart out. "Anybody would do the same thing. He's a nice little boy. Well, so long. *Bye-bye.* He wants a Mighty Max. That's probably what he was searching for."

"Yes, he does want Mighty Max. Bye. Thanks again," said the mom.

"Bye-bye," the little boy mimicked, waving his hand. "Bye-bye."

"Hope I see ya some other time," said the Sojourner Truth School killer. "Bye-bye." *You morons! You incredible idiots. You pathetic simps.*

He walked away from the family. Never looked back once. He was wetting his pants, but he was also beginning to laugh. He couldn't stop himself from laughing. Here was another thing in his favor — even if he was caught someday — *they wouldn't believe that he was the Truth School killer. No way in hell.*

Chapter 15

AH, THIS WAS MUCH BETTER. Life was good again. I opened my eyes and Jannie was there, staring at me from about three feet away. Jannie had Rosie the cat in her arms. Jannie likes to watch me sleep sometimes. I like to watch her sleep, too. Fair is fair.

"Hey there, sweetness and light," I said to her. "You know the song, 'Someone To Watch Over Me'? You remember that one?" I hummed a couple of bars for her.

Jannie nodded her head yes. She knew the song. She'd heard me play it on the piano downstairs, on our porch. "You have *guests*," she announced.

I sat up in bed. "How long have they been here?"

"They just came. Nana sent me and Rosie up to get you. She's making them coffee. You, too. You have to get up."

"Is it Sampson and Rakeem Powell?" I asked.

Jannie shook her head. She seemed unusually shy this morning, which isn't really like her. "They're white men."

I was starting to wake up in a hurry. "I see. You happen to catch the names?" Suddenly, I thought I knew the names. I solved the mystery myself — at least, I thought I had.

Jannie said, "Mr. Pittman and Mr. Clouser."

"Very good," I complimented her.

Not good, not good at all, I was thinking about my "guests." I didn't want to see the chief of detectives, or the police commissioner — especially not in my house.

Especially not for the reason I imagined that they were here to see me.

Jannie bent and gave me my morning kiss. Then a second kiss.

"Oh, what lies there are in kisses," I winked and said to her.

"Nope," she said. "Not my kisses."

It took me less than five minutes to get as ready as I was going to get for this. Nana was entertaining our visitors in the parlor. Commissioner Clouser had come to my house twice before. This was a first for the chief of detectives. The Jefe. I assumed that Clouser had forced him to come.

Chief Pittman and Commissioner Clouser were sipping Nana's steaming coffee, smiling at a story she was spinning for them. I wondered what it was she had decided to get off her chest. This was a dangerous time — for Pittman and Clouser.

"I was just rebuking these gentlemen for allowing Emmanuel Perez to roam our streets for so long," she told me as I entered the parlor. "They promised not to let that sort of thing happen again. Should I believe them, Alex?"

Both Pittman and Clouser chuckled as they looked at me. Neither of them realized this was no chuckling matter, and that my grandmother was no one to mess with or, even worse, condescend to in her house.

"No, you shouldn't believe one word they say. Are you finished now?" I asked her, returning her sweet, phony smile with one of my own.

"I didn't think I could trust either of them. I wanted to get their promise *in writing*," Nana said.

I nodded and smiled, as if she'd just made a joke, which I knew she hadn't. She was dead serious. The Jefe and Commissioner Clouser both laughed heartily. They thought Nana Mama was a stitch. She isn't. She's the whole nine yards.

"Can the three of us talk in here?" I asked her. "Or should we go outside for our discussion?"

"I'll go in my kitchen," Nana evil-eyed me and said. "So nice to meet you, Chief Pittman, Commissioner Clouser. Don't forget your promise. I won't."

Once she had left the room, the commissioner spoke right up. "Well, congratulations are in order, Alex. I understand that you found all kinds of kiddie porn in Emmanuel Perez's apartment."

"Detective Sampson and I found the pornography," I said. Then I was silent. I had decided not to make this easy for them. Actually, I agreed one hundred percent with the point Nana had been trying to make.

"I'm sure you're wondering what we're doing here, so let me explain," Chief of Detectives Pittman spoke up. He and I were not close, to put it mildly. Never had been, never would be. Pittman is a bully and also a closet racist, and those are his better points. He could never seem to see a belt without wanting to hit below it.

"I'd appreciate it," I said to The Jefe. "I was thinking that maybe you had just been in the neighborhood and you dropped by for my grandmother's coffee. It's worth a trip."

Pittman didn't come close to breaking a smile. "We received a formal request from the FBI late last night. They've asked that you work on the investigation of Senator Fitzpatrick's murder. Special Agent Kyle Craig strongly suggested that your background and recent experience might serve the investigation well. Obviously, it's an important case, Alex."

I let Chief Pittman finish, then I slowly shook my head no. "I've got a half-dozen open homicides here in Southeast," I said. "The case I just worked on should have been solved months ago. *Then another little girl wouldn't have died for no goddamn reason.* A homicide detective got reassigned off the killer's trail back then. Now a little girl is dead. Six years old."

"This is a major case, Alex," the commissioner said. He had snow-white hair. His face was bright red, which happened when he was angry or disturbed. The two of us went back some. Usually, we went along, got along. Maybe not this time.

"Tell the FBI that I can't be spared for this Jack and Jill mess. I'll call Kyle and make my peace with him. Kyle will understand. I'm on several homicide cases in Southeast. People die here, too. We have our own messes, and even *major* cases."

"Let me ask you something, Alex," the police commissioner said. He smiled gently as he spoke. Lots of beautifully capped white teeth. I could have played some sweet Gershwin on them, though maybe some key-slamming Little Richard would have been more satisfying.

"Do you still want to be a cop?" he asked.

That one landed, and it stung. It was a sucker punch, but a pretty good one.

"I want to be a good cop," I said to him. "I want to do some good if I possibly can. Same as always. Nothing's changed."

"That's the right answer," the commissioner said as if I were a child who needed his instruction. "You're on the Jack and Jill investigation. It's been decided in very high places. You have experience with these kinds of murders, with lunatic psychotics. You are officially off all your other cases. Now, be a *very* good cop, Alex. The FBI is almost certain Jack and Jill are going to kill again."

So was I, so was I.

And I felt the very same thing about the Sojourner Truth School killer.

Chapter 16

I RESISTED the unique charms of the Jack and Jill case for one more day. Half a day, anyway. I tried to clear a few things on my watch in Southeast. I was furious about what had happened with Clouser and Pittman.

Shanelle Green had died because more detectives hadn't been assigned to find Chop-It-Off-Chucky, hadn't given Alvin Jackson the time of day. The whole sorry affair was race-related, no way around it, and it made me both angry and sad.

I came home early and spent the evening with Nana and the kids. I wanted to make sure they were okay after the murder at the Sojourner Truth School. At least that horror tale had been solved. But I still wasn't over the child killing. I couldn't get past it for a lot of reasons.

For half an hour or so, I gave Damon and Jannie their weekly boxing lesson in the basement. To Damon's credit, he's never complained that the sessions include his sister. He just puts on the gloves.

They're becoming tough little pugs, but more important, they're learning when not to fight. Not many kids mess with them at school, but that's mainly because they're nice kids and know how to get along.

"Watch that footwork, Damon," I told him. "You're not supposed to be putting out a fire with your feet."

"You're supposed to be *dancing*," Jannie threw a little verbal jab at her brother. "Step, right. Back. Step, step, left."

"I'll do a dance on you in a minute," Damon warned her off, and then they both laughed like hell.

A little later, we were upstairs in front of the tube. Jannie was crossing her small arms, squinting her brown eyes, and making a tough-as-nails face at me. It was her official, nonnegotiable bedtime, but she had decided to lodge a protest.

"No, Daddy. Nope, nope, *nopeee*," she said. "Your watch is too fast."

"Yes, Jannie. Yep, yep, *yepeee*." I held my ground, held my own against my chief nemesis. "My watch is too slow."

"No, siree. No way," she said.

"Yes, indeedee. No escaping it. You're busted."

The long arm of the law finally reached out and corralled another repeat offender. I grabbed Jannie off the couch and carried my little girl up to bed at eight-thirty on the dot. Law and order reigns at the Cross house.

"Where we going, Daddy?" she giggled against my neck. "Are we going out for ice cream? I'll have pralines 'n' cream."

"In your dreams."

As I tightly held Jannie in my arms, I couldn't help thinking about little Shanelle Green. When I had seen Shanelle in that schoolyard, I was scared. I'd thought of Jannie. It was a vicious circle that kept playing inside my head.

I lived in fear of the human monsters coming to our house. One of them had come here a few years back. Gary Soneji. That time no one had been hurt, and we had been very lucky.

Jannie and I had worked out a prayer that we both liked. She knelt beside her bed and said the words in a beautiful little whisper.

Jannie said, "God up in heaven, my grandma and my daddy love me. Even Damon loves me. I thank you, God, for making me a nice person, pretty and funny sometimes. I will always try to do the right thing, if I can. This is Jannie Cross saying goodnight."

"Amen, Jannie Cross," I smiled and said to my girl. I loved her more than life itself. She reminded me of her mother in the best possible way. "I'll see you in the morning. I can't wait."

Jannie grinned and her eyes widened suddenly. She popped back up in bed. "You can see me some more *tonight*. Just let me stay up," she said. "I *scream* for ice cream."

"You *are* funny," I said and kissed her goodnight. "And pretty and smart." Man, I love her and Damon so much. I knew that was why the child murder had really gotten under my skin. The madman had struck too close to our house.

Maybe for that reason Damon and I went for a walk a little later that night. I draped my arm over my son's shoulders. It seemed as if every day he got a little bigger, stronger, harder. We were good buddies, and I was glad it had worked out this way so far.

The two of us strolled in the direction of Damon's school. On the way, we passed a Baptist church with angry, dark-red and black graffiti markings: *I don't care 'bout Jeez, 'cause Jeez don't care 'bout me.* That was a common sentiment around here, especially among the young and restless.

One of Damon's schoolmates had died at the Sojourner Truth School. What a horrible tragedy, and yet he had already seen so much of it. Damon had witnessed a death in the street, one young man shooting another over a parking space, when he was only six years old.

"You ever get afraid to be at the school? Tell me the truth. Whatever you *really* feel is okay to say, Damon," I gently reminded him. "I get afraid sometimes, too. Beavis and Butt-head scares me. Ren and Stimpy, too."

Damon smiled, and he shrugged his shoulders. "I'm afraid sometimes, yeah. I was shivering on our first day back. Our school isn't going to close down, is it?"

I smiled on the inside, but kept a straight face. "No, there'll be classes as usual tomorrow. Homework, too."

"I did it already," Damon answered defensively. Nana has him a little too sensitive about grades, but that probably isn't so terribly bad. "I get mostly all A's, just like you."

"Mostly all A's," I laughed. "What kind of sentence is that?"

"Accurate." He grinned like a young hyena who had just been told a pretty good joke on the Serengeti.

I grabbed Damon in a loose, playful headlock. I gently slid my knuckles over the top of his short haircut. Noogies. He was okay for now. He was strong, and he was a good person. I love him like crazy, and I wanted him to always know that.

Damon wiggled out of the headlock. He *danced* a fancy Sugar Ray Leonard–style two-step and fired a few quick, testing punches at my stomach. He was showing me what a tough little cub he was. I had no doubt about it.

Right about then I noticed someone leaving the school building. It was the same woman I'd seen in the early morning of Shanelle Green's murder. The one who had blown me away then. She was watching Damon and me tussle on the sidewalk. She had stopped walking to watch us.

She was tall and slender, almost six feet. I couldn't see her face very well in the shadows of the school building. I remembered her from the other morning, though. I remembered her self-confidence, a sense of mystery I'd felt about her.

She waved, and Damon waved back. Then she headed down to the same dark blue Mercedes, which was parked up against the wall of the building.

"You know her?" I asked.

"That's the new principal of our school," Damon informed me. "That's Mrs. Johnson."

I nodded. *Mrs. Johnson.* "She works late. I'm impressed. How do you like Mrs. Johnson?" I asked Damon as I watched her walk to her car. I remembered that Nana had talked about the principal and been very positive about her, calling her "inspirational" and saying she had a sweet disposition.

She was certainly attractive, and seeing her made my heart ache just a little. The truth was, I missed not having someone in my life. I was getting over a complicated friendship I'd had with a woman — Kate McTiernan. I had been working a lot, avoiding the whole issue that fall. I was still avoiding it that night.

Damon didn't hesitate with his answer to my question. "I like her. Everybody likes Mrs. Johnson. She's tough, though. She's even tougher than you are, Daddy," he said.

She didn't look so tough with her Mercedes sedan, but I had no reason not to believe my son. She was definitely brave to be in the school alone at night. Maybe a little too brave.

"Let's head on home," I finally said to Damon. "I just remembered this is a school night for you."

"Let's stay up and watch the Bullets play the Orlando Magic," he coaxed and grabbed onto my elbow.

"Oh — sure. No, let's get Jannie up and we'll all pull an all-nighter," I said and laughed loudly. We both laughed, sharing the jokey moment.

I slept in with the kids that night. I was definitely not over the murder at the Truth School. Sometimes, we'll throw blankets and pillows on the floor and sleep there as if we were homeless. It gives Nana fits, but I believe she thrives on her fits, so we make certain she has one every other week or so.

As I lay there with my eyes open, and both kids sleeping peacefully, I couldn't help thinking about Shanelle Green. It was the last thing I needed to think about. *Why had someone brought the body back to the schoolyard?* I wondered. There are always loose ends on cases, but this one made no sense, so it concerned me. It was a piece that didn't fit in a puzzle that was supposed to be finished.

Then I began thinking about Mrs. Johnson for a moment or two. That was a better place to be. *She's even tougher than you are, Daddy.* What a glowing recommendation from my little man. It was almost a dare. *Everybody likes Mrs. Johnson,* Damon had said.

I wondered what her first name was. I made a wild guess — *Christine*. The name just came to me. *Christine*. I liked the sound of it in my head.

I finally nodded off to sleep. I slept with the kids in the pile of blankets and pillows on the bedroom floor. No monsters visited us that night. I wouldn't let them.

The dragonslayer was on guard. Tired and sleepy and oversentimental, but ever so watchful.

Chapter 17

THIS WAS REALLY NUTS, insane, demented. *It was so great!* The killer wanted to go for it again, right now. Right this minute. He wanted to do *the two of them*. What a gas that would be. What a large charge. A real shockeroo.

He had watched them from afar — *father and son*. He thought of his own father, the totally worthless prick.

Then he saw the tall, pretty schoolteacher wave and get into her car. Instinctively, he hated her, too. Worthless black bitch. Phony teacher smile spread all over her face.

POW! POW! POW!

Three perfect headshots.

Three exploding head melons.

That's what they all deserved. Summary executions.

A really rude thought was forming in his mind as he watched the scene near the school. He already knew a lot of things about Alex Cross. *Cross was his detective, wasn't he? Cross had been assigned to his case, right? So Cross was his meat. A cop, just like his own father had been.*

The really interesting thing was that nobody had paid much attention to the first killing. The murder had almost gone unnoticed. The papers in Washington had barely picked it up. Same with TV. Nobody cared about a little black girl in Southeast. Why the hell should they?

All they cared about was Jack and Jill. Rich white people afraid for their lives. *Scar-y!* Well, fuck Jack and Jill. He was better than Jack and Jill, and he was going to demonstrate it.

The school principal drove past his hiding place in a cluster of overgrown bushes. He knew who she was, too. Mrs. Johnson of the Truth School. The Whitney Houston of Southeast, right? Screw her, man.

His eyes slowly drifted back to Alex Cross and his son. He felt anger rising inside him, steam building up. It was as if his secret button had been pushed again. The hair on his neck was standing at attention. He was beginning to see red, feeling spraying mists of red in his brain. *Somebody's* blood, right? Cross's? His son's? He loved the idea of them dying together. He could see it, man.

He followed Alex Cross and his kid home — in his rage state — but keeping a safe distance. He was thinking about what he was going to do next.

He was better than Jack and Jill. He'd prove it to Cross and everyone else.

Chapter 18

THE FESTIVE charity gala for the Council on Mental Health was being held at the Pension Building on F Street and Fourth on Friday night. The grand ballroom was three stories, with huge marble columns everywhere, and more than a thousand guests noisily seated around a glistening working fountain. The waiters and waitresses wore Santa Claus hats. The band broke into a lively swing version of "Winter Wonderland." What great fun.

The guest speaker for the evening was none other than the Princess of Wales. Sam Harrison was there as well. *Jack was there.*

He observed Princess Di closely as she entered the glittering, stately ballroom. Her entourage included a financier rumored to be her next husband, the Brazilian ambassador and his wife, and several celebrities from the chic American fashion world. Ironically, two of the models in the group appeared to suffer from anorexia nervosa — the flip side of bulimia, the nervous disorder that had plagued Diana for the previous dozen years.

Jack moved a few steps closer to Princess Di. He was intrigued, and had serious questions about the quality of her security arrangement. He watched the Secret Service boys make a discreet sweep, then remain on duty nearby, earphones at the ready.

A formal toastmaster had been brought all the way from England to properly salute the queen — the council's president — and host Walter Annenberg. The ambassador spoke briefly, then a lavish, though overcooked and underspiced, dinner followed: baby lamb with sauce Niçoise and haricots verts.

When the princess finally rose to speak during dessert, an orange almond tart with orange sauce and Marsala cream, Jack was less than thirty feet away from her. She wore an expensive gold sheath of taffeta with sequins, but he found her somewhat gawky, at least to his taste. Her large feet made him think of the cartoon character Daisy Duck. *Princess Daisy,* that was his moniker for Di.

Diana's speech at the gala was very personal, if familiar, to those who had followed her life closely. A troubled childhood and adolescence, a debilitating search for perfection, feelings of self-revulsion and low personal esteem. All this had led to what she spoke of as her "shameful friend," bulimia.

Jack found the speech strangely off-putting and cloying. He wasn't at all touched by Diana's self-pity, or the near hysteria that seemed to reside just below the surface of her performance — perhaps her entire life.

The audience clearly had a different reaction, even the usually cool-as-ice Secret Service guards seemed to react emotionally to the popular Di. The applause when she had finished speaking was thunderous and seemed heartfelt and sincere.

Then the entire room stood up, Jack included, and continued the warm, noisy tribute. He could almost have reached out and touched Di. *Here's to bulimia,* he wanted to call out. *Here's to worthwhile causes of all kinds.*

It was time for him to move into action again. It was time for number two in the Jack and Jill story. Time for a lot of things to begin.

It was also his turn to be the star tonight — to solo, as

it were. He had been watching another well-known personality that evening at the party. He had watched her, studied her habits and mannerisms on a few other occasions as well.

Natalie Sheehan was physically striking, much more so than Di, actually. The much-admired TV newswoman was blond, about five eight in heels. She wore a simple, classic, black silk dress. She oozed charm, but especially class. *First* class. Natalie Sheehan had been aptly described as "American royalty," "an American princess."

Jack started to move at a little past nine-thirty. Guests were already dancing to an eight-piece band. The breezy chitchat was flowing freely: Marion Gingrich's business dealings, trade problems with China, John Major's problems du jour, planned ski trips to Aspen, Whistler, or Alta.

Natalie Sheehan had downed three margaritas — straight up, with salt around the rim. He had watched her. She didn't show it, but she had to be feeling something, had to be a little high.

She's an extremely good actor, Jack was thinking as he came up beside her at one of the complimentary bars. *She's a master of the one-night stand and the one-weekend affair.* Jill had researched the hell out of her. *I know everything about you, Natalie.*

He took two sidelong steps, and suddenly they were face to face. They nearly collided, actually. He could smell her perfume. Flowers and spices. Very nice. He even knew the delightful fragrance's name — ESCADA *acte 2*. He'd read that it was Natalie's favorite.

"I'm sorry. Excuse me," he said, feeling his cheeks redden.

"No, no. I wasn't looking where I was going. Clumsy me," Natalie said and smiled. It was her killer TV close-up smile. Really something to experience firsthand.

Jack smiled back, and suddenly his eyes communicated recognition. *He knew her.* "You never forgot a name, or a face, not in eleven years of broadcasting," he said to Natalie Sheehan. "That's an accurate quote, I believe."

Natalie didn't miss a beat. "You're Scott Cookson. We met at the Meridian. It was in early September. You're a lawyer with . . . a prestigious D.C. law firm. Of course."

She laughed at her small joke. Nice laugh. Beautiful lips and perfectly capped teeth. *The* Natalie Sheehan. His target for the evening.

"We *did* meet at the Meridian?" she said, checking her facts like the good reporter she was. "You are Scott Cookson?"

"We did, and I am. You had another affair to attend after that, at the British embassy."

"You seem never to forget a face or factoid, either," she said. The smile remained fixed. Perfect, glowing, almost effervescent. The TV star in real life, if this was real life.

Jack shrugged, and acted shy, which wasn't so hard to do with Natalie. "Some faces, some factoids," he said.

She was classically beautiful, extremely *attractive at any rate,* he couldn't help thinking. The warm heartland smile was her trademark, and it worked very well for her. He had studied it for hours before tonight. He wasn't completely immune to her charms — not even under the circumstances.

"Well," Natalie said to him. "I *don't* have another party after this one. Actually, I'm cutting back on parties. Believe it or not. This is a good cause, though."

"I agree. I believe in good causes."

"Oh, and what's your favorite cause, Scott?"

"Society for the Prevention of Cruelty to Animals," he said. "That's my pet cause."

He tried to look pleasantly surprised that she would remain talking with him. He could play parlor games as well as anyone — when he had to, when he wanted to.

"If I might be just a little bold," he said, "would you consider the two of us cutting back together?" His very natural and unassuming smile undercut the forward-sounding line. It was a come-on just the same. There was no disguising that. Natalie Sheehan's answer was tremendously important, to both of them.

She stared at him, slightly taken aback. *He'd completely blown it*, he thought. Or maybe *she* was acting now.

Then Natalie Sheehan laughed. It was a hearty laugh, almost raucous. He was sure that no one in America had ever heard it in her prim and proper role as a network television reporter.

Poor Natalie, Jack thought. *Number two.*

Chapter 19

NATALIE TOOK another margarita for the trip home. "A roadie," she told him and laughed that deep, wonderful laugh of hers again.

"I learned how to party a little bit at St. Catherine's Academy in Cleveland. Then at Ohio State," she confided as they walked to the garage under the Pension Building. She was trying to show him that she was different from her television persona. Looser, more fun. He got that much, got the message. He even liked her for it. He was noticing that her usually crisp and exact enunciation was just a little off now. She probably thought it was sexy, and she was right. *She was actually very nice, very down-to-earth*, which surprised him a little.

They took her car, as Jill had accurately predicted. Natalie drove the silverblue Dodge Stealth a little too fast. All the while she talked rapid-fire, too, but kept it interesting: GATT, Boris Yeltsin's drinking problems, D.C. real estate, campaign-financing reform. She showed herself to be intelligent, informed, high-spirited, and only slightly neurotic about the ongoing struggle between men and women.

"Where are we going?" he finally thought he should ask. He

already knew the answer, of course. The Jefferson Hotel. Natalie's honey trap in D.C. Her place.

"Oh, to my laboratory," she said. "Why, are you nervous?"

"No. Well, maybe a little nervous," he said and laughed. It was the truth.

She brought him upstairs to her private office in the Jefferson Hotel on Sixteenth Street. Two beautiful rooms and a spacious bath overlooked downtown. He knew that she also had a house in Old Town Alexandria. Jill had visited there. Just in case. Just to be thorough. *Measure twice. Measure five times, if necessary.*

"This place is my treat for myself. A special spot where I can work right here in the city," she told him. "Isn't the view breathtaking? It makes you feel as if you own the whole city. It does for me, anyway."

"I see what you mean. I love Washington myself," Jack said. For a moment he was lost, peering off into the distance. He did love this city and what it was supposed to represent — at least, he had once upon a time. He still remembered his very first visit here. He had been a marine private, twenty years old. *The Soldier.*

He quietly surveyed her workspace. Laptop computer, Canon Bubblejet, two VCRs, gold Emmy, pocket OAG. Fresh-cut flowers in a pink vase beside a black ceramic bowl filled with foreign pocket change.

Natalie Sheehan, this is your life. Kind of impressive; kind of sad; kind of over.

Natalie stopped and looked at him closely, almost as if she were seeing him for the first time. "You're very nice, aren't you? You strike me as being a very genuine person. The genuine article, as they say, or used to say. You're a nice guy, aren't you, Scott Cookson?"

"Not really," he shrugged. He rolled his sparkling blue eyes and an engaging little half-smile appeared. He *was* good at this: getting the girl — if it was necessary. Actually, though, under normal circumstances, he never ran around. He was at heart a one-woman guy.

"Nobody's really nice in Washington, right? Not after you've lived here for a while," he said and continued to smile.

"I suppose that's true. I guess that's basically accurate," she snorted out a raucous laugh, then laughed again. At herself? He could see that Natalie was disappointed a little in his answer. She wanted, or maybe she needed, something genuine in her life. Well, so did he; and *this* was it. The game was exquisite, and it was definitely the genuine article. It was so important. It was history. And it was happening right now in this Jefferson Hotel suite.

This irresistible, dangerous game he was playing, this was his life. It was something with meaning, and he felt fulfilled. No, he *felt,* for the first time in years.

"Hi there, Scott Cookson. Did we lose you for a sec?"

"No, no. I'm right here. I'm a here-and-now kind of person. Just admiring the wonderful view you have here. Washington in the wee hours."

"It's our view for tonight. Yours and mine."

Natalie made the first physical move, which was also as he had predicted and was therefore reassuring to him.

She came up close to him, from behind. She placed her long slender arms around his chest, bracelets jangling. It was extremely nice. She was highly desirable, almost overpoweringly so, and she knew it. He felt himself become aroused, become extremely hard down the left side of his trousers. That kind of arousal was like a small itch compared to everything else he was feeling now. Besides, he could use it. *Let her feel your excitement. Let her touch you.*

"Are you okay with this?" she asked. She actually *was* nice, wasn't she? Thoughtful, considerate. It was too bad, really. Too late to change the plan, to switch targets. Bad luck, Natalie.

"I'm very okay with this, Natalie."

"Can I take your tie off, tasteful as it is?" she asked.

"I think that ties should be done away with altogether," he answered.

"No, ties definitely have a place. First Communions, funerals, coronations."

Natalie was standing very close to him. She could be so sweetly, gently seductive — and that was sad. He liked her more than he'd thought he would. Once upon a time, she had probably been the simple Midwestern beauty she now half pretended to be. He had felt nothing but revulsion for Daniel Fitzpatrick, but he felt a great deal tonight. Guilt, regret, second thoughts, compassion. *The hardest thing was killing up close like this*.

"How about white pima cotton shirts? Are you a white-shirt man?" Natalie asked.

"Don't like white shirts at all. White shirts *are* for funerals and coronations. And charity balls."

"I agree a thousand percent with that sentiment," Natalie said as she slowly unbuttoned his white shirt. He let her fingers do the walking. They trailed down to his belt. Teasing. Expert at this. She rubbed her palm across his crotch, then quickly took her hand away.

"How about high heels?" Natalie asked.

"Actually, I like those on the right occasion, and on the right woman," he said. "But I like going barefoot, too."

"Nicely put. Give a girl her choice. I like that."

She kicked off just *one* black slingback, then laughed at her joke. A *choice* — one shoe on, one off.

"Silk dresses?" she whispered against his neck. He was rock-hard now. His breathing was labored. So was Natalie's. He considered making love to her first. Was that fair game? Or was it rape? Natalie had managed to confuse the issue for him.

"I can do without those, depending on the occasion, of course," he whispered back.

"Mmm. We seem to agree on a lot of things."

Natalie Sheehan slid out of her dress. Then she was in her blue lacy underwear, one shoe, black stockings. Around her neck was a thin gold chain and cross that looked as if it had come with her all the way from Ohio.

Jack still had his trousers on. But no white shirt, no tie. "Can we go in there?" she whispered, indicating the bedroom. "It's really nice in there. Same view, only with a fireplace. The fireplace even *works*. Something actually works in Washington."

"Okay. Well, let's start a fire then."

Jack picked her up as if she weighed nothing, as if they were both elegant dancers, which in a way they were. He didn't want to care about her, but he did. *He forced the thought out of his mind. He couldn't think like that, like a schoolboy, a Pollyanna, a normal human being.*

"Strong, too. Hmmm," she sighed, finally kicking off the other shoe.

The picture window in the bedroom was astonishing to behold. The view was north up Sixteenth Street. The streets and Scott Circle below were like a lovely and expensive necklace, jewelry by Harry Winston or Tiffany. Something Princess Di might wear.

Jack had to remind himself that he was stalking Natalie. Nothing must stop this from happening now. The final decision had been made. The die was cast. Literally.

He forced himself not to be sentimental. Just like that! He could be so cold, and so good at this.

He thought about throwing the high-spirited and beautiful newswoman through the plate glass window of her bedroom. He wondered if she would crash through or just bounce back off the glass.

Instead, he set Natalie down gently on a bed covered with an Amish quilt. He pulled out handcuffs from his jacket pocket.

He let her see them.

Natalie Sheehan frowned, her blue eyes widening in disbelief. She seemed to deflate, to depress, right before his eyes.

"Is this some kind of sick joke?" She was angry with him, but she was also hurt. She figured he was a freak, *and she was right beyond her wildest nightmares.*

His voice was very low. "No, this isn't a joke. This is very serious, Natalie. You might say that it's newsworthy."

There was a sudden and very sharp knock at the door to the demi-apartment. He held up a finger for Natalie to be quiet, very quiet.

Her eyes showed confusion, genuine fear, an uncustomary loss of her cool demeanor.

His eyes were cold. They showed nothing at all.

"That's *Jill*," he told Natalie Sheehan. "I'm *Jack*. I'm sorry. I really am."

Chapter 20

I EASED MY WAY inside the Jefferson Hotel just before eight in the morning. A little Gershwin was rolling through my head, trying to soothe the savage, trying to smooth out the jagged edges. Suddenly, I was playing the bizarre game, too. *Jack and Jill. I was part of it now.*

The cool dignity of the hotel was being scrupulously maintained; at least, it was in the elegant front lobby. It was difficult to grasp the reality that a bizarre and unspeakable tragedy had struck here, or that it ever could.

I passed a fancy grillroom and a shop displaying couture fashion. A century-old clock gently chimed the hour; otherwise, the room was hushed. There was no sign, not a hint, that the Jefferson — indeed the entire city of Washington — was in shock and chaos over a pair of grisly, high-profile murders and threats of still more to come.

I am continually fascinated by facades like the one I encountered at the Jefferson. Maybe that's why I love Washington so much. The hotel lobby reminded me that most things aren't what they appear to be. It was a perfect representation for so much that goes on in D.C. Clever facades fronting even more clever facades.

Jack and Jill had committed their second murder in five days. In this serene and very posh hotel. They had threatened several more murders — and no one had a clue why, or how to stop the celebrity stalking.

It was escalating.

Clearly, it was.

But why? What did Jack and Jill want? What was their sick game all about?

I had already been on the phone very early that morning, talking to my strange friends in abnormal psych at Quantico. One of the advantages I have is that they all know I have a doctorate in psych from Johns Hopkins and they're willing to talk with me, even to share theories and insights. So far, they were stumped. Then I checked in with a contact of mine at the FBI's evidence analysis labs. The evidence hounds didn't have much of anything to go on, either. They admitted as much to me. Jack and Jill had all of us chasing our tails in double time.

Speaking of which, I had been ordered by the chief of detectives to work up "one of your famous psych profiles" on the homicidal couple, if that's what they really were. I felt the task was futile at this point, but I hadn't been given a choice by The Jefe. Working at home on my PC, I ran a wide swath through the available Behavioral Science Unit and Violent Criminal Apprehension Program data. Nothing obvious or very useful popped up, as I suspected it wouldn't. It was too early in the chase, and Jack and Jill were too good.

For now at least the correct steps were (1) gather as much information and data as possible; (2) ask the right questions, and plenty of them; (3) start collecting wild hunches on index cards that I would carry around until the end of the case.

I knew about several stalker cases, and I ran the information down in my head. One inescapable fact was that the Bureau now had a database of more than fifty thousand potential and actual stalkers. That was up from less than a thousand in the 1980s. There didn't seem to be any single stalker profile, but many of them shared traits: first and foremost, obsession with the media; need for recognition; obsession with violence and religion; difficulty forming loving relationships of their own. I thought of Margaret Ray, the obsessed fan who had broken into David Letterman's home in Connecticut numerous times. She had called Letterman "*the dominant person in my life.*" I watch Letterman sometimes myself, but he's not *that* good.

Then there was the Monica Seles stabbing in Hamburg, Germany.

Katarina Witt had nearly suffered the same fate at the hand of a "fan."

Sylvester Stallone, Madonna, Michael Jackson, and Jodie Foster had all been seriously stalked and attacked by people who claimed to adore them.

But who were Jack and Jill? Why had they chosen Washington, D.C., for the murders? Had someone in the government harmed one or both of them in some real or imagined way?

What was the link between Senator Daniel Fitzpatrick and the murdered television newswoman Natalie Sheehan? What could Fitzpatrick and Sheehan possibly have in common? They were liberals — could that be something? Or were the killings random, and therefore nearly impossible to chart? *Random* was a nasty word that was sticking in my head more and more as I thought about the case. *Random* was a very bad word in homicide circles. Random murders were almost impossible to solve.

Most celebrity stalkers didn't murder their prey — at least, they didn't use extreme violence right away. That bothered the hell out of me about Jack and Jill. How long had they been obsessed with Senator Fitzpatrick and Natalie Sheehan? How had they ultimately chosen their victims? *Don't let these be random selections and murders. Anything but that.*

I was also intrigued by the fact that there were two of them, working closely together.

I had just come off a dizzying, high-profile case in which two friends, two males, had been kidnapping and murdering women for more than thirteen years. They had been cooperating, but also competing with each other. The psychological principle involved was known as twinning.

So what about Jack and Jill? Were they freak-friends? Were they romantically involved? Or was their bond something else? Was it a sexual thing for them? That seemed like a reasonable possibility. Power dominance? A really kinky parlor game, maybe the ultimate sex fantasy? Were they a husband-and-wife team? Or maybe spree killers like Bonnie and Clyde?

Was this the beginning of a gruesome crime spree? A multiple-murder spree in Washington?

Would it spread elsewhere? To other large cities where celebrities tend to cluster? New York? Los Angeles? Paris? London?

I stepped off the elevator on the seventh floor of the Jefferson Hotel and looked into a corridor of dazed and confused faces. Judging from the looks at the crime scene, I was pretty much up to speed.

> **Jack and Jill came to The Hill**
> **To kill, to kill, to kill.**

Chapter 21

"THE GOOD DOCTOR CROSS, the master of disaster. Well, I'll be. Alex — hey, Alex — *over here!*"

I was lost in a bad jumble of thoughts and impressions about the murders when I heard my name. I recognized the voice immediately, and it brought a smile to my lips.

I turned and saw Kyle Craig of the FBI. Another dragonslayer, this one originally from Lexington, Massachusetts. Kyle was not your typical FBI agent. He was a totally straight shooter. He wasn't uptight, and he usually wasn't bureaucratic. Kyle and I had worked together on some very bad cases in the past. He was a specialist in high-profile crimes that were marked by extreme violence or multiple murders. Kyle was an expert in the nasty, scary stuff most Bureau agents didn't want to be involved with on a regular basis. Beyond that, he was a friend.

"They've got all the big guns out on this one," Kyle said as we shook hands in the foyer. He was tall, still gaunt. Distinctive features and strikingly black hair, coal black hair. He had a long hawk's nose that looked sharp enough to cut.

"Who's here so far, Kyle?" I asked him. He would have everything scoped out by now. He was smart and observant, and his instincts were usually good. Kyle also knew who everybody was and how they fit into the larger picture.

Kyle puckered up. He made a face as if he had just sucked on a particularly sour lemon. "Who the hell isn't here, Alex? Detectives from D.C., your own *compadres*. The Bureau, of course. DEA, believe it or not. The blue suit is CIA. You can tell by the clipped wings. Your close friend Chief Pittman is in visiting with Ms. Sheehan's lovely corpse. They're in the boudoir as we speak."

"Now *that's* scary," I said and smiled thinly. "About as grotesque as you can get."

Kyle pointed to a closed door, which I assumed was the bedroom. "I don't think they want to be disturbed. A rumor circulating at Quantico has it that Chief of Detectives Pittman is a necrophiliac," he said with a deadpan look. "Could that be true?"

"Victimless crimes," I said.

"How about a little respect for the dead," Kyle said, peering down his nose at me. "Even in death, I'm certain Ms. Sheehan would find a way to rebuff your chief of detectives."

I wasn't surprised that The Jefe himself had come to the Jefferson. This was developing into the biggest D.C. homicide case in years. It definitely would be if Jack and Jill struck again soon — as they had promised.

Reluctantly, I parted company with Kyle and walked toward the closed bedroom door. I opened it slowly, as if it might be booby-trapped.

The one and only Chief George Pittman was in the bedroom with a man in a gray suit. Probably a forensics guy. They both glanced around at me. Pittman was chomping on an unlit Bauza cigar. Pittman frowned and shook his head when he saw who it was. Nothing he could do about it. It was Commissioner Clouser's invitation-order that I be on the case. It was obvious that The Jefe didn't want me here.

He muttered "the late Alex Cross" to the other suit. So much for polite introductions and light banter.

The two of them turned back to the famous corpse on the bed.

Chief Pittman had been abusive for no apparent reason. I didn't let it bother me too much. It was business-pretty-much-as-usual with the rude, bullying prick. *What a useless bastard, a real horse's ass.* All he ever did was get in the way.

I breathed in slowly a couple of times. Got into the job, the homicide scene. I walked over to the bed and started my routine: the collection of raw impressions.

A G-string was pulled partly over Natalie Sheehan's head, and the waistband was wrapped around her throat. Panties covered her nose, chin, and mouth. Her wide blue eyes were fixed on the ceiling. She was still wearing black stockings and a blue bra that matched the panties.

Here was evidence of kinkiness again, and yet I didn't quite believe it. Everything was too orderly and arranged. Why would they want us to suspect kinky sex might be involved? Was that something? Were Jack and Jill frustrated lovers? Was Jack impotent? We needed to know whether anyone had sex with the victim.

It was a particularly disturbing death scene. Natalie Sheehan had been dead for about eight hours, according to Kyle's information. She was no longer beautiful, though, not even close. Ironically, she had taken her biggest news story with her to the grave. She knew Jack — and maybe Jill.

I could remember watching her on TV, and it was almost as if someone I knew personally had been murdered. Maybe that's why there's such fascination with celebrity murder cases. We see people like Natalie Sheehan on almost a daily basis; we come to think that we know them. And we believe they lead such interesting lives. Even their deaths are interesting.

I could already see that there were some obvious and striking similarities to the murder of Senator Fitzpatrick. The element of kinky sadism for one thing. Natalie Sheehan was manacled to the bedposts with handcuffs. She was seminude. She also seemed to have been "executed," just as the senator had been.

The news celebrity had received one close-range gunshot to

the left side of her head, which hung to one side as if her long neck had been broken. Maybe it had been.

Was this the Jack and Jill pattern? Organized, efficient, and cold-blooded as hell. Kinky for some reason known only to them. Pseudokinky? Sexual obsession, or a sign of impotence? What was the pattern telling us? What was it communicating?

I was beginning to formulate a psychological personality print for the killers. The method and style of the killings were more important to me than any physical evidence. Always. Both murders had been carefully planned — methodical, very structured, and *leisurely* — Jack and Jill were playing a cold-blooded game. So far, there had been no significant slipups that I knew of. The only physical evidence left at the scenes was *intentional* — the notes.

Sexual fantasy was obvious — both in exhibiting the female on her bed and in the senator's case, male mutilation. *Did Jack and Jill have trouble with sex?*

My initial impression was that both killers were white, somewhere between the ages of thirty and forty-five — probably closer to the latter, based on the high level of organization in both murders. I suspected well above average intelligence, but also persuasiveness and physical attractiveness. That was particularly telling, and bizarre to me — since the killers had managed to get *inside* the celebrities' apartments. It was the best clue we had.

There was much more for me to take in, and I did, madly scribbling away in my notepad. Occasionally, The Jefe looked my way and glared at me. Checking up on me.

I wanted to go at him. He represented so many things that were wrong with the department, the Washington P.D. He was such a controlling macho asshole, and not half as bright as he thought he was.

"Anything, Cross?" he finally turned and asked in his usual clipped manner.

"Not so far," I said.

That wasn't the truth. What definitely occurred to me was that Daniel Fitzpatrick and Natalie Sheehan might both have been "promiscuous," in the old-fashioned sense of the word. Maybe Jack and Jill "disapproved" of them. Both bodies had been left exposed, in compromising and very embarrassing positions. The killers seemed preoccupied with sex — or at least the sex lives of famous people.

Exposed . . . or to expose . . . , I wondered. *Exposed for what reason?*

"I'd like to look at the note," I told Pittman, trying to be civil and professional.

Pittman waved a hand in the direction of an end table on the far side of the bed. His gesture was dismissive and rude. I wouldn't treat the rawest rookie patrolman that way. I had shown more respect to Chop-It-Off-Chucky.

I walked over and read the note for myself. It was another poem. Five lines.

> Jack and Jill came to The Hill
> To right another error.
> To make it short
> Her news report
> Was filled with her own terror.

I shook my head back and forth a few times, but didn't say anything about the note to Pittman. To hell with him. The rhyme didn't tell me much of anything yet. I hoped it would eventually. Actually, the rhymes were clever, but without emotion. What had made these two killers so *clever and cold?*

I continued to search the bedroom. I was infamous in homicide circles for spending a lot of time at crime scenes. Sometimes I'd spend a whole day. I planned to do the same thing here. Most of the dead woman's effects seemed to tie in with her career, almost as if she had no other life. Videocassettes, expense sheets from her network, a pilfered stapler with CBS engraved on it. I observed the murder scene, and the dead woman, from several angles. I wondered if the killers had taken anything with them.

I couldn't concentrate the way I wanted to, though. Chief Pittman had gotten on my nerves. I had let him get to me.

Why had both victims been left exposed? What was it that connected them in death — at least in the minds of the murderers? The killers felt compelled to graphically point out certain things to us. In fact, everything about Fitzpatrick and Sheehan was in public view now. Thanks to Jack and Jill.

This is so bad, I thought and had to reach down deep for a breath.

Worst of all, I was completely hooked on the case. I was definitely hooked.

Then everything took a turn for the worse in the bedroom. A bad and unexpected turn.

I was standing near George Pittman when he spoke again, without looking at me. "You come back after we're finished, Cross. Come back later."

The Jefe's words hung like stale smoke in the air. I had trouble believing that he'd actually said them. I have always tried to act with some respect toward Pittman. It's been hard, nearly impossible most of the time, but I've done it anyway.

"I'm talking to you, Cross," Pittman raised his voice a notch. "You hear what I said? Do you hear me?"

Then the chief of detectives did something he shouldn't have, *something so bad,* something I couldn't look past. He reached out and pushed me with the heel of his hand. Pushed me hard. I stumbled back a half-step. Caught my balance. Both my fists slowly rose to my chest.

I didn't stop to think. Maybe some stored-up venom and powerful dislike made me act. That was part of it.

I reached out and grabbed Pittman with both hands. This unspoken thing between us, the pattern of disrespect from him, had been building for a couple of years — at least that long. Now it flared big-time and ugly. It exploded inside the dead woman's bedroom.

George Pittman and I are about the same age. He's not as tall as I am, but he's probably heavier by thirty pounds. He has the squat, blocklike build and look of a football linebacker from the early sixties. *He's bad at his job and he shouldn't have it. He resents the hell out of me because I'm decent at what I do. Fucker!*

I grabbed and picked him up, right off the floor. I look fairly strong, but I'm actually a lot stronger. Pittman's eyes widened in disbelief and sudden fear.

I slammed him hard against the bedroom wall. Then I banged him into the wall a second time. Nothing lethal or too damaging, but definitely a bell-ringer, an attention-grabber.

Each time his body hit, the staid Jefferson Hotel seemed to shake to its very foundation. The Jefe's body went slack. He didn't fight back. He couldn't believe what I'd just done. To be honest, neither could I.

I loosened my grip on Pittman. I finally let him go, and he wobbled on his feet. I knew I hadn't hurt him much physically, but I had hurt his pride. I had also made a big mistake.

I didn't say a word. Neither did the other gray suit in the room. I took some solace in the fact that Pittman had pushed first. He had started this, and for no reason. I wondered if the other suit had seen it that way, but I doubted it.

I left the crime-scene bedroom. Pittman never spoke to me.

I wondered also if I had just left the Washington Police Department.

Chapter 22

"THIS IS AN ALERT! Something is going down at Crown. Up and at 'em, everybody! We've got trouble at Crown. This is a real alert! This is not a drill! *This is for real.*"

Half a dozen Secret Service agents took the sudden alert very seriously. They watched *Jack* through Rangemaster binoculars, three sets of them.

Jack was on the move.

They couldn't believe what they were witnessing. Not one of the agents could believe this very bad scene playing out before them. The alert was definitely for real, though.

"It's Jack, all right. What is he — crazy?"

"We have full visual contact with Jack. Where the hell is he going? Goddamn him. *What's going on?*"

The six watchers comprised three highly professional teams. They were all first-teamers, among the best and brightest of more than two thousand Secret Service agents working around the world. They sat inside dark-colored Ford sedans parked on Fifteenth Street Northwest. This was getting very serious, and very scary, in a hurry.

This is a real alert.

This is not a drill.

"Jack is definitely leaving Crown now. It's twenty-three forty. At this moment, we have Jack in our crosshairs," one of the agents spoke into the car mike.

"Yeah. Jack can be a real tricky fellow, though. He's proven it before. *Keep* him right in your sights. Where's the lovely Jill, home base?"

"This is home base," a female agent's voice came onto the line immediately.

"Jill is nice and comfy up on the third floor of Crown. She's reading Barbara Bush on Barbara Bush. She's in her jammies. Not to worry about Jill."

"We're absolutely sure about that?"

"Home base is sure about Jill. Jill's in bed. Jill is being a good girl, for tonight anyway."

"Good for Jill. How the hell did Jack get out?"

"He used that old tunnel between the basement of Crown and the Treasury Building. That's how he got out!"

This is an alert.

This is not a drill.

Jack is on the move.

"Jack is approaching Pennsylvania Avenue now. He's near the Willard Hotel. He just glanced back over his shoulder. Jack's paranoid, as well he should be. I don't think he saw us. *Oh, shit,* somebody just flashed their high beams in front of the Willard. *A vehicle is pulling out — and pulling up alongside Jack!* Red Jeep! Jack is getting inside the fucking red Jeep."

"Roger. So much for having Jack in our damn crosshairs. We'll follow him pronto. Virginia plates on the Jeep. License number two-three-one HCY. Koons dealer sticker. Start a trace on the Jeep, now."

"We're following the red Jeep. We're on Jack's ass. Full alert for the Jackal. *Repeat: full alert for the Jackal.* This is not a drill!"

"Do not lose Jack tonight of all nights. *Do not lose Jack* under any circumstances."

"Roger. We have Jack in plain sight."

Three dark sedans took off in hot pursuit of the Jeep. *Jack* was the Secret Service's code name for President Thomas Byrnes. *Jill* was the code name for the First Lady. *Crown* had been the Service's code word for the White House for nearly twenty years.

Most of the current-duty agents genuinely liked President Byrnes. He was a down-to-earth guy, a very regular person as recent presidents went. Not too much bullshit about him. Occasionally, though, the President took off on an unannounced date with some lady friend, either in D.C. or on the road. The Secret Service referred to this as "the president's disease." Thomas Byrnes was hardly the first to suffer from this malady. John Kennedy, Franklin Delano Roosevelt, and especially Lyndon Johnson had been the worst offenders. It seemed to be a perk of high office.

The coincidence of the names chosen by the two psychopathic killers in D.C., the so-called celebrity stalkers, wasn't lost on the Secret Service. The Secret Service didn't believe in coincidences. They had already met four times on the matter — long, difficult meetings in the Emergency Command Center in the West Wing basement of the White House. The name for any would-be assassins of the president was *Jackal*. *Jackal* had been used by the Secret Service for more than thirty years.

The "coincidence" of the names worried the PPD, the Presidential Protection Division, a great deal — especially when President Byrnes decided to go out on one of his unannounced walks, which for obvious reasons didn't include any of his bodyguards.

There were two *Jacks and* two *Jills.*

The Secret Service did not, could not, accept this as a coincidence.

"We've lost the red Jeep around the Tidal Basin. We've lost Jack," an agent's voice suddenly exploded over the car-radio speakers.

Everything was chaos. Full-alert chaos.

This was not a test.

PART II
THE DRAGONSLAYER

Chapter 23

ON MONDAY NIGHT something finally broke on Jack and Jill. It was something potentially big. I hoped it wasn't a hoax.

I'd just gotten home to try and catch a bite of dinner with the kids when the phone rang. It was Kyle Craig. He told me a videotaped message, reportedly from Jack and Jill, had been delivered to the CNN studios. The killers had made a home movie for the world to see. Jack and Jill had also sent cover letters to the *Washington Post* and the *New York Times*. They were planning to "explain" themselves that night.

I had to rush out before Nana's roast chicken hit the supper table. Jannie and Damon gave me their not-again looks. They were right to think that way.

I hurried to the Union Station section of Washington, around H and North Capitol. I didn't want to be late for the party that Jack and Jill were throwing. This was another example of the two of them demonstrating their control over us.

I arrived at CNN headquarters just in time for the screening and only moments before the video was to be aired on *Larry King Live*. Senior agents from the FBI and Secret Service were crowded into a low-key, cozy CNN viewing room. So were various techies, administrators, and lawyers from the news network. Everybody looked incredibly tense and uptight.

The room was completely silent as the filmed message from Jack and Jill began. I was afraid to blink. We all were.

"You believe this shit?" somebody finally muttered.

Jack and Jill had been filming us! That was the first shock of the night. *They had actually filmed the police outside Senator Fitzpatrick's apartment building a few days earlier. They had been right there in the crowd of onlookers, the ambulance-chasers.*

The film was a jarring, documentary-style collage of black and white, with some color. The opening shots were from several angles outside Senator Fitzpatrick's building. It was like a well-made student film, but a little artsy. Then something even more unexpected and powerful came on the screen.

The murderers had filmed the last moments of Senator Fitzpatrick's life, seconds before his murder, I guessed. There were haunting shots of the senator alive. It got worse from there.

We saw graphic shots of Daniel Fitzpatrick, naked, handcuffed to his bed. We heard his voice. "Please don't do this," he pleaded with his captors. Then we heard the click of a trigger. A shot was fired only an inch or two from Fitzpatrick's right ear. Then came a second shot. The senator's head exploded on film. People gasped at the awful image and sound that carried the senator into eternity.

"Oh, Jesus! Jesus!" a woman screamed. Several people looked away from the screen. Others covered their eyes. I stayed with it. I couldn't miss anything. This was all vital information for the case that I was trying to understand. This was more valuable than all the DNA testing, serology, and fingerprinting in the world.

The tone of the film suddenly changed after the footage of Fitzpatrick's vicious murder. Images of ordinary people on the streets of unidentified cities and small towns followed the chilling death sequence. A few of the people on camera waved, some smiled broadly, most seemed indifferent as they were being filmed, presumably by Jack and Jill.

The film continued to weave together black-and-white and color footage, but not in a disorderly fashion. Whoever had stitched it together had a decent skill for editing.

One of them is an artist, or at least has strong artistic tendencies, I thought to myself and made a mental note. *What kind of artist would be involved in something like this?* I was familiar with several theories about links between creativity and psychopaths. Bundy, Dahmer, even Manson, could be considered "creative" killers. On the other hand, Richard Wagner, Degas, Jean Genet, and many other artists had exhibited psychopathic behavior in their lives, but they didn't kill anyone.

Then, about sixty-five seconds into the film, a narration began. We heard two voices: a man's and a woman's. Something dramatic was happening. It caught all of us by surprise.

Jack and Jill had decided to speak to us.

It was almost as if the killers were right there in the studio. The two of them alternated speaking as the film collage continued, but both voices had been electronically filtered, presumably so they couldn't be recognized. I would move on unscrambling the voices as soon as the show was over. But the show sure wasn't over yet.

JACK: For a long time, people like us have sat back and taken the injustices dished out by the elite few in this country. We have been patient and suffering and, for the most part, silent. What is the cynical saying — *don't just do something, sit there?* We have waited for the American system of checks and balances to take hold and work for us. But the system has not worked for a long, long time. Nothing seems to work anymore. Does anyone seriously dispute that?

JILL: Unscrupulous people, such as lawyers and businessmen, have learned to take advantage of our innocence and our goodwill and, most of all, our generosity of spirit. Let us repeat that important thought — *highly* unscrupulous people have learned to take advantage of our innocence, our goodwill, and our wonderful American spirit. Many of them are in our government, or work closely with our so-called leaders.

JACK: Look at the faces before you in this film. These are the disenfranchised. These are the people without any hope, or any belief in our country anymore. These are the victims of *the violence that originates in Washington, in New York, in Los Angeles*. Do you recognize the disenfranchised? Are you one of the victims? *We are*. We're just another Jack and Jill in the crowd.

JILL: Look at what our so-called leaders have done to us. Look at the despair and suffering our leaders are responsible for. Look at the sickness of cynicism they've created. The dreams and hopes they have wantonly destroyed. Our leaders are systematically destroying America.

JACK: Look at the faces.

JILL: Look at the faces.

JACK: Look at the faces. Now do you understand why we are coming to get you? Do you see? . . . Just *look at the faces*. Look at what you have done. Look at the unspeakable crimes you have committed.

JILL: Jack and Jill have come to The Hill. This is why we're here. Beware to all those who work and live in the capital, and attempt to control the rest of us. You've been playing with all of our lives — now we're going to play with yours. It's our turn to play. It's Jack and Jill's turn.

The film ended with striking images of masses of homeless people in Lafayette Square, right across from the White House. Then another poem, another warning rhyme.

> Jack and Jill came to The Hill
> On a grave and somber mission.
> You've made them mad
> The time's so bad
> To be a politician.

JACK: These are the times that try men without souls. You know who you are. *So do we.*

"How long does their little masterpiece run?" One of the television producers wanted an answer to the most practical of questions. CNN was supposed to be on the air *live* with the film in less than ten minutes.

"Just over three minutes. Seemed like forever, I know," a technician with a stopwatch reported. "If you're thinking about editing it down, tell me *right now.*"

I felt a chill after hearing the rhyme, even though the viewing room was warm. No one had left yet. The CNN people were talking among themselves, discussing the film, as if the rest of us weren't even there. The talk-show host was looking pensive and troubled. Maybe he understood where mass communications was heading, and realized it couldn't be stopped.

"We're live in *eight minutes*," a producer announced to his crew. "We need this room, people. We're going to make dupes for all of you."

"Souvenirs," someone in the crowd quipped. "I saw Jack and Jill on CNN."

"They're not serial killers," I said in a soft mumble, more for myself than anyone else. I wanted to *hear* what the thought, the hunch, sounded like out loud.

I was in the minority, but my belief was strong. *They're not pattern killers, not in the ordinary sense.* They were extremely organized and careful, though. They were clever or personable enough to get close to a couple of famous people. They had a hang-up with kinky sex, or maybe they just wanted us to think so. They had some kind of overarching cause.

I could still hear their words, their eerie voices on the tape: "*On a grave and somber mission.*"

Maybe this wasn't a game to them. *It was a war.*

Chapter 24

IT WAS the worst of times; it was the worst of times. On Wednesday morning, just two days after Shanelle Green's murder, a second murdered child was found in Garfield Park, not far from the Sojourner Truth School. This time the victim was a seven-year-old boy. The crime was similar. The child's face had been crushed, possibly with a metal club or pipe.

I could walk from my house on Fifth Street to the horrifying murder scene. I did just that, but I dragged my feet. It was the fourth of December and children were already thinking of Christmas. This shouldn't have been happening. Not ever, but especially not then.

I felt bad for another reason, besides the murder of another innocent child. *Unless someone was copycatting the first murder, and that seemed highly unlikely to me, the killer couldn't have been Emmanuel Perez, couldn't have been Chop-It-Off-Chucky.* Sampson and I had made a mistake. We had run down the wrong child mclester. We were partly responsible for his death.

The wind swirled and howled across the small park as I entered across from the bodega. It was a miserable morning, terribly cold and darkly overcast. Two ambulances and a half-dozen police cruisers were parked on the grounds inside the rim of the park.

There were at least a hundred people from the neighborhood at the crime scene. It was eerie, ghastly, completely unreal. Police and ambulance sirens screamed in the background, a terrifying dirge for the dead. I shivered miserably, and it wasn't only from the cold.

The horrifying crime scene reminded me of a bad time a few years back when we had found a little boy's body the day before Christmas. The image was everlasting in my mind. The boy's name was Michael Goldberg, but everybody had called him Shrimpie. He was only nine years old. The murderer's name was Gary Soneji, and he had escaped from prison after I caught him. He had escaped, and he had disappeared off the face of the earth. I'd come to think of Soneji as my Dr. Moriarty, evil incarnate, if there was such a thing, and I had begun to believe that there was.

I couldn't help thinking and wondering about Soneji. Gary Soneji had a perfect reason to commit murders near my home. He had vowed to pay me back for his time spent in prison: *every day, every hour, every minute.* Payback time, Dr. Cross.

As I ducked under the crisscrossing yellow crime-scene tapes, a woman in a white rain poncho yelled out to me, "You're supposed to be a policeman, right? So why the hell won't you do something! Do *something* about this maniac killing our children! Oh yeah, and have a happy, goddamn holiday!"

What could I possibly say to the angry woman? That real police work wasn't like *N.Y.P.D. Blue* on television? We had no leads on the two child killings so far. We had no Chop-It-Off-Chucky to blame anymore. There was no getting around a simple fact: Sampson and I had made a mistake. A bad hombre was dead, but probably for the wrong reason.

The news coverage continued to be very limited, but I recognized a few reporters at the tragic scene: Inez Gomez from *El Diario* and Fern Galperin from CNN. They seemed to cover everything in Washington, occasionally even murders in Southeast.

"Does this have anything to do with the child murder last

week, Detective? Did you get the real murderer? Is this a serial killer of little kids?" Inez Gomez shot off a clipped barrage of questions at me. She was very good at her job, smart and tough and fair most of the time.

I said nothing to any of the reporters, not even to Gomez. I didn't even look their way. There was an ache at the center of my chest that wouldn't go away.

Is this a serial killer of little kids? I don't know, Inez. I think it might be. I pray that it isn't. Was Emmanuel Perez innocent? I don't believe so, Inez. I pray that he wasn't.

Could Gary Soneji be the killer of these two children? I hope not. I pray that isn't the case, Inez.

Lots of prayers this cold, dismal morning.

It was too harsh for early December, too much snow. Somebody on the radio said they've been shoveling so much in D.C., it felt like an election year.

I pushed my way through the crowd to the dead child lying like a broken doll on an expanse of frost-covered grass. The police photographer was taking pictures of the small boy. He had a short haircut like Damon's, what Damon called a "baldie."

Of course, I knew it wasn't Damon, but the effect was incredibly powerful. It was as if I had been punched in the stomach, hard. The sight took all the breath out of my chest and stomach, and left me wheezing. Cruelty isn't softened by tears. I had learned that lesson many times by then.

I knelt down low over the murdered boy. He looked as if he were sleeping, but having a terrible nightmare. Someone had closed his eyes, and I wondered if it could have been the killer. I didn't think so. More likely it was the work of some Good Samaritan or possibly a good-hearted, but very careless, policeman. The little boy had on worn, loose gray sweats that had holes in the knees and tattered Nike sneakers. The right side of his face had been virtually destroyed by the killer blow, just like Shanelle's. The face was crushed, but also pocked with jagged holes and tears. Bright red blood was pooled under his head.

The maniac likes to decimate beautiful things. It gave me an idea. Is the killer disfigured in some way himself? Physically? Emotionally? Maybe both.

Why does he hate small children so much? Why is he killing them near the Sojourner Truth School?

I opened the little boy's eyes. The child stared up at me. I don't know why I did it. I just needed to look.

Chapter 25

"DR. CROSS . . . Dr. Cross . . . I know this boy," said a shaky voice. "He's in our lower school. His name is Vernon Wheatley."

I looked up and saw Mrs. Johnson, the principal at Damon's school. She held back a sob; she grabbed the sob back *hard*.

She's even tougher than you are, Daddy. That's what Damon had said to me. Maybe he was right about that. The school principal wouldn't cry, wouldn't allow herself to.

The medical examiner was standing next to Mrs. Johnson. I knew her, too. She was a white woman, Janine Prestegard. Looked to be about the same age as Mrs. Johnson. Mid-thirties, give or take a few years. They had been talking, consulting, probably consoling each other.

What was there about the Sojourner Truth School? *Why this school? Why Damon's school?* Shanelle Green and now Vernon Wheatley. What did the principal know, if anything? Did the school principal believe she could help solve these terrifying murders? She had known both victims.

The medical examiner was arranging for an autopsy to determine the cause of death. She looked shaken by the savage attack the child had suffered. The autopsy of a murdered child is as bad as it gets.

Two detectives from the local precinct waited nearby. So did the morgue team. Everything was so quiet, so sad, so horribly bad, at the scene. There is nothing any worse than the murder of a child. Nothing I've seen, anyway. I remember every one that I've been to. Sampson sometimes tells me I'm too sensitive to be a homicide detective. I counter that every detective should be as sensitive and human as possible.

I rose to my full height. At six three I was only a few inches taller than Mrs. Johnson.

"You've been at both murder scenes," I said to her. "You live around here? You live nearby?"

She shook her head. She looked straight up into my eyes. Her eyes were so intense, so large and round. They held mine and wouldn't let go. "I know a lot of people in the neighborhood. Someone called me at home. They felt I should know. I grew up near here in the Eastern Market section," she volunteered. "This is the same killer, isn't it?"

I didn't answer her question. "I may need to talk to you about the murders later," I said. "We might have to talk to some of the children at school again. I won't do that unless we have to, though. They've been through enough. Thank you for your concern. I'm sorry about Vernon Wheatley."

Mrs. Johnson nodded and kept looking at me with incredibly penetrating eyes. *Who exactly are you?* they seemed to ask. *You've been at both murder scenes, too.*

"How can you do this kind of work?" she suddenly blurted out.

It was an unexpected and startling question. It should have seemed tactless, but somehow it didn't. It happened to be my own personal mantra. *How do you do this work, Alex? Why are you the dragonslayer? Who exactly are you? What have you become?*

"I don't really know." I told her the truth.

Why had I admitted the weakness to her? I rarely did that with anyone, not even with Sampson. It was something about her eyes. They demanded the truth.

I lowered my eyes and turned away from her. I had to. I went back to my note taking. My head was thick with questions, bad questions, bad thoughts, and worse feelings about the murder. The two murders. The two cases.

Why does he hate children so much? I kept asking myself. *Who could possibly hate these little children so much?* He had to have been badly abused himself. Probably a male in his twenties. Not too organized or careful.

I had the thought that we would catch this one — but would we catch him soon enough?

Chapter 26

I WAS WAITING for possible disciplinary action from the department, waiting for the whisper of the ax. It didn't come right away. Chief Pittman was holding his sharp knife over my head. The Jefe was playing with me. Cat and mouse.

Maybe the higher powers wouldn't let him act . . . on account of Jack and Jill. That was it. It had to be. They felt that they needed me on the celebrity stalkings and murders.

While I waited in limbo, there was plenty of work to do. I passed the hours checking and rechecking the FBI's Behavioral Science Unit data for anything that might possibly connect the two child murders to any others in Washington — or anywhere else, for that matter. Then I repeated almost the same process on Jack and Jill. *If you want to understand the killer, look at his work.* Jack and Jill were organized. The child killer was disorganized and sloppy. The cases couldn't have been more different.

I continued to feel that I couldn't work two complex homicide cases like these at the same time. I believed it was time for my so-called deal with the department to start working both ways.

I made some phone calls late in the afternoon. I called in a few chips, favors I was owed inside the department. What did I have to lose?

That night four homicide detectives from the 1st District met me in the deserted parking lot behind the Sojourner Truth School. Each was a genuine badass in the department. All in all, four troublemakers. Four very good cops, though. Probably the best I knew in Washington.

The detectives I'd chosen all lived right in Southeast. They each took the child murders personally and wanted the gruesome case solved quickly — no matter what their other priority assignments were.

Sampson was the last one to arrive, but he was only a few minutes past the ten o'clock starting time. The secret get-together would definitely have been shut down by the chief of detectives. I was about to set up an off-duty unit to help find the killer of Shanelle Green and Vernon Wheatley. We weren't vigilantes, but we were close.

"*The late* John Sampson," Jerome Thurman quipped and let out a high-pitched laugh when Sampson finally entered the tight circle of homicide detectives. Thurman was close to two hundred seventy pounds, not much of it soft. He and Sampson liked to go at each other, but they were good friends. It had been that way since we all played roundball in the D.C. high school leagues a thousand or so years ago.

"My watch says ten on the dot," Sampson said, without peeking at his ancient Bulova.

"Then ten o'clock it is," contributed Shawn Moore. Moore was a hard-driving, young detective with three kids of his own. His family lived less than a mile from the Truth School, as it's usually called in the neighborhood. One of his boys went there with Damon.

"I'm glad you all could come out to play on this chilly night," I said after the ribbing and small talk had settled down. I knew that these detectives got along and had respect for one another. I also knew this meeting would never get back to The Jefe through any of them.

"Sorry to get you out here so late. Best we don't be seen together. Thanks for coming, though. This schoolyard seemed like the right place for what we have to talk about. I'll make it as short as possible," I said, looking around at all the faces.

"You'd *better,* Alex," Jerome warned me. "Freezin' my fat ass off."

"You've all heard about the seven-year-old boy found in Garfield Park this morning?" I asked the detectives. "Boy by the name of Vernon Wheatley."

Heads nodded solemnly around the circle. Bad homicide news always travels quickly.

"Well, I've been thinking about these child murders a lot. I've run the evidence we have through the Violent Criminal Apprehension Program and also the Behavioral Science Unit databanks. Nothing comes up that's a match. I have a preliminary psych profile working. I hope that I'm wrong, but I'm afraid there's a pattern killer working in this neighborhood. This is probably a serial killer of children. I'm almost sure of it."

"How bad a situation are we talking, Alex?" Rakeem Powell leaned in and asked me.

I knew what Rakeem was getting at. He and I had worked on a tough pattern-killer case a few years back. "I think this one is already in heat, Rakeem. The two murders came within days. There was a high level of violence. He seems to be in a rage, or damn close to it. I say *he,* though it might be a she."

"Violent for a female," Sampson said. He cleared his throat. "Too much . . . blood . . . crushed skulls . . . little kids." He shook his head no. "Doesn't feel like a woman to me."

"I tend to agree," I said, "but you never know these days. Look at *Jill.*"

"How many detectives assigned to the child murders?" Jerome Thurman asked through thick lips that were pursed and stuck way out from his face, like those candy lips kids wear and then eat when they tire of having fat lips.

"Two teams." I told them the bad news. "Only one is full-time, though. That's the reason I wanted us to meet. The chief of detectives is resisting any theory that the same person killed both children. Emmanuel Perez is still on the books as the killer of the girl."

"That dumb motherfuck asshole," Jerome Thurman growled angrily. "That bastard's as useless as titties on a bull."

The other detectives cursed and grumbled. I had expected a negative reaction to anything The Jefe said or did. Still, I wasn't into cheap shots. Much as I was tempted.

"How sure are you about this being the same killer, Alex?" Rakeem asked. "You said your profile is preliminary. I know this shit takes time."

I sniffed in the cold, then went on. "The second child, the little boy, had his face badly smashed in, Rakeem. Only one side of the face, though. It was exactly like the murdered little girl's face. Same side, the right. No significant variation that I could find. The medical examiner corroborates that. The "unsub" probably feels that he has a good and a bad side. The bad side gets punished—destroyed, is more like it.

"The final thing, and this is just a best guess at this point, I think he's a beginner at this. But devious and clever just the same . . . a risk taker. He'll make a mistake. I think we can get him soon, if we work together. But it has to be soon. *I think we can nail this one!*"

Sampson finally spoke up. "You going to talk about what's *really* going down here, Alex, or you want me to?"

I smiled at what Sampson had said, the cranky way he'd said it. "No, I thought I'd leave the real dirty work to you."

"As usual," he said. "Here's what Alex *hasn't* said so far. Just to get it out on the dance floor. The *real* reason one team of detectives is assigned to these murders goes something like this. One, it happened in the area of the projects, and we know all the shit flows downhill in D.C. and eventually ends up here. Two, Jack and Jill is sucking up everybody's time in the department. Rich white people are being killed. They're scared shitless up on Capitol Hill and such. So of course we drop everything else. Two little black kids don't matter much, not in the greater scheme, not in the *big picture*."

"Sampson and I have been working on the Truth School murders." I picked up his thread, just lowered the volume a touch. "Strictly off the books. We have to do our own surveillance," I added, so that everybody knew the deal. "We need some help now. This is a major homicide case. Unfortunately, there are *two* major cases in Washington at this time."

"Only *one* case on my mind," Rakeem Powell said. "One guess which case it is."

"You know you've got the Fatman on board." Jerome Thurman raised his high-pitched voice and punched his stubby club of an arm into the air. "I'm in. I'm on your *nonpayroll* with all its nonbenefits and risks for forced early retirement. Sounds great."

"My boy goes to the Sojourner Truth School, Alex," Shawn Moore said. "I'll make the time for this. Hope I can fit in Jack and Jill."

We laughed at the jokes. It was our hardass approach to the difficult problems at hand. The five of us were in. We just didn't have any idea what we were in for.

There were definitely two major murder cases in Washington — and now there were two task forces to try and solve them. One and a half task forces, anyway.

"Cocktails, anyone?" Jerome Thurman asked in the softest, most cultivated voice. You'd have thought we were at the old Cotton Club in Harlem as he passed around his beat-up Washington Redskins game flask.

We all took a hit; more like two or three.

We were blood brothers.

Chapter 27

I WORKED the Jack and Jill case from five in the morning until three o'clock in the afternoon. Me and about ten thousand other harried law officers around D.C. I was checking for a possible link between Senator Fitzpatrick and Natalie Sheehan. We even looked at news photos taken of them in the past months. Maybe somebody interesting would show up in the background of a shot. Or even better, show up twice. I had a detective visiting all of the kinky sex shops around D.C. He called the assignment the ultimate Jack-off.

I met Sampson at the Boston Market restaurant on Pennsylvania Avenue at three-thirty. It was time for our second job. Our *other* homicide case, the "back burner" case. This arrangement was definitely much better — not great, but a significant improvement over the past few days of frustration and utter madness for me.

"I think you might be right on the button about one thing, Alex," Sampson told me over a lunch of double-glazed meat loaf and mashed potatoes made from scratch. "The Truth School killer is an amateur. He's sloppy. Maybe a first-timer at this. He left prints all over the second crime scene, too. The techies got his prints, some hair, threads off his clothing. Based on the prints, the killer is a small man — or possibly a woman. If this squirrel isn't careful, he or she is going to get their squirrel ass caught."

"Maybe the killer wants to," I said between bites of a meat loaf sandwich spiced with decent tomato sauce. "Or maybe the killer just wants us to think he's a first-timer. That could be the act. Soneji might play it like that."

Sampson grinned broadly. It was his best killer smile. "Do you have to double- and triple-think everything, Sugar?"

"Of course I do. That's my job description. That's Alex's cross," I said and offered my own killer smile.

"Oh, ho!" said Man Mountain and grinned again. Man, I loved being with him, loved to make him laugh.

"Anything in from the rest of the team?" I asked him. "Jerome? Rakeem?"

"They're all working the case, but still no tangible results. Nothing yet from the go-team."

"We need surveillance at the boy's funeral and at Shanelle's gravesite. The killer might not be able to stay away. A lot of them can't."

Sampson rolled his eyes. "We'll do what we can. Do our best. Surveillance at a child's gravesite. Shee-it."

At quarter past four, the two of us split. I headed over to the Sojourner Truth School.

The principal's car was sitting in the small, fenced-in parking lot. I remembered that Mrs. Johnson sometimes worked late after classes. That was good for me. I wanted to talk to her about Shanelle Green and Vernon Wheatley. What connection was there between the Truth School and the killer? What could it be?

I knew approximately where the principal's office was located in the annexed building, so I walked directly there. It was a very nice school, for just about any area of the city. Outside, near the street, a chain-link fence with razor wire ran the perimeter of the schoolyard, but the inside was festive, very bright, imaginatively decorated.

I read several hand-lettered posters and banners as I walked. CHILDREN FIRST. GROW WHERE YOU ARE PLANTED. SUCCESS COMES IN CANS, NOT CANNOTS. Cornball, but nice. Inspiring for the children, and for me as well.

That particular week the hallway display cases were filled with "animal shelters," which were dioramas made by the kids, each one illustrating an animal and its habitat. It struck me that the Sojourner Truth School was a terrific habitat itself. Under normal circumstances, it was a sweet place for Damon to grow and learn.

Unfortunately, two little babies from this school had been murdered in the last week.

That made me furiously angry, and it also frightened me more than I wanted to admit. When I was growing up, tough as it was supposed to have been in D.C., kids seldom if ever died at our school. Now, for a lot of reasons, it happened all the time in schools. Not only in Washington but in L.A.'s schools. New York's. Chicago's. Maybe even Sioux City's.

What the hell was going on from sea to shining sea?

The heavy wooden door to the inner administrative office was open, but the assistant appeared to have left. On her desk was a collection of Caucasian, African-American, and Asian play dolls. A sign read: *Barbara Breckenridge, I can really tap-dance.*

I felt like a housebreaker, a neighborhood break-and-enter artist, a bad character of some sort or other. Suddenly, I was concerned about the principal working late by herself in the school.

Anyone could walk in here, just as I had done. The Sojourner Truth School killer could walk in here some night. It would be so easy. *This easy.*

I turned the corner into the main office and was about to announce my presence when I saw Mrs. Johnson. I thought of my made-up name for her — *Christine.*

She was busy at work at an old-fashioned rolltop desk that looked at least a hundred years old. She was *lost* in the work, actually.

I watched her for a couple of seconds. She wore gold-wire glasses to do her paperwork. She was humming the "Shoop Shoop" song from *Waiting to Exhale*. Sounded nice.

There was something enormously right, even touching, about the scene — the dedicated teacher, the educator, at work. A smile passed across my lips. *She's even tougher than you are, Daddy.*

I still wondered about that. She didn't look tough at the moment. She looked serene, happy in her work. She looked at peace, and I envied her that.

I finally felt a little awkward standing in the doorway unannounced. "Hi there. It's Detective Alex Cross," I said. "Hello. Mrs. Johnson?"

She stopped humming and looked up. There was the slightest glint of fear in her eyes. Then she smiled. Her smile was warm and welcoming. Very nice to be on the receiving end of one of her easy smiles.

"Ahh, it *is* Detective Cross," she said. "And what brings you to the principal's office?" she said in a put-on voice of authority.

"I guess I need some help from the principal. Extra help with my homework." That was true enough, I suppose. "I need to talk with you a little about Vernon Wheatley, if that's possible. I also wanted to get your okay to speak with some of the teachers again, to see if any of them heard anything from the kids after Vernon's murder. Somebody might have seen *something* that would help us, even if they don't think they did. Maybe something the kids heard their parents say."

"Yes, I figured the same thing," Mrs. Johnson said. "Somebody here at the school could have a clue, something useful, and might not know it."

I liked everything I saw about Mrs. Johnson, but as soon as I saw it, I pushed it out of my mind. *Wrong time, wrong place, and wrong woman.* I'd done some questionable things in my life, and I'm no angel, but trying to fool with a married woman wasn't going to be one of them.

"There's not too much new to report, I'm afraid," she said.

"I've been working a little overtime on your account. I grilled the teachers at lunch today. *Interrogated* them, actually. I told them that they should tell me if they heard or saw anything suspicious. They talk to me about most things. We have a pretty close-knit group here."

"Are any of the teachers still here? I could talk to them now if they are. I don't know this for sure, but I suspect the killer might have watched the school at some point," I said to her. I didn't want to frighten Mrs. Johnson or the other teachers, but I did want them on the alert and cautious. I believed that the killer probably had scouted the school.

She shook her head slowly back and forth. Then she cocked it softly to the left. She seemed to be looking at me in a new way. "Almost all of them are long gone by four. They like to leave together, if possible. Safety in numbers."

"That makes a lot of sense to me. It isn't a great neighborhood. Well, it is and it isn't."

"And being here at five or so, with a lot of unlocked doors, doesn't make any kind of sense," she said. It was what I had been thinking ever since I arrived at her office door.

I didn't say anything, didn't comment on the unlocked doors. Mrs. Johnson was certainly free to live her life in whatever way she chose. "Thanks for checking with the teachers for us," I said to her. "Thanks for the overtime work."

"No, thank you for coming by," she said. "I'm sure this must be very hard for you and for Damon. For your whole family. It certainly is for all of us at the school."

She finally took off the wire-rim glasses and slid them into the pocket of her work smock. She looked good with or without glasses.

Intelligent, nice, pretty.

Off-limits, out-of-bounds, off your radar charts, I reminded myself. I could almost feel a ruler rap across my knuckles.

Faster than I would have thought possible, she slid a snubnose .38 Special out of an open drawer on the right side of the desk.

She didn't point it in my direction, but she easily could have. *Easily.*

"I lived in this neighborhood for a lot of years," she explained. Then she smiled and put the gun away. "I try to be prepared for whatever might happen," she said calmly. "And shit *does* happen around here. I knew you were there in the doorway, Detective. The kids claim I have eyes in the back of my head. Actually, I do."

She laughed again. I did like her laugh. Anyone with a pulse would. *Say goodnight, Alex.*

I had mixed feelings about civilians owning guns, but I was sure hers was registered and legal. "You learn to use that revolver in the neighborhood?" I asked.

"No, actually, I learned at the Remington Gun Club out in Fairfax. My husband was, is, worried about my coming to work here, too. You men seem to think alike. Sorry, *sorry*," she said and smiled again. "I try to catch myself when even I say outrageous sexist things like that. I don't like that. No how, no way. *Sorry.*"

She stood up and flicked off the Mac laptop on her desk. "I'll walk you to the front door," she said. "Make sure you get out safely, since it's well after four."

"That's a good idea." I went along with her little joke. She had me smiling some, anyway. That was pretty good, under the circumstances of the past few days. "Are you always this funny? This loose?"

She tilted her head again. It was something she did often. Then she nodded confidently. "Always. *At least* this funny. Those were my two vocational choices: comedienne or educator. Obviously, I chose comedienne. More laughs here. Honest laughs. Most days, anyway."

The two of us walked down the deserted halls of the school together. Our footfalls made clapping sounds that echoed loudly. The "Shoop Shoop" song played inside my head, the tune she'd been humming in her office. There were lots more questions I wanted to ask her, but I knew I shouldn't be asking some of them. They had nothing to do with the murder case.

When we got to the school's front door, a husky, middle-aged security guard was there to let me out. He surprised me. I hadn't seen him on my way in.

He had a thick wooden nightstick and a walkie-talkie. It was the look and feel of D.C. schools that I knew all too well. Guards, metal detectors, steel-mesh screens covering every window. No wonder the people of the neighborhood hate and fear all established institutions, even their own schools.

"Goodnight, sir," the school guard said with a most congenial smile. "You be leaving soon, Mrs. Johnson?"

"Pretty soon," she said. "You can go home if you want to, Lionel. I have my Uzi inside."

Lionel laughed at her joke. She had very good delivery, good timing. I'll bet she could have done some stand-up work if she'd wanted.

"Goodnight, Mrs. Johnson," I said. I couldn't help adding, "Please be careful until this case is over."

She stood just inside the heavy wooden door. She looked so wise, and she *was* attractive, in my way of viewing the world. "It's 'Christine,'" she said, "and I will be careful. I promise. Thank you for stopping by."

Christine! Jesus! It was the same name I'd made up for her. Probably I'd heard it somewhere before, from Damon or Nana, but it seemed so strange. Kind of magical, actually. Would have made James Redfield happy as hell.

I went home that evening thinking about the two child murders, and Jack and Jill, but also about the principal of the Sojourner Truth School. She was wise, funny, and pretty, too. She could take care of herself — even handle a gun.

Mrs. Johnson.

Christine.

Shoop. Shoop. Shoop. Shoop.

Chapter 28

IN THIS DANGEROUS AGE, everybody needs to think, *It won't happen to me. Not to me. What are the odds of it actually happening to me?*

The motion picture actor Michael Robinson thought it was absurd and more than a little self-absorbed for him to be concerned or afraid of the maniac killers on the loose in Washington. What did the malicious Jack and Jill threats have to do with him, anyway? The answer, it seemed clear to him, was nothing at all.

Still, he was a trifle skittish and jumpy, so he tried to enjoy the adrenaline rush, to go with the nasty flow of the moment, of the times we live in.

A little before midnight, the Hollywood star finally got up his nerve and called for a date from the VIP escort service. A "snack" before bedtime. He had used the service many times before while visiting D.C. The discreet, toney, very expensive sex-for-hire service had his requirements down pat. M.R. was in its file, compliments of the star's full-service business agent in Los Angeles.

After he made the phone call, the forty-nine-year-old actor tried to read an expensive adventure-romance script he'd

commissioned, but then got up and walked to the window of
his penthouse suite at the Willard Hotel on Pennsylvania Avenue. He knew his fans would find it scandalous that he was
paying for a lover, but that was their hang-up, not his.

The truth was, he found it far less complicated, and far easier
on the psyche, to pay a thousand or fifteen hundred than to get
involved in wooing, and then painfully separating from, lovers
while on the road.

Actually, he was in a good mood tonight, feeling very level
and grounded, he thought as he stared out on the street. He
just needed some company, a little TLC, and some uncompli-
cated sex. All three of his requirements would be met shortly, he
hoped.

In a way, he was still time-warped back in his hometown of
Wichita, circa 1963, when he was a high school senior. The fan-
tasies and desires he'd had then were still unresolved and op-
erating full-tilt boogie inside him. There was one difference: he
knew what he wanted tonight and he would get it without much
trouble, guilt, or the gnashing of teeth.

He glanced around the hotel suite and decided to tidy it up before the escort arrived. The neurotic tidying-up made him smile.
How incredibly bourgeois he still was. *You can take the boy out
of Kansas*, Michael Robinson thought.

He heard two quick raps on the door, and the noise caught him
by surprise. The service had said the escort would be there within
the hour, which usually meant at least that long, sometimes
longer.

"Just a minute," he called out. "Be right there. One minute."

Michael Robinson glanced at his watch. The "date" had arrived in about thirty minutes. Well, fine. He was ready for some
quick nookie and then a night of blessed sleep. He was having
breakfast with the chairman of the Democratic National Com-
mittee early the next morning. He'd been asked to do a fund-
raiser for the Democrats. The chairman was a starfucker of
another variety. They all were, really. Everybody wanted what

he thought he couldn't have, and everybody couldn't have Michael Robinson. Well, *almost* everybody.

He peeked through the hotel-door spyhole. Well, well, well. He definitely liked what he saw in the hallway; even through a fish-eye lens, the escort looked good. He felt a spike of adrenaline kick in. He opened the door and his fifteen-million-dollar-per-picture smile was automatically engaged.

"Hi, I'm Jasper," the handsome escort said. "It's very nice to meet you, sir."

Michael Robinson doubted that the escort was "Jasper." He thought that a name like Jake or Cliff would fit the escort better. He was a tad older than Robinson had expected, possibly in his mid-thirties, but he was more than acceptable. He was near perfect, actually. Michael Robinson was already hard, and he was lubricated. *Armed and dangerous,* he called the ready state.

"How are you doing tonight?" The actor put out his hand and lightly touched the other man's arm. He wanted "Jasper" to know that he was down-to-earth, unaffected, and most of all, a warm person. He truly *was* all of that. *USA Today* had recently published a list of the "nicest" stars in Hollywood. He was on it, courtesy of his business agent and lawyer, who spoke exceedingly well of him.

Jack unleashed his best smile as he entered Michael Robinson's *Lifestyles of the Rich and Famous* hotel suite. He shut the door behind him. He figured he had about half an hour before the real escort arrived from the service. That would be enough time.

At any rate, Jill was watching the lobby of the Willard, just in case the male prostitute arrived early. She would take care of things downstairs. Jill was excellent with the details, all the loose ends. Jill was excellent, period.

"I'm a real fan," Jack said to the big Hollywood star. "I've been following your career closely, actually."

Michael Robinson spoke in a near-whisper that would have shocked male and female fans of his action-romance films. "Oh, really, Jasper? That's always so nice for me to hear. It's kind of you to say, anyway."

"I swear to God, it's true." Sam Harrison continued his act. "My name is Jack, by the way. Jill is down in the lobby. Maybe you've heard of us?"

Jack pulled out a Beretta with a silencer and aimed it between the actor's startled deep-blue eyes. He fired. It fit the pattern of Jack and Jill. People in high places. Execution-style murder. Kinky touches and poem to follow.

> Jack and Jill came to The Hill
> To kill, to kill, to kill.

Chapter 29

ONE SPECIFIC, and particularly fascinating, detail about the murders was weighing heavily on my mind, troubling the hell out of me. I thought about it as I turned onto crowded Pennsylvania Avenue and double-parked in front of the Willard Hotel — the latest helter-skelter murder scene.

I thought about the troubling detail as I marched inside and headed up to Michael Robinson's suite.

I thought about it as the smooth-riding elevator whooshed open on the seventh floor, where half a dozen uniforms were standing around, and rolls of crime-scene tape ribboned the hallway like a tangle of distasteful Christmas wrapping.

There wasn't much evidence of passion in the first two killings, I was thinking. Especially the second murder. The murders were so cold-blooded and efficient. The arrangement of the bodies of the victims seemed to have been art-directed. The kinkiness of the scenes seemed too directed and orderly. This is the exact opposite of the Sojourner Truth School murders, which were violent explosions of pent-up anger and pure rage.

I didn't get the full significance yet, and neither did anyone else I spoke to about the murder case. Not inside the D.C.

police, and not at the Federal Bureau in Quantico. If, as a detective, I had one basic rule about premeditated murders, it was this: they were almost always based on passion. There usually had to be extreme love. Or hate. Or greed . . . but these killings seemed to have none of that. It kept bugging me.

Why Michael Robinson? I wondered as I walked toward the hotel room where he had been murdered. *What are these two bizarre psychopaths doing here in Washington? What sick and cruel game are they playing . . . and why do they crave millions of spectators for their sensational blood sport?*

I spotted Kyle Craig once again. The FBI senior agent and I talked for several moments outside the suite. All around us, usually sangfroid D.C. cops appeared in mild shock. A lot of them were probably disappointed Michael Robinson fans.

"The medical examiner figures he's been a famous corpse for about seven hours. So it happened around twelve last night," Kyle told me, giving me the lay of the land. "Two shots fired to his head, Alex. Close range, just like the others. Take a look at the tattooing for yourself. Whoever did the shooting is a real heartless bastard."

I agreed with what Kyle was saying.

Heartless.

No passion.

No rage.

"How was Michael Robinson found?"

"Oh, that's another good part, Alex. A new wrinkle. They *phoned* it in to the *Post*. Told the newspaper where to pick up the trash this morning."

"Is that a quote?" I asked Kyle.

"I don't have the exact quote they used, but 'pick up the trash' was definitely part of it," Kyle said.

I was interested in any irreverence or cynicism Jack and Jill might use in describing the killings. They were obviously into wordplay. They were *artistes.* I also wondered if they might be out there on Pennsylvania Avenue, watching us again. Filming us as we bumbled and stumbled over one another inside the Willard. I wondered if they were preparing a second film, with their usual wide-release distribution method in mind. Surveillance had been posted outside, so if they were there, we had them.

I entered the living room of the suite, and I was relieved to see that Chief of Detectives Pittman was nowhere on the scene. The film actor Michael Robinson was there, however. As they say, he had been born to play the role — perhaps his greatest.

His naked body was in a sitting position on the floor, the head against the couch. It seemed as if the actor had been propped up to see anyone entering the room, and maybe that was the killers' idea. His eyes stared out at me. *To see, or to be seen?* I wondered. He was not a pretty sight. I took note of the lividity. The blood had already pooled in the lowermost parts of his body, which now had an ugly purplish red color.

Another celebrity had been *exposed. Brought down to earth. Punished for some real or imagined sin? What connection was there with Fitzpatrick and Sheehan? Why a senator, a newswoman, and an actor?*

Three murders in such a short time. Celebrities are supposed to be safer than the rest of us, more protected at least, and above all this. It got to me, seeing Michael Robinson dead and violated. There was something visceral and system-shocking about what the killers were doing.

What was the bizarre, complex message from Jack and Jill? That nobody was safe anymore? I rolled the outrageous thought around in my head. It was a good starting place, a concept to work with.

Nobody is safe? Jack and Jill were telling us they could come for anyone, at any time. They knew how to get *inside.*

There was another note with the body. Another Jack and Jill rhyme. It was on the night table, where the weird and ghoulish killers, or killer, had left it for us to find.

Jack and Jill came to The Hill
To do some deadly deeds.
They weren't far wrong
To judge how long
A bleeding liberal bleeds.

One of Michael Robinson's agents was in the room. He'd flown down from New York. He was a good-looking man, with silver-blond hair. He wore a long cashmere coat over an Armani suit. I noticed his eyes were red and swollen. He seemed to have been crying. *Two* medical examiners were working on the film actor's body. I suppose you could call all that attention going out in style. Only the best for Michael Robinson.

There were some other obvious connections to the Fitzpatrick and Sheehan murders. There was a tawdry, kinky side to all three killings. Each had been an execution. And maybe most important so far, they were all "bleeding liberals," weren't they? They had all been *exposed* for what they were.

"Dr. Alex Cross? Excuse me, you're Dr. Alex Cross, aren't you?"

I turned to a tall, rangy man who had spoken my name. He was clean-cut and his bearing was almost military. About forty, I guessed. He wore a black raincoat over a dark gray suit. A buttoned-down look. Definitely senior law enforcement of some kind, I figured.

"Yes, I'm Alex Cross," I said to him.

"I'm Jay Grayer from the Secret Service," he introduced himself formally. There was something about the very erect way that he held himself. Extreme confidence. Or was it moral certitude? A stiff pole up his behind?

"I'm senior agent of the First Family detail."

"What can I do for you?" I asked Agent Grayer. Alarms were already sounding in my head. I felt I was about to get a much fuller understanding of why I had been put on the Jack and Jill investigation. By whom, and for exactly what reason.

"You're wanted at the White House," he said. "I'm afraid it's

a command performance, Dr. Cross. It's about the Jack and Jill
investigation. There's a problem we have to let you know about."

"I'll bet it's a big problem, too," I said to Agent Grayer.

"Yes, I'm afraid it is. It's a very big problem, Dr. Cross. We have
something we need to share with you."

I had suspected as much. I'd had a quiet fear way in the back
of my mind. Now it was up front.

I was being summoned to the White House.

*They wanted the dragonslayer there. Did they understand what
that meant?*

Chapter 30

THE ONLY THING anybody seems to share very readily in Washington these days is trouble.

I could hardly argue with the command from on high, though. I dutifully accompanied Jay Grayer up the street to 1600 Pennsylvania Avenue. *Ask not what I can do for my country.*

The White House was only a short jaunt from the Willard Hotel. Despite the relative performance of some of the recent occupants, the White House continues to cast its spell over a lot of people, including me. I had been inside only twice, on canned guided tours with my kids, but even they had been larger-than-life and moving. I almost wished Damon and Jannie could be with me.

We were quickly passed through the blue-canopied guardhouse on West Executive Drive. Agent Grayer was allowed to park his car in the garage under the White House. He seemed modestly proud of the perk. He explained that the garage was still considered a primary bomb shelter, but also an escape route in case of an attack.

"Good to know," I said and smiled. Grayer smiled back. It was forced conviviality, but at least we were both making an effort.

"I'm sure you're curious as to why you've been asked to come. I would be."

"I don't think I've been invited to tea," I said stiffly. "But, yes, I'm very curious."

"The reason is the Soneji and Casanova cases," Grayer explained to me as we took an elevator one flight up from the garage. "Your reputation precedes you here. You're aware that the FBI has never captured a single serial killer, for all their expertise? We want you on the team."

"What team is that?" I asked.

"You'll see in a few seconds. This is definitely the A team, though. Be ready for some crazy shit. The Bureau has staked out the hotel room where John Hinckley stayed. Just in case the killers might decide to stay there. Pay homage, or something like that."

"Not such a terrible idea," I told Grayer. He looked at me as if I were crazy, too. "Not a particularly good idea, either," I said. He cracked a grin.

Half a dozen men and two women in business attire were gathered in the West Wing office of the White House chief of staff. I sensed a lot of tension in the room, but everyone was working hard to hide it. I was introduced as the representative of the Washington police. *Welcome to the team. Say hello to the dragonslayer.*

The others at the table cordially introduced themselves. Two more senior agents from the Secret Service, a woman named Ann Roper and a youngish, good-looking man named Michael Fescoe; the director of intelligence from the FBI, Robert Hatfield; General Aiden Cornwall from the Joint Chiefs of Staff and the U.S. Army; the national security advisor, Michael Kane; the White House chief of staff, Don Hamerman. The other woman turned out to be a senior officer in the CIA. The inspector general. Her name was Jeanne Sterling. Her presence meant that a foreign power's involvement in Jack and Jill was being considered. There was a twist I hadn't considered before.

It was fast company for a homicide detective from Southeast
D.C., even for a deputy chief. But I figured I was pretty fast company, too. I had seen nasty things that none of them had, or would
ever want to.

Let the sharing begin.

Glistening sweet rolls, butter in ice, and coffee in silver pots
had been put out for our unusual breakfast club. It was obvious
that some of the others had worked together before. I had learned
a long time ago that if you can't spot the pigeon in a poker game,
then you're probably it.

The national security advisor called the gathering to order a
minute or so past ten. Don Hamerman was a wiry, blond man
in his mid-thirties who appeared to be tightly strung. That definitely fit the White House staff profile in recent years: very young
and very uptight. On the move. On the make, get set, go.

"I'm going to use overheads for this presentation, folks. That's
the way we do it here in the Big House," Hamerman said and
managed a thin, forced smile. He had an unsettling kinetic energy. He reminded me of high-flying D.C. public relations types,
and even of Michael Robinson's overwrought agent back at the
Willard.

I gathered from his remark that White House meetings were
usually bureaucratic and somewhat formal, rather than loosy-
goosy. Everyone seemed to enjoy the small joke, anyway.

Actually, the forced cordiality disturbed me. I was still flashing on the death-mask expression of Michael Robinson. It
wasn't an image I liked bringing with me into the White House.

Michael Robinson's naked corpse was probably still in the
Willard Hotel with the morgue team, ready to be tagged and
bagged.

"I have about an hour's worth of briefing material — tops.
With full discussion, let's say we're at two hours," Hamerman
continued. "That will take us close to noon, but I believe the
unfortunate circumstances warrant a tight briefing up front."

What unfortunate circumstances, exactly? I wanted to interrupt

Hamerman, but I kept my cool. It was neither the time nor the place.

Cups of coffee and several cigarette packs were already laid out on the worktable. Everyone was prepared for a tough siege. I guessed that was the way it was done at the Big House.

Hamerman placed his first overhead on the gently purring machine. The display screen said *Jack and Jill Investigation*.

Not much to argue about so far.

"As you know, there have been three brutal celebrity murders in Washington in the past week. The latest was the shooting sometime last night of the actor Michael Robinson at the Willard. The stalkers call themselves Jack and Jill. They leave artsy mash notes at their murder scenes. They like to play games with the media. They seem to relish the spotlight *a lot*.

"They also seem to know what they're doing. They've successfully committed three high-profile murders and haven't left us squat to work with. They appear to be signature or serial killers, though of a particularly high order. That's debatable, or so I'm led to understand. But it's one theory.

"Here's the first *kicker*," Hamerman said and arched his thin, blond eyebrows. "What some of you don't know is that 'Jack and Jill' is also the Secret Service code name used for President and Mrs. Byrnes. It has been since the President took office. We are not comfortable accepting this fact as mere coincidence."

The blond woman from the CIA lit a cigarette. I remembered her name. *Jeanne Sterling.* She blew out a pale gust of smoke. I heard her mutter "shit." My sentiments exactly. This was the worst news we'd had so far. Also, I didn't appreciate the fact it had been kept from us until this moment.

"We believe it is a very real possibility that an assassination attempt could be made on either President Byrnes or Mrs. Byrnes. Or perhaps on both of them," Hamerman said.

The words were absolutely chilling to hear. I glanced around the table and saw the frozen expressions of concern.

"We have taken, or are taking, every precaution that we can

think of. The President's exposure outside the White House will be extremely limited for the time being. He's been told everything about the unfortunate situation, and so has Mrs. Byrnes. They're taking it well. They're both very smart, very impressive people. They will not panic. I can promise you that. I'll do the panicking for both of them.

"Let me talk about some facts we *don't* have about the so-called stalkers Jack and Jill. Actually, there are several thousand investigators assigned to the case, and we know surprisingly little. Jack and Jill may be heading toward the White House next, and we don't have the foggiest idea why. Or who they might be. Or what the hell is *in this for them*."

Don Hamerman peered around the table. He was definitely wired. The other word to describe him, the one that came to my mind anyway, was *supercilious*.

"Please feel free to correct me on any point I make. Feel free to add any updated information you might have," he said with a tiny sneer.

Except for a few sighs, no one spoke. No one seemed to know any more than I did. No one had a worthwhile clue so far. That was the scariest thing of all.

The possibility existed that the President and First Lady were the ultimate targets for Jack and Jill . . . or maybe not even the ultimate targets?

Jack and Jill came to The Hill. What in the name of God for? To wipe out all the bleeding liberals? To punish sinners? Was the President a sinner in their minds?

"Jay, do you want to say something now?" Hamerman asked Secret Service Agent Grayer.

Grayer nodded and stood up at the worktable. He leaned against it with his hands. He looked a little pale. "There's a very tough problem here," he said to us. "The danger is real, believe me. This is as scary as anything I've seen in my time at the White House. You see, I was the first one inside Senator Fitzpatrick's apartment after the killing. I was there, alone, at six o'clock that morning. I called the Metro police . . . the same is true for Ms. Sheehan and for Michael Robinson. Each time, Jack and Jill has *called the Secret Service first.* They've contacted us right here at the White House. They told us . . . that they're *practicing for the big one.*"

Chapter 31

ON FRIDAY NIGHT Jack and Jill checked into a high-priced suite at the Four Seasons Hotel, one of the Washington area's best. No one was scheduled to die at the exclusive hotel. Not that they knew of, anyway. Actually, the killers were taking the weekend off — *while everyone else in Washington, the police geniuses especially, stewed in their own juices.*

What a fabulous treat the weekend was. What a delicious notion. The six-hundred-dollar-a-night suite overlooked a corner of Georgetown, and they never left it for a moment. A masseuse came Friday night for a double shiatsu session. Sara had a facial and a manicure on Saturday morning. Room service sent up a personal chef Saturday night, and he prepared their meal in their room. Sam had also provided for four dozen white roses to be delivered when they arrived. It was paradise regained. They felt they deserved it for what they had accomplished so far.

"This is so unbelievably decadent. It's a postmodern, grossly socially incorrect fairy tale," Sara said at a luxurious high point late on Sunday night. "I love every minute of it."

"But do you love every inch of it?" Sam asked her. Only he could get away with a touchy line like that — and *he did.*

Sara smiled and felt a rush of heat inside her body. She looked at him with warm and inquiring eyes. "As a matter of fact, I do."

He was deep inside her, thrusting slowly and gently, and she was wondering if he truly loved her. She wished for it with all her being, but she didn't believe it, couldn't believe it. She was, after all, Sara the gimp, Sara the drudge, Sara the drone.

How could he have fallen in love with her? And yet sometimes it seemed that he had. *Is this part of the game for him, too?* Sara wondered.

Her fingers ran all over his chest, played with individual hairs. She touched him everywhere: his beautiful face, his throat, stomach, buttocks, his dangling testicles, which seemed as large as a bull's. Sara arched up toward him, wanting to be as close as she possibly could, wanting every inch, yes, wanting everything of him that there was. *Even his real name,* which he wouldn't tell her.

"We've earned this weekend," Sam said. "It's also necessary, Sara. Rest and relaxation are a real part of war, an important part. Jack and Jill is going to get progressively harder from here on. Everything escalates now."

Sara couldn't help smiling as she stared up at Sam's face. God she loved being with him. Under him, over him, sideways, upside down. She loved his touch — sometimes strong, sometimes so surprisingly gentle. She loved, *yes,* every inch of him.

She'd never felt like this before, never thought that she would. She would have bet anything against its happening. In a way, she *had* bet everything, hadn't she? For the cause, but also for Sam, for this.

Sam was such a closet romantic, too. It was so unexpected from The Soldier, from any man she had known before. The suite at the Four Seasons was his idea, just because she had mentioned — *mentioned it once* — that it was her favorite hotel in Washington.

"Say," she said to him now, whispering during their love-making, "do you want to know my favorite hotel in the whole wide world?"

He got the joke — he got all of her humor and twisted ironies. His large blue eyes sparkled. He grinned. He had brilliantly white teeth, and such a shy, disarming smile. She thought he was much better looking than Michael Robinson had been. Sam was a real-life action hero. *The Soldier.* In a real war for survival, the most important war of our times. They both believed that to be the truth.

"Please, *don't* tell me the answer," he said with a laugh. "*Don't you dare tell me* your favorite hotel in the world. You know I'll have to take you there somehow if you do. Don't tell me, Sara!"

"The Cipriani in Venice," Sara blurted out, laughing.

She had never actually been there, but she'd read so much about it. She had read about everything, but experienced so little until recently. Sara the hopeless bookworm, Sara the bibliophile, Sara the cipher. Well, no more. Now she lived as almost no one had before. Sara the gimp lives!

"Okay, then. When this is all over — and this *will* end — we'll go to Venice, for a holiday. I promise you. The Cipriani it is."

"And Sunday brunch at the Danieli," she whispered against his cheek. "Promise?"

"Of course. Where else but the Danieli for brunch? That's a given. As soon as this is finished."

"It's going to get worse, isn't it?" she said, hugging his powerful body a little tighter.

"Yes, I'm afraid so. But not tonight, Jilly. Not tonight, my love. So let's not ruin this by thinking too much about tomorrow. Don't make a wonderful weekend into a bad Monday."

Sam was right, of course. He was a wise man, too. He started to move again on top of her. He flowed like a fast river current over the top of her. He was such a generous and beautiful lover; he was both teacher and student; he knew how to give and take in bed. Most important, Sam knew how to bring her out of herself. God, she had needed that — forever, it seemed. *To get outside of herself. Not to be the gimp anymore. Not ever again.* She promised herself that.

Sara pursed her lips tightly. In pleasure? In pain? She wasn't even sure anymore. She shut her eyes, then quickly opened them. *She wanted to look.*

He held himself over her, as if he were pausing during a push-up. "So you've never been to the Cipriani, Monkey Face?" he asked. His cheeks weren't even flushed. He effortlessly held himself over her. His body was so beautiful, strong and agile, rock-solid. Sara was in good shape also, but Sam was superb.

He called her "Monkey Face," from Hitchcock's *Suspicion*. It wasn't really such a great movie, but it had hit the spot for them, hit *their* spot. Ever since they'd seen it, she'd been the Joan Fontaine character, Lena. He was Johnny, who had been played by Cary Grant. Johnny had called Lena "Monkey Face."

At the end of the film, Lena and Johnny had driven off into a sunset on the Riviera, presumably to live happily ever after. The Hitchcock movie was an elegant, witty, mysterious game, just as this was.

Their game. The most exquisite game two people had ever played together.

Will we drive off into the sunset after all this? Sara Rosen wondered. *Oh, I think not. I don't suppose that we will. What will happen to us, then? Oh, what will happen to us? What will become of Jack and Jill?*

"I've only been to the Cipriani in my dreams," she confessed to Sam. "Only in dreams. But, yes, *I've been there* many, many times."

"Is *this all* a dream, Monkey Face?" Sam asked. His look was serious for a moment. She couldn't help thinking how precious every moment like this was, and how fleeting. She had secretly yearned for this all of her life, for one truly romantic experience.

"I think it's a dream, yes. It's *like* a dream anyway. Please don't wake me, though, Sam."

"It's not a dream," Sam whispered. "I love you. You are the most lovable woman I've ever met. You are, Sara. You're like staying at the Cipriani every day for me. Please believe that, Monkey Face. Believe in us. I do."

He clasped Sara from behind and pulled her closer. She savored the sweetness of his breath, the smell of his cologne, the smell of *him*.

He began to move inside her and she felt herself melting into a liquid force. She did love him — she did, she did, she did. Her hands ran all over him, touching, possessing. There had never been anything like this before in her life, nothing even close.

She slithered up and down on his long, powerful pole, his strength, his exquisite maleness. Sara couldn't stop herself now, and she didn't want to. She was choking with her own passion.

She heard her voice crying out and almost didn't recognize herself. She was joined with him in a simple rhythm that got faster and faster as the two of them came closer to being one — *Jack and Jill, Jack and Jill, Jack and Jill, Jack and Jill!*

Chapter 32

THEIR FAIRY TALE ended with a quiet, almost disheartening *thud,* and Sara felt herself crashing back to earth, tumbling, being rushed along in a powerful tide. Monday morning meant a return to the dreary work world again, to real life.

Sara Rosen had held "normal," boring jobs around Washington for fourteen years, ever since she'd graduated from Hollins College in Virginia. She had a day job now. A perfect job for their purposes. The dreariest and weariest of jobs.

That morning, she rose early to get ready. She and Sam had separated on Sunday night at the Four Seasons. She missed him, missed his humor, missed his touch, missed everything about him. Every inch.

She had gotten lost in that thought. *Inches. Millimeters. The essence of Sam. His tremendous inner strength.* She glanced at the luminescent face of the clock on her bed stand. She groaned out loud. *Quarter to five. Dammit, she was already late.*

Her bathroom had a yoga corner with a custom-made leather mat. No time for that, though her body and mind ached for the discipline and the release.

She took a quick shower and washed her hair with Salon

Selectives shampoo. She put on a navy Brooks Brothers suit, low pumps, a leather-strapped Raymond Weil watch. She needed to look sharp, look alert, look freshly scrubbed this morning.

Somehow, she always came out like that anyway. Sara the freshly starched.

She hurried outside, where a grimy yellow cab was already waiting at the curb, wagging a tail of smoke. The wind whooped and howled up and down K Street.

At five-twenty, the yellow cab pulled up in front of her workplace. The Liberty Cab driver smiled and said, "A famous address, my lady. So, are you somebody famous?"

She paid the driver and collected change from a five-dollar bill. "Actually, I might be someday," she said. "You never know."

"Yeah, maybe I'm somebody, too," the driver said with a crooked smile. "You never know."

Sara Rosen climbed out of the cab and felt the early December wind in her face. The pristine building before her looked strangely beautiful and imposing in the early-morning light. It appeared to be shining, actually, glowing from the inside out.

She showed her ID card, and security let her pass inside. She and the guard even shared a quick laugh about her being a workaholic. And why not? Sara Rosen had worked inside the White House for nine years.

PART III
THE PHOTOJOURNALIST

Chapter 33

THE PHOTOJOURNALIST was the last piece in the complex puzzle. He was the final player. He was working in San Francisco on December 8. Actually, the photojournalist was playing the game in San Francisco. Or rather, he was playing around the outer edges of the game.

Kevin Hawkins sat in a scooped-out, gray plastic chair at Gate 31. He contentedly played chess with himself on a PowerBook. He was winning; he was losing. He enjoyed it either way.

Hawkins loved games, loved chess, and he was close to being one of the better players in the world. It had been that way ever since he'd been a bright, lonely, underachieving boy in Hudson, New York. At quarter to eleven he got up from his seat to go play another kind of game. This was his favorite game in the world. *He was in San Francisco to kill someone.*

As he walked through the busy airport, Kevin Hawkins snapped off photograph after photograph — *all in his mind.*

The prizewinning photojournalist was outfitted in his usual studied-casual manner: tight black cord jeans with a black

T-shirt, tribal bracelets from several trips to Zambia, a diamond stud earring. A Leica camera was looped around his neck on a leather strap decorated with engravings.

The photojournalist slipped into a crowded bathroom in Corridor C. He observed a ragged line of men slouched at the urinals. *They are like pigs at a trough,* he thought. Like water buffalo, or oxen, taught to stand on their hind legs.

His eye composed the shot and snapped it off. A beauty of order and sly wit. *The Boys at the Bowl.*

The urinal scene reminded him of a clever pickpocket he had once seen operate in Bangkok. The thief, a keen student of human nature, would snatch wallets while gents were in midstream at a urinal and were reluctant, or unable, to go after him.

The photojournalist couldn't forget the comical image whenever he entered an airport men's room. He rarely forgot any image, actually. His mind was a well-run archive, a rival to Kodak's vast storehouses of pictures in Rochester.

He peered at his own image, a rather haggard and pasty-white face, in one of the cloudy bathroom mirrors. *Unimpressive in every way,* he couldn't help but think. His eyes were war-weary, an almost washed-out blue. Gazing at his eyes depressed him — so much so that he sighed involuntarily.

He saw no other mind pictures to take in the mirror. Never, ever, a picture of himself.

He started to cough and couldn't stop. He finally brought up a thick packet of despicable, yellowish paste. *His inner core,* he thought. His animus was slowly leaking out.

Kevin Hawkins was only forty-three, but he felt like a hundred. He had lived too hard, especially the last fourteen years. His life and times had been so very intense, often flamboyant and occasionally absurd. He had been *burned,* he often imagined, from every conceivable angle. He had played the *game of life and death* too hard, too well, too often.

He started to cough again and popped a Halls into his mouth.

Kevin Hawkins checked the time on his Seiko Kinetic wristwatch. He quickly finger-combed his lank, grayish blond hair and then left the public bathroom.

He merged smoothly with the thick corridor traffic rolling past on the killing floor. It was almost time, and he was feeling a nice out-of-body buzz. He hummed an old, absolutely ridiculous song called "Rock the Casbah." He was pulling a dark Delsey suitcase hinged on one of those cheap roller contraptions that were so popular. The "walking" suitcase made him look like a tourist, like a nobody of the first order.

The red-on-black digital clock over the airport passageway read 11:40. A Northwest Airlines jet from Tokyo had landed just a few minutes earlier. It had come into Gate 41, right on schedule. *Some people just know how to fly.* Wasn't that Northwest's tag line?

The gods were smiling down on him; Kevin Hawkins felt a grim, humorless smile of his own. The gods loved the game, too. *Life and death. It was their game, actually.*

He heard the first strains of a noisy commotion coming from the connecting Corridor B. The photojournalist kept walking ahead, until he was past the point where the two wide corridors connected.

That was when he saw the phalanx of bodyguards and wellwishers. He *clicked* off a shot in his mind. He got a peek at Mr. Tanaka of the Nipray Corporation. He *clicked* another shot.

His adrenaline was flowing like lava from Kilauea in Hawaii, where he'd once shot for *Newsweek. Adrenaline. Nothing like it.* He was addicted to the stuff.

Any second now.

Any second.

Any nanosecond — which, he knew, is to a second as a second is to about thirty years.

There was no X-marks-the-spot on the terminal floor, but Kevin Hawkins knew this was the place. He had it all visualized, every critical angle was vivid as hell in his mind's eye. All the intersect points were clear to him.

Any second. Life and death.

There *might as well* have been a big black **X** painted on the airport floor.

Kevin Hawkins felt like a god.

Here we go. Cameras loaded and at the ready. Lock and load! Someone's going to die here.

Chapter 34

WHEN THE SEMIOFFICIAL ENTOURAGE was approximately twelve feet from the busy corridor-crossing, a small bomb detonated. The explosion sent a cloud of gray-black smoke into Corridor A. Screams pierced the air like whining sirens.

The bomb had been inside a dark blue suitcase left next to the news and magazine kiosk. Kevin Hawkins had placed the innocent-looking suitcase directly in front of a sign that advised travelers to WATCH YOUR LUGGAGE AT ALL TIMES.

The deafening, *booming* noise and sudden chaos startled the bodyguards surrounding Mr. Tanaka. It made them erratic, and therefore predictable. Security teams, even the best of them, could be fooled *if you forced them to improvise.* Travelers and airport personnel were screaming, seeking cover where there was none to be had. Men, women, and children pressed themselves to the floor, faces hard against cold marble.

People haven't seen real panic until they've witnessed it in a large airport, where everyone is already close to the edge of primal fears.

Two of the bodyguards covered the corporate chairman, doing a half-decent job, Hawkins saw.

He clicked another mind photo. Stored it in his photo file for future reference.

This was good stuff, valuable as hell. How an excellent security team reacted under stress during an actual attack.

Then the efficient, if uninspired, bodyguards began to hurriedly move their "protected person" out of danger, out of harm's way. They obviously couldn't go forward into the smoky, bombed-out corridor. The security team chose to go back — their only choice, the one Kevin Hawkins knew they would make under duress.

They pulled along Mr. Tanaka as if he were a large, ungainly puppet or doll, which he pretty much was. They almost physically carried the important businessman, holding him under his arms so that both his feet left the floor at times.

Mind photo of that: *expensive black tasseled loafers skipping across the marble floor.*

The trained bodyguards had *one goal:* get the "protected person" out of there. The photojournalist let them proceed about thirty feet before he pushed the detonator in the shoulder bag housing his camera gear. It was that easy. The best plans were one-button simple. Like a camera. Like a camera suitable for a child.

A second suitcase he had left alongside the corridor near the men's room exploded with double the thunder and lightning of the first, causing more than twice the damage. It was as if an invisible missile had been guided directly into the center of the airport.

The destruction was instantaneous, and it was brutal. Bodies, and even body parts, flew in every imaginable direction. Tanaka didn't survive. Neither did any of the four diligent and highly underpaid bodyguards.

The photojournalist was tightly wedged in amidst the rushing wall of men and women trying to escape toward the airport exits. His was just another terrified face in the stormy human sea.

And, yes, he could look very terrified. He knew more than any of them what fear looked like. He had photographed uncontrolled fear on so many faces. He often saw those awful looks of terror, those silent screams, in his dreams.

He held back a tight, grim smile as he turned onto Corridor D and headed toward his own plane. He was going to Washington, D.C., that evening and hoped the delays caused by the murder wouldn't be massively long.

The risk had been a necessary one, actually. This had been a rehearsal, *the last rehearsal*.

Now, on to far more important things. The photojournalist had a very big job in D.C. The code name was easy enough for him to remember.

Jack and Jill.

Chapter 35

"THE EIGHTEEN-ACRE ESTATE around the White House in-cludes many diversions: a private movie theater, gym, wine cel-lar, tennis courts, bowling lanes, rooftop greenhouse, and a golf range on the South Lawn. The house and property are cur-rently assessed at three hundred forty million by the District of Columbia." I could almost do the spiel myself.

I showed my temporary pass, then carefully drove down into the parking garage under the White House. On the way in I had noticed some renovation to the main building and also extensive groundwork, but overall the White House looked just fine to me.

My head was not so fine. It was uneasy. Filled with chaotic thoughts. I had slept only a couple of hours the night before, and that was becoming a pattern. The morning's *Washington Post* and *New York Times* lay folded on the car seat beside me.

The *Post* headline asked WHO'S NEXT FOR JACK AND JILL? It seemed like a question directed right at me. WHO'S NEXT?

I thought about a possible attempt on the life of President Thomas Byrnes, as I walked from the small parking garage to the elevator. A lot of people were extremely high on the President and his programs. Americans had clamored for change for a long time, and President Byrnes was delivering it in large doses. Of course, what most people want "change" to mean is more money in their pockets, instantly, without any sacrifice on their part.

So who might be angry and crazed enough at the President to want him murdered? I knew that was why I was at the White House. I was here to conduct a homicide investigation. In the White House. A search for a couple of killers who could be planning to murder the President.

I met Don Hamerman in the West Wing Entrance Hall. He was still acting extremely high strung and anxious, but that seemed to be his persona. It also fit the times. The chief of staff and I talked for a few minutes in the hallway. He went out of his way to tell me that I had been handpicked for the investigation because of my expertise with high-profile killers, especially psychopaths.

He seemed to know an awful lot about me. As he talked, I imagined that he'd probably gotten the coveted brownnoser award in his senior year at Yale or Harvard, where he had also learned to talk with a whiny, upper-class drawl.

I had absolutely no idea what to expect that morning. Hamerman said he was going to line up some "interviews" for me. I sensed some of his frustration in trying to organize an investigation like this inside the White House. A murder investigation.

He left me alone inside the Map Room on the ground floor. I paced around the famous room, absently checking out the elaborately carved Chippendale furniture, an oil portrait of Ben Franklin, a landscape painting titled *Tending Cows and Sheep*. I already had a busy day ahead. I had appointments set up at the city morgue and with Benjamin Levitsky, the number two at the FBI's intelligence unit.

I continued to be frustrated about the Truth School child murders. For the moment, that was Sampson's concern. Sampson's and our part-time posse of detectives'. But I couldn't keep it off my mind.

Suddenly, someone entered the Map Room along with the national security advisor. I was taken by surprise. I was blown away, actually. No words could possibly describe the feeling.

Don Hamerman stiffly announced, "President Byrnes will see you now."

Chapter 36

"GOOD MORNING. Is it Doctor or Detective Cross?" President Thomas Byrnes asked me.

I had a sneaking suspicion that Dr. Cross would serve me much better at the White House. Like Dr. Bunche, Dr. Kissinger, or even Doc Savage. "I guess that I prefer Alex," I said to him.

The President's face lit up in a broad smile, and it was the same charismatic one I had seen many times on television and on the front pages of newspapers.

"And I prefer Tom," the President said. He extended his hand and the two of us shook off our surnames. His grip was firm and steady. He held eye contact with me for several seconds.

The President of the United States managed to sound both cordial and appropriately serious at the same time. He was about six feet tall, and he was trim and fit at fifty. His hair was light brown, trimmed with silver-gray. He looked a little like a fighter pilot. His eyes were very sensitive and warm. He was already known as our most personable president in many years, and also our most dynamic.

I had read and heard a lot about the man I was meeting for the first time. He had been the successful and much-admired head of the Ford Motor Company in Detroit before he decided to go for an even higher executive office. He had run for the presidency as an Independent, and true to the polls of the past few years, the people had voted for fresh, independent thinking — or maybe they were just voting against the Republican and Democratic Parties, as some pundits believed. So far, he had shown himself to be a contemporary thinker, but a bit contrarian, a genuine maverick in high office. As an independent mover and shaker, the President had made few friends in Washington, but lots of enemies.

"The director of the FBI highly recommended you," he said. "I think Stephen Bowen's a pretty good man. What do you think? Any opinion of him?"

"I agree with you. The Bureau has changed a lot in the past couple of years under Bowen. We work well with them now. That didn't used to be the case."

The President nodded. "Is this a real threat, Alex, or are we just taking wise precautions?" he asked me. It was a tough, blunt question. I also thought it was the right question to ask.

"I think the concern of the Secret Service is definitely a wise precaution," I said. "The coincidence of the names Jack and Jill being the same as your code names with the Secret Service, that's very disturbing. So is the killers' pattern of going after famous people here in Washington."

"I guess I fit that damn description. Sad but true," President Byrnes said and frowned. I had read that he was an intensely private man and down-to-earth as well. He seemed that way to me. Midwestern in the best sense. I guess what surprised me the most was the warmth that came from the man.

"As you have admitted yourself, you're 'shaking up the toy box.' You've already disturbed a lot of people."

"Stay tuned, there are *a lot more* major disturbances to come. This government badly needs to be reengineered. It was designed for life in the eighteen hundreds. Alex, I'm going to cooperate in any way I can with the police investigation. I don't want anyone else to be hurt, let alone die. I've certainly thought about it, but I'm not ready to die yet. I think Sally and I are decent people. I hope you'll feel that way the more you're around us. We're far from perfect, but we are decent. We're trying to do the right thing."

I was already feeling that way about the President. He had quickly struck a good chord with me. At the same time, I wondered how much of what he'd said I could believe. He was, after all, a politician. The best in the land.

"Every year, several people try to break into the White House, Alex. One man succeeded by tagging onto the end of the marine marching band. Quite a few have tried to ram the front gates with cars. In ninety-four, Frank Eugene Corder flew a single-engine Cessna in here."

"But so far, nothing like this," I said.

The President asked the real question on his mind. "What's your bottom line on Jack and Jill?"

"No bottom line yet. Maybe a morning line," I told him. "I disagree with the FBI. I don't see them as pattern killers. They're highly organized, but the pattern seems artificial to me. I'll bet they're both attractive, white, with well above normal IQ. They have to be articulate and persuasive to get into the places that they did. They want to accomplish something even more spectacular. What they've done so far is only groundwork. They enjoy the power of manipulating both us and the media. That's what I have so far. It's what I'm prepared to talk about, anyway."

The President nodded solemnly. "I have a good feeling about you, Alex," he said. "I'm glad we met for a couple of minutes here. I was told that you have two children," he said. He reached into his jacket and handed me a presidential tie clasp and a pin especially designed for kids. "Keepsakes are important, I think. You see, I believe in tradition as well as in change."

President Byrnes shook my hand again, looked me directly in the eye for a moment, and then left the room.

I understood that I had just been welcomed to the team, and the sole purpose of the team was to protect the President's life. I found that I was powerfully motivated to do just that. I looked down at the tie clasp and pin for Damon and Jannie and was strangely moved.

Chapter 37

"SO DID YOU get to meet the royal couple yet?" Nana Mama asked when I entered her kitchen about four that afternoon.

She was making something in a big gray stewpot that smelled like the proverbial ambrosia. It was white bean soup, one of my favorites. Rosie the cat was prowling around on the counters, purring contentedly. *Rosie in the kitchen.*

At the same time Nana cooked at the counter, she was doing the crossword puzzle in the *Washington Post.* A book of her word jumbles was also out in view. So was *No Stone Unturned — The Life and Times of Maggie Kuhn.* Complicated woman, my grand-mother.

"Did I meet who?" I pretended not to understand her crystal-clear and very pointed question to me. I was playing the game that the two of us have had going for many years, and probably will until death do us part somehow, sometime, someway.

"Meet *whom,* Dr. Cross. The President and Mrs. President, of course. The well-to-do white folks who live in the *White* House, looking down on the rest of us. Tom and Sally up in Camelot for the nineties."

I smiled at her usual high-spirited and occasionally bittersweet banter. I looked in the fridge. "I didn't come home for the third and fourth degree, you know. I'm going to make a sandwich from this brisket. It looks moist and tender. Or are looks deceiving?"

"Of course they are, but this brisket is moist and you could cut it with a soup spoon. Seems as if they work very short hours over at the White House, considering all that they have to do. Somehow, I suspected as much. But I could never prove it until now. So *who* did you meet?"

I couldn't resist. I had been going to tell her this much anyway. "I met and talked with the President this morning."

"You met *Tom?*"

Nana pretended to take a punch in the manner of the heavyweight boxer George Foreman. She did a stumbling stutter-step back from the counter. She even cracked a tiny smile. "Well, tell me all about *Tom,* for heaven's sake. And Sally. Does Sally wear a black pillbox hat inside the White House in the daytime?"

"I think that was Jacqueline Kennedy. Actually, I liked President Byrnes," I said as I commenced making a thick brisket sandwich on fresh rye with bib lettuce, tomatoes, and a dab of mayonnaise, lots of pepper, a whisk of salt.

"You would. You like everybody unless they kill somebody," Nana said as she began to slice up some more tomatoes. "Now that you've met Mr. President, you can get back on the Sojourner Truth School case. That's very important to the people in this house. The *Gray* House. No black people care very much about the President and his problems anymore. Nor should they."

"Is that a fact, Mrs. Farrakhan?" I said as I bit into my sandwich. Delicious, as promised. Cut it with a soup spoon, melts in the mouth.

"Should be a fact, if it isn't. It's close to a fact, anyway. I'll admit that it's a sad state of affairs, but it's the sad state we all live in. Don't you agree? You *must.*"

"You ever hear of mellowing with age?" I asked her. "Your brisket is terrific, by the way."

"You ever hear of getting better, not getting older? You ever hear of taking care of one's own kind? You ever hear about teeny-tiny, darling black children being murdered in our neighborhood, Alex, and nobody doing enough to make it stop? Of course the brisket is excellent. You see, I *am* getting better."

I reached into my trouser pocket and took out the clasp and pin that the President had given me. "The President knew I had two children. He gave me these keepsakes for them." I handed them over to Nana. She took them, and for once in her life, she was speechless.

"Tell them that these are from Tom and that he's a fine man trying to do the right thing."

I finished half of my overstuffed sandwich and took the remaining half with me out of the kitchen. If you can't stand the heat and all that. "Thanks for the delicious sandwich, and the advice. In that order."

"Where are you going now?" Nana called after me. She was winding up again. "We were talking about an important matter. Genocide against black people right here in Washington, our nation's capital. They don't care what happens in these neighborhoods, Alex. *They* is *them,* and *them* is *white,* and you're collaborating with the enemy."

"Actually, I'm going out to put in a few hours on the Truth School murder case," I called back as I continued toward the front door, and blessed escape from the tirade. I couldn't see Nana Mama anymore, but I could hear her voice trailing behind me like a banshee cry, or maybe the caw of a field crow.

"Alex has finally found his senses!" she exclaimed in a loud, shrill voice. "There's hope after all. There's hope. Oh, thank you, Black Lord in Heaven."

The old goat can still get my goat, and I love her for it. I just don't want to listen to her annoying rap sometimes.

I beeped the car horn of my old Porsche on the way out of the driveway. It's our signal that everything is all right between us. From inside the house, I heard Nana call out: "*Beep* back at you!"

Chapter 38

I WAS BACK on the mean streets of inner Washington, the underside of the capital. I was a homicide detective again. I loved it with a strange passion, but there were times when I hated it with all my heart.

We were doing all that could humanly be done on both cases. I had set up surveillance on the Truth School during the day and also had day and night surveillance on Shanelle Green's gravesite. Often psycho killers showed up at victims' graves. They were ghouls, after all.

The circus was definitely in town.

Two of them.

Two completely different kinds of murder pattern. I had never seen anything like it, nothing even close to this chaos.

I didn't need Nana Mama to remind me that I wanted to be out on the street right now. As she had said, *Someone is killing our children.*

I was certain that the unspeakable monster was going to kill again. In contrast to Jack and Jill, there *was* rage and passion in his work. There was a raw, scary craziness, the kind I could almost taste. The killer's probable amateur status wasn't reassuring, either.

Think like the killer. Walk in the killer's shoes, I reminded myself. That's how it all starts, but it's a lot tougher than it sounds. I was gathering as much information and data as I possibly could.

I spent part of the afternoon ambushing several of the local hangarounds who might have picked up something on the murders: convivial street people, swooning pipeheads, young runners for the rock and weed dealers, a few low-level rollers themselves, store owners, snitches, Muslims selling newspapers. I gave some of them a tough time, but nobody had anything useful for me.

I kept at The Job anyway. That's the way it goes most days. You just keep at it, keep your head down and screwed on straight. About quarter past five, I found myself talking to a seventeen-year-old homeless youth I knew from working the soup kitchen at St. Anthony's. His name was Loy McCoy, and he was a low-level crack runner now. He had helped me once or twice in the past.

Loy had stopped coming by for free food once he had started moving nickel and dime bags of crack and speed around the neighborhood. It's hard to blame kids like Loy, as much as I would like to some days. Their lives are unbelievably brutal and hopeless. Then one day someone comes along and offers them fifteen or twenty bucks an hour to do what's going to happen anyway. The more powerful emotional hook is that their dope bosses believe in them, and in many cases nobody has believed in any of these lost kids before.

I called Loy over, away from the posse of fools he was hanging with on L Street. They all wore black, machine-knit wool caps pulled low over their eyes and ears. Gold toothcaps, hoop earrings, baggy trousers, the works. His gang was talking about the movie based on the old Flintstones cartoon, or maybe about the actual cartoons. *Yabba dabbas* was one of the catchphrases used to describe police patrolmen and detectives in the 'hood. *Here comes the yabba dabba.* Or, *he's a yabba dabba doo motherfucker.* I had recently read a sad statistic that seventy percent of Americans got nearly one hundred percent of their information from television and the movies.

Loy smirked as he slow-shuffled up to me at the street corner. He was maybe six one, but about only a hundred and forty pounds. He had on baggy, layered winter clothes, artfully torn, and he was "grittin" me today, trying to stare me down, put me down.

"Yo, you say c'mon over, I got to come?" Loy asked in a defiant tone that I found both irritating and monumentally sad. "Whyzat? I pay my *taxes*," he rapped on. "I ain't holdin'. Ain't none of us holdin'."

"None of your bullshit attitude works on me," I told him. "You better lose it right now." I knew that his mother was a heroin addict and that he had three little sisters. All of them lived at the Greater Southeast Community Hospital shelter, which was like having the tunnels under Union Station as your home address.

"Say your business, an' I get back to my business," Loy said, remaining defiant. "My time's money, unnerstand? Axt me what you got to axt."

"Just one question for you, Loy. Then you can go back to your big money business dealings."

He kept "grittin" me, which can get you shot in this neighborhood. "Why I have to answer any questions? What's in it for me? What you have to deal?"

I finally smiled at Loy and he cracked a half-smile himself, showing off his shiny gold caps. "You give me something, maybe I'll remember. Then maybe I'll owe you one sometime," I said.

"Yo," he came right back at me. "Wanna know a big fat secret, *Detective*? I don't *need* your markers. And I don't much care about these murdered kids' homo-cides you lookin' into." He shrugged as if it were no big deal on the street. I already knew that.

I waited for him to finish his little speech, and also to process my offer. The sad thing was that he was bright. Crazy smart. That was why the crack boss had hired him. Loy was smart enough, and he probably even had a decent work ethic.

"I can't talk to you! Don't have to, neither!" he finally did a little exasperated spin and threw up both his skinny arms. "You think I owe you 'cause once upon a time you fed us Manhandler soup-slop at the po'boy kitchen? Think I owe you? I don't owe you shit!"

Loy started to strut away. Then he looked back at me, as if he had just one more irritating wisecrack to hurl my way. His dark eyes narrowed, caught mine, and held on for a second. *Contact. Liftoff.*

"Somebody saw an old man where that little girl got kilt," Loy blurted out. It was the biggest news we had so far on the Truth School case. It was the *only* news, and it was what I had been looking for all these days working the street.

He had no idea how fast I was, or how strong. I reached out and pulled him close to me. I pulled Loy McCoy *very* close. So close I could smell the sweet peppermint on his breath, the scent of pomade in his hair, the mustiness of his badly wrinkled winter clothes.

I held him to my chest as if he were a son of mine, a prodigal son, a young fool who needed to understand that I wasn't going to allow him to be this way with me. I held him real tight and I wanted to save him somehow. I wanted to save all of them, but I couldn't, and it was one of the big hurts and frustrations of my life.

"I'm not fooling around here, now. Who told you that, Loy? You talk to me. Don't fuck with me on this. *Talk to me, and talk to me now.*"

His face was inches from mine. My mouth was almost pressed against his cheek. All of his street swagger and the attitude had disappeared. I didn't like being a tough guy with him, but this was important as hell.

My hands are large and scarred, like a boxer's, and I let him see them. "I'm waiting for an answer," I whispered. "I *will* take you in. I will ruin your day and night."

"Don't know *who*," he said between wheezing breaths. "Some people in the shelter be sayin' it. I just heard it, you know. Old homeless dude. Somebody saw'm hangin' in Garfield. *White* dude in the park."

"A white man? On the southeast side of the park? You sure about that?"

"That's right. What I said. What I *heard*. Now, let me *go*. C'mon, man, let go!"

I let him pull away from me, walk away a few steps.

Loy regained his composure and cool as soon as he realized that I wasn't going to hurt him, or even take him in for questioning.

"That's the story. You *owe* me," he said. "I'm gonna *collect*, too." I don't believe Loy saw the irony in what he was saying.

"I owe you," I said. "Thanks, Loy." *I hope you don't ever have to collect.*

He winked at me. "Be all you can be, al-riii!" he said and laughed and laughed as he walked back to the other crack runners.

Chapter 39

AN OLD HOMELESS MAN near the murder scene. In Garfield Park. That was something solid to work with, finally. I had paid some dues and gotten a return on investment.

A white man. A white suspect.

That was even more promising. There weren't too many white males hanging out in the Garfield Park area. That was for sure.

I called Sampson and told him what I'd found out. He'd just come on duty for the night shift. I asked John how it was going on his end. He said that it wasn't going, but maybe now it would. He would let the others in our group know.

At a little past five, I stopped by the Sojourner Truth School again. There were several forces strongly pulling me in the direction of the school. The new information about the homeless white man and the constant feeling that just maybe my nemesis Gary Soneji might be involved. That was part of it. Then there was Christine Johnson. Mrs. Johnson.

Once again, nobody was sitting at the desk in the outer office. The multiracial dolls on the desk looked abandoned. So did some "face doodles" and a couple of *Goosebump* books. The heavy wooden door into the main office was shut tight.

I couldn't hear anyone inside, but I knocked anyway. I heard a drawer bang shut, then footsteps. The door opened. It wasn't locked.

Christine Johnson had on a cashmere jacket and long wool skirt. Her hair was pulled back and tied with a yellow bow. She was wearing her glasses. Working barefoot. I thought of a line — from Dorothy Parker, I think — *Men seldom make passes/At girls who wear glasses*.

Seeing her lifted my spirits, brought me up immediately. I didn't know exactly why, but it did.

It occurred to me that she worked late at the school a lot. That was her business, but I wondered why she spent so much time here.

"Yes, I'm working late again. You caught me in the act. Red-handed, guilty as charged. A friend of yours dropped by the school this morning," she said. "A detective John Sampson."

"He's in charge of the case," I said.

"He seems very dedicated and concerned. Surprising in a lot of ways. He's reading Camus," she said.

I wondered how he had worked *that* into their conversation. Among other noble pursuits, Sampson is dedicated to meeting interesting and attractive women, like Christine Johnson. It wouldn't bother him that she was married, unless it bothered her. Sampson can be chivalrous to a fault, but only if it's appreciated.

"Sampson reads a lot, always has since I've known him. My grandmother taught him in school, before I met him, actually. He's the original Pagemaster."

Christine Johnson smiled, showed me all those beautiful teeth of hers. "You're familiar with the movie *Pagemaster*? I guess you must see them all."

"I do see them all. Anything the kids 'have to, have to see, Daddy!' We gave *Pagemaster* a six. But we're not as down on Master Macauley Culkin as some people seem to be."

She continued to smile and seemed to be an extremely nice person. Smart enough to do many things — patient and concerned enough to do this difficult job in the city. I envied her students.

I got right down to the business I had at the school. "The reason I stopped by is that there's a possible ID on the killer — a start, anyway. I heard about it this afternoon, not too long ago."

Christine Johnson listened closely to what I had to say. Her brow furrowed deeply. Her brown eyes were intense. She was a good listener, which, if I remembered correctly, was unusual for a school principal.

"An older man, a white man, was seen in the vicinity of where Shanelle Green was originally abducted in Garfield Park. He was described as a street person. Possibly a homeless man. Not very big, with a full white beard, wearing a brown or black poncho."

"Should I tell that to the teachers? What about the children?" she asked as I finished the description.

"I'd like to have someone stop by here tomorrow morning to talk to the teachers again," I said. "We don't know if this lead is anything, but it could be important. It's the best thing we have so far."

"An ounce of prevention," she said, then smiled. Actually, she laughed at herself. "That's what is known, derogatively, as 'teacher talk.' You can catch a dose of it if you hang around here too much. Too many clichés. You sometimes find yourself talking to other adults as if they were five or six years old. It drives my husband *crazy*."

"Is your husband a teacher, too?" I asked. It just came out. *Shit.*

She shook her head and seemed amused for some reason. "No, no. George is a lawyer. He's a lobbyist on Capitol Hill, actually. Fortunately, he's only trying to push the interests of energy businesses. Occidental Petroleum, Pepco Energy Company, the Edison Electric Institute. I can live with that." She laughed. "Well, most of the time I can." Her look was innocent, but not naive. Maybe just a little conspiratorial.

"Well, I wanted to pass on the news about our suspect. Maybe we have a real suspect this time," I said. "I've got to run."

"*Don't*," Christine Johnson said, and I stopped short, startled a little.

Then she smiled that knowing smile of hers. Quietly dazzling and appealing as could be.

"Absolutely no running in the halls," she winked at me. "*Gotcha!*" Cute.

I laughed and was on my merry way, back to work after a brief moment of sweetness and light. I did like her quite a lot. Who wouldn't? Maybe we could be friends somehow, someway, but probably not.

Nothing was coming out right; nothing was working very well. *An old homeless white man* was the best we could do. It wasn't bad police work, but it wasn't enough. Not even close. Two impossible cases. Jesus!

I pulled my car way down the street and watched the Truth School for a couple of hours that night. *My son's school.* Maybe a homeless white man would come by — *but one didn't.*

I left the stakeout about half an hour after Christine Johnson left hers.

Chapter 40

"WHAT DO YOU THINK of our magic carpet ride so far? On a scale of one to eleven?" Jack asked Jill, Sam asked Sara. They were floating high over the Maryland countryside.

"It's absolutely beautiful. It's as thrilling as can be. Unbelievable. The simple joy of flying like a bird."

"Hard to imagine that this is work. But it is, Monkey Face. This could be important for us, for everything we're doing, for the game."

"I know that, Sam. I'm paying attention."

"I know you are. Always so diligent."

The two of them were sitting close together inside the tiny cockpit of a Blanik L-23 sailplane. They had flown the sailplane out of Frederick Municipal Airport in Maryland, about an hour from downtown Washington. It was the perfect treat for her, Sara couldn't help thinking. The perfect metaphor. The gimp was flying. Unbelievable. Her entire life was that way now.

Down below, she could see Frederick, with its many examples of German Colonial architecture. She could actually make out several of the cutesy-pie shops on Antique Walk in town. The sky was filled with cumulus, like cotton balls moving lightly over a calm sea. Sara had told Sam that she'd gone up in a sail-plane once, and it was "just about the best thing I've ever done." He'd said, "We'll go tomorrow afternoon. I know just the place, Monkey Face. Perfect! I want to fly over Camp David, where the President goes to stay. I want to look down on President Byrnes's retreat. I want to drop an imaginary bomb on his ass."

Sam Harrison already knew a great deal about Camp David, but the view from the air could be useful anyhow. An attack on the presidential retreat was a very real possibility in the future — especially if the Secret Service continued to keep President Byrnes tightly under wraps, as they had for the past few days.

Everything about Jack and Jill was so much harder now, but he had expected that. It was why they had several plans, not just one. The President of the United States was going to die — it was just a matter of when and where. The *how* had already been decided. Soon the when and where would be taken care of as well.

"Isn't this risky, flying so close to Camp David?" Sara asked. He smiled at the question. He knew that she had been biting her tongue as they floated north from Frederick, inching closer and closer to the presidential outpost, closer and closer to danger, maybe even disaster.

"So far, it's not too risky. Sailplanes and hot-air balloons do it all the time. Catch a distant peek at where the President stays. He's not here right now, so they're not as paranoid on the ground. We can't get too close, though. Ever since that plane landed at the White House, this airspace is protected with missiles. I doubt they'd shoot down a sailplane, but who knows?"

They could see the buildings at Fort David below, just a little to the northeast in Catoctin Mountain Park. There were three Army Jeeps left in the open. No one seemed to be out on the well-wooded grounds today, though. Camp David itself looked rather odd: a strange cross between Army barracks and a rustic vacation place. Not too formidable. Nothing they couldn't work with, if need be, if the final plan demanded it.

"Camp David. Named after Eisenhower's grandson," Jack said. "Pretty good president, Ike. Generals usually are."

Jack touched the holstered Beretta on his ankle. The gun was reassuring. But nothing was going to happen to the President right now, or to Jack and Jill. No, the game was about to go off in another direction. That was the beauty of it — no one could predict where it would go. *It was a game, designed as one, played as one.*

He felt Sara's hand lightly touch his cheek. "How much longer do we have?" she asked. He suspected that she didn't want the sailplane ride to end.

"They'll *never* catch us," he said and smiled.

"No, *the ride,* silly," she laughed and patted his arm. "How much longer do we have up here?"

"You're not bored already? We're nowhere near the world's altitude record — about forty-nine thousand feet, if I recall. Need a hell of a wave lift for that." Suddenly, he seemed concerned that she might not be having a good time. That was just like Sam.

"No, no," she laughed and put her arm around his neck. Sara held him tightly. "I love it up here, love flying, love being with you. Thank you — for everything."

"You're welcome, Monkey Face," he whispered against her cheek.

Two incredible killers.

Jack and Jill.

Flying over the President's famous retreat at Camp David.

See you soon, Mr. President. There's nothing you can do to stop this from happening. Nowhere you can hide from us. Trust us on that. Haven't we kept all of our promises so far?

Chapter 41

ON THE HOUR-LONG DRIVE back to Washington, Sam seemed distracted and distant. Sara cautiously watched him out of the corner of her eye. It was as if he were still up in the sailplane. His brow was furrowed, his deep-blue eyes set on the road ahead.

He could get like this sometimes; but then again, so could she. *Sara the worrier. Sara the drudge.*

They both understood and mostly accepted the good and the bad points about each other. The game of Jack and Jill was getting much tougher now for both of them. Every move was chancy and fraught with danger. They could be caught before the mission was completed. The hunters were literally all over the place. One of the largest manhunts in history was under way. Not only in Washington, D.C., but everywhere around the world.

"I was just thinking about the game and how it's going, an honest evaluation. I was considering — a game inside our game," Sam finally said. "Something more sophisticated. Completely unexpected by our trackers."

Sara watched him detaching from his reverie, coming away from it, coming back to her.

"Yes, I could see that you were somewhere other than here on the beltway with me and all of these commuters. That much was pretty obvious."

Sam grinned. "Sorry. You probably smelled the wood burning, too." He was incredibly self-effacing — something else she enjoyed about him. He didn't seem to realize that he was something special; or if he did, he kept it to himself. God, it was so easy when they were together, so hard when they were apart. Sara wondered how she had survived before she met Sam. The answer was, Basically, she hadn't. She had been alive, but she didn't have a life. Now, she did.

"You're concerned about the progress of the game from here on, the exact sequence," she said. "It's furrowed your brow. Poor dear Sam. What's your idea?"

He smiled and shook his head. He often told her how perceptive and intelligent she was. Not many men had ever said that to Sara Rosen — practically none, in fact. Her intelligence scared most men. Even worse, she was verbal. So men usually needed to keep her down, to put her down constantly, to belittle anything she said that they weren't entirely one hundred percent comfortable with.

Sam wasn't that way. He seemed to understand exactly what she needed. *Is that part of the game, too?* she wondered. *Part of his game?*

"There's going to be tremendous heat from the police and FBI coming our way soon," he said, staring straight ahead at the gray ribbons of roadway. "What's gone before was nothing, Sara, absolutely *nothing*. The manhunt will increase exponentially from here on. They want to capture us badly. The FBI is assembling the best team possible, and make no mistake, it will be an impressive group. Sooner or later, they'll find something on us. It's inevitable that they will."

Sara nodded in agreement. Still, he had frightened her. "I know that. I'm ready for it; at least, I think I am. You have an idea how to deal with this blistering heat that's coming our way?"

"Yes, I think I do. It's something I've been thinking about for a while, but I believe I've solved it. Let me try this one out on you. Tell me what you think."

See? He did want her opinions. Always. He was so different from the others.

He looked over at her, made eye contact. "It's so simple, really. We need perfect alibis. I have an idea how to accomplish that. It involves a slight change in our game plan, but I think it's worth it."

She tried to keep the concern out of her voice. "What kind of change? You don't want to go after the target we already agreed on?"

"I want to change the next target, yes, but I want to change something else as well. I want to get someone else to do the next kill. That way, we'll both have airtight alibis. I think it's a powerful twist. I think it could be the clincher for us. If anyone is onto either of us, this will throw them off completely."

They were coming down Wisconsin Avenue and into Washington. The city looked like a J. M. W. Turner painting, Sara decided. Hazy light, caught just right. "I like your thinking a lot. It's a good plan. Who would you get?" she asked.

"I've already made a contact," Sam said. "I think I have the perfect person for this little twist. He thinks the way we do, believes in the cause. He happens to be right here in Washington.".

Chapter 42

A SECRET SERVICE AGENT named James McLean, one of Jay Grayer's lieutenants, walked me around the White House. More than a million visitors come here every year, but this was the show none of them got. This was the real deal.

Instead of the usual tour of Library, East, Blue, Green, and Red Rooms, I got to see the private family quarters on the second and third floors. I requested a viewing of the President's offices in the West Wing, as well as Vice President Mahoney's in the Executive Office Building.

As the two of us wandered through the impressive Center Hall, with its bright yellow color scheme, I half expected either "Ruffles and Flourishes" or "Hail to the Chief" to suddenly ring out.

Agent McLean was filling me in on details about security at the White House. The grounds were covered by audio and pressure sensors, electronic eyes, and infrared. A SWAT team was on the roof at all times now. Helicopters were less than two and a half minutes away. Somehow, I wasn't comforted by the tight security.

"What do you think of all this?" McLean asked as he led me into the Cabinet Room. It was dominated by serious-looking leather chairs, each bearing a brass plaque with the cabinet member's title. A very impressive place to visit.

"What I'm thinking is that every person working here has to be checked out," I said.

"They've all been checked, Alex."

"I know that. They haven't been checked by me, though. We need to check them all over again. I'd like each of them run against an interest in poetry or literature, even college degrees in literature; any kind of filmmaking experience; painting, sculpting, any endeavor requiring creativity. I'd like to know what magazines they subscribe to. Also their charitable contributions."

If McLean had an opinion on all that, he kept it to himself. "Anything else?" he asked.

We were looking out over the Rose Garden. I could see office buildings off in the distance, so I assumed they could see us. I didn't like that too much.

"Yeah, I'm afraid so," I went on. "While we're doing those background checks, we need to look at everyone in the crisis group. You can start with me."

Agent James McLean stared at me for a long moment.

"You're shitting me, aren't you?" he finally spoke his mind.

I spoke my mind, too. "I shit you not. This is a murder investigation. This is how it's done."

The dragonslayer had come to the White House.

Chapter 43

THE PHOTOJOURNALIST had chosen a conservative dark gray suit and a striped rep's tie for the sold-out performance of *Miss Saigon* at the Kennedy Center.

He had cut his grayish blond hair short; the ponytail was long gone. He no longer wore a diamond stud earring. It was doubtful whether anyone he knew would have recognized him. Just as it should be, as it had to be from now until the end of the game.

"Seems like old times," Kevin Hawkins sang softly as he crossed a parking lot facing *USA Today* headquarters across the river in Rosslyn.

"Keep those big presses running," he muttered under his breath. "Might have something for you later. Might just have a big, late-breaking story tonight at the Kennedy Center. *Quien sabe?*"

He was so glad to be back in Washington, where he'd lived at various times in the past. He was happy to be back in the game as well. *The game of games,* he couldn't help thinking, and believing it in his heart. Code name: Jack and Jill. Intrigue just didn't get any better than this. It couldn't.

There were two essential parts to his psychological buildup as he approached the difficult evening ahead. The first part was to make himself as cautious, as suspicious, as paranoid, as he possibly could. The second part, equally important, was to pump himself up with a full megadose of confidence so that he would succeed.

He could not fail. He would not fail, he told himself. His job was to murder someone — often a well-known someone, sometimes in public view — and not get caught.

In public view.

And not get caught.

So far, he had never been caught in the act.

He found it curious, though not particularly disturbing anymore, that he had little or no conscience, no guilt about the killings; and yet he could be perfectly normal in many other areas of his life. His sister, Eileen, for example, called him the "last believer" and the "last patriot." Her children thought he was the nicest, kindest Uncle Kevin imaginable. His parents back in Hudson adored him. He had plenty of nice, normal, *close* friends all around the globe. And yet here he was, ready for another cold-blooded kill. Looking forward to it, actually. *Craving it.*

His adrenaline was pumping, but he felt less than nothing about the intended victim tonight. There were billions of people on the earth, far too many of them. What did one less human mean? Not a whole lot, any goddamn way you looked at it. If you took a logical view of the world.

At the same time, he was extremely cautious as he entered the glittery Kennedy Center, with its gleaming crystal chandeliers and Matisse tapestries. He glanced up at the chandeliers in the Grand Foyer. With their hundreds of different prisms and lamps, they probably weighed a ton apiece.

He was going to murder in public view, under the bright lights, under all these prisms and lamps.

And not get caught!

What an incredible magic trick. How good he was at this.

His seat had been purchased for him, the theater ticket left in a locker at Union Station. The seat was in the back of the orchestra. It was almost underneath the "President's Box." Very nice. Just about perfect. He purposely arrived just as the houselights dimmed.

He was actually surprised when the intermission came. *So fast!* The time had really flown. The melodramatic stage play really moved along.

He glanced at his wristwatch: 9:15. The intermission was right on schedule. The houselights came up and Hawkins idly observed that the crowd was highly enthused about the hit musical.

This was good news for him: genuine excitement, ebullience, lots of noisy small talk filling the air. He slowly rose from his cushy seat. *Now for the night's real drama,* he was thinking.

He entered the Grand Foyer with the huge chandeliers that resembled stalactites. The carpeting was a plush red sea beneath his feet. Up ahead was the proud bronze bust of John Kennedy.

Very fitting and appropriate.

Just so. Just right.

Jack and Jill would be the biggest thing since Kennedy, and that was more than thirty years ago. He was happy to be a part of it. Thrilled, actually. He felt honored.

For tonight's performance, the part of Jack will be played by Kevin Hawkins.

Watch closely now, theater fans. This act will be unforgettable.

Chapter 44

THE GRAND FOYER of the Kennedy Center was mobbed with uppity Washingtonian assholes. Theater people, Jesus. It was mostly an older crowd — season subscribers. Tables were set up selling junky T-shirts and high-priced programs. A woman with a gaudy red umbrella was guiding a tour of high school kids through the intermission crowd.

There was a very nasty and difficult trick to this killing, Kevin Hawkins knew.

He had to get unbelievably close to the victim, physically close, before he actually committed the murder.

That bothered him a lot, but there was no way around it. *He had to get right on top of the target, and he could not fail at this part of the job.*

The photojournalist was thinking about it as he successfully blended into the noisily buzzing theater crowd.

He eventually spotted Supreme Court Justice Thomas Henry Franklin. Franklin was the youngest member of the current Court. He was an African-American. He looked haughty, which fitted his reputation around Washington. He was not a likable man. Not that it mattered.

Snapshot! Kevin Hawkins took a mind photo of Thomas Henry Franklin.

On the justice's left arm was a twenty-three-year-old woman. *Snapshot. Snapshot.*

Hawkins had done his homework on Charlotte Kinsey, too. He knew her name, of course. He knew that she was a second-year law student at Georgetown. He knew other dark secrets about Charlotte Kinsey and Justice Franklin as well. He had watched the two of them together in bed.

He took another moment to observe Thomas Franklin and the college girl as they talked in the Grand Foyer. They were as animated and bubbly as any of the other couples there. Even more so. What great fun the theater could be!

He took several more mind photos. He would never forget the image of the two of them talking together like *that. Snapshot.* And *that. Snapshot.*

They laughed very naturally and spontaneously, and appeared to like each other's company. Hawkins found himself frowning. He had two nieces in Silver Spring. The thought of the young law student with this middle-aged phony irked the hell out of him!

The irony of his harsh judgment brought a sudden smile to his lips. The morality of a stone-cold killer — *how droll! How insane. How very cool.*

He watched the two of them move onto the large terrace off the lobby. He followed several paces behind. The Potomac stretched out before them and was black as night. A dinner-cruise boat from Alexandria — the *Dandy* — was floating by.

The sheer curtains between the lobby and terrace flapped dramatically in the crisp river wind. Kevin Hawkins carefully moved toward the Supreme Court justice and his beautiful date. He took more mind photos of the two of them.

He noted that Justice Franklin's white shirt was a size too small, grabbing at his neck. The yellow silk tie was too loud for his subdued gray suit. Charlotte Kinsey had a quick, sweet smile that was irresistible. She had lovely rounded breasts. Her long black hair swirled in the river breeze.

He physically brushed against the two of them. *He got that close to Charlotte and Thomas.* He actually touched the law student's long shiny hair. He could smell her perfume. Opium or Shalimar. *Snapshot.*

He was right there. So close. He was practically on top of them, in every sense of the phrase.

His mind's eye continued to snap off photo after photo of the two of them. He would never forget any of this, not a single frame of the intimate murder scene.

He could see, hear, touch, smell; and yet he couldn't feel a thing.

Kevin Hawkins resisted all human impulses now. No pity. No guilt. No shame. And no mercy.

The law student carried a leather bag on her left shoulder. It was slightly open, just a sliver, just enough. Ah, carefree, casual, careless youth.

The photojournalist was good with his hands. *Still* good. Still steady. Still very quick. Still one of the best.

He slid something into her bag. *C'est ça.* That was it! Success. The first of the night.

Neither she nor Justice Franklin noticed the fleeting movement, or *him,* as he passed by in the crowd. He was the river breeze, the night, the light of the moon.

He felt incredible exhilaration at that special moment. There was nothing in the world like this. The power in taking, *stealing,* another human life was like nothing else in the full palette of human experiences.

The hard part was over, he knew. The close work. Now the simple act of murder.

To murder in public view.

And not get caught.

His heart suddenly jumped, bucked horribly. Something was going wrong. Very wrong. As wrong as could be. Wrong, wrong, wrong!

Jesus, Charlotte Kinsey was reaching into her bag.

Snapshot.

She'd found the note he'd left there — the note from Jack and Jill! Wrong, wrong, wrong!

Snapshot.

She was looking at it curiously, wondering what it was, wondering how it had gotten in her handbag.

She began to unfold the note, and he could feel his temples pounding horribly. She had gotten the justice's attention. He glanced down at the note as well.

Nooooo! Jesus, nooo, he wanted to scream.

Kevin Hawkins operated on pure instinct. The purest. No time to second-guess himself now.

He moved forward very quickly and surely.

His Luger was out, dangling below his waist. The gun was concealed because of the closeness of the crowd, the forest of legs and arms, pleated trousers, fluffed dresses.

He raised and fired the Luger just once. Tricky angle, too. Far from ideal. He saw the sudden blossom of crimson red. The body jolted, then crumbled and fell to the marble floor.

A heartshot! Certainly a miracle, or close to it. God was on his side, no?

Snapshot!

Snapshot!

His heart almost couldn't take it. He wasn't used to this sudden improvising.

He thought about getting caught, after all of these years, and on such an unbelievably important job. He had a vision of total failure. He felt . . . *he felt something.*

He dropped the Luger into the jumble of legs, trousers, satin and taffeta gowns, high-heeled slippers, highly polished dark cordovans.

"Was that a gunshot?" a woman shrieked. "Oh, God, Phillip. *Someone's been shot.*"

He backed away from the spectacle as just about everyone else did. The Grand Foyer looked as if it were ablaze.

He was part of them, part of the fearful, bolting crowd. He had nothing to do with the terrifying disturbance, the murder, the loud gunshot.

His face was a convincing mask of shock and disbelief. God, he knew this look so well. He had seen it so many times before in his lifetime.

In another tense few moments, he was outside the Kennedy Center. He was heading toward New Hampshire Avenue at a steady pace. He was one with the crowd.

"Seems Like Old Times" raced through his head, playing much too fast, at double or triple speed. He remembered humming the tune on his walk in. And as the photojournalist knew, the old times were definitely the best.

The old times were coming back now, weren't they?

Jack and Jill had come to The Hill.

The game was so beautiful, so delicate and exquisite.

Now for the greatest shocker of them all.

Chapter 45

AGENT JAY GRAYER called me at home from his car phone. I was in the middle of reading approximately two hundred background security checks done on White House personnel by the Secret Service uniformed division. The deputy director was speeding downtown to the Kennedy Center complex, doing ninety on the beltway. I could hear the siren blaring from his car.

"They struck again. Jesus, they made a hit at the Kennedy Center tonight. Right under our noses. It's another real bad acid trip, Alex. Just come." He definitely sounded out of control.

Just come.

"They hit during intermission of *Miss Saigon*. I'll meet you there, Alex. I'm seven to ten minutes away."

"Who was it this time?" I asked the sixty-four-thousand-dollar question. I almost didn't want to hear the answer. No, not almost. I *didn't* want to hear the victim's name.

"That's part of the problem. This whole thing is nuts. It wasn't really anybody, Alex."

"What do you mean, 'it wasn't really anybody'? That doesn't make sense to me, Jay."

"It was a law student from Georgetown University. A young

woman named Charlotte Kinsey. She was only twenty-three years old. They left one of their notes again. It's them for sure."

"I don't get it. I do not get this," I muttered over the phone. "*Goddammit.*"

"Neither do I. The girl might have caught a bullet meant for somebody else. She was out with a Supreme Court justice, Alex. Thomas Henry Franklin. Maybe the bullet was meant for him. That would fit the celebrity pattern. Maybe they've finally made a mistake."

"I'm on my way," I told Jay Grayer. "I'll meet you inside the Kennedy Center."

Maybe they finally made a mistake.

I didn't think so.

Chapter 46

IT WASN'T REALLY ANYBODY, ALEX. How the hell could that be?

A twenty-three-year-old law student from Georgetown was dead. Christ. It didn't make sense to me, didn't track at all. It changed everything. It seemed to blow the pattern.

I drove from our home to the Kennedy Center in record time. Jay Grayer wasn't the only one partly out of control. I stuck a flasher on the roof of my car and rode like hell on wheels.

The second half of *Miss Saigon* had been canceled. The murder had taken place less than an hour before, and there were still hundreds of onlookers at the crime scene.

I heard "Jack and Jill" mumbled several times as I made my way to the Grand Foyer. Fear was a tangible, almost physical, presence in the crowd. A lot of elements of the murder at the Kennedy Center were torturing me when I arrived at the crime scene at quarter past ten. There were some similarities with the other Jack and Jill killings. A rhyming note had been left. The job had been done coldly and professionally. *A single shot.*

But there were huge differences this time. They seemed to have destroyed their pattern.

Copycat killer? Maybe. But I didn't think so. Yet nothing could, or should, be dismissed. Not by me, and not by anyone else on the case.

The new twists nagged at me as I pushed my way through the curious, horrified, even dumbstruck, crowd on New Hampshire Avenue. The law student hadn't been a national figure. So why had she been killed? Jay Grayer had called her a *nobody*. Grayer said she wasn't the daughter of anybody famous, either. She had been out to the theater with Supreme Court Justice Thomas Henry Franklin, but that didn't seem to count as a celebrity stalk-and-kill.

Charlotte Kinsey had been a nobody.

The killing just didn't fit the pattern. Jack and Jill had taken a huge risk committing the murder in such a public place. The other killings had been private affairs, safer and more controllable.

Shit, shit, shit. What were they up to now? Was this whole thing changing? Escalating? Why had they varied their pattern? Were the killers moving into another, more random phase?

Had I missed their original point? Had we all missed the real pattern they were creating? Or had they made a mistake at the Kennedy Center?

Maybe they finally made a mistake.

That was our best hope. It would show that they weren't invincible. *Let this be a goddamn mistake! Please let it be their first.* Just the same, whoever it was made a clever escape.

The six-hundred-foot-long lobby had been emptied of all but police officials, the medical examiner's staff, and the morgue crew. I saw Agent Grayer and walked over to him. Jay looked as if he hadn't slept in weeks, as if he might never be able to sleep again.

"Alex, thanks for getting down here so quickly," the Secret Service agent said. I liked working with him so far. He was smart and usually even-tempered, with absolutely no bullshit about him. He had an old-fashioned dedication to his job, and especially to the President, both the office and the man.

"Anything worthwhile turn up yet?" I asked him. "Besides another corpse. The poem."

Grayer rolled his eyes toward the glittering chandeliers hanging above us. "Oh yeah. Definitely, Alex. We found out some more about the murdered student. Charlotte Kinsey was just starting her second year at Georgetown Law. She was bright as hell, apparently. Did her undergraduate at New York University. However, she only had average grades as a Hoya, so she didn't make Law Review."

"How does a law student fit into the pattern? Unless they *were* shooting at Justice Franklin and actually missed. I've been trying to make some connection on the way over. Nothing comes to mind. Except that maybe Jack and Jill are playing with us?"

Grayer nodded. "They're definitely playing with us. For one thing, your illicit sex theory is still intact. We know why Charlotte Kinsey didn't excel at Georgetown. She was spending quality time with some very important men here in town. Very pretty girl, as you'll see in a second. Shiny black hair down to her waist. Great shape. Questionable morals. She'd have made a *terrific* attorney."

The two of us walked over to the dead woman's body. The law student was lying facing away from us.

Beside the body was a bag she had been carrying. I couldn't see the bullet hole, and Charlotte Kinsey didn't even appear to be hurt. She looked as if she'd just decided to take a nap on the floor of the terrace at the Kennedy Center. Her mouth was open slightly, as if she wanted one last breath of the river air.

"Go ahead, tell me now," I said to Jay Grayer. I knew that he had something more on the murder. "Who is she?"

"Oh, she's somebody, after all. The girl was President Byrnes's mistress," he said. "She was seeing the President, too. He skipped out of the White House and saw her the other night. That's why they killed her. Bingo, Alex. Right in our face."

My chest felt seriously constricted as I bent over the dead

woman. Claustrophobia again. She was very pretty. Twenty-three years old. Prime of her life. One shot to the heart had ended that.

I read the note they had left in the law student's handbag.

> Jack and Jill came to The Hill
> Your mistress had no clue, Sir.
> She was a pawn
> But now she's gone
> And soon we'll get to you, Sir.

The poetry seemed to be getting a little better. Certainly it was bolder. And so were Jack and Jill. God help us all, but especially President Thomas Byrnes.

And soon we'll get to you, Sir.

Chapter 47

THE MORNING after the murder, I drove eight miles down to Langley, Virginia. I wanted to spend some time with Jeanne Sterling, the CIA's inspector general and the Agency's representative on the crisis team. Don Hamerman had made it clear to me that the Agency was involved because there was the *possibility* a foreign power might be behind Jack and Jill. Even if it were a long shot, it had to be checked. Somehow, I suspected there might be more to the CIA's involvement than just that. This was my chance to find out.

Supposedly, the Agency had a lead that was worth checking out. Since the Aldrich Ames scandal, and the resulting Intelligence Authorization Act, the CIA had to share information with the rest of us. It was now the law.

I remembered the inspector general very well from our first meeting at the White House. Jeanne Sterling had listened mostly, but when she spoke, she was highly articulate and spotlight-bright. Don Hamerman told me she had been a professor of law at the University of Virginia years before joining the Agency. Now her job was to help clean up the Agency from the inside. It sounded like an impossible task to me, certainly a daunting one.

Hamerman told me she had been put on the crisis team for one reason: she was the Agency's best mind.

Her office was on the seventh floor of the modern gray building that was the hub of CIA headquarters. I checked out the Agency's interior design: lots of extremely narrow halls, green-hued fluorescent lighting everywhere, cipher locks on most of the office doors. Here it was in all its glory: the CIA, the avenging angel of U.S. foreign policy.

Jeanne Sterling met me in the gray-carpeted hallway outside her office. "Dr. Cross, thank you for coming down here. Next time, I promise we'll do it up in Washington. I thought it best if we meet here. I think you'll understand by the time we're finished this morning."

"Actually, I enjoyed the drive down, needed the escape," I admitted to her. "Half an hour by myself. Cassandra Wilson on the tape deck. 'Blue Light 'Til Dawn.' Not so bad."

"I think I know exactly what you mean. Trust me, though, this won't be a trip in search of the wild goose. I have something interesting to discuss with you. The Agency was called in on this with good reason, Dr. Cross. You'll see in a moment."

Jeanne Sterling was certainly far removed from the stereotypical CIA Brahmin of the fifties and sixties. She spoke with a folksy, enthusiastic, mid-Southern accent, but she sat on the Agency's Directorate of Operations. She was considered crucial to the CIA's turnaround; indeed, its very survival.

We entered her large office, which had a commanding view of woods on two sides and a planted courtyard on another. We sat at a low-slung glass table covered with official-looking papers and books. Photographs of her family were up on the walls. Cute kids, I couldn't help noticing. Nice-looking husband, tall and lean. She herself was tall, blond, but a little heavier than she ought to be. She had a friendly smile with a slight overbite, and just a hint of the farmer's daughter about her.

"Something important *has* come up," she said, "but before I get into it, I just heard that the gun used at the Kennedy Center wasn't the same one used for the previous murders. That raises a question or two; at least, in my mind it does. Could the Kennedy Center murder have been a copycat killing?"

"I don't think so," I said. "Not unless the copycat and Jack or Jill happen to have the same handwriting. No, the latest rhyme was definitely from them. I also think it qualifies as a celebrity stalking."

"One more question," Jeanne Sterling said. "This one is completely off the beaten track, Alex. So bear with me. Our analysts have been searching, but we're not aware of any useful psychological study that's looked at professional assassins. I'm talking about studies on the contract killers used by the Army, the DEA, the Agency. Are you aware of anything? Even we don't have a comprehensive study on the subject."

I had a feeling we were easing into what Jeanne Sterling wanted to discuss. Maybe that was also why the head of internal affairs for the Agency was involved with the crisis team. Contract killers for the Army and CIA. I knew that they existed and that a few lived in the area surrounding Washington. I also knew they were registered somewhere, but not with the D.C. police. Perhaps for that reason they were sometimes referred to as "ghosts."

"There's not much written about homicide in any of the psych journals," I told Jeanne Sterling. "A few years back, a professor I know at Georgetown ran an interesting search. He found several thousand references to suicide, but less than fifty homicide references in the journals he sampled. I've read a couple of student papers written at John Jay and Quantico. There isn't very much on assassins. Not that I'm aware of. I guess it's hard to get subjects to interview."

"I could get a subject for you to interview," Jeanne Sterling said. "I think it might be important to Jack and Jill."

"Where are you going with this?" I had a lot of questions for her suddenly. Familiar alarms were sounding inside my head.

A soft, pained look drifted across her face. She inhaled very slowly before she spoke again. "We've done extensive psychological testing on our lethal agents, Alex. So has the Army, I've been assured. I've even read some of the test reports myself."

My stomach continued to tighten. So did my neck and shoulders. But I was definitely glad I'd taken the time to visit Langley.

"Since I've been in this job, about eleven months, I've had to open a number of dark, eerie closets here at Langley and elsewhere. I did over three hundred in-depth interviews on Aldrich Ames alone. You can imagine the cover-ups that we've had over the years. Well, you probably can't. I couldn't have myself, and I was working here."

I still wasn't sure where Jeanne Sterling was going with this. She had my full attention, though.

"We think one of our former contract killers might be out of control. Actually, we're pretty sure of it, Alex. That's why the CIA is on the crisis team. *We think one of ours might be Jack.*"

Chapter 48

JEANNE STERLING and I went for a ride through the surrounding countryside. The CIA inspector general had a new station wagon, a dark blue Volvo that she drove like a race car. Brahms was playing softly on the radio as we headed for Chevy Chase, one of Washington's small, affluent bedroom communities. I was about to meet a "ghost." A professional killer. One of ours.

Oh brother, oh shit.

"Plot and counterplot, ruse and treachery, true agent, double agent, false agent . . . didn't Churchill describe your business something like that?"

Jeanne Sterling cracked a wide smile, her large teeth suddenly very prominent. She was a very serious person, but she had a quick sense of humor, too. The inspector general. "We're trying to change from the past, both the perception and the reality. Either the Agency does that or somebody will pull the plug. That's why I invited the FBI and the Washington police in on this. I don't want the usual internal investigation, and then charges of a cover-up," she told me as she engineered her car underneath towering, ancient trees that evoked Richmond or Charlottesville. "The CIA is no longer a 'cult,' as we've been called by several self-serving congressmen. We're changing everything. Fast. Maybe even too fast."

"You disapprove?" I asked her.

"Not at all. It has to happen. I just don't like all the theater surrounding it. And I certainly don't appreciate the media coverage. What an incredible assemblage of jerk-offs."

We had crossed inside the beltway and were entering Chevy Chase now. We were headed for a meeting with a man named Andrew Klauk. Klauk was a former contract killer for the Agency: the so-called killer elite, the "ghosts."

Jeanne Sterling continued to drive the way she talked, without effort and rapidly. It was the way she seemed to do everything. A very smart and impressive person. I guess she needed to be. Internal affairs at the CIA had to be extremely demanding.

"So, what have you heard about us, Alex?" she finally asked me. "What's the scuttlebutt? The intelligence?"

"Don Hamerman says you're a straight arrow, and that's what the Agency needs right now. He believes Aldrich Ames hurt the CIA even more than we read. He also believes Moynihan's 'End of the Cold War' bill was an American tragedy. He says they call you Clean Jeanne out here at Langley. Your own people do. He's a big fan of yours."

Jeanne Sterling smiled, but the smile was controlled. She was a woman very much in control of herself: intellectually, emotionally, and even physically. She was substantial and *sturdy*, and her striking amber eyes always seemed to want to dig a little deeper into you. She wasn't satisfied with surface appearances or answers: the mark of a good investigator.

"I'm not really such a goody-goody." She made a pouty face. "I was a pretty fair caseworker in Budapest my first two years. Caseworker is our sobriquet for 'spy,' Alex. I was a spy in Europe. Harmless stuff, information-gathering mostly.

"After that I was at the War College. Fort McBain. My father is career Army. Lives with my mother in Arlington. They both voted for Oliver North. I fervently believe in our form of government.

I'm also hooked on making it work better somehow. I think we actually can. I'm convinced of it."

"That sounds pretty good to me," I told her. It did. All except the Oliver North part.

We were just pulling up to a house that was very close to Connecticut Avenue and the Circle. The place was Colonial revival, three stories, very homey and nice. Beautiful. Attractive moss crawled over the hipped roof and down the north side.

"This is where you live?" I smiled at Jeanne. "But *you're not* Miss Goody Two-shoes? You're not Clean Jeanne?"

"Right. It's all a clever facade, Alex. Like Disneyland, or Williamsburg, or the White House. To prove it to you, there's a trained killer waiting for us inside," Jeanne Sterling said, and winked.

"There's one in your car, too." I winked back at her.

Chapter 49

THE LATE-DECEMBER AFTERNOON was unusually bright and sunny. The temperature was in the high fifties, so Andrew Klauk and I sat in the backyard at Jeanne Sterling's lovely home in Chevy Chase.

A simple, wrought-iron fence surrounded the property. The gate was forest green, recently painted, slightly ajar. A breech in security.

CIA hitmen. Killer elite. Ghosts. They do exist. More than two hundred of them, according to Jeanne Sterling. A freelance list. A weird, scary notion for the 1990s in America. Or anywhere else, for that matter.

And yet here I was with one of them.

It was past three when Andrew Klauk and I began our talk. A bright yellow school bus stopped by the fence, dropping off kids on the quiet suburban street. A small towheaded boy of ten or eleven came running up the driveway and into the house. I thought that I recognized the boy from the photos at her office. Jeanne Sterling had a boy and a little girl. Just like me. She brought her casework home, just like me. Scary.

Andrew Klauk was a whale of a man who looked as if he

could move very well, anyway. A whale who dreamed of dancing. He was probably about forty-five years old. He was calm and extremely self-assured. Piercing brown eyes that grabbed and wouldn't let go. Penetrated deeply. He wore a shapeless gray suit with an open-neck white shirt that was wrinkled and dingy. Brown Italian leather shoes. *Another kind of killer, but a killer all the same,* I was thinking.

Jeanne Sterling had raised a very provocative question for me on our drive: What was the difference between the serial killers I had pursued in the past and the contract killers used by the CIA and Army? Did I think one of these sanctioned killers could actually *be Jack* of Jack and Jill?

She did. She was certain that it was a possibility that needed to be checked out, and not just by her own people.

I studied Klauk as the two of us talked in a casual, sometimes even lighthearted, manner. It wasn't the first time I'd conversed like that with a man who murdered for a living, with a mass murderer, so to speak. This killer, however, was allowed to go home nights to his family in Falls Church, and lead what he described as a "normal, rather guilt-free life."

As Andrew Klauk told me at one point: "I've never committed a crime in my life, Dr. Cross. Never got a speeding ticket." Then he laughed — a bit inappropriately, I thought. He laughed a little too hard.

"What's so funny?" I asked him. "Did I miss something?"

"You're what, two hundred pounds, six foot four? That about right?"

"Pretty close," I told him. "Six three. A little under two hundred. But who's counting?"

"Obviously, I am, Detective. I'm grossly overweight and look out of shape, but I could take you out right here on the patio," he informed me. It was a disturbing observation on his part, provocatively stated.

Whether or not he could do it, he needed to tell me. That was the way his mind worked. Good to know. He'd succeeded in shaking me up a little just the same, in making me extra cautious.

"You might be surprised," I said to him, "but I'm not sure if I get the point you're trying to make."

He laughed again, a tiny, unpleasant nose snort. Scary guy to drink lemonade with. "That's the point. I could and I *would*, if it was asked of me by our country. That's what you don't get about the Agency, and especially about men and women in my position," he said.

"Help me to get it," I said. "I don't mean you should try to kill me here in the Sterlings' backyard, but keep talking."

His tight smile turned to a wide-open grin. "Not try. Trust me on that one."

He was a truly scary man. He reminded me a little of a psychopathic killer named Gary Soneji. I had talked to Soneji just like this. Neither of them had much affect in their faces. Just this cold fixed glare that wouldn't go away. Then sudden bursts of laughter. My skin was crawling. I wanted to get up from the table and leave.

Klauk stared at me for a long moment before he went on. I could hear Jeanne Sterling's kids inside the house. The refrigerator door opening and closing. Ice tinkling against glass. Birds whooping and twittering in background trees. It was a strange, strange scene. Indescribably eerie for me.

"There is one basic proposition in covert action. In subversion, sabotage, being better at it than the other guy. *We can do anything we want*." Klauk said it very, very slowly, word by word.

"And we often do. You're a psychologist and a homicide detective, right? What's your objective take on this? What are you hearing from me?"

"No rules," I said to him. "That's what you're telling me. You live, you work, in a closed world that virtually isn't governed. You could say that your world is completely antisocial."

He snorted a laugh again. I was a decent student, I guess. "Not a fucking one of them. Once we're commissioned for a job — *there are no rules*. Not a one. Think about it."

I definitely would think about it. I started right then and there. I considered the idea of Klauk trying to kill me — if our country asked him to. *No rules. A world peopled by ghosts.* And even scarier was that I could sense he believed every word he'd said.

After I finished with Klauk, for that afternoon at least, I talked with Jeanne Sterling for a while more. We sat in an idyllic, multiwindowed sunroom that looked out on the idyllic backyard. The subject of conversation continued to be murder. I hadn't come down yet from my talk with the assassin. The ghost.

"What did you think of our Mr. Klauk?" Jeanne asked me.

"Disturbed me. Irritated me. Scared the hell out of me," I admitted to her. "He's really unpleasant. Not nice. He's a jerk, too."

"An *incredible* asshole," she agreed. Then she didn't say anything for a couple of seconds. "Alex, somebody *inside the Agency* has killed at least three of our agents. That's one of the skeletons I've dug up so far in my time as inspector. It's an 'unsolved crime.' The killer isn't Klauk, though. Andrew is actually under control. He *isn't* dangerous. *Somebody else is.* To tell you the complete truth, the Directorate of Operations has demanded that we bring in somebody from the outside on this. We definitely think one of our contract killers could be Jack. Who knows, maybe Jill is one of ours, too."

I didn't talk for a moment, just listened to what Jeanne Sterling had to say. *Jack and Jill came to The Hill.* Could Jack be a trained assassin? What about Jill? And then, why were they killing celebrities in Washington? Why had they threatened President Byrnes?

My mind whirled around in great looping circles. I thought about all the possibilities, the connections, and also the disconnects. Two renegade contract killers on the loose. It made as much sense as anything else I had heard so far. It explained some things about Jack and Jill for me, especially the absence of passion or rage in the murders. Why were they killing politicians and celebrities, though? Had they been commissioned to do the job? If so, by whom? To what end? What was their *cause*?

"Let me ask you a burning question, Jeanne. Something else has been bothering me since we got here."

"Go ahead, Alex. I want to try and answer all your questions. If I can, that is."

"Why did you bring him here to talk? Why take Andrew Klauk right into your own house?"

"It was a safe place for the meeting," she said without any hesitation. She sounded so unbelievably certain when she said it. I felt a chill ease up my spine. Then Jeanne Sterling sighed loudly. She knew what I was getting at, what I was feeling, as I sat inside her home.

"Alex, he *knows* where I live. Andrew Klauk could come here if he wanted to. Any of them can."

I nodded and left it at that. I knew the feeling exactly; I lived with it. It was my single greatest fear as an investigator. My worst nightmare.

They know where we live.

They can come to our houses if they want to . . . anytime they want to.

Nobody was safe anymore.

There are no rules.

There are "ghosts" and human monsters, and they are very real in our lives. Especially in my life.

There was Jack and Jill.

There was the Sojourner Truth School killer.

Chapter 50

AT A LITTLE PAST SEVEN the next morning, I sat across from Adele Finaly and unloaded everything that I possibly could on her. I unloaded — *period*. Dr. Adele Finaly has been my analyst for a half-dozen years, and I see her on an irregular basis. As needed. Like right now. She's also a good friend.

I was ranting and raving a little bit. This was the place for it, though. "Maybe I want to leave the force. Maybe I don't want to be part of any more vile homicide investigations. Maybe I want to get out of Washington, or at least out of Southeast. Or maybe I want to trot down and see Kate McTiernan in West Virginia. Take a sabbatical at just about the worst possible time for one."

"Do you really want to do any of those things?" Adele asked when I had finished, or at least had quieted down for a moment. "Or are you just venting?"

"I don't know, Adele. Probably venting. There's also a woman I met whom I could become interested in. She's *married*," I said and smiled. "I'd never do anything with a married woman, so she's perfectly safe for me. She couldn't be safer. I think I'm regressing."

"You want an opinion on that, Alex? Well, I can't give you one. You certainly have a lot on your plate, though."

"I'm right smack in the middle of a very bad homicide investigation. Two of them, actually. I just came off another particularly disturbing one. I think I can sort that part out for myself. But, you know, it's funny. I suspect that I still want to please my mother and father, and it *can't* be done. I can't get over the feeling of abandonment. Can't intellectualize it. Sometimes I feel that both my parents died of a kind of terminal sadness, and that my brothers and I were part of their sorrow. I'm afraid that I have it, too. I think that my mother and father were probably as smart as I am, and that they must have suffered because of it." My mother and father had died in North Carolina, at a very young age. My father had killed himself with liquor, and I hadn't really gotten over it. My mom died of lung cancer the year before my father. Nana Mama had taken me in when I was nine years old.

"You think sadness can be in the genes, Alex? I don't know what to think about that myself. Did you see that *New Yorker* piece on twins by any chance? There's some evidence for the genes theory. Scary note for our profession."

"Detective work?" I asked her.

Adele didn't comment on my little joke.

"Sorry," I said. "Sorry, sorry."

"You don't have to be sorry. You know how happy it makes me when you get any of your anger out."

She laughed. We both did. I like talking to her because our sessions can bounce around like that, laughter to tears, serious to absurd, truth to lies, just about anything and everything that's bothering me. Adele Finaly is three years younger than I am, but she's wise beyond her years, and maybe my years as well. Seeing her for a skull session works even better than playing the blues on my front porch.

I talked some more, let my tongue wag, let my mind run free, and it felt pretty good. It's a wonderful thing to have somebody in your life whom you can say absolutely anything to. Not to have that is almost unthinkable to me.

"Here's a connection I've made recently," I told Adele. "Maria is murdered. I grieve and I grieve, but I never come close to getting over the loss. Just like I've never gotten past the loss of my mother and father."

Adele nods. "It's incredibly hard to find a soul mate." She knows. She's never been able to find one herself, which is sad.

"And it's hard to lose one — a soul mate. So, of course, now I'm petrified about losing anyone else whom I care deeply for. I shy away from relationships — *because they might end in loss*. I don't leave my job with the police — *because that would be a kind of loss, too*."

"But you're thinking about these things a lot now."

"All the time, Adele. Something's going to happen."

"Something has. We've run way over our time," Adele finally said.

"Good," I said and laughed again. Some people turn on Comedy Central for a good laugh. I go to my shrink.

"*Lots* of hostility. How nice for you. I don't think you're regressing, Alex. I think you're doing beautifully."

"God, I love talking to you," I told her. "Let's do this in a month or so, when I'm really screwed up again."

"I can't wait," Adele said and rubbed her small, thin hands together greedily. "In the meantime, as Bart Simpson has said many times, 'Don't have a cow, man.'"

Chapter 51

DETECTIVE JOHN SAMPSON couldn't remember working so many brutal, absolutely shitty days in a row. He couldn't remember it ever being so godawful, goddamn bad. He had an overload of really bad homicides *and* he had the Sojourner Truth School killer case, which didn't seem to be going anywhere.

On the morning after the Kennedy Center killing, Sampson worked the upscale side of Garfield Park, the "west bank." He was keeping his eyes out for Alex's *homeless suspect,* who'd been spotted the afternoon of Shanelle Green's murder, though not since, so even that lead was growing cold. Alex had a simple formula for thinking about complex cases like this one. First, you had to answer the question that everybody had: *What kind of person would do something like this? What kind of nutcase?*

He had decided to visit the Theodore Roosevelt School on his street canvass. The exclusive military academy used Garfield Park for its athletics and some paramilitary maneuvers. There was a slim possibility that a sharp-eyed cadet had seen something.

A white-haired homeless motherfucker, Sampson thought as he climbed the military school's front graystone steps. *A sloppy and disorganized thrill killer who left fingerprints and other clues at both crime scenes, and still nobody could nail his candyass to the wall. Every single clue leads to a dead end.*

Why was that? What were we getting all wrong here? What were they messing up on? Not just him. Alex and the rest of the posse, too.

Sampson went looking for the commandant at the school, The Man In Charge. The detective had served four years in the Army, two of them in Vietnam, and the pristine school brought to mind ROTC lieutenants in the war. Most of them had been white. Several had died needlessly, in his opinion — a couple of them, his friends.

The Theodore Roosevelt School consisted of four extremely well-kept, red-brick buildings with steep, slate-shingle roofs. Two of the roofs had chimneys spouting soft curls of gray smoke. Everything about the place shouted "structure," "order," and "dead, white louies" to him.

Imagine something like this school, only in Southeast around the projects, he thought as he continued his solitary walk around the school. The image made him smile. He could almost see *five hundred or so homies resplendent in their royal blue dress uniforms, their spit-shined boots, their plumed dress hats. Really something to contemplate. Might even do some good.*

"Sir, can I help you?" A scrawny towheaded cadet came up to him as he started down what looked to be an academic hall in one of the buildings.

"You on guard here?" Sampson asked in a soft drawl that was the last vestige of a mother who'd grown up in Alabama.

The toy soldier shook his head. "No, sir. But can I help you anyway?"

"Washington police," Sampson said. "I need to speak with whoever's in charge. You arrange that, soldier?"

"Yes, *sir!*"

The cadet saluted him, of all people, and Sampson had to fight back the day's first, and maybe only, smile.

Chapter 52

MORE THAN THREE HUNDRED scrubbed and steampressed cadets from the middle school and the academy's high school were crammed into Lee Hall at nine o'clock in the morning. The cadets wore their regular school uniform: loose-fitting gray pants, black shirt and tie, gray waist-jacket.

From his stiff wooden seat in the school auditorium, the Sojourner Truth School killer saw the towering black man entering Lee Hall. He recognized him instantly. That sucker was Detective John Sampson. He was Alex Cross's friend and partner.

This was not a good thing. This was very bad, in fact. The killer immediately began to panic, to experience the outer edges of fear. He wondered if the Metro police were coming for him right now. *Did they know who he was?*

He wanted to run — but there was no way out of here now. He had to sit this one out, to gut it out.

The killer's initial reaction was to feel shame. He thought he was going to be sick. Throw up or something. He wanted to put his head between his legs. He felt like such a chump to get caught like this.

He was seated about twenty yards from where that stuffed

shirt Colonel Wilson and the detective were standing around as if something incredibly fucking important were about to happen. Every passing cadet saluted the adults, like the robotic morons that they were. A buzz of apprehension began to fill the room.

Was something earth-shattering going to happen? The thought screaming inside the killer's head. *Were the police about to arrest him in front of the entire school? Had he been caught?*

How could they have traced anything to him, though? It didn't make sense. That thought calmed him somewhat.

A false calm? A false sense of security? he wondered and lowered himself slightly in the stiff wooden seat, wishing that somehow he could disappear.

Then he sat straight up in his seat again. *Oh, shit. Here we go!*

He watched closely as the homicide detective slowly walked toward the podium with Colonel Wilson. His heartbeat was like the rhythm section in a White Zombie song.

The assembly began with the usual, dumb cadet resolutions, "honesty, integrity in thought and deed," all that crap. Then Colonel Wilson began to talk about the "cowardly murders of two children in Garfield Park." Wilson went on: "The Metro police are canvassing the park and surrounding environs. Maybe a cadet at Theodore Roosevelt has unwittingly seen something that might help the police with their investigation. Maybe one of you can help the police in some way."

So that was why the imposing homicide detective was here. A goddamn fishing expedition. The ongoing frigging investigation of the two murders.

The killer was still holding his breath, though. His eyes were very large and riveted to the stage as Sampson went over to the podium mike. The tall black man *really* stood out in the room of nothing but uniforms and short haircuts and mostly pink faces. He was *huge*. He was also kind of cool-looking in his black leather car coat, gray shirt, black necktie. He towered over the podium, which had seemed just the right height for Colonel Wilson.

"I served in Vietnam, under a couple of lieutenants who looked about your age," the detective said into the mike. His voice was calm and very deep. He laughed then, and so did most of the cadets. He had a lot of presence, a whole world of presence. He definitely seemed like the real deal. The killer thought that Sampson was laughing down at the cadets, but he couldn't be sure.

"The reason I'm here at your school this morning," the detective went on, "is that we're canvassing Garfield Park and everything that it touches. Two little kids were savagely killed there, both within the past week. The skulls of the children were crushed. *The killer is a fiend*, in no uncertain terms."

The killer wanted to give Sampson the finger. *The killer isn't a fiend. You're the fiend, mojoman. The killer is a lot cooler than you think.*

"As I understand it from Colonel Wilson, many of you go home from school through the park. Others run cross-country, and you also play soccer and lacrosse in the park. I'm going to leave my number at the precinct with the office here at school. You can contact me at any time, day or night, at the number if you've seen anything that could be helpful to us."

The Sojourner Truth School killer couldn't take his eyes off the towering homicide detective who spoke so very calmly and confidently. He wondered if he could possibly be a match for this one. Not to mention motherhumping Detective Alex Cross, who reminded him of his own real father — *a cop.*

He thought that *he* could be a match for them.

"Does anybody have any questions?" Sampson asked from the stage. "Any questions at all? This is the time for it. This is the place. Speak up, young men."

The killer wanted to shout from his seat. He had an overwhelming impulse to throw his right arm high in the air and volunteer some real help. He finally *sat* on his hands, right on his fingers.

I unwittingly saw something in Garfield Park, sir. I might just know who killed those two kids with an eighteen-inch, tape-reinforced baseball bat.

Actually, to be truthful, I killed them, sir. I'm the child killer, you feeble asshole! Catch me if you can.

You're bigger. You're much bigger. But I'm so much smarter than you could ever be.

I'm only thirteen years old. I'm already this good! Just wait until I get a little older. Chew on that, you dumb bastards.

PART IV

A-HUNTING WE WILL GO

Chapter 53

I LAY ON THE COUCH with Rosie the cat and a full sack of nightmares. Rosie was a beautiful, reddish brown Abyssinian. She was wonderfully athletic, independent, feral, and also a great nuzzler. She reminded me of the much larger cats of Africa in the way she moved. One weekend morning she just showed up at the house, liked it, and stayed.

"You're not going to leave us one day, are you, Rosie? Leave us like you came?" Rosie shook her whole body. "What a dopey question," she was telling me. "No, absolutely not. I'm part of this family now."

I couldn't sleep. Even Rosie's purring didn't relax me. I was a few aches beyond bone-tired, but my mind was racing badly. I was counting murders, not sheep. About ten o'clock I decided to go for a drive to clear my head. Maybe get in touch with my chi energy. Maybe get a sharper insight into one of the murder cases.

I drove with the car windows open. It was minus three degrees outside.

I didn't know exactly where I was going — and yet unconsciously, I did know. *Shrink shrinks shrink.*

Both murder cases were running hard and fast inside my head.

They were on dangerous parallel tracks. I kept reviewing and re-reviewing my talk with the CIA contract killer Andrew Klauk. I was trying to connect what he'd said to the Jack and Jill murders. Could one of the "ghosts" be Jack?

I *found* myself on New York Avenue, which is also Route 50 and eventually turns into the John Hanson Highway. Christine Johnson lived out this way, on the far side of the beltway in Prince Georges County. I knew where Christine lived. I'd looked it up in the casenotes of the first detective who interviewed her after Shanelle Green's murder.

This is a crazy thing, I thought as I drove in the direction of her town — Mitchellville.

Earlier that night, I'd talked to Damon about how things were going at school now, and then about the teachers there. I eventually got around to the principal. Damon saw through my act like the little Tasmanian devil that he is sometimes.

"You like her, don't you?" he asked me, and his eyes lit up like twin beacons. "You do, don't you, Daddy? Everybody does. Even *Nana* does. She says Mrs. Johnson is your type. You like her, right?"

"There's nothing not to like about Mrs. Johnson," I said to Damon. "She's married, though. Don't forget that."

"Don't *you* forget," Damon said and laughed like Sampson.

And now here I was driving through the suburban neighborhood relatively late at night. What in hell was I doing? What was I thinking of? Had I been spending so much time around madmen that finally some of it rubbed off? Or was I actually following one of my better instincts?

I spotted Summer Street and made a quick right turn. There was a mild squeal of tires that pierced the perfect quiet of the neighborhood. I had to admit it was beautiful out in suburbia, even at night. The streets were all lit up. Lots of Christmas lights and expensive holiday props. There were wide curbs for rain runoff. White sidewalks. Colonial-style lampposts on all the street corners.

I wondered if it was hard for Christine Johnson to leave this safe, lovely enclave to come to work in Southeast every day. I wondered what her personal demons were. I wondered why she worked such long hours. And what her husband was like.

Then I saw Christine Johnson's dark blue car in the driveway of a large, brick-faced Colonial home. My heart jumped a little. Suddenly, everything became very real for me.

I continued up the blacktop street until I was well past her house. Then I pulled over against the curb and shut off the headlights. Tried to shut down the roaring inside my head. I stared at the rear of somebody's shiny white Ford Explorer parked out on the street. I stared for a good ninety seconds, about how long the white Explorer would have lasted before it was stolen on the streets of D.C.

I had the conscious thought that maybe this was not such a good idea. Doctor Cross didn't exactly approve of Doctor Cross's actions. This was real close to being inappropriate behavior. Parking in the dark in a posh, suburban neighborhood like this wasn't a real sound concept, either.

A few therapist jokes were running around inside my head. *Learn to dread one day at a time. You're still having a lousy childhood. If you're really happy, you must be in denial.*

"Just go home," I said out loud in the darkened car. "Just say no."

I continued to sit in the darkness, though, listening to the occasional theatrical sigh, the loud debate buzzing inside my head. I could smell pine trees and smoke from someone's chimney through the open car window. My engine was clicking gently as it cooled. I knew a little about the neighborhood: successful lawyers and doctors, urban planners, professors from the University of Maryland, a few retired officers from Andrews Air Force Base. Very nice and very secure. No need for a dragonslayer out here.

All right then, go see her. Go see *both* of them, Christine and her husband.

I supposed that I could bluff my way through some trumped-up reason why I had to come out to Mitchellville. I had the gift of gab when I needed it.

I started the car again, the old Porsche. I didn't know what I was going to do, which way this was going to lead. I took my foot off the brake, and the automobile crept along on its own. *Slowly, I crept.*

I continued for a full block like that, listening to the crunch of a few leaves under the tires, the occasional pop of a small stone. Every noise seemed very loud and magnified to me.

I finally stopped in front of the Johnson house. Right in front. I noticed the bristle-brush, manicured lawn, and well-trimmed yews.

Moment of truth. Moment of decision. Moment of crisis.

I could see lights burning brightly inside the house, tiny fires. Somebody seemed to be up at the Johnson house. The dark blue Mercedes sedan was sitting peacefully against the closed garage door.

She has a nice car and a beautiful home. Christine Johnson doesn't need any terrible trouble from you. Don't bring your monsters out here. She has a lawyer husband. She's doing real fine for herself.

What did she say her husband's name was — *George?* George the lawyer lobbyist. George the *rich* lawyer lobbyist.

There was only one car in the driveway. Her car. The garage door was closed. I could picture another car in there, maybe a Lexus. Maybe a gas grill for cookouts, too. Power lawn mower, leaf blower, maybe a couple of mountain bikes for weekend fun.

I shut off the engine and got out of my car.

The dragonslayer comes to Mitchellville.

Chapter 54

I WAS DEFINITELY CURIOUS about Christine Johnson, and maybe it was a little more complicated than that. *You like her, don't you, Daddy? Maybe? Yes, I did like her — a lot.* At any rate, I felt as if I needed to see her, even if it made me feel tremendously awkward and foolish. A good thought struck me as I climbed out of the car: *how much more foolish to walk away.*

Besides, Christine Johnson *was* part of the complex homicide case I was working on. There was a logical enough reason for me to want to talk to her. Two students from her school had been murdered so far. Two of her babies. Why that school? Why had a killer come there? So close to my home?

I walked to the front door and was actually glad that all the shimmering houselights were turned on bright. I didn't want her husband, or any of the neighbors in Mitchellville, to spot me approaching the house in a cloak of shadows and darkness.

I rang the bell, heard melodious chimes, and waited like a porch sculpture. A dog barked loudly somewhere inside the house. Then Christine Johnson appeared at the front door.

She had on faded jeans, a wrinkled yellow crewneck sweater, white half-socks, and no shoes. A tortoiseshell comb pulled her hair back to one side, and she was wearing her glasses. She looked as if she were working at home. Still working at this late hour. *Peas in a pod, weren't we?* Well, not exactly. I was a long way from my pod, actually.

"Detective Cross?" She was surprised; understandably so. I was kind of surprised to be standing there myself.

"Nothing has happened on the case," I quickly reassured her. "I just have a few more questions." That was true. *Don't lie to her, Alex. Don't you dare lie to her. Not even once. Not ever.*

She smiled then. Her eyes seemed to smile as well. They were very large and very brown, and I had to stop staring at them immediately. "You do work too late, too hard, even under the current circumstances," she said.

"I couldn't turn this horrible thing off tonight. There are two cases, actually. So here I am. If this is a bad time, I'll stop by at the school tomorrow. That's no problem."

"No, come on in," she said. "I know how busy you are. I can imagine. Come in, please. The house is a mess, like our government, all the usual boilerplate copy applies."

She led me back through an entranceway with a cream marble floor and past the living room with its comfortable-looking sectional sofa and lots of earth colors: sienna, ocher, and burnt umber.

There was no guided tour, though. No more questions about why I was there. A little too much silence suddenly. My chi energy was draining off somewhere.

She took me into the huge kitchen. She went to the refrigerator, a big, double-door jobbie that opened with a loud *whoosh*. "Let me see, we've got beer, diet cola, sun tea. I can make coffee or hot tea if you'd like. You *do* work too hard. That's for sure."

She sounded a little like a teacher now. Understanding, but gently reminding me that I might have areas of improvement.

"A beer sounds pretty good," I told her. I glanced around the kitchen, which was easily twice the size of ours at home. There were rows of white custom cabinets. A skylight in the ceiling. A flyer on the fridge promoting a "Walk for the Homeless." She had a very nice home — she and George did.

I noted an embroidered cloth on a wall stretcher. Swahili words: *Kwenda mzuri.* It's a farewell that means "go well." A gentle hint? Word to the wise?

"I'm glad to hear you'll have a beer," she said smiling. "That would mean you're at least *close* to knocking off for the day. It's almost ten-thirty. Did you know that? What time is it on *your* clock?"

"Is it that late? I'm real sorry," I said to her. "We can do this tomorrow."

Christine brought me a Heineken and iced tea for herself. She sat across from me at an island counter that subdivided the kitchen. The house was far from being the mess she'd warned me about when I came in. It was nicely lived-in. There was a sweet, charming display of drawings from the Truth School on one wall. A beautiful mud cloth on a stretcher also grabbed my eye.

"So. What's up, doc?" she asked. "What brings you outside the beltway?"

"Honestly? I couldn't sleep. I took a drive. I drove out this way. Then I had the bright idea that maybe we could cover some ground on the case . . . or maybe I just needed to talk to some-body." I finally confessed, and it felt pretty good. Directionally good, anyway.

"Well, that's okay. That's fine. I can relate to that. I couldn't sleep myself," she said. "I've been wound tight ever since Shanelle's murder. And then poor Vernon Wheatley. I was pruning the plants, with *ER* on the television for background noise. Pretty pathetic, don't you think?"

"Not really. I don't think it's so strange. *ER* is good. By the way, you have a beautiful house out here."

I could see the living room TV set from the kitchen. A mammoth Sony playing the medical drama. A black retriever, a young dog, wandered in from the direction of a narrow hallway with oatmeal-colored carpeted stairs. "That's Meg," Christine told me.

"She was watching *ER*, too. Meg loves a good melodrama." The dog nuzzled me, then licked my hand.

I don't know why I wanted to tell her, but I did.

"I play the piano at night sometimes. There's a sun porch in our house, so the awful racket doesn't bother the kids too much. Either that or they've learned to sleep right through it," I said. "A little Gershwin, Brahms, Jellyroll Morton at one in the morning never hurt anyone."

Christine Johnson smiled, and seemed at ease with this kind of talk. She was a very self-assured person, very centered. I'd noticed that right from the first night. I had sensed it about her.

"Damon has mentioned your nocturnal piano playing a few times at school. You know, he *occasionally* brags about you to the teachers. He's a very nice boy, in addition to being a brainiac. We like him tremendously."

"Thank you. I like him a lot myself. He's lucky we have the Sojourner Truth School nearby."

"Yes, I think he is," Christine agreed. "A lot of D.C. schools are a complete disgrace, and so sad. The Truth is a small miracle for the children who attend."

"Your miracle?" I asked her.

"No, no, no. A lot of people are responsible, least of all me. My husband's law firm has contributed some guilt money. I just help to keep the miracle going. I *believe* in miracles, though. How long has it been since your wife died, Alex?" she suddenly changed gears. But Christine Johnson made the question conversational and low-key and very natural to ask, even if it wasn't. Still, it took me by surprise. I sensed I didn't have to answer if I didn't want to.

"It's going to be five years soon," I told her, partly holding my breath as I did. "This March, actually. Jannie was still a little baby. She was less than a year old. I remember coming in and holding her that night. She had no idea that she was comforting me."

The two of us were getting comfortable talking at the kitchen counter. We were both opening up quite a lot. Small talk at first. Then bigger talk. Sojourner Truth School killer talk. Maybe something helpful for the investigation. It went on like that until almost midnight.

I finally told her I needed to be heading home. She didn't disagree. The look in her eyes told me that she understood everything that had gone on here tonight, and all of it was okay with her.

At the front door, Christine surprised me again. She pecked me on the cheek.

"Come back, Alex," she said, "if you need to talk again. I'll be here tending to my shrubs in my ostentatious house. *Kwenda mzuri*," she said.

We left it like that. *Go well*. A strange tableau at a strange time in our lives. I had no idea whether her lawyer husband was home or not. Was he up in the bedroom sleeping? Was his name really George? Were they still together?

It was another mystery to solve some other day, but not that day.

On the drive home, I pondered whether I should feel bad about the unconventional, surprise visit to Christine Johnson's house. I decided that I shouldn't, that I wouldn't even get embarrassed about it at a later date. She'd made that possible for me. She was incredibly easy to be around. Absolutely incredible. It was painful in a way.

When I got home, I played the piano for another hour or so. Beethoven, then Mozart. Classical felt right to me. I went up and peeked in on Damon and Jannie. I gently pecked their cheeks, as Christine Johnson had pecked mine. I finally fell asleep on the downstairs couch. I didn't feel sorry for myself there, but I did feel very alone.

I slept until several shrill rings of the phone woke me, shooting adrenaline through my body like electric current.

It was Jack and Jill again.

Chapter 55

TYSONS GALLERIA in Tysons Corner was, along with the neighboring Tysons Corner Mall, one of the largest shopping complexes in the United States, maybe in the world. Sam Harrison had parked in the enormous Galleria lot at a little past 6:00 A.M.

At least a hundred cars were already there, though Versace and Neiman Marcus, FAO Schwarz and Tiljengrist wouldn't open until ten. Maryland Bagels *was* open and smells from the popular local bakery filled the air. Jack hadn't come to Tysons Corner for a piping-hot blueberry bagel, though.

From the parking area of the mall, he jogged to Chain Bridge Road in McLean. He wore a blue and white Fila jacket and running shorts and looked as if he belonged in the $400,000-to-$1,500,000-per-house neighborhood. That was one of the important rules in his game: *Always appear to belong, to fit in, and soon you will.*

With his short blond hair and trim build, he looked as if he might be a commercial pilot with USAir or Delta. Or perhaps just one of the neighborhood's many professionals, a doctor or lawyer — whatever. He definitely seemed to belong. He fit in seamlessly.

He had known from the start that he would have to carry out this murder alone. Jill shouldn't be out here in McLean Village. This was the really bad one for him personally. This one was over the top, even for Jack and Jill, even for the game of games.

The murder this morning would be extremely dangerous. This target might know that someone was coming for him. Number four was going to be a hard one, done the hard way. He thought about all this as he steadily jogged toward his final destination in the pretty and peaceful Washington suburb.

As he crossed onto Livingston Road, he attempted to clear his mind of everything except the terrible murder that lay ahead of him.

He was Jack once again, the brutal celebrity stalker. He was going to prove it in just a few minutes.

This one was going to be tough, the hardest so far. The man he was about to kill had been one of his best friends.

In the game of life and death, that didn't matter.

He had no best friends. He had no friends at all.

Chapter 56

I AM SAM, Sam I am, he was thinking as he ran.

But he wasn't really Sam Harrison.

He didn't have blond hair, or wear trendy jogging suits with logos on the breast pocket, either.

Who in hell am I? What am I becoming? he asked himself as his feet struck the pavement hard.

He knew that the house at 31 Livingston Road was guarded by a sophisticated security system. He would have expected nothing less.

He ran at a quickening pace now. Eventually, he veered off the macadam road and disappeared into underbrush and pine trees. He kept running through the woods.

He was in good shape and hadn't broken much of a sweat yet. The cold weather helped. He was alert, fresh, ready for the game to resume, ready to murder again.

He figured that he could get up close, perhaps as near as ten yards from the house without being seen. Then a quick dash to the garage.

For that short period, he would be out in the open. Completely exposed. There was no way around it and, God knows, he had tried to figure out an alternative attack plan.

He was about to attack a house in McLean. How incredible that seemed. This was like a war. A war fought at home. A revolutionary war.

There were two other large Colonial-style houses that he could see from the light woods. No lights on yet; no one seemed to be up anywhere on Livingston Road. So far, his luck was holding okay. His luck, or his skill, or maybe a combination of both.

As far as he could tell, no one was awake at 31 Livingston. He couldn't be sure until he was inside the house itself, and then it would be too late to turn back.

The FBI could be waiting in there or lurking right in these woods. Nothing would surprise him now. Anything could happen, at any time, to either him or Jill.

He decided to walk out from the woods, looking calm, looking casual. *As if he belonged.* He didn't make much noise as he gently raised the garage door. He quickly ducked under the partially open door and he was *inside.*

He went straight to the Nutone security box and punched in the code. So much for high security in the suburbs. There was no effective protection, really. Not from people like him.

He entered the main part of the house. His heart pounded like a battering ram inside his chest. There was a sheen of sweat on his neck now. He could picture Aiden's face. He could see Aiden as if he were standing there beside him.

Everything was peaceful and quiet and orderly inside the house. Fridge gently humming. Kids' artwork and a school lunch menu attached to the door with magnets. That made his heart sink. *Aiden's kids.*

Aiden Junior was nine years old. Charise was six. The wife, Merrill, was thirty-four, fifteen years younger than her husband. It was her second marriage, his third. They'd seemed very much in love the last time he had seen them together.

Jack moved quickly into the living room. He stopped breathing.

Someone was in the living room!

Jack whirled to the left. He yanked up his pistol and pointed it at the man. *Jesus God, it was only a goddamn mirror!* He was looking at his own image.

He managed to catch his breath, then continued on his mission, his heart still thundering. He hurried through the living room. It was so familiar, lots of memories seeping into his consciousness. Painful thoughts. He pushed them aside.

He began to climb up plush carpeted stairs, then stopped for a second. For the first time, he had doubts.

There can't be any doubts! Doubt and uncertainty weren't allowed! Not in this. Not in Jack and Jill.

He remembered the upstairs hallway, knew the house very well. He'd been here before — as a "friendly."

The master bedroom was the last door on the right.

There would be weapons in the bedroom. A .357 in the drawer of the night table. An automatic taped under the bed.

He knew. He knew. He knew everything.

If Aiden had already heard him, everything would be over. The game would end right there. This would be it for Jack and Jill.

Nutcruncher time. Weird thoughts. Too many of them.

He had finally gone to see *Pulp Fiction* the night before. It hadn't relaxed him, though he'd laughed out loud several times. *Sick story; he was even sicker; America was sickest of all.*

Don't think anymore, he warned himself. *Just do this. Do it efficiently. Do it now! Do it fast! Get out!*

Jack kills American celebrities! Various and sundry bigshots. That's what he does. Be Jack!

But he wasn't really Jack!

He wasn't really Sam Harrison!

Don't think, he commanded himself again as he hurried down the upstairs hallway to the master bedroom.

Be Jack.

Kill.

Chapter 57

JACK — whoever the hell he was — was three or four steps from the master bedroom when its varnished wood door suddenly opened.

A tall, balding man stepped out into the hall. Very hairy arms and legs. Bare, bony feet; toes splayed. Only half awake. In the middle of a jaw-cracking yawn.

He had on blue plaid boxer shorts, nothing else. A good build, still athletic-looking; just a hint of a spare tire above the boxers' elastic band. Still formidable after all the years of D.C. power lunches.

General Aiden Cornwall!

"You! *You son of a bitch!*" he whispered as he suddenly saw Jack in the upstairs hallway. "I knew it might be you." Yes, Aiden Cornwall knew *everything* in an instant. He had solved the mystery; a lot of mysteries, actually. He understood Jack and Jill. Where it was going. And why it was going there: *why it had to be this way. Why there could be no turning back.*

Jack fired the silenced Beretta twice and the target collapsed. Jack quickly stepped forward and caught the lifeless body before it could thud loudly against the floor.

He held the body in his arms, lowering it slowly to the carpet. *His friend,* whatever that meant now. He stayed down on his knees for a long moment. His heart was exploding.

He hadn't realized how hard this one was going to be until now. Not until this instant.

He looked down into the startled gray blue eyes of the *former* member of the Joint Chiefs, part of the White House's Jack and Jill emergency task force.

One of the hounds had been taken out. Just like that. Jack and Jill had struck back boldly at the manhunters! They had shown their strength again.

He took a note from his pocket. He left a calling card on Aiden Cornwall's chest.

> Jack and Jill came to The Hill
> To storm your picket fences.
> Once safe and sound
> They easily found
> The flaw in your Defenses.

A noise in the hall! He looked up. Aiden's boy! "Oh, Jesus God, no," he whispered out loud. "Oh, God, no." He felt sick all over. He wanted to run from the house.

The boy had recognized him. How could he not? Young Aiden even knew his children. He knew too much. *Dear God, have mercy on me. Please have mercy.*

Jack fired the Beretta again.

This was war.

Chapter 58

I WAS CALLED to an emergency crisis team meeting at the White House at 8:00 A.M. on December 10. I had been causing some trouble over the past few days there. My internal investigation was making waves, ruffling feathers. The big cats on The Hill didn't like being under suspicion — but all of them were, at least in my book.

Jay Grayer grabbed me the moment I arrived inside the West Wing. Jay's eyes were flat and cold and hard. His grip was strong on my shoulder. "Alex, I need to talk to you for a minute," he said. "It's important."

"What's going on now?" I asked the Secret Service agent. He didn't look well. There were dark puffs under both his eyes. Something else had happened. I could tell.

"Aiden Cornwall was murdered early this morning. It happened at his house out in McLean. It was Jack and Jill. They called us again. Called it in to us like we're mission control." He shook his head in sadness and disbelief. "They killed Aiden's nine-year-old son, Alex."

I found myself rocking back on my heels. The news from Jay Grayer didn't make sense to me; it didn't track with the Jack and

Jill style to this point. Goddamn them! They kept changing the rules. They had to be doing it on purpose.

"I want to go there right now," I told him. "I need to see the house. I need to be out there, not here."

"I hear you, but wait a minute, Alex," he said. "Hold on. Let me tell you the rest of what's going on. It gets worse."

"How could it get any worse?" I asked him. "Jesus, Jay."

"Trust me, it does. Just listen for a minute."

Agent Grayer continued to talk in a subdued whisper in the White House hallway as we walked together toward the Emergency Command Center, where the others were gathering. He pulled me aside a few paces from the meeting room. His voice was still an urgent whisper.

"The President is always awakened at quarter to five by the agent in charge. Happens every morning. This morning, the President dressed and went down to the library, where he reads the early papers as well as an executive summary that's prepared for him before he rises."

"What happened this morning?" I asked Jay. I was beginning to perspire. "*What happened,* Jay?"

He was very thorough and procedural. "At five o'clock the phone in the library rang. It was Jill on the private line. She was calling to talk with the President. She got through to him, *and that just isn't possible.*"

My head involuntarily shook back and forth. I agreed with Jay Grayer: this couldn't be happening. The idea, the concept, of the President as a murder target was a hugely disturbing one. The fact that, so far, we were helpless to stop it was much, much worse.

"I think I understand why the call couldn't happen, but tell me anyway," I said. I needed to hear it from him.

"Every single call to the White House goes through a private switchboard. Then the call is monitored by a second operator in White House Communications, which is actually part of our Intelligence Division. Every call *except this one.* The call completely bypassed the control system. Nobody knows how the hell it happened. But it *happened*."

"This phone call that couldn't have happened — was it recorded?" I asked Grayer.

"Yes, of course it was. It's already being processed at FBI headquarters and also at Bell Atlantic out in White Oak. Jill used another filtering device to modify her voice, but there might be ways to get around that. We've got half the Baby Bell's high-tech lab on it."

I shook my head again. I'd heard it, but I couldn't believe any of this. "What did Jill have to say?"

"She began by identifying herself. She said, '*Hi, this is Jill speaking.*' I'm sure that got the President's attention better than his usual cup of joe in the morning. Then she said, '*Mr. President, are you ready to die?*'"

Chapter 59

I NEEDED TO SEE the house. I needed to be inside the place where General Cornwall and his son had been murdered. I needed to feel everything about the killers, their modus operandi.

I got my wish. I reached McLean before nine that morning. The December day was very gray and overcast. The Cornwall house looked surreal, stark and cold, as I approached and then entered through the front door. It was cold on the inside, too. Either the Cornwall family was denying that winter was coming or they were saving money on heat.

The double murders had been committed on the second floor. General Aiden Cornwall and his nine-year-old son still lay on their backs in the upstairs hallway.

It was a cold, calculated, very professional killing. The grisly murder scene looked like something from a casebook, maybe even one of my notebooks. It was forensic textbook stuff, almost too much so.

FBI technicians and medical examiners were all over the house. There were probably twenty people inside.

It began raining hard just after I arrived at the house. The cars and TV news trucks that came after me all had their headlights on. It was eerie as hell.

Jeanne Sterling found me in the upstairs hallway. For the first time, the CIA inspector general seemed rattled. The severe, constant pressure was getting to all of us. *Some people were after the President of the United States, and they were very good at this.* They were extremely brutal as well.

"What's your gut reaction, Alex?" asked Jeanne.

"My reaction won't make any of our jobs easier," I said. "The only truly sustaining pattern I've seen is that Jack and Jill really don't have a pattern. Other than the notes, the poems. There certainly doesn't seem to be any sexual angle to these two murders. Also, from what I understand, Aiden Cornwall was a conservative, not a liberal like the other victims. That's a shift that might knock down a whole lot of theories about Jack and Jill."

As I was talking to Jeanne Sterling, I had another insight into the notes Jack and Jill had left. *The poetry might be telling us something important. The FBI linguistic agents hadn't found anything yet, but I didn't care. Whoever was writing the rhymes, probably Jill, wanted us to know something. . . . Was there a definite order to what they were doing? The desire to create instead of destroy? The poetry had to mean something. I was almost sure of it.*

"How about on your end, Jeanne? Anything?"

Jeanne shook her head and bit her lower lip with her big teeth. "Not a thing."

Chapter 60

IT HAD BEEN a very long day and it was still going strong and hard. At ten o'clock that night, I arrived at the FBI offices on Pennsylvania Avenue. My mind was running way too fast as I rode the elevator up to twelve. The lights in the building were blazing like tiny campfires above D.C. I figured that Jack and Jill had a lot of people staying up late that night. I was only one of them.

I'd come to the FBI offices to listen to the phone message Jill had sent to the President early that morning. All the important evidence was being made available to me. I was being let *inside*. I was even being allowed to make waves inside the White House. I knew all about horrible multiple killers; most of the rest of the team hadn't had that pleasure.

No rules.

I was brought by Security to an audio/electronics office on twelve. An NEC tape machine was waiting for me. A copy of Jill's voice tape was already in. The tape machine was on. Running hot.

"This is a dupe, Dr. Cross, but it's close enough for your listening purposes," I was told. An FBI techie, long hair and all, went on to inform me they were certain that the voice on the tape had been altered or filtered electronically. The FBI experts didn't believe the caller could possibly be identified from the tape. Once again, Jack and Jill had carefully covered their trail.

"I talked to a contact at Bell Labs," I said. "He told me the same thing. Couple more experts confirm that and I'll believe it."

The nonconformist-looking FBI technician finally left me alone with the taped phone call. I wanted it that way. For a while I just sat in the office and stared out at the Justice Department across Pennsylvania Avenue.

Jill was right there with me.

She had something about herself to reveal, something she needed to tell us. Her deep, dark secret.

The tape had been cued up. Her voice startled me in the silent, lonely office.

Jill spoke.

"Good morning, Mr. President. It's December ten. Exactly five A.M. Please don't hang up on me. This is Jill. Yes, *the* Jill. I wanted to speak to you, to make this situation very personal for you. Are we okay so far?"

"It's way past 'personal.'" President Byrnes spoke calmly to her. "Why are you murdering innocent people? Why do you want to kill me, *Jill?*"

"Oh, there's a very good reason, a fully satisfactory explanation for all our actions. Maybe we just like the power trip of frightening the so-called *most powerful people in the world*. Maybe we like sending you a message from all the *little* people you've frightened with your command decisions and almighty mandates from on high. At any rate, no one who's been killed was *innocent*, Mr. President. They all deserved to die, for one reason or another."

Then Jill laughed. The sound of the electronically altered voice was almost childlike.

I thought of Aiden Cornwall's young son. Why did a nine-year-old boy deserve to die? At that moment, I hated Jill — whoever she was, whatever her motives.

President Byrnes didn't back down. The President's voice was measured, calm. "Let me make one thing clear to you: you don't frighten me. Maybe you ought to be afraid, Jill. You *and* Jack. We're getting close to you now. There's nowhere on earth you can hide. There isn't one safe spot on the globe. Not anymore."

"We'll certainly keep that in mind. Thanks so much for the warning. Very sporting of you. And you please keep this in mind — you're a dead man, Mr. President. Your assassination is already a done deal."

That was the end of the tape. Jill's final words to President Byrnes, spoken so coolly, so brazenly.

Jill the morning deejay. Jill the poet. Who are you, Jill?

Your assassination is already a done deal.

I wanted to interview President Byrnes again. I wanted to talk with him right now. I needed him in this office, listening to the sick, threatening tape with me. Maybe the President knew things that he wasn't telling any of us. Someone must.

I played the frightening taped message several more times. I don't know how long I sat in the FBI office, staring out over the becalmed lights of Washington, D.C. They were somewhere out there. Jack and Jill were out there. Possibly planning an assassination. But maybe not. Maybe that wasn't it at all.

You're a dead man, Mr. President.

Your assassination is already a done deal.

Why were they warning us?

Why warn us about what they planned to do?

Chapter 61

IT WAS PAST TEN-THIRTY, but I still had one more important stop I wanted to make. I called Jay Grayer and told him I was on my way to the White House. I wanted to see President Byrnes again. Could he make it happen?

"This can wait until the morning, Alex. It should wait."

"It shouldn't wait, Jay. I've got a couple of theories that are burning a hole in my brain. I need the President's input. If President Byrnes says that it waits until the morning, then it waits. But talk to Don Hamerman and whoever else needs to be talked to about it. This is a murder investigation. We're trying to *prevent* murders. At any rate, I'm on my way over there."

I arrived at the White House, and Don Hamerman was waiting for me. So was John Fahey, the chief counsel, and James Dowd, the attorney general and a personal friend of President Byrnes. They all looked put out and also very tense. This apparently wasn't how things were done in the Big House.

"What the hell is this all about?" Hamerman confronted me angrily. I had been waiting to see what his bite was like. I'd seen worse, actually.

"If you want, I'll wait until tomorrow. But my instincts tell me not to," I told him in a soft but firm voice.

"Tell *us* what you want to say to him," James Dowd spoke up. "Then we'll decide."

"I'm afraid that it's only for the President to hear. I need to talk with him, *alone,* just like we did the first time we met."

Hamerman exploded. "Jesus Christ, you arrogant son of a bitch. We're the ones who let you in here in the first place."

"Then you're the ones to blame, I guess. I told you that I was here to conduct a murder investigation and that you wouldn't like some of my methods. I told the President the same thing."

Hamerman stormed away from us, but he returned in a couple of minutes. "He'll see you up on the third floor. This shouldn't take more than a couple of minutes of his time. It *won't* take more than a few minutes."

"We'll see what the President has to say about that."

Chapter 62

THE TWO OF US met in a solarium that is attached to the living quarters on the third floor. The room had been a favorite of Reagan's. Outside the windows, the lights of Washington were shining brightly. I felt as if I were living a chapter out of *All the President's Men*.

"Good evening, Alex. You needed to see me," the President said, and seemed calm and cheerful enough. Of course, there was no way for me to judge his true feelings. He was dressed casually in khakis and a blue sport shirt.

"I apologize for coming in and causing a lot of upset and inconvenience," I said to him.

The President raised his hand to stop me from apologizing further. "Alex, you're here because we wanted you to do exactly what you're doing. We didn't think anybody on the inside would have the balls. Now, what's on your mind? How can I help you?"

I relaxed a little bit. *How could the President help me?* That was a question most of us had always wanted to hear. "I spent the day thinking about this morning's phone call, and also the murders out in McLean. Mr. President, I don't think we have *a lot of time left*. Jack and Jill are making that pretty clear. They're impatient, very violent; they're taking more and more risks. They also have a psychological need to rub it in our face every time that they can."

"Are they just flattering their egos, Alex?"

"Possibly, but maybe they want to *diminish your power.* Mr. President, I wanted to see you alone because what I have to say needs absolute confidentiality. As you know, we've been checking out everyone who works at the White House. The Secret Service has been cooperative. So has Don Hamerman."

The President smiled. "I'll bet Don has."

"In his own way, he has. A watchdog is a watchdog, though. Based on our findings so far, we've placed three members of the current staff under surveillance by the Secret Service. We would rather watch than dismiss them. They've been added to the seventy-six others currently under surveillance around Washington."

"The Secret Service always has a number of potential threats to the President under surveillance," Thomas Byrnes said.

"Yes, sir. We're just taking precautions. I don't have particularly high hopes for the three staff members. They're all males. Somehow I thought we might turn up Jill. But we didn't."

The President's look darkened. "I would have liked to meet Jill and have a private chat with her. I'd have liked that a lot."

I nodded. Now came the really difficult part of our little talk. "I have to broach a tough subject, sir. We need to talk about some of the other people around you, *the people closest to you.*"

Thomas Byrnes sat forward in his chair. I could tell that he didn't like this at all.

"Mr. President, we have reason to suspect that someone with access into the White House, or possibly with power and influence here, might be involved in all of this. Jack and Jill are certainly getting into high places with the greatest of ease. The people close to you have to be checked, and checked very closely."

Both of us were suddenly quiet. I could almost visualize Don Hamerman waiting outside, chewing on his silk tie.

I broke the awkward silence.

"I know that we're talking about things you would rather not," I said.

The President sighed. "That's why you're here. That's why you're here."

"Thank you," I told him. "Sir, you have no reason not to trust me on this. As you said yourself, I'm an outsider. I have nothing to gain."

Thomas Byrnes sighed a second time. I sensed that I had reached him, at least for the moment. "I trust many of these people with my life. Don Hamerman is one of them, my bulldog, as you correctly surmised. *Whom don't I trust?* I'm not completely comfortable with Sullivan or Thompson at the Joint Chiefs. I'm not even sure about Bowen at the FBI. I've made serious enemies on Wall Street already. Their reach inside Washington is very deep and very powerful. I understand that organized crime is none too pleased with my programs, and they are much more organized now than they've ever been. I'm challenging an old, powerful, very fucked-up system — and *the fucked-up system doesn't like it*. The Kennedys did that — especially Robert Kennedy."

I was having trouble catching my breath all of a sudden. "Who else, Mr. President? I need to know all your enemies."

"Helene Glass in the Senate is an enemy. . . . Some of the reactionary conservatives in the Senate and House are enemies. . . . I believe . . . that Vice President Mahoney is an enemy, or close to one. I made a compromise before the convention to put him on the ticket. Mahoney was supposed to deliver Florida and other parts of the South. He *did* deliver. I was supposed to deliver certain considerations to patrons of his. I haven't delivered. I'm screwing with the system, and that isn't done, Alex."

I listened to Thomas Byrnes without moving a muscle. The effect of talking to the President like this was numbing and disturbing. I could see by the look on his face what it cost Thomas Byrnes to admit some of what he had to me.

"We should put surveillance on these people," I said.

The President shook his head. "No, I can't allow it. Not at this time. I can't do that, Alex." The President rose from his chair. "How did your kids like the keepsakes?" he asked me.

I shook my head. I wouldn't be held off like that. "Think about the vice president, and about Senator Glass, too. This is a murder investigation. Please don't protect someone who might be involved. Please, Mr. President, help us . . . whoever it is."

"Goodnight, Alex," the President said in a strong, clear voice. His eyes were unflinching.

"Goodnight, Mr. President."

"Keep at it," he said. Then he turned away from me and walked out of the solarium.

Don Hamerman entered the room. "I'll see you out," he said stiffly. He was cold — unfriendly.

Perhaps I also had an enemy in the White House.

Chapter 63

NO WAY, JOSE! Couldn't be. Could not be. This just could not be happening. Welcome to the *X-Files* meets *The Twilight Zone* meets the Information Superhighway.

At five one and two hundred ten pounds, Maryann Maggio was a powerhouse. She thought of herself as a "censor of the obscene and dangerous" on the Prodigy interactive network. Her job with Prodigy was to protect travelers on the Information Superhighway. An emergency was developing before her eyes right now. There was an intruder on the network.

This couldn't be happening. She couldn't take her eyes off her IBM desktop screen. "This is the interactive age, all right. Well, people, get ready for it," she muttered at the screen. "There's a train wreck a-comin'."

Maryann Maggio had been a censor with IBM-owned Prodigy for nearly six years. By far, the most popular service on Prodigy was the billboards. The billboards were used by members to broadcast personal messages for other members to react to, learn from, plan their vacations, find out about a new restaurant, that sort of thing.

Usually the messages were pretty harmless, covering topical

subjects, questions and answers on anything from welfare reform to the ongoing murder trial of the month.

But not the messages that she was staring at right now. This called for Infante the Censor, the protector of young minds, as she sometimes thought of herself. "Big Sister," according to her bearded, three-hundred-pound husband, Terry the Pirate.

She had been monitoring messages from a particular subscriber in Washington, D.C., since around eleven that night. In the beginning, the quirky messages were borderline judgment calls for her to make. Should she censor or hold back? After all, Prodigy now had to compete with the Internet, which could get pretty damn wild and wacky.

She wondered if the sender knew this. Cranks sometimes knew the rules. They wanted to push the edge of the envelope. Sometimes they just seemed to need human contact, even contact with her. The censor of their thoughts and actions. *Big Sister is watching.*

The first messages had asked other subscribers for their "sincere" point of view on a controversial subject. A child-murder case in Washington, D.C., was described. Then subscribers were asked whether the child murders or the Jack and Jill case deserved more attention from the police and from the press. Which case was more important, morally and ethically?

Maryann Maggio had been forced to pull two of the early messages. Not because of their content per se, but because of the repeated use of four-letter words, especially the dreaded *f* word and the *s* word and one of the *c* words.

When she pulled the messages, though, it seemed to cause an unbelievable emotional explosion from the subscriber in Washington. First came a long, nasty diatribe about the "obscene and unnecessary censorship plague on Prodigy." It urged subscribers to switch to CompuServe and other rival on-line services. Of course, CompuServe and America Online had their censors, too.

The messages continued to fly out of Washington faster than

the D.C.–New York shuttle. One called for Prodigy to "fire the ass of your absurdly incompetent censor." Maryann Maggio censored it.

Another message used the *f* word eleven times in two paragraphs. She censored that fucker, too.

Then the message sender became more than just another foul-mouthed, annoying loose cannon on the service. At 1:17 the subscriber in Washington began to claim responsibility for the two brutal child murders.

The subscriber claimed that he was the murderer, and he would prove it, *live on Prodigy.*

"Big Sister" pulled the message immediately. She also called her supervisor to her cubicle at the Prodigy center in White Plains, New York. Her huge body was shaking all over like jelly by the time her boss arrived, bringing black coffee for both of them. Black coffee? Maryann needed a couple of Little John's "fully loaded" pizzas to get her through this total disaster.

Suddenly, a brand-new message flashed across the screen from the Washington subscriber, who seemed articulate and intelligent enough, but incredibly angry and really, really crazy. The latest message listed gory details about the murder of a black child, "details only the D.C. police would know," the subscriber wrote.

"Jesus, Maryann, what a nasty, weird creep," the Prodigy supervisor said over Maryann Maggio's shoulder. "Are all the messages like this one?"

"Pretty much, Joanie. He's toned down his language some, but the violence is really graphic stuff. Vampire creepy. Been that way since I clipped his wings."

The latest message from Washington continued to scroll before their eyes. The description *seemed* to be of an actual murder of a small black child in Garfield Park. The killer claimed to have used a sawed-off baseball bat reinforced with electrical tape. He claimed to have struck the child twenty-three times, and to have *counted* every single blow.

"Stop this awful, freakish crap now. Pull the damn plug on him!" the supervisor quickly made her decision.

Then the supervisor made an even more important decision. She decided the Washington Police Department had to be alerted about the suspicious subscriber. Neither she nor Maryann Maggio knew whether the child murders were real, but they sure sounded that way.

At one-thirty in the morning, the Prodigy supervisor reached a detective at the 1st District in D.C. The supervisor made a note of the detective's rank and also his name in her own log: Detective John Sampson.

Chapter 64

I HAD GOTTEN TO BED at a little past one. Nana came and woke me at quarter to five. I heard her slippers scuffing across the bare wood of the bedroom floor. Then she spoke in a low whisper just above my ear. Made me feel as if I were six years old again.

"Alex? Alex? You awake?"

"Mm, hmm. You bet. I am now."

"Your friend's down in the kitchen. Eating bacon and tomatoes out of my skillet like there's no tomorrow, and he would know, wouldn't he? He still eats it faster than I can cook it."

I held in a soft, painful moan. My eyes blinked twice and felt badly puffed and swollen each time they opened. My throat was scratchy and sore.

"Sampson's here?" I finally managed to say.

"Yes, and he says he might have a lead on the Truth School killer. Isn't that a good way to start your day?"

She was taunting me. Same as always. It wasn't even five o'clock in the morning and Nana had her rusty shiv in me already.

"I'm up," I whispered. "I don't look like it, but I'm up."

Less than twenty minutes later, Sampson and I pulled up in front of a brick townhouse on Seward Square. He admitted that he *needed* me at the scene. Rakeem Powell and a white detective named Chester Mullins, who wore an ancient porkpie hat, were standing outside their own cars, waiting for us. They looked extremely tense and uncomfortable.

The street was on the moderately upscale side of Seward Square Park, less than a mile and a half from the Sojourner Truth School. This was probably Mullins's home beat.

"It's the white-on-white Colonial motherlode on the corner," Rakeem said, pointing to a big house about a block away. "Man, I like working in these high-rent neighborhoods. You'all smell the roses?"

"That's window-cleaning solution," I said.

"There goes my career with FTD," Rakeem Powell laughed, and so did his partner Chester.

"Might not be the Partridge Family living in that nice house up yonder," Sampson cautioned the two detectives. "Beautiful surroundings, peaceful street and all, maybe a homicidal maniac shitheel waiting for us inside, though. You copy?"

Sampson turned to me. "What are you thinking about, Sugar? You having your usual nasty thoughts on this? Feeling the gris-gris?"

Sampson had told me what he knew on the short ride over to Seward Square. A subscriber to the Prodigy interactive service, an Army man, Colonel Frank Moore, had been sending messages about the child killings over the service. He appeared to know details about the murders that only the police and the real killer knew. He *sounded* like our freak.

"I don't like what I'm hearing from you so far, Mister John. The killings suggest he's in a rage state, and yet he's fairly careful. Now he's reaching out for help? He's virtually leading us to his doorstep? I don't know if I get that. And I don't like it too much, either. That's what I'm feeling so far, partner."

"I was thinking the same thing." Sampson nodded and kept staring at the house in question. "At any rate, we're here. Might as well check out what the colonel wanted us to see."

"Not mutilated bodies," Rakeem Powell said and frowned

deeply. "Not at five on a Monday morning. Not more little kids stashed somewhere in that big house."

"Alex and I will take the back door in," Sampson said to Rakeem. "You and Popeye Doyle here can cover the front. Watch the garage. If this is the killer's house, you might expect a surprise or two. Everybody wide-awake? Wakee-wakee!"

Rakeem and the white man in the hat nodded. "Bright-eyed and bushy-tailed," Rakeem said with fake enthusiasm.

"We have you covered, Detectives." Chester Mullins finally said something.

Sampson nodded calmly. "Let's do it then. Not daylight yet, maybe he's still in his coffin."

Five-twenty A.M. and my adrenaline was pumping wildly. I had already met all the human monsters I cared to meet in my lifetime. I didn't need any more on-the-job experience in this particular area.

"Am I here to watch your ass?" I asked as Man Mountain and I moved toward the big house perched on the corner.

"You got it, Sugar. I need you on this. You got the magic touch with these psycho-killers," Sampson said without looking back at me.

"Thanks. I think," I muttered. There was a real loud noise roaring in my head, as if I'd just taken nitrous oxide at the dentist's. *I really didn't want to meet another psychopath; I didn't want to meet Colonel Franklin Moore.*

We cut across a spongy lawn leading to a long, deep porch with an ivy trellis.

I could see a man and woman standing in the kitchen. Two people were already up inside.

"Must be Frank and Mrs. Frank," Sampson muttered.

The man was eating something as he leaned over the kitchen counter. I could make out a box of strawberry Pop-Tarts pastry, a carton of skim milk, and the morning's *Washington Post*.

"*Very* Partridge Family," I whispered to John. "I really don't like this at all. He's leading us all the way, right to the door."

"Homicidal maniac," he said through brilliantly white, gritted teeth. "Don't let the Pop-m-ups fool you. *Only* psychos eat that shit."

"Not easily fooled," I said to Sampson.

"So I hear. Let's do it then, Sugar. Time to be unsung heroes again."

We both crouched down below the level of the kitchen windows — no easy task. We couldn't see the man and woman from there, and they couldn't see us.

Sampson grasped the doorknob and slowly turned it.

Chapter 65

THE BACK DOOR into the Moore house was unlocked, and Sampson pushed it right in. The two of us exploded into the homey kitchen with its smells of freshly toasted Pop-Tarts and coffee. We were in the Capitol Hill section of Washington. The house and kitchen looked it. So did the Moores. Neither Sampson nor I was fooled by the trappings of normalcy, though. We'd seen it before, in the homes of other psychos.

"Hands on top of your heads! Both of you. Put your arms up slow and easy," Sampson yelled at the man and woman we had surprised in the kitchen.

We had our Glocks trained on Colonel Moore. He didn't look like too much of a threat: a short man, thin and balding, middle-aged paunch, eyeglasses. He wore a standard-issue Army uniform, but even that didn't help his image too much.

"We're detectives with the Metro D.C. police," Sampson identified the two of us. The Moores looked in shock. I couldn't blame them. Sampson and I can be shocking under the wrong circumstances, and these were definitely the wrong circumstances.

"There's been some kind of really bad, really crazy mistake," Colonel Moore finally said very slowly and carefully.

"I'm Colonel Franklin Moore. This is my wife, Connie Moore. The address here is 418 Seward Square North." He slowly enunciated each word. "Please lower your weapons, Officers. You're in *the* wrong place."

"We're at the correct address, sir," I told the colonel. *And you're the crank caller we want to talk to. Either you're a crank or you're a killer.*

"And we're looking for Colonel Frank Moore," Sampson filled in. He hadn't lowered his revolver an inch, not a millimeter. Neither had I.

Colonel Moore maintained his cool pretty well. That concerned me, set my inner alarms off in a loud jangle.

"Well, can you please tell us what this is all about? And please do it quickly. Neither of us has ever been arrested. I've never even had a traffic violation," he said to both Sampson and me, not sure who was in charge.

"Do you subscribe to Prodigy, Colonel?" Sampson asked him. It sounded a little crazy when it came out, like everything else lately.

Colonel Moore looked at his wife, then he turned back to us. "We do subscribe, but we do it for our son, Sumner. Neither of us has much time in our schedules for computer games. I don't understand them much and don't want to."

"How old is your son?" I asked Colonel Moore.

"What difference does that make? Sumner is thirteen years old. He's in the ninth grade at the Theodore Roosevelt School. He's an honor student. He's a great kid. What is this all about, Officers? Will you please tell us why you're here?"

"Where is Sumner now?" Sampson said in a very low and threatening voice.

Because maybe young Sumner was listening somewhere near in the house. Maybe the Sojourner Truth School killer was listening to us right now.

"He gets up half an hour to forty-five minutes later than we do. His bus comes at six-thirty. Please? *What is this about?*"

"We need to talk to your son, Colonel Moore," I said to him. Keep it real simple for right now.

"You have to do better —" Colonel Moore started to say.

"No, we don't have to do better," Sampson interrupted him. "We need to see your son right now. We're here on a homicide investigation, Colonel. Two small children have already been killed. Your son may be involved with the murders. *We need to see your son.*"

"Oh, dear God, Frank," Mrs. Moore spoke up for the first time. Connie, I remembered her name. "This can't be happening. Sumner couldn't have done anything."

Colonel Moore seemed even more confused than when we first burst in, but we had gotten his full attention. "I'll show you up to Sumner's room. Could you please holster your weapons, at least?"

"I'm afraid we can't do that," I told him. The look in his eyes was inching closer to panic. I didn't even look at Mrs. Moore anymore.

"Please take us to the boy's bedroom now," Sampson repeated. "We need to go up there quietly. This is for Sumner's own protection. You understand what I'm saying?"

Colonel Moore nodded slowly. His face was a sad, blank stare. "Frank?" Mrs. Moore pleaded. She was very pale.

The three of us went upstairs. We proceeded in single file. I went first, then Colonel Moore, followed by Sampson. I still hadn't ruled out Franklin Moore as a suspect, as a potential madman, as the killer.

"Which room is your son's?" Sampson asked in a whisper. His voice barely made a sound. Last of the Masai warriors. On a capital-murder case in Washington, D.C.

"It's the second door on the left. I promise you, Sumner hasn't done anything. He's thirteen years old. He's first in his class."

"Is there a lock on the bedroom door?" I asked.

"No . . . I don't think so . . . there might be a hook. I'm not sure. He's a good boy, Detective."

Sampson and I positioned ourselves on either side of the

closed bedroom door. We understood that a murderer might be waiting inside. *Their good boy might be a child killer. Times two.* Colonel Moore and his wife might have no idea about their son, and what he was truly all about.

Thirteen years old. I was still slightly stunned by that. Could a thirteen-year-old have committed the two vicious child murders? That might explain the amateurness at the crime scenes. But the rage, the relentless violence? The hatred?

He's a good boy, Detective.

There was no lock, no hook, on the boy's door. *Here we go. Here we go.* Sampson and I burst into the bedroom, our guns drawn.

The room was a regular teenager's hideout, only with more computer and audio equipment than most I'd seen. A gray cadet dress uniform hung on the open closet door. Someone had slashed it to shreds!

Sumner Moore wasn't in his bedroom. He wasn't catching an extra half-hour of sleep that morning.

The room was empty.

There was a typewritten note on the crumpled bedsheets, where it couldn't be missed.

The note simply said *Nobody is gone.*

"What is this?" Colonel Moore muttered when he read it. "What is going on? *What is going on?* Can somebody please explain? What's happening here?"

I thought that I got it, that I understood the boy's note. Sumner Moore was *Nobody* — that was how he felt. And now, *Nobody was gone.*

An article of clothing lying beside the note was the second part of the message to whoever came to his room first. He had left behind Shanelle Green's missing blouse. The tiny electric-blue blouse was covered with blood.

A thirteen-year-old boy was the Truth School killer. He was in a state of total rage. And he was on the loose somewhere in Washington.

Nobody was gone.

Chapter 66

THE SOJOURNER TRUTH SCHOOL killer traipsed along M Street reading the *Washington Post* from cover to cover, looking to see if he was famous yet. He had been panhandling all morning and had made about ten bucks. *Life be good!*

He had the newspaper spread wide open, and he wasn't much looking where he was going, so he bumped into various assholes on his way. The *Post* was full of stories about goddamn Jack and Jill, but nothing about him. Not a paragraph, not a single word, about what he'd done. What a frigging joke newspapers were. They just lied their asses off, but everybody was supposed to believe them, right?

Suddenly, he was feeling so bad, so confused, that he wanted to just lie down on the sidewalk and cry. He shouldn't have killed those little kids, and he probably wouldn't have if he'd stayed on his medication. But the Depakote made him feel dopey, and he hated it as if it were strychnine.

So now his life was completely ruined. He was a goner. His whole life was over before it had really begun.

He was on the mean streets, and thinking about living out here permanently. *Nobody is here. And nobody can stop Nobody.*

He had come to visit the Sojourner Truth School again. Alex Cross's son went there and he was pissed as hell at Cross. The detective didn't think much of him, did he? He hadn't even come to the Teddy Roosevelt School with Sampson. Cross had dissed him again and again.

It was approaching the noon recess at the Truth School and he decided to stroll by, maybe to stand up close to the fenced yard where they had found Shanelle Green. *Where he had brought the body.* Maybe it was time to tempt the fates. See if there was a God in heaven. Whatever.

Rock-and-roll music was pounding nonstop in his head now. Nine Inch Nails, Green Day, Oasis. He heard "Black Hole Sun" and "Like Suicide" from Soundgarden. Then "Chump" and "Basket Case" from Green Day's *Dookie.*

He caught himself, pulled himself back from the outer edge.

Man, he had gone ya-ya for a couple of minutes there. He had completely zoned out. *How long had he been out of it?* he wondered.

This was getting bad now. Or was it getting very good? Maybe he ought to take just a wee bit of the old Depakote. See if it brought him back anywhere near our solar system.

Suddenly, he spotted the black bitch Amazon woman coming toward him. It was already too late to move out of the way of the cyclone.

He recognized her right away. She was the high-and-mighty principal from the Sojourner Truth School. She had a bead on him, had him in her sights. Man, she should have been wearing a NO FEAR T-shirt to play that kind of game. *You put the bead on me — then I'll put the bead on you, lady. You don't want my bead on you. Trust me on that, partner.*

She was yelling, raising her voice anyway. "Where do you go to school? Why aren't you there now? You can't stand around here." She called loudly as she kept walking straight toward him.

FUCK YOU, BLACK BITCH. MIND YOUR OWN BUSINESS. WHO THE HELL DO YOU THINK YOU'RE TALKING TO?

YOU . . . TALKIN' . . . TO . . . ME?

"Do you hear me, mister? You deaf or something? This is a drug-free area, so move on. *Now.* There's absolutely no loitering near this school. That means *you*, in the fatigue jacket! Move on. Go on, get out of here."

Just fuck you, all right? I'll move on when I'm good and ready.

She came right up to him, and she was big. A lot bigger than he was, anyway.

"Move it or lose it. I won't take any crap from you. None at all. Now get out of here. You heard me."

Well, hell. He moved on without giving her the satisfaction of word one. When he got up the block, he saw all the schoolkids being let outside into the yard with the high fence that didn't mean squat in terms of protection. *Can't keep me out*, he thought.

He looked for Cross's little boy, searched the schoolyard with his eyes. Found him, too. No sweat. Tall for his age. Beautiful, right? Kute as hell. Damon was his name-o, name-o.

The school principal was still out in the playground — staring up the street at him, bad-eyeing him. Mrs. Johnson was her name-o.

Well, she was a dead woman now. She was already ancient history. Just like old Sojourner Truth — the *former* slave, *former* abolitionist. *They all are*, the killer thought as he finally moved on. He had better things to do than loitering, wasting his precious time. He was a big star now. He was important. He was somebody.

Happy, happy. Joy, joy.

"You believe that," he said to nobody in particular, just the generic voices crackling inside his head, "then you must be crazier than I am. I ain't happy. There ain't no joy."

As he turned the corner, he saw a police car coming up the street toward the school. It was time to get the hell out of there, but he would be back.

Chapter 67

THE FOLLOWING AFTERNOON I gathered up my files and all my notes on Jack and Jill. I headed to Langley, Virginia, again. No music in the car that morning. Just the steady *whhrrr* of my tires on the roadway. Jeanne Sterling had asked to see what I had come up with so far. She'd called half a dozen times. She promised to reciprocate this time. *You show me yours, I'll show you mine. Okay?* Why not? It made a lot of sense.

An Agency assistant sporting a military-style crew cut, a woman in her twenties, escorted me into a conference room on the seventh floor. The room was filled with bright light and was a far cry from my cube in the White House basement. I felt like a mouse out of its hole. Speaking of the White House, I hadn't heard from the Secret Service about any plan to investigate possible enemies of the President in high places. I would stir that pot again when I got back to D.C.

"On a clear day you used to be able to see the Washington Monument," Jeanne Sterling said as she came striding in behind me. "Not anymore. The air quality in Fairfax County is abysmal. What's your reaction to the files on our killer elite, so far? Shock? Surprise? Boredom? What do you think, Alex?"

I was starting to get used to Jeanne's rapid-fire style of speaking. I could definitely see her as a law school professor. "My first reaction is that we need weeks to analyze the *possibility* that one of these people might be a psychotic killer. Or that one of them might be Jack," I told her.

"I agree with you on that," she nodded. "But just suppose we had to compress our search into about twenty-four fun-filled hours, which is about what we have to work with. Now then, are there any prime suspects in your mind? You have something, Alex. What is it?"

I held up three fingers. I had three somethings so far.

She smiled broadly. Both of us did. You had to learn to laugh at the madness or it could bring you so far down, you'd never make it back up again.

"Okay. All right. That's what I like to hear. Let me guess," she said, and went ahead. "Jeffrey Daly, Howard Kamens, Kevin Hawkins."

"Well, that's interesting," I said. "That might tell us something at least. Maybe we better start with the one name that's on both of our shortlists. Tell me about Kevin Hawkins."

Chapter 68

JEANNE STERLING spent about twenty minutes briefing me on Kevin Hawkins. "You'll be gratified to hear that we have Hawkins under surveillance already," she said as we rode a swift, smooth elevator down to the basement garage, where our cars were parked.

"See, you don't need my help, after all," I said. I was buoyed by the prospect of any kind of progress on the case. I was actually feeling positive for the first time in several days.

"Oh, but we do, Alex. We haven't brought him in for an interview, because we don't have anything concrete on him. Just nasty, nasty suspicions. That and a need to catch somebody. Let's not forget about that. Now *you're* suspicious, too."

"That's all I have at this point," I reminded her. "Suspicions."

"Sometimes that's enough, and you know it. Sometimes it has to be."

We arrived at the small private garage underneath the CIA complex at Langley. The space was filled mostly with family vehicles like Taurus station wagons, but there were a few high-testosterone sports cars as well. Mustangs, Bimmers, Vipers. The cars matched up fairly well with the personnel I had seen upstairs.

"I guess we should take both our cars," Jeanne suggested, and it made sense to me. "I'll drive back here when we're through. You can go on into D.C. Hawkins is staying with his sister in Silver Spring. He's at the house now. It's about half an hour on the beltway, if that."

"You're going to take him in now?" I asked her. It sounded like it to me.

"I think we should, don't you? Just to have a little chat, you know."

I went to my car. She walked to her station wagon. "This man we're going to see, he's a professional killer," I called to her across the garage floor.

She called back, her voice echoing against concrete and steel. "From what I gather, he's one of our very best. Isn't that a fun thought?"

"Does he have an alibi for any of the Jack and Jill murder dates?"

"Not that we know of. We'll have to ask him more about it — in detail."

We got into our respective cars and started up the engines. I was beginning to notice that the CIA inspector general wasn't a bureaucrat; she certainly wasn't afraid to get her hands dirty. Mine, either. We were going to meet another "ghost." Was he Jack? Could it be that easy? Stranger things had happened.

It took the full thirty minutes to get over to Hawkins's sister's house in Silver Spring, Maryland. The houses there were somewhat overpriced, but it was still considered a middle-class area. Not my middle class. Somebody else's.

Jeanne pulled her Volvo wagon up alongside a black Lincoln parked three-quarters of a block from the sister's house. She powered down the passenger-side window and talked to two agents inside the parked car. One of her surveillance teams, I guessed. Either that or she was asking directions to the assassin's hideout, which struck me as humorous. One of the few laughs I'd had recently.

Suddenly, I saw a man come out of the sister's Cape Cod–style house.

I recognized Kevin Hawkins from his file pictures. No doubt about it.

He threw a quick glance down the street, and he must have seen us. He started to run. Then he hopped on a Harley-Davidson motorcycle parked in the driveway.

I shouted, "Jeanne," out my open window and gunned my engine at the same time.

I began to chase . . . *Jack?*

Chapter 69

THE FIRST THING Kevin Hawkins did on the motorcycle was to cut sharply sideways over the sliver of frost-covered lawn separating two split-level ranch houses. He raced past a few more houses, one of them with an aboveground pool covered by a baby-blue tarp for the winter.

I aimed my old Porsche along the same inland route that Hawkins was taking. Fortunately, the past few days had been cold, and the ground was mostly solid. I wondered if anybody from the houses had spotted the motorcycle and car crazily zigzagging through their backyards.

The motorcycle took a sharp right onto the development road past the last row of houses. I followed close behind. My car was bouncing high. Then it scraped bottom loudly against the high curb. It thudded hard onto the road pavement, and my head struck the rooftop.

As we approached an intersecting street, the Volvo station wagon and the Lincoln joined the race. A few neighborhood kids who were playing flag football in spite of the miserable weather stopped to gawk wide-eyed at the real-life police chase roaring up the suburban street.

I had my Glock out and the window rolled down. I wasn't going to fire unless he did. Kevin Hawkins wasn't wanted for any specific crime yet. No warrants had been served. Why was he running? He sure was acting guilty about something.

Hawkins leaned the Harley into a steep curve as he downshifted into fourth. I remembered another life and time spent on a fast motorcycle. I recalled its amazing maneuverability. The rawness of the speed. The feeling when your skin begins to tighten against your skull. I remembered Jezzie Flanagan, and *her* motorcycle.

Hawkins's bike made a deep, guttural roar as it climbed the hilly road like a ground rocket.

I tried to keep up, and was doing a pretty decent job. Amazingly, so was the Volvo wagon and the sedan. The chase scene was complete madness, though — suburbia suddenly racing out of control.

Was Jack up ahead?

Was Hawkins Jack?

I watched Kevin Hawkins stretch himself flat over the handlebars of the bike. He knew how to ride. What else did the trained killer know how to do?

He was accelerating into fifth, approaching ninety or so on a narrow suburban road repeatedly marked for thirty-five.

Then up ahead — *traffic!*

The bane of our existence was suddenly the most glorious and welcome sight in the world to me.

A traffic jam!

Several cars and vans were already backed up in the direction we were coming from.

A bright orange mini–school bus was stopped in the opposite lane. It was discharging a thin line of children, as it did probably every day about this time.

Hawkins hadn't slowed the cycle much, though. Suddenly, he was riding the double line in the road. He hadn't slowed the cycle at all.

I realized what he was going to do.

He was going to split the stopped traffic, and keep on going.

I started to brake and cursed loudly. I knew what I had to do.

I swerved off the road again, traveling cross-country over more lawns. A woman in a black pea jacket and jeans screamed at me from her porch and waved a snow shovel.

I headed toward where the main road looped down ahead to meet the lane I had been stuck in traffic in only a few seconds ago.

Jeanne Sterling followed in her station wagon. So did the Lincoln sedan. Madness and chaos helter-skelter in Silver Spring.

Was this Jack up ahead? Were we about to nab the celebrity stalker and killer?

I had high hopes. We were so close to him. Less than a hundred yards.

I kept my eyes pinned on the bouncing, speeding motorcycle. Suddenly, it went down!

The bike slid on one side, sending up a sheet of bright orange and white sparks against the roadway black. A few kids were still walking in a line between the bus and the stopped traffic.

Then Hawkins went down!

He had gone down to avoid hitting the children.

He had swerved to avoid hitting the kids!

Hawkins was down on the road.

Could this be Jack up ahead?

If not, who in the name of God was he?

I was out of the car, holding my Glock, racing like a madman toward the bizarre accident scene. I was slip-sliding on the ice and snow, but I wouldn't let it slow me down.

Jeanne Sterling and her two agents were out of their cars as well, but they weren't doing as well in the slush. I was losing my cover.

Kevin Hawkins managed to pull himself up from the sprawling heap. He looked back. He saw us coming. Guns everywhere.

He had a gun out, but he didn't fire. He was only a few feet away from the school bus and the children.

He left the kids alone, though. Instead, he ran to a black Camaro convertible at the head of the line of stopped cars.

What the hell was he up to now?

I could see him yelling into the driver-side window of the stopped sports car. Then *blam*, he fired directly into the open window.

Hawkins yanked open the car door, and a body fell out.

Jesus Christ, he'd shot the driver dead! Just like that.

I had seen it, but I couldn't believe it.

The contract killer took off in the Camaro. He'd killed someone for his car. But he'd nearly killed himself to avoid hitting a row of innocent children.

No rules . . . or rather, make up your own.

I stopped running and stood helplessly in the middle of the street in Silver Spring. *Had we just been that close to catching Jack? Had it almost been over?*

Chapter 70

NANA MAMA was still up when I got home about eleven-thirty that night. *Sampson was with her.*

Adrenaline fired through my body the moment I saw them waiting for me. The two of them looked even worse than I felt after a long bear of a day.

Something was wrong. Something was very wrong at our house. I could tell it for sure. Sampson and Nana didn't have casual visits after eleven o'clock at night.

"What's going on? What happened?" I asked as I came in through the kitchen door. My stomach was dropping, plunging. Nana and Sampson sat at the small dining table. They were talking, conspiring over something.

"What is it?" I asked again. "What the hell is going on?"

"Someone's been calling on the telephone all night tonight, Alex. Then they just hang up when I answer the phone," my grandmother told me as I sat at the kitchen table beside her and Sampson.

"Why didn't you call me right away?" I asked, firmly but gently. "You have my beeper number. That's what it's for, Nana."

"I called John," Nana answered the question. "I knew you were busy protecting the President and his family."

I ignored her usual rancor. This wasn't the time for that, or for a tiff. "Did the caller ever say anything?" I asked. "Did you actually speak to anyone?"

"No. There were twelve calls between eight-thirty and ten or so. None since then. I could hear someone breathing on the line, Alex. I almost blew my whistle on them." Nana keeps a silver referee's whistle near the phone. It's her own solution to obscene calls. This time I almost wished she had blown the damn whistle.

"I'm going to bed now," she said and sighed softly, almost inaudibly. For once, she actually looked her age. "Now that you're both here."

She strained as she pushed herself up out of the creaking kitchen chair. She went over to Sampson first. She bent just a little and kissed him on the cheek.

"'Night, Nana," he whispered. "There's nothing to worry about. We'll take care of everything, bad as it seems right now."

"John, John," she gently scolded him. "There's a great deal of worry about, and we both know it. Don't we, now?"

She came and kissed me. "Goodnight, Alex. I'm glad you're home now. This murderer stalking our neighborhood worries me so. It's very bad. Very bad. Please trust my feelings on this one."

I held her frail body for a few seconds, and I could feel the anger building inside. I held her tightly and thought about how terrible this was, *what she was intimating*, this evil incarnate following me home. No one in his right mind goes after a cop's family. I didn't believe the killer was in his right mind, though.

"Goodnight, Nana. Thank you for being here for us," I whispered against her cheek, smelled her lilac talc. "I hear what you're saying. I agree with you."

When she had left the room, Sampson shook his head. Then he finally smiled. "Tough as ever, man. She's really something else. I love her, though. I love your grandma."

"I do, too. Most of the time."

I was staring up at the ceiling light, trying to focus on something that I could comprehend — like electricity, lamps, moldings. No one can really understand a homicidal madman. They are like visitors from other planets — literally.

I was almost speechless, for once in my life. I felt violated, incredibly angry, and also afraid for my family. Maybe these phone calls were nothing, but I didn't know that for sure.

I got a couple of beers from the fridge, popped them open for the two of us. I needed to talk to Sampson, anyway. There hadn't been a free moment all day long.

"She's afraid for the kids' sake. That gets the fur up on her neck. Claws out," Sampson said, then took a long sip of beer.

"Sharp claws, man." I finally managed a half-smile in spite of the incredibly bad circumstances and my weariness.

We both listened to the silence of the old house on Fifth Street for a long moment. It was finally punctuated by the familiar dull clanging of the heating pipes. We took pulls on our bottles of ale. No invasive phone calls came now. Maybe Nana's whistle wasn't such a bad idea.

"How are you and the all-stars doing with the search for the Moore kid?" I asked Sampson. "Anything today? Anything new from the rest of our group? I know our surveillance is breaking down. Not enough manpower."

Sampson shrugged his broad shoulders, moved in his seat. His eyes turned hard and dark. "We found traces of makeup in his room. Maybe he used makeup to play the part of an old man. We will find him, Alex. You think he's the one who called here tonight?"

I spread my hands, then I nodded my head. "That would make sense. He definitely wants special attention, wants to be seen as important, John. Maybe he feels Jack and Jill is taking attention away from him, stealing the spotlight from his show. Maybe he knows I'm working Jack and Jill, and he's angry with me."

"We'll just have to ask the young cadet," Sampson said. He smiled a truly malevolent smile, one of his best, or worst, ever.

"Sure wish I was popular like you, Sugar. No freaks call me late at night. Write me mash notes at my house. Nothing like that."

"They wouldn't dare," I said. "Nobody's that crazy, not even the Truth School killer."

We both laughed, a little too loudly. Laughter is usually the best and only defense in a really tough murder investigation. *Maybe Jack and Jill had called me at home. Or Kevin Hawkins had called here. Or maybe even Gary Soneji, who was still out there somewhere, waiting to settle his old score with me.*

"Technician will be at the house first thing in the morning. Put a crackerjack hookup on your phone. We'll put a detective in here, too. Until we find the boy wonder anyway. I talked to Rakeem Powell. He's glad to do it."

I nodded. "That's good. Thanks for coming by and being here for Nana."

Things had taken a turn for the worse. They were threatening me in my own house now, threatening my family. Someone was. The freaks were right at my doorstep.

I couldn't get to sleep after Sampson left that night.

I didn't feel like playing the piano. No music in me for the moment. I didn't dare call Christine Johnson. I went up and looked in on the kids. Rosie the cat followed me, yawning and stretching. I watched them, much as Jannie had watched me sleep the other morning. I was afraid for them.

I finally dozed off about three in the morning. There were no more phone calls, thank God.

I slept on the porch with the Glock in my lap. Home, sweet home.

Chapter 71

I HEARD THE KIDS squawking and squealing first thing the next morning. They were laughing loudly, and it both raised my spirits and mildly depressed me.

I immediately remembered the situation we were in: *the monsters were at our doorstep. They knew where we lived.* There were no rules now. Nobody, not even my own family, was safe.

I thought about the Moore boy for a moment or two as I lay on the old sofa on the porch. Strangely, nothing in his past history fit in with the two murders. It just didn't track. I considered the monstrous idea of a thirteen-year-old boy committing purely existential murders. I had a lot of material stored in my head on the subject. I vaguely recalled André Gide's *Lafcadio's Adventures* from grad school. The twisted main character had pushed a stranger from a train just to prove that he was alive.

I glanced at the portable alarm clock beside my head. It was already ten past seven. I could smell Nana's strong coffee wafting through the house. I refused to let myself get down about the lack of progress. There was a saying I kept around for just such occasions. *Failure isn't falling down . . . it's staying down.*

I got up. I went to my room, showered, put on some fresh clothes, rumbled back downstairs. *I wasn't staying down.*

I found my two favorite Martians spiraling around the kitchen, playing some kind of tag game at seven in the morning. I opened my mouth and did my imitation of the silent scream from Edvard Munch's painting *The Shriek.*

Jannie laughed out loud. Damon mimed a silent scream of his own. They were glad to see me. We were still best pals, best of friends.

Somebody had called our house last night.

Sumner Moore?

Kevin Hawkins?

"Morning, Nana," I said as I poured a cup of steaming coffee from her pot. The best to you each morning and all that. I sipped the coffee and it tasted even more wonderful than it smelled. The woman can cook. She can also talk, think, illuminate, irritate.

"Morning, Alex," she said, as if nothing bad had happened the night before. Tough as nails. She didn't want to upset the kids, to alarm them in any way. Neither did I.

"Somebody will be by to look at our phone." I told her what Sampson and I had discussed the night before. "Somebody will be around for a few days, too. A detective. Probably it will be Rakeem Powell. You know Rakeem."

Nana didn't like that news one bit. "Of course I know Rakeem. I taught Rakeem in school for heaven's sake. Rakeem has no business here, though. This is *our home,* Alex. This is so terrible. I just don't think I can stand it . . . that it's happening *here.*"

"What's wrong with our telephone?" Jannie wanted to know.

"It works," I told my little girl.

Chapter 72

THE TWO MURDER CASES were beginning to feel like a single, relentless nightmare. I couldn't seem to catch my breath anymore. My stomach was in knots and apparently would stay that way for the duration of the investigation. The situation was Kafkaesque, and it was wearing down the entire Metro police force. No one could remember anything like it.

I had decided to keep Damon home with Nana and Detective Rakeem Powell for a few days. Just to be on the safe side. Hopefully, we'd find thirteen-year-old Sumner Moore soon, and half the horror story would be ended.

I continued to suspect either that Sumner Moore wanted to be caught or that he would be soon. The carelessness in both murders indicated it. I hoped that he wouldn't kill another child before we found him.

I considered moving Nana and the kids to one of my aunts', but held back. Rakeem Powell would stay with them at the house. That seemed enough chaos and disruption to force into their lives. For the moment, anyway.

Besides, I was almost certain Nana wouldn't have moved to

one of her sisters' without a huge battle and casualties. *Fifth Street was her home*. She would rather fight than switch. Occasionally, she had.

I drove to the White House very early in the morning. I sat in a basement office with a mug of coffee and a two-foot-thick stack of classified papers to read and ponder. These were literally hundreds of CIA reports and internal memos on Kevin Hawkins and the other CIA "ghosts."

I met with Don Hamerman; the attorney general, James Dowd; and Jay Grayer at a little past nine. We used an ornate conference room near the Oval Office in the West Wing. I recalled that the White House had originally been built to intimidate visitors, especially foreign dignitaries. It still had that effect, especially under the current circumstances. The "American mansion" was huge, and every room seemed formal and imposing.

Hamerman was surprisingly subdued at the meeting. "You made quite an impression on the President," he said. "You made your point with him, too."

"What happens now?" I asked. "What actions do we take? Obviously, I'd like to help."

"We've initiated some extremely sensitive investigations," Hamerman said. "The FBI will be handling them." Hamerman looked around the room. It seemed to me that he was reaffirming his power, his clout.

"Is that it, what you wanted to tell me?" I asked him after a few seconds of silence.

"That's it for now. You got it started. That's something. It's a really big deal."

"It is a big deal," I said. "It's a fucking murder investigation in the White House!" I got up and went back to my office. I had work to do. I kept reminding myself that I was part of the "team."

Hamerman peeked his head into the office about eleven-thirty. His eyes were wider and wilder than usual. I thought that maybe he'd changed his mind about the latest investigation — or had his mind changed for him.

He didn't look himself.

"The President wants to see us immediately."

Chapter 73

PRESIDENT BYRNES personally greeted each of us on the crisis team as we entered the Oval Office, which was indeed oval. "Thank you for coming. Hello, Jay, Ann, Jeanne, Alex. I know how busy you are, and the tremendous pressure you're all working under," he said as we walked in and began to take seats.

The crisis team had been assembled, but President Byrnes clearly dominated the room and the unscheduled meeting. He was dressed in a dark blue chief executive's business suit. His sandy-brown hair was freshly barbered, and I couldn't help wondering if it had just been cut that morning, and if it had, where did he get the time?

What had happened now? Had Jack and Jill contacted the White House again?

I glanced across the room at Jeanne Sterling. She shrugged her shoulders and widened her eyes. She didn't know what was up, either. No one seemed to know what the President had on his mind, not even Hamerman.

When we were seated, President Byrnes spoke. He stood directly in front of a pair of flags, army and air force. He seemed in control of his emotions, which was quite a feat.

"Harry Truman used to say," he began, "'if you want a friend in Washington, buy a dog.' I think I've experienced the precise feelings that inspired his wit. I'm almost sure that I have."

The President was an unusually engaging speaker. I already knew as much from his address at his convention and other televised talks — his version of FDR's fireside chats. He was clearly able to bring his oratory talents to a much smaller room and audience, even a tough, cynical crowd like the one before him. "What a royal pain in the butt this job can be. Whoever coined the phrase 'If drafted, I will not run; if elected, I will not serve' had the right idea. Believe me on that one."

The President smiled. He had an ability to make anything he said sound personal. I wondered if he planned it. How much of this was a first-rate acting job?

The President's intense blue eyes circled the room, stopping for a moment on each face. He seemed to be judging us, but more important, communicating with us individually. "I've been thinking a great deal about this current, unfortunate situation. Sally and I have talked about it upstairs, late into the night, several nights in a row. I've been thinking about Jack and Jill too much, in fact. For the past few days, this miserable three-ring circus has been the focus, and a major distraction to the executive branch of our government. It's already disrupted cabinet meetings and played havoc with everyone's schedule. This situation simply can't be allowed to continue. It's bad for the country, for our people, for everybody's mental health, including my own and Sally's. It makes us look weak and unstable to the rest of the world. A threat by a couple of kooks can't be permitted to disrupt the government of the United States. We can't allow that to happen.

"As a consequence, I've made a tough decision, which ultimately has to be mine to make. I'm sharing it with you this morning, because the decision will affect all of you as well as Sally and me."

President Byrnes let his eyes quickly roam around the room

again. I didn't know where this was going yet, but the process was fascinating to me. The President led us a step, then he checked to make sure we were still with him. He was clearly issuing an order, but he made it seem as if he were still seeking some consensus in the room.

"We simply have to return to business-as-usual at the White House. We have to do that. The United States can't be held hostage to real or imagined dangers or threats. That's the decision I'm making, and it goes into effect at the end of today. We have to move on, to move ahead with our programs."

As the President told us his decision, there was uneasy movement in the room. Ann Roper groaned out loud. Don Hamerman dropped his head down low, close to his knees. I kept my eyes pinned on the President.

"I fully understand that this makes your jobs more difficult, to say the very least. How in hell can you protect me if I won't cooperate, won't follow your recommendations? Well, I can't cooperate anymore. Not if it means sending a message to the world that a couple of psychopaths can completely alter our government. Which is *exactly what is happening*. It's happened, folks.

"Starting tomorrow, I'm back on my regular schedule. There will be no further debate on that subject. Sorry, Don." He looked at his chief of staff as he officially rejected his advice.

"I've also decided to make my scheduled visit to New York City on Tuesday. Sorry again, Don, Jay. I wish the best to all of us on our appointed tasks. You do your jobs, please. I'll try to do mine. We will have *absolutely no regrets*, no matter what happens from this point on. Is that understood?"

"Understood, sir." Everyone in the room nodded yes. Every eye was intensely focused on the President, mine included. President Byrnes had been both impassioned and impressive.

Absolutely no regrets, I repeated the phrase inside my head. I was sure I'd remember it for the rest of my life, no matter what happened, no matter what Jack and Jill had planned from here on.

Thomas Byrnes had just put his life on the line, *really on the line*.

The President had just put his life in our hands.

"By the way, Don," President Byrnes said to Hamerman as the meeting was starting to break up. "Have somebody run out and get me a goddamn dog. I think I need a friend."

We all laughed, even if we didn't quite feel up to it.

Chapter 74

THAT NIGHT it snowed about an inch in Washington. The temperature dropped way down into the teens. The Truth School killer woke up feeling scared. Feeling very alone. Feeling *trapped*. Feeling quite sad, actually.

No happy, happy. No joy, joy.

He was in a cold, greasy sweat that grossed him out completely. In a dream that he remembered now, he had been murdering people, then burying them under a fieldstone fireplace at his grandparents' country home in Leesburg. He'd been having that same dream for years, ever since he could remember, *ever since he was a kid.*

But was it a dream, or had I committed the grisly murders? he wondered as he opened his eyes. He tried to focus on the surroundings. *Where the hell am I?*

Then he remembered where he was, where he had come to sleep for the night. What a mindblower! What a cool idea he'd had.

The song, *his song,* blared inside his head:

> I'm a loser, baby.
> So why don't you kill me?

This hiding place was cool as shit. Or maybe he was just being too stupid and careless. Cool as shit? Or dumb and dumber? You be the judge.

He was in his own house, up on the third floor.

He wrapped his mind around the idea that he was "safe and sound" for now. Man, he loved the power of that thought.

He was in total control. He *was* mission control. He could be as big and important as Jack and Jill. Hell, he could be bigger and better than those trippy assholes. He knew that he could. He could stomp Jack and Jill's asses.

He felt around on the floor for his trusty backpack. *Where the hell is his stuff? . . . Okay. There it is. Everything is cool.* He fumbled inside — located his flashlight. He flicked the ON switch.

"Let there be light," he whispered. "*Wah-lah!*"

Awhh, too bad sports fans — he was definitely in the attic of his home. This wasn't a dream. He *was* the Truth School killer, after all. He shined the bright light down on his wristwatch. It was a twelfth-birthday present. It was the kind of sophisticated watch that pilots wore. *Wow,* he was so damn impressed! Maybe he could study to be a jet pilot after this was all behind him. Learn to fly an F-16.

It was 4:00 A.M. on the jet pilot's watch! *Must be 4:00 A.M., then.*

"The hour of the werewolf," he whispered softly. It was time to come down out of the attic. It was time to continue to make his mark in the world. Something cool and amazing had to happen now.

Perfect murders.

Had to, had to, had to.

Chapter 75

HE LET the bulky foldaway stairs drop down very slowly to the second floor of the house. His house. If his foster parents happened to get up for a pee right now — BIG PROBLEMS FOR HIM.

BIG SURPRISE FOR THEM, THOUGH.

MAJOR SHITSTORM FOR EVERYBODY CONCERNED.

He was having a little trouble with his breathing. None of this was easy now. He needed to set the heavy, unwieldy stairs down quietly on the second floor, but there was a little *thud* right at the end.

"Damn you. *Loser,*" he whispered.

He still couldn't exactly catch his breath. His body was covered with a thick coat of sweat, the kind horses break on a morning workout. He had seen that phenomenon on his grand-parents' farm. Never forgot it: *sweat that almost turned into this frothy cream, right before your eyes.*

"Pusillanimous," he whispered, mocking his own coward-ice. "Chickenshit bastard. Punk of the month. Loser, man." His theme song again.

He tried to let some of the icy panic and nervousness pass.

He took long, slow, deep breaths as he paused at the top of the folding stairs. This was so freaky. It was helter fucking skelter, in real life, in real time.

He finally began to climb down the wobbly wooden stairway, on *wobbly wooden legs* that felt like stilts. He was being as careful and quiet as he could be.

He felt a little better as he got to the bottom. Terra firma.

He walked on his tiptoes down the upstairs hallway to the door of the master bedroom. He opened the door and was immediately struck with a blast of really cold air.

His foster father kept the window open, even in December, even when it fucking snowed. *He would.* The arctic cold probably kept his silver-blond crew cut short. Saved him on haircuts. What a super jerk-off the guy was.

"Do you screw her in the cold dark?" he whispered under his breath. That sounded about right, too.

He walked up real close to their king-size bed. *Real close.* He stood at their altar of love, their sacred throne.

How many times had he imagined a moment like this? *This* very moment.

How many other kids had imagined this same scene a thousand thousand times? But then done nothing about it. *Losers!* The world was full of them.

He was on the verge of one of his worst rages, *a real bad one.* The hair on the back of his neck was standing at attention. TEN-SHUN. It felt like it, anyway.

He could *see red* everywhere in the bedroom. Like this misting red. It was almost as if he were viewing the room through a nightscope.

He . . . was . . . just . . . about . . . to . . . go . . . off . . . wasn't . . . he?

He could feel himself . . . exploding . . . into . . . a . . . billion . . . pieces.

Suddenly, he screamed at the top of his voice. *"Wake up and smell the fucking Folger's coffee!"*

He was sobbing now, too. For what reason, he didn't know. He couldn't remember crying like this since he was a real little kid, *real* little.

His chest hurt as if he'd been punched hard. Or hit with an eighteen-inch ballbat. He realized that he was starting to wimp out. Mister Softee was coming back. He felt like Holden Caulfield. Repentant. Always triple-thinking every goddamn move both before and after he made it.

"POW," he screamed at the top of his voice.

"POW," he screamed the word again.

"POW.

"POW.

"POW.

"POW.

"POW.

"POW.

"POW.

"POW.

"POW.

"POW."

And with every bloodcurdling yell, he pulled the trigger of the Smith & Wesson. He put another 9mm bullet into the two sleeping figures. *Twelve shots,* if he was counting correctly, and he was counting everything very correctly. *Twelve shots,* just like Jose and Kitty Menendez got.

The Roosevelt military education finally came in handy, he couldn't help thinking. His teachers had been right, after all. Colonel Wilson at the school would have been proud of the marksmanship — but most of all, the firm resolve, the very simple and clear plan, the extraordinary courage he had shown tonight.

His foster parents were annihilated, completely vanquished, almost disintegrated by all the firepower he'd brought to the task. He felt nothing — except maybe pride in what he had done, in his fine workmanship.

Nobody was here. Nobody did this, man.

He wrote it in their blood.

Then he ran outside to play in the snow. He got blood all over the yard, all over everything. *He could, you know.* He could do anything he wanted to now. There was no one to stop Nobody.

Chapter 76

ANOTHER MURDERED CHILD has been discovered.

A male. Less than an hour ago.

John Sampson got the news about seven o'clock in the evening. He couldn't believe it. *Could not, would not,* accept what he had just been told. Friday the thirteenth. Was the date deliberate?

Another child murdered in Garfield Park. At least, the body was left there. He wanted Sumner Moore bad, and he wanted him now.

Sampson parked on Sixth Street and began the short walk into the desolate and dreary park. *This is getting worse,* he thought as he walked toward the red and yellow emergency lights flashing brightly up ahead.

"Detective Sampson. Let me through," he said as he pushed his way inside a circle of police uniforms.

One of the uniforms was holding a gray-and-white yapping mutt on a leash. It was a weird touch at a weird scene. Sampson addressed the patrolman. "What's with the dog? Whose dog?"

"Dog uncovered the victim's body. Owner let it loose for a run after she got home from work. Somebody covered up the dead kid with tree branches. Not much else. Like he wanted somebody to find it."

Sampson nodded at what he'd heard so far. Then he moved on, stepped closer to the body. The victim was clearly older than either Vernon Wheatley or Shanelle Green. Sumner Moore had graduated from murdering very small children. The creepy little ghoul was on a full rampage now.

A police photographer was taking pictures of the body, the camera's harsh flashes dramatic against the blanket of snow covering the park.

The boy's mouth and nose were wrapped with silver duct tape. Sampson took a deep breath before he stooped down low next to the medical examiner, a woman he knew named Esther Lee.

"How long you think he's been dead?" Sampson asked the M.E.

"Hard to say. Maybe thirty-six hours. Decomposition is slowed a lot in this cold weather. I'll know more after the autopsy. The boy took a brutal beating. Lead pipe, wrench, something nasty and heavy like that. He tried to fight the killer off. You can see defensive bruises on both hands, on his arms. I feel so bad for this boy."

"I know, Esther. Me, too."

What John Sampson could see of the boy's neck was discolored and badly bloated. Tiny black bugs crawled along the hairline. A thin line of maggots spilled from a split in the scalp above the right ear.

Sampson sucked it up, grimaced, and forced himself to move around to the other side of the boy's body. Nobody knew it, not even Alex, but this was the part of homicide that he just couldn't handle. DOAs. Bodies in decomposition.

"You won't like it," Esther Lee told him before he looked. "I'm warning you."

"I know I won't," he muttered. He blew warmth on his hands, but it didn't help much.

He could see the boy's face now. He could see it — but he

couldn't believe it. And he certainly didn't like it. Esther Lee was right about that.

"Jesus Christ," he said out loud. "Jesus. Jesus. Jesus. Make this terrible thing stop."

Sampson stood up straight. He was six nine again, only it wasn't tall enough, wasn't big enough. He couldn't believe what he had just seen — *the boy's face*.

This killing was too much even for him, and he had seen so much in D.C. during the past few years.

The murdered boy was Sumner Moore.

PART V
NO RULES. NO REGRETS.

Chapter 77

NOTHING EVER BEGINS at the time we believe it does. Still, this is what I think of as the beginning.

Jannie and I sat in the kitchen and we talked the talk, our own special talk. The words didn't matter much, just the sentiments.

"You know, this is an anniversary for us," I said to her. "Special anniversary." I touched her cheek. So soft. Soft as a butterfly's belly.

"Oh, *really?*" Jannie said and gave me her most skeptical Nana Mama look. "And what anniversary might that be?"

"Well, I'll tell you. This just happens to be the *five-hundredth* time that I've read you *The Stinky Cheese Man*."

"Okay, fine," she said and smiled in spite of herself, "so read the story already! I love the way you read it." I read the story again.

After we were done with our *Stinky Cheese*, I spent some time with Damon, and then with Nana. Then I went upstairs to pack.

When I came back down, I talked out on the porch with Rakeem Powell. Rakeem was waiting to be relieved. Sampson was coming over for the night. Man Mountain was late as usual, and we hadn't heard from him yet, which was a little unusual, but I knew he would be there.

"You okay?" I asked Rakeem.

"I'm fine, Alex. Sampson will get here eventually. You take care of yourself."

I went out to my car. I stepped inside and put in a tape that felt right for the moment at hand — for my mood, anyway. It was the finale to Saint-Saëns's second piano concerto. I had always dreamed of being able to play the piece on the porch piano. Dream on, dream on.

I listened to the blazing music as I drove out to Andrews airfield, where *Air Force One* was being prepared.

President Byrnes was going to New York City, and I was going with him.

No regrets.

Chapter 78

THERE HAVE BEEN many conflicting accounts, but this is what happened and how it happened. I know, because I was there.

On Monday evening, nine days before Christmas, we landed in a grayish blue fog and light rain at La Guardia Airport on Long Island. No specific information about President Byrnes's travel plans had been announced to the press, but the President was keeping his commitment to speak in New York the following morning. Thomas Byrnes was known for keeping his commitments, keeping his word.

It had been decided to go from La Guardia into Manhattan by car, rather than by helicopter. The President wasn't hiding anymore. *Had Jack and Jill counted on just that kind of courage, or arrogance, from him?* I wondered. Would Jack and Jill follow the President to New York? I was almost sure that they would. It fit everything we knew about them so far.

"Ride with us, Alex," Don Hamerman said as we hurried across the tarmac, a cold December rain blowing hard in our faces. Hamerman, Jay Grayer, and I had gotten off *Air Force One* together. During the plane ride we sat together, planning how to protect President Byrnes from an assassination attempt in New

York. Our talk was so intense that I missed out on the specialness of the ride.

"We're traveling in the car directly behind the President. We can continue our little chat on the way into Manhattan," Hamerman said to me.

We climbed into a somber, blue Lincoln Town Car that was parked less than fifty yards from the jet. It was close to ten in the evening, and that part of the airfield had been secured. There were Secret Service men, FBI agents, and New York City policemen milling around everywhere.

Surrounding the five limousines of the presidential motorcade were at least three dozen NYPD blue-and-white squad cars, not to mention a few Harley motorcycles. The Secret Service agents stared into the foggy night as if Jack and Jill might suddenly appear on the runway at La Guardia.

I had learned that the NYPD would have a minimum of five thousand uniformed officers on the special-service detail for the length of the President's visit. More than a hundred detectives would also be assigned. The Secret Service had tried to convince the President to stay at the Coast Guard base on Governors Island, or at Fort Hamilton in Brooklyn. The President had insisted on making a statement by staying in Manhattan. *No regrets.* His words in the Oval Office played over and over in my head.

I settled back into the cushy and comfortable leather seat of the town car. I could sense the power. What it was like to ride in a motorcade directly behind the President's car, which the Secret Service called "Stagecoach."

A couple of NYPD police cruisers pulled out in front of the pack. Their red and yellow roof lights began to revolve in quick kaleidoscopic circles. The presidential motorcade started to wind its way out of La Guardia Airport.

Don Hamerman spoke as soon as we were moving. "No one has seen Kevin Hawkins in the past three days, right? Hawkins seems to have fallen off the face of the earth," he said. His voice was full of frustration, anger, and the usual petulance. He enjoyed bullying people beneath him, but neither Grayer nor I would put up with it.

"No one knows the route we're taking," Hamerman said. "We didn't have a final route until a few minutes ago."

I couldn't keep quiet. "We know the route. People in the NYPD know it, or they will momentarily. Kevin Hawkins is good at uncovering secrets. Kevin Hawkins is good, period. He's one of *our best*."

Jay Grayer was peering out of the rain-streaked window into the fast lane of the New York highway we were traveling on. His voice sounded far away. "What's your instinct about Hawkins?" he asked me.

"I think Kevin Hawkins is definitely involved somehow. He's extreme right-wing. He's associated with some groups that are opposed to the President's policies and plans. He's been in trouble before. He's suspected of a homicide inside the CIA. It all fits."

"But something's bothering you about him?" Grayer asked. He'd learned how to read me pretty well already.

"According to everything I've read, he's never worked closely with anyone before. Hawkins has always been a loner, at least until now. He seems to have problems relating to women, other than his sister in Silver Spring. I don't understand how Jill would fit in with him. I don't see Hawkins suddenly working with a woman."

"Maybe he finally found a soul mate. It happens," Hamerman said. I doubted that Hamerman ever had.

"What else pops out about Hawkins?" Jay Grayer continued to probe. He shut his eyes as he listened.

"All his FBI psych profiles and workups suggest a potential loose cannon. I don't know how they justified keeping him active for all those years in Asia and South America. Here's the interesting part. Hawkins can get committed to causes that he believes in, though. He strongly believes in the importance of intelligence for our national defense. President Byrnes doesn't, and he's said so publicly several times. That could explain the Jack and Jill scenario. *Could* explain it. Hawkins is experienced and resourceful enough to pull off an assassination. He definitely could be Jack. If he is, he will be very hard to stop."

We were starting to cross the Fifty-ninth Street Bridge into Manhattan. New York, New York. The presidential motorcade was a strange, eerie parade of wailing sirens and bright flashing lights. The island of Manhattan lay straight ahead of us.

New York looked amazingly huge and imposing, capable of swallowing us whole. *Anything can happen here,* I was thinking, and I'm sure Don Hamerman and Jay Grayer were, too.

Bam!

Bam!

Bam!

The three of us jumped forward in the backseat of the town car. I had my hand on my gun, ready for almost anything, ready for Jack and Jill.

We all stared in horror at the President's car up ahead — *Stagecoach*. There was total silence in our car. Awful silence. Then we began to laugh.

The loud noises hadn't been gunshots. They just sounded like it. They were false alarms. But it was chilling all the same.

We had passed over worn and warped metal gratings on the ramp coming off the bridge. Everyone in our car had experienced an instant heart attack at the sudden and unexpected noise. Undoubtedly, the same thing had happened in the President's car.

"Jesus," Hamerman moaned loudly. "That's what it would be like. Oh, God Almighty."

"I was there at the Washington Hilton when Hinckley shot Reagan and Brady," Jay Grayer said with a tremor in his voice. I knew that he was back there once again, with Reagan and James Brady. Experiencing a flashback, the kind no one wanted to have.

I wondered about Grayer's personal stake in this. I wondered about everybody on our team.

I watched the President's car as it swept down onto the crowded, brightly lit streets of New York City. The American flags on the fenders were flapping wildly in the river breeze.

No regrets.

Chapter 79

THE PHOTOJOURNALIST had arrived early on Monday, December 16, for his work in New York.

He had decided to drive from Washington. It was much safer that way. Now he walked along Park Avenue, where the presidential motorcade would travel tomorrow morning, only a few hours from now. He was relaxing before the historic day, taking in the sights and sounds of New York City in the holiday season.

Kevin Hawkins had occasional flashes, mind photos of memorabilia he had studied on the JFK killing, the murders of Martin Luther King and Robert Kennedy, even the badly botched shooting of Ronald Reagan.

He knew one thing for certain: this particular assassination wouldn't be botched. *This was a done deal. There was no way out for Thomas Byrnes. No escape.*

He was closing in on the Waldorf-Astoria Hotel, where he knew the President and his wife would be staying. It was typical for this president to go against the advice of his security advisors. It fit his profile perfectly.

Don't listen to the experts. Fix what isn't broken. Arrogant fool, useless bastard. Traitor to the American people.

The night was cool and fine, the light rain having finally stopped. The air felt good against his skin. He was certain that he wasn't going to be spotted as Kevin Hawkins. He'd taken care of that. There were easily a couple of hundred NYPD uniforms around the hotel. It didn't matter. No one would recognize him now. Not even his own mother and father.

The picturesque divided avenue outside the hotel was relatively crowded at this time of night. Some spectators had come in hopes of seeing the President shot. They didn't know when the President would be arriving, but they knew the likely hotels in midtown. The Waldorf was a good guess.

The local tabloids, and even the *New York Times,* had run huge headlines about Jack and Jill and the ongoing drama. In typical fashion, the press had gotten it mostly wrong — but that would be helpful to him soon.

Kevin Hawkins joined in with the strangely noisy and almost festive crowd, several of whom had wandered over from holiday visits to the Christmas tree at Rockefeller Center. The unruly ambulance-chasers gathered outside the hotel told smugly ironic jokes, and he despised them for their big-city cynicism, their attitude. He despised them even more than the useless president he had come to this city to kill.

He stayed at the outer edge of the crowd, just in case he suddenly had to move fast. He didn't want to be around there too late, but the presidential motorcade was running behind the schedule he had, *the schedule he had been given.*

Finally, he saw heads and necks in the crowd craning to the far left. He could hear the roar of cars coming up Park Avenue. The motorcade was approaching the hotel. It had to be the motorcade coming.

The dozen or so cars stopped at the canopied entrance on Park Avenue. Then Kevin Hawkins almost couldn't believe what he was seeing.

The arrogant bastard had chosen to walk inside from the street rather than use the underground garage. He wanted to be seen —

to be photographed. He wanted to show his courage to all the world . . . to show that Thomas Byrnes wasn't afraid of Jack and Jill.

The photojournalist watched the cocksure and vainglorious chief executive as he was ushered from his limousine. He could have taken out Thomas Byrnes right there! Once the hotshot, former automobile executive had made the decision to return the presidency to "business as usual," the assassination was virtually guaranteed.

Amateurs made such amateurish decisions, Hawkins knew. Always. It was a fact that he counted on in his work.

I could do him right now. I could take out the President right here on Park Avenue.

How does that make me feel? Excited — pumped. No guilt. What a strange man I have become, Kevin Hawkins thought.

That was really why he was there that night — to test his emotional responses.

This was his dress rehearsal for the big event. The only rehearsal he would need, or get.

The Secret Service team smoothly and expertly got the President safely inside the hotel. Their coverage was excellent. Three tight rings around the PP, the protected person.

The presidential detail was very good, but not good enough. No one could be. Not for what Kevin Hawkins had in mind.

A kamikaze attack! A suicide attack. The President would not be able to escape from it. No one could. It was a done deal.

He watched the rest of the shiny blue and black sedans unload, and he recognized nearly every face. He took his usual mind photos. Dozens of shots to remember — all inside his head.

Finally, he saw Jill. She looked so cool and utterly unconcerned. She was such a great psycho in her own right, wasn't she? Jill stood there in the middle of all the fuss and bustle. Then she disappeared inside the Waldorf with the rest of them.

The photojournalist finally sauntered away, down Park toward what had once been the Pan Am Building and now belonged to

MetLife. A float with Snoopy driving Santa's sleigh stood out on the building's rooftop.

The President ought to buy some term life insurance tonight, he thought, *whatever the price. The assassination is as good as done. It was guaranteed.*

But what Kevin Hawkins didn't even suspect, didn't realize, was that *he too* was being watched. He was under close observation, at that very moment, in New York City.

Jack was watching Kevin Hawkins stroll down Park Avenue.

Chapter 80

JACK BE *NIMBLEST*.

Jack be *quickest*.

After he had watched Kevin Hawkins disappear on Park Avenue, Sam Harrison left the crowded area near the Waldorf. New York was already as stirred up about Jack and Jill as Washington, D.C. That was good. It would make everything easier.

There was something he had to do now. He had to do this, no matter what the risks. It was the most important thing to him.

At the corner of Lexington Avenue and Forty-seventh Street, he stopped at a pay phone booth. Surprisingly, the damn contraption actually worked. Maybe the only one that did in midtown.

As he dialed, he watched a garish street hooker plying her trade across Lexington. Nearby, a middle-aged gay man was picking up a blond teenager. Urban cowboys and girls sashayed into a peculiar New York bar called Ride'm High. He mourned for the old New York, for America as it had been, for real cowboys and real men.

He had important and necessary work to do in New York. Jack

and Jill was heading toward its climax. He was confident that the real truth would go to his grave with him. It had to be like that.

The truth had always been far too dangerous for the public to know. The truth didn't usually set people free, it just got them crazier. Most people just couldn't handle the truth.

He finally reached a number in Maryland. There was a very small risk in the phone call, but he had to take it. He had to do this one thing for his own sanity.

A little girl's voice came on the phone. Immediately, he felt the most incredible relief, but also a joy he hadn't experienced in days. The girl sounded as if she were right there in New York.

"This is Karon speaking. How may I help you?" she said. He had taught her to answer the phone.

He closed his eyes tight, and all of New York's depressing tawdriness, everything he was about to do was suddenly, effectively, shut out. Even Jack and Jill was gone from his thoughts for the briefest of moments. He was in a safety zone. He was home.

His little girl was what really counted for him now. She was the only thing that mattered. She'd been permitted to wait up late for his call.

He wasn't Jack as he cradled the phone receiver against his chin.

He wasn't Sam Harrison.

"It's Daddy," he said to his youngest child. "Hello, pumpkin-eater. I miss you to bits. How are you? Where's Mommy?" he asked. "Are you guys taking good care of each other? I'll be home real soon. Do you miss me? I sure miss you."

He had to get away with this, he thought as he talked to his daughter, and then to his wife. Jack and Jill had to succeed. He had to change history. He couldn't go home in a body bag. In disgrace. As the worst American traitor since Benedict Arnold.

No, the body bag was for President Thomas Byrnes. He deserved to die. So had all the others. They were all traitors in their own way.

> Jack and Jill came to The Hill
> To kill, to kill, to kill.

And soon — very soon — it would be finished.

Chapter 81

SOMETHING was clearly wrong at the hotel. We hadn't been at the Waldorf for more than a few minutes when I knew there was a serious breach in security. I could see the way the Secret Service agents closed around President Byrnes and his wife as they entered the glittery hotel foyer.

Thomas and Sally Byrnes were hurriedly being escorted to their suite of rooms on the twenty-first floor. I knew the drill by heart. NYPD detectives had been working closely with the Secret Service detail. They had checked every conceivable and inconceivable method of infiltration into the Waldorf, including subways, sewers, and all the underground passages. Bomb-sniffing dogs had been marched through the midtown hotel just before our arrival. The dogs had also been taken that afternoon to the Plaza and the Pierre, other possible choices for the President's stay.

"Alex." I heard from behind. "Alex, over here. In here, Alex." Jay Grayer beckoned with his hand. "We've got a little problem already. I don't know how they managed it, but they're definitely here in New York. Jack and Jill are here."

"What the hell is going on here, Jay?" I asked the Secret

Service agent as we hurried past glass cases filled with quart-size perfume bottles and expensive clothing accessories.

Jay Grayer led me to the hotel's administrative offices, which were directly behind the front desk on the lobby floor. The room was already filled with Secret Service, FBI agents, and New York City police honchos. Everybody seemed to be listening to earphones or hand transmitters. They looked stressed-out, including the hotel management, with their own director of security and the proud claim that every president since Hoover had stayed at the Waldorf.

Grayer finally turned to me and said, "A delivery of flowers came about ten minutes ago. They're from our friends Jack and Jill. There's another rhyme with the flowers."

"Let's take a look at it. Let me see the message, please."

The note was on a mahogany desk next to an arrangement of blood-red roses. I read it as Grayer looked over my shoulder.

> Jack and Jill went up The Hill
> And surprised the Chief with flowers.
> We're here in town
> We're counting down
> Your last remaining hours.

"They want us to *believe* they're a couple of kooks," I said to Jay.

"Do you?"

"I sure as hell don't, but they're sticking with it. It's consistent as hell and it's all a plan. They *definitely* know what they're doing, and we *definitely* don't."

And Jack and Jill were *definitely* in New York City.

Chapter 82

THE HEAVY WOODEN DOOR into President Thomas Byrnes's master bedroom opened at a few minutes past midnight. The Waldorf's presidential suite consisted of four bedrooms and two sitting rooms in the tower portion of the hotel. No other hotel guests were staying on that floor, or the floors immediately above and below.

"Who is it?" The President looked up from the book he was reading to try and calm his nerves. The book was the massive *Truman* by David McCullough. The President nearly dropped the heavy tome when the door opened unexpectedly.

Thomas Byrnes smiled when he saw who was standing between the doorway and a large antique armoire.

"Oh, it's you. I thought it might be Jill. I think she secretly likes me. Just a gut feeling I have," he said and chuckled.

Sally Byrnes forced a smile. "Only me. I wanted to say goodnight. And to see if you were all right, Tom."

The President looked fondly at his wife. They had been sleeping in separate bedrooms for the past few years. They'd had problems. But they were still close friends. He believed they still loved each other, and always would.

"You didn't come to tuck me in?" he asked. "That's a shame."

"Of course I did. That, too. Tonight, you deserve a tuck-in."

Her husband smiled in a way that reminded both of them of better times, *much* better times. He could be a charmer when he wanted to be. Sally Byrnes knew that all too well. Tom could also be a major heartbreaker. Sally knew that, too. It had been that way for most of their years together. *The agony and the ecstasy,* she called the relationship. In truth, though, to be fair, it had been more ecstasy than agony. They both believed that, and knew what they had was rare.

Thomas Byrnes lightly patted the edge of the bed, which was king-size with a partial canopy. Sally came and sat beside him. He reached for her hand, and she gave it to him willingly. She loved to hold hands with her Tom. She always had. She knew she still loved him in spite of past hurts and all their other troubles. She could forgive him for his affairs. She knew they meant nothing to him. She was secure in herself. Sally Byrnes also understood her husband better than anybody else. She knew how disturbed he was right now, how deeply frightened, and how vulnerable.

And she did love him, the whole complex package — the arrogance, the diffidence, the insecurities, the very large ego at times. She knew that he loved her and that they would always be best friends and soul mates.

"Tell you something weird," he said as he pulled her closer, as he tenderly held his wife of twenty-six years.

"Tell me. I expect nothing less than full disclosure, *Mr. King.*" It was a phrase they had both laughed over in the London stage play *The Madness of George III.* The queen had called George III "Mr. King" in bed.

"I think it's somebody we know. I had a talk about it with that homicide detective. He's the only one who had the balls to come to me with bad news. I think it could be somebody close to us, Sally. That makes it all the more horrible."

Sally Byrnes tried not to show her fear. Her eyes traveled up and around the high-ceilinged bedroom. There was a chair rail halfway up the walls. Baby-blue-and-cream wallpaper rose above the rail. God, how she wished they could go home to Michigan. That's what she really wanted more than anything, for her and Tom to go back home.

"Have you told that to Don Hamerman?"

"I'm telling you," he whispered. "You, I can trust. You, I *do* trust."

Sally kissed his forehead softly, then his cheek, and finally his lips. "You sure about that?"

"Hundred percent," he whispered. "Although you have some good reasons to want to get me. Better reasons than most. Better than Jack and Jill, I'll bet."

"Hold me tight," she said. "Don't ever let go."

"Hold *me* tight," the President continued to whisper to his wife. "Don't you ever let go. I could stay like this with you forever. And please, Sally, forgive me."

It's somebody close. It's somebody very close to me. President Thomas Byrnes couldn't turn off the disturbing thought as he held his wife. *Somebody close.*

"What would you like for Christmas, Tom? You know the press — they always want to know."

President Byrnes thought for a moment.

"Peace. For this to be over."

Chapter 83

IT WAS TIME to prove he was better than Jack and Jill. In his heart, he knew that he was. No contest. Jack and Jill were basically full of crap.

The Cross house stood in dark, shifting shadows on Fifth Street in Washington's Southeast. It looked as if everyone inside had finally fallen asleep. *We'll soon see. We'll just see about that,* the killer thought to himself.

His name was Danny Boudreaux, if you really wanted to know the truth. He watched the streetlamp-lit scene from a clump of gum trees sprouting in an otherwise empty lot.

He was thinking about how much he hated Cross and his family. Alex Cross reminded him of his real father, who'd also been a cop devoted to his stupid job and who had left him and his mother because of it. Deserted them as if they were so much spit on the sidewalk. Then his mother had killed herself, and he'd wound up with foster parents.

Families made him sick, but bigshot Cross tried to be such a perfect daddy. He was such a phony, a real scam artist. Worse than that, Cross had severely underestimated him and also "dissed" him several times.

Danny Boudreaux had been a classmate of Sumner Moore at Theodore Roosevelt. Sumner Moore had always been the perfect suck-up cadet, the perfect student, the perfect student-athlete asshole. Moore had been his goddamn *tutor* since the previous summer. Danny Boudreaux had to go to the Moore house twice a week. He'd hated Sumner Moore from day one for being such a condescending and stuck-up little prick. He'd hated the whole condescending Moore family. Well, he'd taught them a lesson. He'd turned out to be the tutor.

His *first* totally outrageous idea had been to make it look as if Sumner Moore, *the perfect cadet,* were the child killer. He'd logged into the Moore's Prodigy account and led the cops right to their house. What a great frigging prank that had been — the best. Then he'd decided to get rid of Sumner. That was the second outrageous idea. He'd enjoyed killing Sumner Moore even more than the little kids.

He wanted to teach Cross a lesson now, too. Cross obviously didn't think the so-called Sojourner Truth School killer was worth much of his precious time. Danny Boudreaux was no Gary Soneji in the eyes of Alex Cross. He was no Jack and Jill. *He was Nobody, right?*

Well, we'll see about that, Dr. Cross. We'll just see how I stack up against Jack and Jill and the others. Watch this one real closely, Doctor Hotshit De-fective. You just might learn something.

In the next hour or so, a lot of people would learn not to underestimate Danny Boudreaux, not to snub him ever again.

Danny Boudreaux crossed Fifth Street, careful to keep his body in tree shadows. He walked right into the well-kept yard that bordered the Cross house.

He was thirteen, but small for his age. He was five three and only a hundred and ten pounds. He didn't look like much. The other cadets called him Mister Softee because he would melt into tears whenever they teased him, which was just about all the time. *For Danny Boudreaux hell week had lasted the whole school year. No, it had lasted for his entire life so far.* Christ, he had enjoyed *killing Sumner Moore! It was like killing his whole goddamn school!*

He smeared gray eye shadow over his face, his neck, and his hands as he waited across from the Cross house. He had on dark jeans and a black shirt, and also a dark camo face mask made by Treebark. He had to fit in with the African-American neighborhood, right? Well, no one had paid much attention to him on Sixth Street, or even walking along E Street on his way to Fifth.

Danny Boudreaux touched the butt of the Smith & Wesson semiautomatic in the deep pocket of his poncho. The gun held a dozen shots. He was loaded for bear. The safety was off. He started crying again. Hot tears were streaming down his face. He wiped them away with his sleeve. No more Mr. Softee.

He did perfect murders.

Chapter 84

NOTHING IN HEAVEN or on earth could save Alex Cross's cute little family now. They were next in line to die. It was the move he had to make. The right move at the right time. *Hey, hey, what do you say?*

Danny Boudreaux inched his way up the back-porch steps of the house. He didn't make a freaking sound.

He could be a damn good cadet when he needed to be. A fine young soldier. He was on maneuvers tonight, that's all it was. He was on a nocturnal mission.

Search and destroy.

He didn't hear any noises coming from inside the house. No late-night TV sounds. No Letterman, Leno, and Beavis and Butthead, NordicTrack commercials. No piano playing, either. That probably meant Cross was sleeping now, too. So be it. *The sleep of the dead, right?*

He touched the doorknob and immediately wanted to pull his fingers away. The metal felt like dry ice against his skin. He held on, though. He turned the knob slowly, slowly. Then he pulled it toward him.

The goddamn door was locked! For some crazy reason he'd imagined it wouldn't be. He could still get in the house through this door, but he might make some noise.

That wouldn't do.

That wasn't *perfect.*

He decided to go around front and check the situation there. He knew there was a sun porch. A piano on the porch. Cross played the blues out there — but the blues were only just beginning for the good doctor. After tonight, the rest of his life would be nothing but the blues.

Still no sound came from inside the house. He knew Cross hadn't moved his family out of harm's way. That showed more disrespect on his part. Cross wasn't afraid of him. Well, he ought to be afraid. Dammit, Cross ought to be scared shitless of him!

Danny Boudreaux reached out to try the door to the sun porch. The young killer broke out in a sweat. Boudreaux could hardly breathe. He was seeing his worst nightmare, and his nightmares were really bad.

Detective John Sampson was staring right at him! The black giant was there on the porch. Waiting for him. Sitting there, all smug as hell.

He'd been caught! Jesus. They'd set a trap for him. He'd fallen for it like a true chump.

But, hey, wait a damn minute. Waitaminute!

Something was wrong with this picture . . . or rather something was very right with the picture!

Danny Boudreaux blinked his eyes, then he stared real hard. He concentrated hard. Sampson was *sleeping* in the big, fluffy armchair next to the piano.

His stockinged feet were propped up on a matching hassock. His holstered gun was on a small side table, maybe twelve inches from his right hand. His *holstered* gun.

Twelve inches. Hmmm. Just twelve little inches, the killer thought, mulled it over.

Danny Boudreaux held on to the doorknob for dear life. He didn't move. His chest hurt as if he'd been punched.

What to do? What to do? What in hell to do? . . . TWELVE MEASLY INCHES . . .

His mind was going about a million miles a second. There were so many thoughts blasting through his brain that it almost shut down on him.

He wanted to go at Sampson. To rush in and take the big moke out. Then hurry upstairs and do the family. He wanted it so much that the thought burned in him, seared the inside of his brain, fried his thought waves.

He slid in and out of his military mind. *The better part of valor and all that shit. Logic conquers all.* He knew what he had to do.

Even more slowly than he'd come up the steps, he backed away from the porch door of the Cross house. He couldn't believe how close he'd come to stumbling right into the huge, menacing detective.

Maybe he could have snuck up on the big moke — blown his brains out. Maybe not, though. The big moke was a really big moke.

No, the Truth School killer wouldn't take the chance. He had too much fun, too many games, ahead of him to blow it like this.

He was too experienced now. He was getting better and better at this.

He disappeared into the night. He had other choices, other business, he could take care of. Danny Boudreaux was on the loose in D.C., and he loved it. He had a taste for it now. There would be time for Cross and his stupid family later.

He'd already forgotten that just minutes before he had been

crying his eyes out. He hadn't taken his medicine in seven days. The hated, despicable Depakote, his goddamn mood-disorder medicine.

He was wearing his favorite sweatshirt again. *Happy, happy. Joy, joy.*

Chapter 85

I WOKE WITH A START and a trembling shiver. My skin was prickling, my heart racing furiously.

Bad dream? Something unholy, real, or imagined? The room was pitch-black, all the lights out, and it took me a second to remember where in the name of God I was.

Then I remembered. I remembered everything. I was part of the team assigned to try and protect the President — except the President had decided to make our job even harder than it had been. The President had decided to travel out of Washington — to show the colors — to demonstrate that he wasn't afraid of terrorists and crackpots of any kind.

I was in New York City — at the Waldorf-Astoria Hotel on Park Avenue. Jack and Jill were in New York, too. They were so sure of themselves that they had sent us a calling card.

I groped around for the lamp on the bedside table, then for the damn lamp switch. Finally, I clicked it on. I looked at the night table clock. Two fifty-five.

"That's just terrific," I whispered under my breath. "That's great."

I thought of calling my kids in Washington. Calling Nana. It

330 / James Patterson

wasn't a real serious idea, but the notion floated across my mind.
I thought about Christine Johnson. Calling her at home. *Absolutely not!* But I did have the thought, and I did like the idea of talking to her on the phone.

I finally pulled on a pair of khakis, stepped into battered Converse sneaks, slipped into an old sweatshirt. I wandered out into the hotel. I needed to be out of my hotel room. I needed to be out of my own *skin.*

The Waldorf-Astoria was sound asleep. As it should be. Except that very uptight Secret Service agents were posted everywhere, in every hallway where I wandered. The presidential detail was on its night watch. They were mostly athletic-looking men, who reminded me of very fit accountants. Only a couple of women were assigned to the detail in New York.

"You going for a late run through midtown New York, Detective Cross?" one of the Secret Service agents asked as I passed by. It was a woman named Camille Robinson. She was serious and very dedicated, as most of the Secret Service agents seemed to be. They seemed to like President Thomas Byrnes a lot, enough to take a bullet for.

"My mind is up and running, for sure," I said and managed a smile. "Probably do a couple of marathons before morning. You okay? Need some coffee or anything?"

Camille shook her head and kept her serious face on. Watchdogs can be female, too. I'd met my share of them. I saluted the diligent agent, then kept on walking.

A few thoughts continued to plague me as I wandered inside the eerily quiet hotel. My mind was running way too hot.

The murder of Charlotte Kinsey was one disturbing puzzle piece. That murder might have been committed by somebody other than Jack and Jill. Could there be a third killer? Why would there be a third killer? How did it fit?

I continued down another long hallway, and down still another track in my mind.

What about larger and more complicated conspiracies? Dallas and JFK? Los Angeles and RFK? Memphis and Dr. King? Where did that insane and depressing line of thinking take me? The list of possible conspirators was impossibly long, and I didn't have the resources to get at most of the suspects, anyway. The crisis group talked about conspiracies a lot. The Federal Bureau was obsessed with conspiracies. So was the CIA ... but a powerful fact remained: thirty years after the Kennedy assassinations, no one was really convinced that either of those murders had been solved.

The more I delved into conspiracy theories, the more I realized that getting to the core was almost impossible. Certainly, no one had yet. I'd talked to several people at the Assassination Archives and Research Center in Washington, and they had come to exactly the same conclusion. Or dead end.

I wandered into the hallway on the twenty-first floor, where the President was sleeping. I had a chilling thought that he might be dead in his room; that Jack and Jill had already struck and left a note, another poem for us to discover in the morning.

"Everything okay?" I asked the agents stationed just outside the door of the presidential suite.

They watched me carefully, as if they were asking themselves, *Why is he here?* "So far," one of them said stiffly. "No problems here."

Eventually, I made it full circle back to my room. It was almost four in the morning.

I slipped inside the room. Lay down on the bed. I thought of my conversation with Sampson earlier that night, hearing about the murder of Sumner Moore. Apparently, the Moore boy wasn't the Truth School killer. I tried not to think about either case anymore.

I finally dozed until six — when the clock radio went off like a fire alarm next to my head.

Rock-and-roll music blared. "K-Rock" in New York. Howard Stern was talking to me. He had worked down in Washington years ago. Howard said, "The prez is in town. Can Jack and Jill be far away?"

Everybody knew about it. The President's motorcade through Manhattan started at eleven. Stagecoach was ready to roll again.

Chapter 86

HISTORY was about to be made in New York City. At the very least, it was white-knuckle time. Definitely that. The game had ceased being a game.

Jack jogged at a strong, steady pace through Central Park. It was a little before six in the morning. He'd been out running since just after five. He had a lot on his mind. D day had finally arrived. New York City was the war zone, and he couldn't imagine a better one.

He observed the very striking Manhattan skyline from where he was running alongside Fifth Avenue, heading south. Above the tall, uneven line of buildings, the sky was the color of charcoal seen through tissue paper. Huge plumes of smoke billowed up from turn-of-the-century buildings.

It was pretty as hell, actually. Close to glorious. Not the way he usually thought of New York City. *It was just a facade, though. Like Jack and Jill,* he was thinking.

As he ran alongside a blue city bus charging down Fifth Avenue, he wondered if he might die in the next few hours. He had to be ready for that, to be prepared for anything.

Kamikaze, he thought. *The final plan was deadly, and it was as surefire as these things could be.* He didn't believe that the target could possibly survive this attack. No one could. There would be other deaths as well. This *was* a war, after all, and people died in war.

Jack finally emerged from the park at Fifth Avenue and Fifty-ninth. He continued to run south, picking up his pace.

A few moments later, he entered the formal and attractive lobby of the Peninsula Hotel in the West Fifties. It was ten past six in the morning. The Peninsula was a little more than twenty blocks from Madison Square Garden, where President Byrnes was scheduled to appear at twenty-five past eleven. The *New York Times* was just being delivered into the hotel lobby. He caught the headline: JACK AND JILL KILLERS FEARED IN NEW YORK AS PRESIDENT VISITS. He was impressed. Even the *Times* was on top of things.

Then Jack saw Jill. Jill was right on time in the lobby. *Always on time.* She was at the Peninsula according to plan. *Always according to plan.*

She had on a silver-and-blue jogging suit, but she didn't look as if she'd raised a sweat coming up from the Waldorf. He wondered if she had run or walked. Or maybe even caught a Yellow Cab.

He didn't acknowledge her in any way. He stepped into a waiting elevator and took it to his floor. Sara would take the next elevator.

He let himself into his room and waited for her. A single knock on the door. She was on schedule. Less than sixty seconds behind him.

"I look terrible," she said. Sara's first words. It was so typical of her self-effacing tone, her view of herself, her vulnerability. *Sara the poor gimp.*

"No, you don't," he reassured her. "You look beautiful, because you *are* beautiful." She didn't look her best, though. She was showing the terrible strain of these last hours. Her face was a mask of worry and doubt, too much makeup and mascara and bright red lipstick. *D day.* She'd sprayed her blond hair, and it looked brittle.

"The Waldorf is hopping already," she reported to him. "They think an assassination attempt definitely will be made today. They're ready for it, at least they think they are. Five thousand regular New York police, plus the Secret Service, the FBI. They have an army on hand."

"Let them think they're ready," Jack said. "We'll see soon enough, won't we? Now come here, you," he smiled. "You don't look terrible at all. Never happen. You look ravishing, Sara. May I ravage you?"

"Now?" Sara weakly protested. It was a whisper. So tiny and vulnerable and unsure. But she couldn't resist his strong, reassuring embrace. She never had been able to, and that was part of the plan as well. Everything had been anticipated, which was why they couldn't fail.

He slid out of his running shirt, exposing a glistening-wet chest. All the tufts of his hair were damp with sweat. He pressed up against Sara. She arched her body hard against him. Their pulses were racing. *Jack and Jill. In New York. So close to the end.*

He could feel her heartbeat quickening, like a small hunted animal's. She couldn't help it. She was so scared now, legitimately so.

"Please tell me that we'll see each other again, even if we won't. Tell me it isn't over after today, Sam."

"It won't be over, Monkey Face. I'm as frightened as you are right now. To feel this way is normal, and sane. You're very sane. We both are."

"In a few hours we'll be on our way out of New York. All of this Jack and Jill will be behind us," she whispered. "Oh, I do love you, Sam. I love you so much that it's scary."

It was scary. More than Sara could possibly know. More than anybody ought to know, *or ever would.* History wasn't for the general public — it never had been.

Slowly and carefully, he slid a Ruger from the rear waistband of his sweatpants. His hands were sweaty. He was holding his breath now. He placed the gun against Sara's head and fired at a slightly downward angle into her temple. Just one shot.

A professional execution.

Without passion.

Almost without passion.

The Ruger was silenced. The noise in the hotel room was no more than a tiny, insignificant spit. The harsh impact of the 9mm bullet took her out of his arms. He shivered involuntarily as he looked down on the lifeless body on the hotel rug.

"Now it's over," he said. "The pain of your life is over, all the bitterness and hurt. I'm sorry, Monkey Face."

He put the final note in Jill's right hand. Then he squeezed her fist so that the note crumpled naturally. He held Sara's hand for the last time.

And Jill came tumbling after. He thought of the words in the children's rhyme.

But Jack would not fall down.

The day of ultimate madness had begun.

Jack and Jill had finally begun.

PART VI

NOBODY IS SAFE
ANYMORE — NOBODY

Chapter 87

THE THICK DOCUMENT in my hands was entitled *Visit of the President of the United States. New York City, December 16 and 17*. It ran to eighty-nine pages and included virtually every moment from when the President would step off *Air Force One* at La Guardia until he reboarded at approximately two in the afternoon and traveled back to Washington.

Included among the pages were sketches, literally of everywhere the President would be: La Guardia Airport, the Waldorf, the Felt Forum inside Madison Square Garden, the motorcade routes, alternate routes.

The Secret Service document stated:

10:55 A.M. The President and Mrs. Byrnes board motorcade

Note: The President and Mrs. Byrnes proceed through a cordon of NYPD officers at the Waldorf-Astoria Hotel
11:00 A.M. Motorcade departs Waldorf via route (code C) to Madison Square Garden, the Felt Forum

Closed arrival.

No press pool coverage.

I occupied my mind with the puzzle of Jack and Jill as the time approached for the President to leave the Waldorf and then travel downtown with the motorcade of limousines, police radio cars, and motorcycles. For the past three days, the FBI, Secret Service, and New York police had been cooperating on a massive plan to try and capture Jack and Jill if they actually came to Madison Square Garden. Nearly a thousand plainclothes agents and detectives would be inside for the President's speech. We all had doubts that it would be enough protection.

A disturbing mania had been running through my head all morning: *No one ever stops an assassin's bullet. No one stops a bullet except the victim.*

What would Jack and Jill do? How would it go down? I believed they would be at Madison Square Garden. I suspected that they planned to do the job up close. And somehow, they planned to escape.

The President and Mrs. Byrnes were escorted to their car at precisely five minutes to eleven. A phalanx of a dozen Secret Service agents shadowed them from the tower suite to an armor-plated limousine waiting in the hotel's underground garage.

I walked closely behind the main escort group. My role here wasn't to physically protect the President. I had already told Jay Grayer how I believed the attempt would be made. *It would be close in. It would be showy. But they would have a plan to escape.*

There had already been a change in plans that morning. *No cordon of high-ranking policemen at the hotel's rear entrance. No photo opportunities.* The President had been convinced not to go through the open Waldorf lobby a second time.

I watched as Mrs. Byrnes and the President walked into the limousine for the two-mile ride. The two of them held hands. It was a touching moment to witness. It fit with everything I knew about Thomas and Sally Byrnes.

No regrets.

The motorcade began to move right on time. It was what the Secret Service called "the formal package motorcade." There were twenty-eight cars. Six held counterassault teams. One car, "Intelligence," held computers to keep contact with surveillance on known threats to the President. I wondered if Jack and Jill had the schedule, even the number of cars.

The motorcade's limos and town cars rode at almost perpendicular angles out of the steep hotel garage. Manhole covers clattered loudly under our tires. The route to the auditorium began on Park Avenue, then jogged west along Forty-seventh Street to Fifth.

I rode with Don Hamerman, two cars behind the President. Even Hamerman was subdued and distant that morning. Nothing had happened yet. Could Jack and Jill possibly have changed their plan? Was this part of covering their trail? Would they surface when we began to doubt that they would? Would they surprise me and attack the motorcade?

I watched everything out the car window. The morning was an eerie, out-of-body experience. The people lining the street were enthusiastic, clapping and cheering as the motorcade passed by. That was one reason why President Byrnes had decided he couldn't hide in the White House any longer. The people, even New Yorkers, wanted a piece of him. He was a good president so far, a popular one, a courageous one, too.

Who wanted to kill Thomas Byrnes, and why? There were so many potential enemies, but I kept returning to the President's own list. Senator Glass, Vice President Mahoney, a few reactionaries in Congress, powerful men connected to Wall Street. He had said that he was trying to change the system, and the system fiercely resented change.

The system fiercely resented change!

Police sirens wailed and seemed to be everywhere around us. It was a screaming wall of noise that was just right for the occasion. My eyes drifted back and forth between the cheering crowds and the quickly moving line of cars, the presidential motorcade.

I was a part of it, and yet I also felt disconnected. I couldn't help thinking of Dallas, John Kennedy, Robert Kennedy, and Dr. King. The past tragedies of our country. Our sorrowful history. I couldn't take my eyes off Stagecoach.

It struck me as almost impossible, as unthinkable, that two of the three major assassinations remained mysterious and unsolved in most people's minds. Two of the three major murder cases of our century had never been satisfactorily cleared.

The VIP garage underneath Madison Square Garden was a concrete bunker, which was painted bright white. There must have been a hundred Secret Service and New York police gathered there to meet us. The Secret Service agents all wore earphones that plugged them into the Service's cellular net.

I watched Thomas and Sally Byrnes slowly get out of their armored car. I watched the President's eyes. He seemed steady and confident and focused. Maybe he knew exactly what he was doing; maybe his way was the only way for this to go.

I was less than a dozen feet away from the President and his wife. Every second they were out in the open seemed an eternity. There were too many people there in the parking garage. *Any of them could be a killer.*

The President and Sally Byrnes were smiling, talking smoothly and easily to important well-wishers from New York. They were both very skilled at this. They understood the tremendously important ceremonial role of the office. The symbolism and the absolute power. That was why they were here. I very much liked their sense of duty and responsibility. Nana was wrong about them. I was convinced they were decent people trying to do their best. I understood how difficult their jobs were. I hadn't realized this before I came to the White House.

Nothing must happen to President Byrnes or Sally Byrnes, I thought — as if an act of will could stop an assassin's bullet, stop terrible things from happening there in the garage or upstairs in the packed Felt Forum.

Any one of these people could be Jack or Jill, I kept thinking as I watched the crowd.

Get the President and his wife out of here. Do it now! Let's go, let's go.

The Kennedy Center in D.C.! The shooting of the law student, Charlotte Kinsey, in a public place, just like this! My mind kept going back to that particular killing.

Something had happened there, something revealing about Jack and Jill. The pattern had been broken! What was the *real* pattern?

We began to walk upstairs to the jam-packed auditorium.

If Jack and Jill are willing to die, they can succeed here. Easily!

And yet it seemed to me that they planned to get away with this. That was the one pattern of theirs that was consistent. I didn't see how that could happen in the middle of Madison Square Garden — not if they chose to attack here.

The real Jack and Jill — the President and the First Lady of the United States — had arrived. On time.

Chapter 88

A DROP OF SWEAT slowly rolled off the tip of my nose.

A tractor-trailer was sitting on my chest.

The thunderous noise coming from inside the concrete-and-steel auditorium added to the escalating confusion and chaos. It was decibels beyond deafening once we were inside. Nearly ten thousand people had filled the auditorium by the time we arrived.

I moved toward the main auditorium stage with the rest of the security entourage. Secret Service agents, FBI, U.S. marshals, and New York police were posted everywhere around the President. I searched everywhere for Kevin Hawkins. Hopefully, at his side, Jill.

President Byrnes never let his smile or his step falter as he entered the auditorium. I remembered his words: "*A threat by a couple of kooks can't be permitted to disrupt the government of the United States. We can't allow that to happen.*"

It was warm in the building, but I was in a cold sweat — as cold as the winds blowing off the Hudson River. We were less than thirty yards from the massive stage that was filled with celebrities and well-known politicians, including both the governor and the city's popular mayor.

Cameras flashed blinding light everywhere, from every imaginable angle. A whine of feedback lashed out from one of the stage microphones. I adjusted a five-pointed star on the left lapel of my suit jacket. The star was color-coded for the day. It identified me as part of the Secret Service team. The day's color was green. For hope?

Jack and Jill had kept all their promises so far. They could have found a way to get weapons inside. There were at least a thousand handguns, but also rifles and shotguns inside the huge amphitheater. The police and other security guards had them.

Any one of them could be Jack or Jill.

Any one of them certainly could be Kevin Hawkins.

Don Hamerman was at my side, but it was too loud for us to talk in anything approaching normal tones. Occasionally, we leaned close and shouted into each other's ear.

Even then, it was difficult to hear more than an isolated word or phrase.

"He's taking too long to walk to the stage!" Hamerman said. I *think* that's what he said.

"I know it. Tell me about it," I shouted back.

"Watch the crowd movement," he yelled at me. "They'll stampede if they see a gun pulled. President's spending too much time out in the crowd. Is he taunting the killers? What does he think that he has to prove?"

The chief of staff was right, of course. The President seemed to be daring Jack and Jill. Still, we might get lucky with the trap inside the crowded hall.

Suddenly, the crowd did start to stampede! The crowd began to part.

"Kill the son of a bitch! Kill him!" I heard the shouts a row or two ahead. I moved quickly, pushing, clawing my way forward in a hurry

"Watch it, you bastard!" a woman turned and yelled in my face.

"Kill him now!" I heard up ahead.

"Let me through!" I shouted as loud as I could.

The man who was causing the scene up ahead had shoulder-length blond hair. He wore a baggy black parka with a black backpack attached.

I grabbed him at the same time as someone else from the other side of the aisle. We brought the blond man down hard and fast. His skull crunched against the cement floor.

"New York police!" the other guy holding the blond man yelled.

"D.C. police, White House detail," I yelled back. I was already patting down the suspect. The New York cop had his gun in the suspect's face.

I didn't recognize the blond as Kevin Hawkins, but there was no way to tell for sure, and absolutely no way for us to take a chance on him. *We had to take him down. There was no choice about that.*

"Kill the bastard! Kill the President!" the blond man continued to scream.

He was absolutely crazy, everything was, not just this asshole on the floor.

"You hurt me!" he started to yell at me and the New York cop. "You hurt my head!"

Madman? I wondered.

Copycat?

Diversion?

Chapter 89

KAMIKAZE ATTACK! It was coming any second now. A killer willing to commit suicide. That was why this couldn't be stopped. It was also why President Byrnes was the walking dead.

Kevin Hawkins hadn't experienced any problems getting into a prime position in the noisy, crowded auditorium. He had used his imagination and visual skills to create an unusual identity for himself.

Hawkins was now a tall brunette woman dressed in a dark blue pantsuit. He wasn't a very good-looking woman, he had to admit, but he was much less likely to draw attention because of it.

Hawkins also had a Federal Bureau of Investigation ID, which was authentic down to the stamp and thickness of the paper. It identified him as Lynda Cole, a special agent from New York. The photojournalist stood at Lynda Cole's seat in the sixth row and calmly observed the crowd.

Snapshot.

Snapshot.

He took several mind photos, one after the other, mostly of his competition. The FBI, the Secret Service, the NYPD. Actually, he didn't believe that he had any real competition.

Kamikaze. Who could stop that? No one could. Maybe God could. And maybe not even God.

He was impressed by the sheer numbers of the opposition, though. They were serious about trying to derail Jack and Jill this morning. And who knew? Maybe they would succeed with their superior numbers and firepower. Stranger things had happened.

Hawkins just didn't believe that they could. Their last real chance had been *before* he'd gotten inside the building — not now. The photojournalist versus the FBI, the Secret Service, the U.S. marshals, and the NYPD. That seemed reasonable enough to him. It seemed like a pretty fair game.

Their elaborate preparations struck him as being ironic. He waited for the target to appear. *Their game plan was an essential part of* his. Everything they were doing now, every step, had been anticipated and was necessary for *kamikaze* to work.

"She's a Grand Old Flag" began to play from the loudspeakers, and Hawkins clapped along with the others. He was a patriot, after all. No one might believe it after today, but he knew that it was so.

Kevin Hawkins was one of the last true patriots.

Chapter 90

NO ONE stops an assassin's bullet.

There was a fire burning inside my chest. I was moving quickly through the crowd — searching for Kevin Hawkins everywhere.

Every nerve in my body was stretched tight and burning. My right hand rested on the hard butt of my Glock. I kept thinking that any one of these people could be Jack or Jill. The handgun seemed insubstantial in the huge, noisy crowd.

I had made it to the second row, just to the right of the ten- to twelve-foot-high stage. The light in the hall seemed to be fading, but maybe it was the light inside my head. The light inside my soul?

The President was just stepping onto the gray metal stairs. He clasped the hand of a well-wisher. The President patted the shoulder of another. He seemed to have forced the idea of danger out of his mind.

Sally Byrnes climbed the stairs in front of her husband. I could see her features clearly. I held the thought that maybe Jack and Jill could, too. Secret Service agents seemed to take up all the available space around the stage.

I was there when it finally happened. *I was so close to President Byrnes.*

Jack and Jill struck with a terrible vengeance.

A bomb went off. The loudest imaginable clap of thunder struck near the stage — maybe even on the stage itself. The explosion was completely unexpected by the bodyguards surrounding the President. It detonated *inside* the defense perimeter.

Chaos! A bomb instead of gunfire! Even though the auditorium had been swept for bombs just that morning, I was thinking as I rushed forward. I noticed that my hand was bleeding — probably from the earlier tussle with the nutcase, but maybe from the bomb.

The worst imaginable sequence of actions began to unfold, and in very fast motion. Pistols and riot-control shotguns were pulled out everywhere in the crowd. No one seemed to know where the bomb had hit yet, or how, or the actual calculations of damage done. *Or what purpose the explosion was meant to serve?*

Everyone dropped to the floor in the first twenty rows and up on the stage.

Thick black smoke billowed toward the ceiling, the glass roof, and overhanging steel girders.

The air smelled like human hair burning. People were screaming everywhere. I couldn't tell how many were hurt. I couldn't see the President anymore.

The bomb had detonated close to the stage. Very close to where President Byrnes had been standing, shaking hands and chatting, just a few seconds before. The ringing was still vibrating in my ears.

I frantically pushed my way toward the stage. There was no way to tell how many people had been injured, or maybe even killed, by the blast. I still couldn't locate the President or Mrs. Byrnes because of the smoke and the bodies suddenly in frenzied motion. TV cameramen were wading in toward the disaster scene.

I finally spotted a cluster of Secret Service agents huddled tightly around the President. They had him up on his feet. Thomas Byrnes was alive; he was safe. The agents were starting to move him out of harm's way. The Secret Service bodyguards acted as a human shield for the President, who didn't appear to be hurt.

I had my Glock out, pointed up at the rafters for safety. I shouted, "Police!"

Several other Secret Service agents and NYPD detectives were doing the same thing. We were identifying ourselves to one another. Trying not to get shot, trying not to shoot anybody else during the terrifying confusion. Several people in the crowd were crying hysterically.

I kept pushing and pulling my way toward the southwest side exit that the Secret Service had used to bring the President in. The escape route had been established beforehand.

Beyond the glowing red EXIT sign, a long concrete tunnel led to a special visitors' parking area on the river side of the building. Bulletproof, armor-plated cars were waiting there. *What else might be waiting?* I wondered. A voice in my head shouted for attention as I moved forward as fast as I could. *Jack and Jill have always been a step ahead of us. They missed him! Why did they miss?*

They don't make mistakes.

I was less than a dozen yards from the President and his Secret Service guards when it hit me, when finally I understood what no one else did yet.

"*Change the route out!*" I yelled at the top of my voice. "*Change the escape route!*"

Chapter 91

NO ONE heard me shouting. I could barely hear my own voice in the melee. There was too much noise and confusion inside Madison Square Garden.

I pushed ahead anyway, desperately following the phalanx that looked like the rabble at a prizefight from my vantage point. The smoke from the bomb had created a kind of strobe-light effect.

"Change the escape route! Change the escape route!" I shouted over and over.

We finally entered the whitewashed concrete tunnel. Every sound echoed bizarrely off the walls. I was right behind the last of the Secret Service agents.

"*Don't go this way! Stop the President!*" I continued to yell in vain.

The tunnel was full of late-arriving special guests and even more security guards. We were pushing forward against a strong tide coming the other way.

It was too late to change the route now. I pushed and shoved my way closer and closer to President and Mrs. Byrnes. I desperately searched the crowd for the face of Kevin Hawkins. There was still a chance to stop him.

Every face I encountered registered shock. The eyes I saw were wide with fear, and they were *searching my face.* Suddenly, there were several *loud pops* in the heart of the tunnel. Gunshots!

Five shots seemed to explode inside the tight phalanx of people around the President. Someone had gotten inside the defense perimeter. My body sagged as if I'd been shot myself.

Five shots. Three quick — then two more.

I couldn't see what had happened up ahead, but suddenly I heard the eeriest sound. It was a high-pitched wail, a keening.

Five shots!

Three — then two more.

The keening sound was coming from where I had last seen fleeting glimpses of President Byrnes, where the shots had exploded just a few seconds before.

I shoved my body, all my weight, against the crowd and forced myself toward the epicenter of the madness.

It felt as if I were trying to swim out of quicksand, to pull myself free. It was almost impossible to walk, to push, to shove.

Five shots. What had happened up ahead?

Then I could see. I saw everything at once.

My mouth felt incredibly dry. My eyes were watering. The bunkerlike tunnel had become strangely quiet. President Thomas Byrnes was down on the gray cement floor. A lot of blood was flowing in rivulets, spreading down his white shirt. Bright red blood drained from the right side of his face, or maybe the wound was high in his neck. I couldn't tell from where I was.

Gunshots. Execution-style.

A professional hit.

Jack and Jill, those bastards!

It was their pattern, or close to it.

I waded forward, roughly, shoving people out of my way. I saw Don Hamerman, Jay Grayer, and then Sally Byrnes. Everything seemed to be happening in slow motion.

Sally Byrnes was trying to get to her husband. The First Lady didn't appear to be hurt. Still, I wondered if she was a target, too. Maybe Jill's target? Secret Service agents were holding Mrs. Byrnes back, trying to protect her. They wanted to keep her away from the bloodshed, from her husband, from any possible danger.

I saw a second body then. The shock was like a low hard punch to my stomach. No one could have anticipated this terrible scene.

A woman was down near the President. She'd been shot in her right eye socket. There was a second wound in her throat. She appeared to be dead. A semiautomatic lay near her sprawled body.

The assassin?

Jill?

Who else could it possibly be?

My eyes were drawn back to the motionless figure of Thomas Byrnes. I was afraid that he was already dead. I couldn't be sure, but I believed he'd been hit at least three times. I saw Sally Byrnes finally reach her husband's body. She was weeping uncontrollably, and she wasn't the only one.

Chapter 92

JACK SAT STILL and calmly watched the maze of bumper-to-bumper cars and tractor-trailers stalled on West Street near the entrance to New York's Holland Tunnel.

He could hear radios blaring on each side of his black Jeep. He observed the troubled and confused faces inside the cars. A middle-aged woman in a forest-green Lexus was in tears. A thousand sirens screamed like banshees on the loose in midtown.

Jack and Jill came to The Hill. Now everyone knew why, or at least they thought they did.

Now everyone understood the seriousness of the game.

Turn off your news reports, he wanted to tell all these well-meaning people approaching the tunnel out of New York. *What's happened has nothing to do with any of you. It really and truly doesn't. You'll never know the truth. No one ever will. You can't handle the truth, anyway. You wouldn't understand if I stopped and explained it to you right here.*

He tried not to think about Sara Rosen as he finally rode into the long, claustrophobic tunnel that snaked beneath the Hudson.

Beyond the tunnel, he drove south on the New Jersey Turnpike, then on I-95 into Delaware and points farther south.

Sara was the past, and the past didn't matter. The past didn't exist, except as a lesson for the future. Sara was gone. He did think about poor Sara as he ate at the Country Cupboard near the Talleyville exit on the turnpike. It was important to grieve. For Jill, not for President Byrnes. She was worth a dozen Thomas Byrneses. She had done a good job, a nearly perfect job, even if she had been used right from the start. And Sara Rosen had definitely been used. She had been his eyes and ears inside the White House. She had been his mistress. Poor Monkey Face.

As he approached Washington about seven that night, he made a vow: he wouldn't sentimentalize about Sara again. He knew he could do that. He could control his own thoughts. He was better than Kevin Hawkins, who had been a very good soldier indeed.

He had been Jack.

But he was no longer Jack.

Jack no longer existed.

He was no longer Sam Harrison, either. Sam Harrison had been a facade, a necessary safeguard, a part of the complex plan. *Sam Harrison no longer existed.*

Now his life could be simple and mostly good again. He was almost home. He had completed his Mission: Impossible, and it was a success. Everything had gone almost perfectly.

Then he *was* home, pulling into the familiar rounded driveway that was filled with colorful seashells and tiny pebbles and a few children's toys.

He saw his little girl come running out of the house, her blond hair streaming. He saw his wife close behind her, also running. Tears rolled down her cheeks and down his own. He wasn't afraid to cry. He wasn't afraid of anything anymore.

Jesus God, mercy, the war was finally ended. The enemy, the evil one, was dead. The good guys had won, and the most precious way of life on earth was safe for a little while longer—for the lives of his children, anyway.

No one would ever know how and why it had happened, or who was really responsible.

Just as it had been with JFK in Dallas.

And RFK in Los Angeles.

And Watergate and Whitewater and most every other significant event in our recent history. In truth, our history was *not knowing*; it was being carefully shielded from the truth. That was the American way.

"I love you so much," his wife whispered breathlessly against the side of his face. "You are my hero. You did such a good, brave thing."

He believed it, too. He knew it deep within his heart.

He wasn't Jack anymore. Jack no longer existed.

Chapter 93

IT WASN'T OVER!

At a little past noon, the Secret Service received news from the NYPD of another homicide. They had strong reason to believe it was related to the shooting of President Byrnes.

Jay Grayer and I rushed to the Peninsula Hotel, which is just off Fifth Avenue in midtown. We were completely numb from the horror of the morning and still couldn't believe the President had been shot. Even so, we had all the details of the latest murder. A chambermaid at the hotel had discovered a body in a suite on the twelfth floor. There was also a poem from Jack and Jill in the room. *A final poem?*

"What is the NYPD saying?" I asked Jay during the ride uptown. "What are the details?"

"According to the initial report, the dead woman might be Jill. Jill could have been murdered — or maybe she committed suicide. They're reasonably certain the note is authentic."

The mysteries inside horrific mysteries continued. Was this death part of the Jack and Jill scheme, too? I thought that probably it was, and that there were even more layers to unravel — layers upon layers — before getting to the core of the horror.

Grayer and I emerged from a gold-plated elevator onto the crime-scene floor. New York police were everywhere. I saw emergency medics, SWAT team members in helmets with Plexiglas face masks, uniforms, homicide detectives. The scene was instant bedlam. I was worried about evidence contamination, leaks to the press.

"The President?" one of the New York detectives asked us as we arrived. "Any word? Any hope?"

"He's still hanging in there. Sure, there's hope," Jay Grayer said; then we moved on, away from the cluster of detectives.

At least a dozen New York police and FBI agents were crowded into the hotel suite. The ominous sounds of police sirens rose from the streets below. Church bells pealed loudly, probably at nearby St. Patrick's Cathedral, just south on Fifth Avenue.

A blond woman's body lay on the plush gray carpet next to an unmade double bed. Her face, neck, and chest were covered with blood. She was wearing a silver-and-blue jogging suit.

A pair of wire-rim eyeglasses were on the rug near her Nike sneakers.

She had been shot execution-style — as the early victims of Jack and Jill had been.

One shot, close to the head.

Very professional. Very cold.

No passion.

"Was she ever on any of our suspect lists?" I asked Grayer. We knew that the dead woman's name was Sara Rosen. She had been cleared as part of the White House staff. She'd escaped detection during *two* "thorough" investigations of the staff, and that was the scariest piece of evidence yet.

"Not that we know of. She was something of a fixture at the White House communications office. Everybody liked her efficiency, her professionalism. She was *trusted*. Jesus, what a mess. What a disaster. She was trusted, Alex."

Part of the left side of her face was gone, ripped away as if by an animal. Jill looked as if she had been caught by surprise. Her eyebrows were arched. There was no fear in her eyes.

She had trusted her killer. Was it Jack who had pulled the trigger? I noticed the smudging around the wound, the gray ring. It was a close-range discharge. It must have been Jack. *Professional. No passion. Another execution.*

But is this really Jill? I wondered as I bent over the body. The contract killer Kevin Hawkins had died at St. Vincent's Hospital downtown. We knew that Hawkins had disguised himself as a female FBI agent to get into Madison Square Garden. He had used the concussion bomb to get his target where he wanted, when he wanted. He'd been waiting in the exit tunnel, dressed as a woman. It had worked. What was Kevin Hawkins's relationship to this woman? What in hell was going on?

"He left a poem. Somebody did. Looks like the others," Jay Grayer said to me. The note was in a plastic evidence bag. He handed it to me. "The last will and testament of Jack and Jill," he said.

"The perfect assassination," I muttered, more to myself than to Grayer. "Jack and Jill both dead in New York. Case closed, right?"

The Secret Service agent stared at me and then slowly shook his head. "This case will never be closed. Not in our lifetime, anyway."

"I was just being ironic," I said.

I read the final note.

> Jack and Jill came to The Hill
> Where Jill did what she must.
> Her reason drove her
> The game is over
> Though dead Jill's cause was just.

"Fuck you, Jill," I whispered over the dead body. "I hope you burn in hell for what you've done today. I hope there's a hell just for you and Jack."

Chapter 94

NOWHERE was the news of the shooting taken any harder than in Washington. Thomas Byrnes was loved and he was hated, but he was one of the city's own, *especially now*.

Christine Johnson was in shock, as were her closest friends and most everyone that she knew. The teachers at Sojourner Truth and the children were completely destroyed by what had happened to the President in New York City. It was so horrifying and stark, but also so unbearably sad and unreal.

Because of the shooting, all D.C. schools had canceled classes for the afternoon. She had been watching the nightmarish TV coverage of the assassination attempt from the first moment she got home from school. She still couldn't believe what had happened. No one could believe it. The President was still alive. No other bulletins were being released.

Christine didn't know whether Alex Cross had been at Madison Square Garden, but she imagined that he had been there. She worried about Alex, too. She liked the detective's sincerity and his inner strength, but especially his compassion and his vulnerability. She liked the way he looked, talked, acted. She also liked the way Alex was bringing up his son, Damon. It made her want children even more herself. She and George had to talk about that. She and George had to talk.

He arrived home before seven that night, which was an hour or two early for him. George Johnson was a hard worker in his corporate law job. He was thirty-seven years old and had a smooth, attractive baby face. He was a good man, although way too self-centered and, truthfully, a little bit of a buppie at times.

Christine loved him, though; she accepted the good and the bad. She was thinking that as she fiercely hugged him at the front door. There was no doubt of it in her mind. She and George had met at Howard University and been together ever since. That was the way she believed it ought to be, and would be as far as she was concerned.

"People are still out there crying in the streets," George said. After the hug, he shucked off his wool Brooks Brothers suit jacket and loosened his tie, but he didn't go upstairs to change. He was breaking all his usual patterns tonight. Well, good for George.

"I didn't vote for President Byrnes, but this has really gotten to me anyway, Chris. What a damn shame." There were tears in his eyes, and that started her up again, too.

George usually kept his feelings to himself, everything all bottled up. Christine was touched by her husband's emotion. She was touched a great deal.

"I've cried a couple of times," she confided to George. "You know me. I did vote for the President, but that's not it. It just seems as though we're losing respect for every institution, everything permanent. We're losing respect for human life at a very fast rate. I even see it in the eyes of six-year-old schoolchildren. I see it every day at the Truth School."

George Johnson held his wife again, held her tight. At five eleven, he was exactly her height. Christine rested her head softly against the side of his. She smelled of light citrus fragrance. She'd worn it to school. He loved her so much. She was like no other woman, no other person he'd ever met. He felt incredibly lucky to have her, to be loved by her, to hold her like this.

"Do you know what I'm saying?" she asked, wanting to talk with George tonight, not willing to let him disappear on her, as he so often did.

"Sure I do," he said. "Everybody feels it, Chrissie. Nobody knows how to begin to make it stop, though."

"I'll fix us something to eat. We can watch the dregs on CNN," she finally said. "Part of me doesn't want to watch the news, but part of me has to watch this."

"I'll help with the grub," George offered, which was rare. She wished that he could be like this more often and that it didn't take a national tragedy to get him in touch with his emotions. Well, a lot of men were like that, she knew. There were worse things in a marriage.

They made a vegetarian gumbo together and opened a bottle of Chardonnay. They had barely finished supper in front of the TV when the front doorbell rang. It was a little before nine, and they weren't expecting anyone, but sometimes neighbors dropped in.

CNN was covering the scene at New York University Hospital, where the President had been rushed after the shooting. Alex Cross had appeared with various other officers who had been at the scene of the shooting, but he wouldn't say much to the media. Alex looked upset, spent, but also, well — noble. Christine didn't mention to George that she knew him. She wondered why. She hadn't told George about Alex's visit to their house late one night. He had slept right through it; but that was George.

Before he could get up off the couch, the doorbell rang a second time. Then, a third ring. Whoever it was wouldn't go away.

"I'll get it, Chrissie," he said. "Don't know who in hell that could be, this time of night. Do you?"

"I don't, either."

"All right, already," he snapped. Christine found herself smiling. George the Impatient was back.

"I'm coming for Christmas' sake. I'm coming, I'm coming.

Hold your water, I'm *coming*," he said as he hobbled toward the door in his stockinged feet.

He peered through the peephole, then turned to look at Christine with a questioning scowl on his face.

"It's some white kid."

Chapter 95

DANNY BOUDREAUX stood on the shiny, white-painted porch of the schoolteacher's house. He was dressed in an oversized army-green rain poncho that made him look bigger than he actually was, somewhat more impressive. The Sojourner Truth School killer in the flesh! He was in his glory now. But even in his megahyper mood, he sensed that something was wrong with him now.

He didn't feel good, and he was getting sad — kind of depressed as hell, actually. The machine was breaking down. The doctors couldn't figure whether he was a bipolar disorder or conduct disorder. If they couldn't, how the hell was he supposed to? So what if he was a little impulsive, had huge mood swings, was a social misfit? The fuse was lit. He was ready to blow. Like, who cared?

He had stopped his dosages of Depakote. Just say no, right? He was humming the "Mmm mm mm" song over and over. Crash Test Dummies. Sad, angry music that just wouldn't stop playing in his head like MTV Muzak.

His "mad button" seemed to be stuck — *permanently.*

He was mad at Jack and Jill. Real mad at Alex Cross. Mad at the principal of the Truth School. Mad at just about everybody on the planet. He was even mad at himself now. He was such a goddamn screwup. Always had been, always would be.

I'm a loser, baby.

So why don't you kill me?

He snapped back to semireality when a black fucker wearing a blue pinstriped shirt, suit trousers, and mellow-yellow suspenders answered the door. Hey, welcome to the Cyburbs!

At first, Danny Boudreaux didn't understand who the hell the round-faced black dude was. He'd been expecting the big-deal school principal Mrs. Johnson, or maybe even Alex Cross, if Cross hadn't gone to New York. He had seen Cross and the principal together on three different occasions. He guessed they were getting it on.

He didn't know why that made him mad, but it did. Cross was just like his goddamn father, his real father. Another fuck-up cop who had deserted him, who didn't think he was worth dogshit. And now Cross was humping this teacher on the side.

Wait, wait, hold on, Danny Boudreaux suddenly got something clear. A flash. *This self-righteous Kunta Kinte dude has to be her husband, right? Of course he was.*

"Yes? Can I help you with something?" George Johnson asked the strange-looking and disheveled young man on the porch. He didn't know the paper-delivery boy in the neighborhood, but maybe this was he. For some strange reason, the white boy reminded him of a disturbing movie called *Kids* that he'd watched with Christine. The boy looked as if he had some trouble in his life right now.

In Danny Boudreaux's humble opinion, the black guy seemed real unfriendly and uppity as hell. Especially for the nobody husband of some nobody schoolteacher. That pissed him off even more. Made him see about twelve different shades of red. Put him over the edge.

He felt one of the worst rages coming on. *Hurricane Daniel was about to strike in Mitchellville.*

"Noooooo!" he nearly yelled at the man. "You can't even help *yourself*. You sure as shit can't help me!"

Danny Boudreaux suddenly yanked out his semiautomatic. George Johnson looked at the gun in disbelief. He stepped back quickly from the door. He threw up both his arms in self-defense.

Without any hesitation, Boudreaux fired twice. "Take that, you silly black rabbit!" he yelled, letting the voices come as they may. The two bullets hit George Johnson in the chest.

He flew back through the open door as if he'd been struck with a sledgehammer. He bounced once off the cream marble floor.

The cat was DOA for sure. Blood was surging from the two holes in his chest.

The Sojourner Truth School killer then walked right into the teacher's house. He stepped over the fallen body as if it were worth nothing. He was feeling *nothing*.

"I'll just go ahead in, thanks," he said to the dead man on the floor. "You've been most helpful."

Christine Johnson had risen from the couch in the living room when she heard the shots. He had forgotten how goddamn tall she was. Danny Boudreaux could see her from the front hallway. She could see him and her husband's body as well.

She didn't look so almighty-in-charge anymore. He had knocked her ass down a peg real quick. She deserved it, too. She'd hurt his feelings the first time they met: She probably didn't even remember the incident.

"Remember me?" he called to her. "Remember hassling me, bitch? At the Truth School? You remember me, don't you?"

"Oh, my God. Oh, George. Oh, God, George," she moaned the words. A dry sob was shaking her body. She looked as if she might collapse. He saw that fucking Jack and Jill was on the tube. Goddammit. They were always trying to one-up him. Even here, even now!

Danny Boudreaux could tell that the schoolteacher wanted to run real bad. There was nowhere to go, though. Not unless she went right through the picture window and out onto her lawn.

She had her hand up to her mouth. Her hand looked as if it were stuck there with Velcro. Probably in shock.

Lady, who isn't these days?

"Don't yell anymore," he warned her in a high-pitched scream of his own. "Don't scream again or I'll shoot you, too. I can and I will. I'll shoot you dead as the doorman."

He closed in on her now. He kept the Smith & Wesson pointed out in front of him. He wanted her to see that he was very comfortable with the weapon, very expert with firearms — which he was, thanks to the Teddy Roosevelt School.

His hand was shaking some, but so what? He wouldn't miss her at this distance.

"Hi there, Mrs. Johnson," he said and gave her his best spooky-guy grin. "I'm the one who killed Shanelle Green and Vernon Wheatley. Everybody's been looking all over for me. Well, I guess *you* found me," he told her. "Congratulations, babe. Nice work."

Danny Boudreaux was crying now, and he couldn't remember why he was so sad. All he knew for sure was that he was furiously angry. With everybody. Everybody had fucked up real bad this time. This was about the worst so far.

No happy, happy. No joy, joy.

"I'm the Truth School killer," he repeated. "You believe that? You got it? It's a true tale. Tale of heartbreak and woe. Don't you even remember me? Am I that forgettable? I sure remember *you*."

Chapter 96

I RUSHED BACK to the Washington, D.C., area that night about eleven o'clock. The Sojourner Truth School killer was rampaging. I had predicted he was going to go off, but being right held no rewards for me. Stopping the explosion might.

Maybe it was no accident that he was blowing the same night as Jack and Jill. He wanted to be better than them, didn't he? He wanted to be important, famous, in the brightest spotlight. *He couldn't bear being Nobody.*

I tried to put my mind somewhere else for the short time I was on the military jet. I was feeling so low, I could have jumped off a dime. I scanned the late papers, which carried front-page stories about President Byrnes and the shooting in New York. The President was in extremely critical condition at New York University Hospital on East Thirty-third Street in Manhattan. Jack and Jill were both reported dead. Doctors at University Hospital didn't know if the President would survive the night.

I was numb, disoriented, overloaded, on the slippery borderline of shock trauma myself. Now it was getting worse. I didn't know for certain if I could handle this, but I hadn't been given a choice.

The killer had demanded to see me. He claimed that I was *his* detective and that he'd been calling my house for the past few days.

A police cruiser was scheduled to meet me at Andrews Air Force Base. From there I'd be taken to nearby Mitchellville, where Danny Boudreaux was holding Christine Johnson hostage. So far, Boudreaux had murdered two small children, a classmate of his named Sumner Moore, and his own foster parents. It was an extraordinary rampage, and the case deserved more resources than it had received from the Metro police.

A police cruiser was waiting at Andrews as promised. Somebody had put together material for me on Daniel Boudreaux. The boy had been under a psychiatrist's care since he was seven. He had been severely depressed. He'd apparently committed bizarre acts of animal torture as early as seven. Daniel Boudreaux's real mother had died during his infancy, and he blamed himself. His real father had committed suicide. The father had been a state trooper in Virginia. *Another cop,* I noted. Probably some kind of transference going on inside the boy's head.

I recognized Summer Street as soon as we branched off the John Hanson Highway. A detective from Prince Georges County sat with me in the backseat of the cruiser. His name was Henry Fornier. He tried to brief me on the hostage situation as best he could under the bizarre circumstances.

"As we understand it, Dr. Cross, George Johnson has been shot, and he may be dead in the house. The boy won't allow the body to be removed or to receive any medical attention," Officer Fornier told me. "He's a nasty bastard, I'll tell you. A real little prick."

"Boudreaux was being treated for his anger, his depression and rage cycles, with Depakote. I'll bet anything that he's off it now," I said. I was thinking out loud, trying to prepare myself for whatever was coming just a few blocks up this peaceful-looking street.

It didn't matter that the Boudreaux boy was thirteen years

old. He had already killed five times. That's what he did: *he killed*. Another monster. A very young, horrifying monster.

I spotted Sampson, who was half a head taller than the other policemen stationed outside the Johnson house. I tried to take in everything. There were scores of police, but also soldiers in riot gear with military camouflage at the scene. Cars and trucks with government license plates were parked all over the street.

I walked right over to Sampson. He knew the things I needed to hear, and he would know how to talk to me. "Hey there, Sugar," he greeted me with a hint of his usual ironic smile. "Glad you could make it to the party."

"Yeah, nice to see you, too," I said.

"Friend of yours wants to see you. Wants to talk the talk with Dr. Cross. You've got the damnedest friends."

"Yeah. I sure do," I said to Sampson. He was one of them. "They're holding back firepower because he's a kid? Is that what's going on so far?"

Sampson nodded. I had it right. "He's just another stone killer, Alex," he said. "You remember that. He's just another killer."

Chapter 97

A THIRTEEN-YEAR-OLD MURDERER.

I began to pay very close attention to the staging area that had been set up around the perimeter of the Johnson house. Even relatively small, local police forces were getting good at this sort of thing. Terror was invading towns with names like Ruby Ridge and Waco, and now, Mitchellville.

A late-model, dark blue van with its back doors open held TV monitors, state-of-the-art sound equipment, phones, a desktop workstation. A techie was crouched near a windblown willow tree listening to the house with a microphone gun. The gun could pick up voices from well over a hundred yards.

Surveillance shots and also assorted photos of the boy were tacked to a board propped against a squad car. A helicopter was spraying high-intensity beams on the rooftops and trees. Here the hostage drama was unfolding as we know and love it.

In suburbia this time.

A thirteen-year-old boy named Daniel Boudreaux.

Just another stone killer.

"Who do they have talking to him?" I asked Sampson as we wandered closer to the house. I spotted a black Lexus parked in the driveway. George Johnson's car? "Who's the negotiator on this?"

"They got Paul Losi down here as soon as they found out about the hostage situation, and how goddamn bad it was."

I nodded and felt a little relief at the choice of a negotiator. "That's good. Losi is tough. He's good under pressure, too. How is the boy communicating from the house?"

"At first, over the phone lines. Then he demanded a megaphone. Threw a real tantrum. Threatened to shoot the teacher and himself on the spot. So the bad boy got his own blowhorn. He uses that now. He and Paul Losi are not exactly what you call 'hitting it off.'"

"How about Christine Johnson? She still okay? What do you hear?"

"Appears to be all right, so far. She's been cool under fire. We think she's holding the bad boy in control somehow, but just barely. She's tough."

That much I knew already. *She's even tougher than you are, Daddy.* I hoped Damon was one hundred percent right. I hoped she was tougher than all of us.

George Pittman wandered up beside Sampson and me while we were talking. The chief of detectives was the last person I wanted to see then, absolutely the last. I still suspected he was the one who had "volunteered" me to the White House. I swallowed any anger I was feeling; swallowed my pride, too.

"FBI has sharpshooters in place," Pittman informed us. "Trouble is, the powers won't let us use them. The little bastard's been out in the open a couple of times."

I stayed even and calm with Pittman. He still had a gun to my head. We both knew it. "Trouble is, the killer is thirteen years old. He's probably suicidal," I said. I was making an educated guess, but I was almost certain it was the right one. He had cornered himself in the Johnson house, then started screaming *come and get me.*

Pittman's face became a dark scowl. His face was tinged with red down to his bull neck. "He thinks the five murders he's committed are funny. Little fucker told the negotiator that already. He laughs about the murders. He's asking for you specifically. Now how do you feel about the sharpshooters?" Pittman came back at me before he walked away.

Sampson shook his head. "Don't even think about going in there to play games with Dennis the Menace," he said.

"I need to understand him better. I have to talk to him to do that," I muttered and looked at the Johnson house. There were plenty of lights on downstairs. None up on the second floor.

"You understand him *too goddamn much* already, though you'd deny it. You understand so much about the crazies, you're going over the edge yourself. You hear me? You understand that?"

I did understand. I had a fair idea of my own strengths and weaknesses. Most of the time, anyway. Maybe not on a night like this one, though.

A voice on a megaphone interrupted us. The Sojourner Truth School killer had decided to speak.

"Hey! Hey, out there! Hey, you dumb bastards! Did you forget something? Remember me?"

I got to hear Danny Boudreaux for the first time. He sounded like a boy. Nasal, high-pitched, ordinary as hell. Thirteen years old.

"You sons of bitches are screwing with my head, aren't you?" he screeched. "I'll answer my own question. Yeah, you are! You're fucking with the wrong falcon."

Paul Losi blew once on his bullhorn. "Hold on. That's really not the case, Danny. You've been in control all the way so far. You know that, Danny. Let's be fair about this."

"Bullshit!" Danny Boudreaux answered back angrily. "That's so much bullshit, it makes me sick to the gills just to hear it. *You* make me sick, Losi. You also make me super pissed-off, you know that, *Losi?*"

"Tell me what the problem is." The negotiator maintained a cool head under fire. "Talk to me, Danny. I want to talk to you. I know you might not believe that, but I do."

"I know you do, asshole. It's your job to keep me on the line. Trouble is, you cheated, you lied, you said you loved me. You *lied!* So now *you're off my team.* Not one more word from you, or I'll murder Mrs. Johnson. It'll be your fault.

"I'll kill her now. I swear to God, I will. Even though she was nice enough to make me a fried egg sandwich before. BANG! . . . BANG! . . . SHE'S DEAD!"

The police were everywhere outside the Johnson house. They began to lower their dark Plexiglas face masks. Riot shields were slowly raised. The forces were getting ready to rush the house. If they did, Christine Johnson would very likely die.

"What is your problem?" the negotiator cautiously asked the boy. "Talk to me. We'll work it out, Danny. We can come to a solution that works for you. What's the problem?"

For a while it was eerily quiet on the front lawn and on the street. I could hear the wind rush through willow and evergreen trees.

Then Danny Boudreaux screamed out.

"What's my problem? What's my problem? You're such a *phony asshole,* is part of my problem. . . . The other part is that *the man* is here. Alex Cross is here, and you didn't tell me. I had to find out on the TV news!

"You have exactly thirty seconds, Detective Cross. Make that *twenty-nine. Twenty-eight.* I can't wait to meet you, sucker. I can't wait for this. *Twenty-seven. Twenty-six. Twenty-five* . . ."

The Sojourner Truth School killer was calling the shots. A thirteen-year-old boy. A command performance.

Chapter 98

"THIS IS ALEX CROSS," I called out to the teenage murderer. I was standing on the outer edge of the Johnson's frostbitten lawn. I didn't need a megaphone for Danny Boudreaux to hear me. *Your detective is here. Everything is going just the way you want it to go.*

"This is Detective Cross," I called out again. "You're right, I'm here. I just arrived, though. I came because you asked for me. We're taking this seriously. Nobody's messing around with you. Nobody would do that."

Not yet, anyway. Give me half a chance, though, and I'll mess with you good. I remembered poor little Shanelle Green. I remembered seven-year-old Vernon Wheatley. I thought about Christine Johnson trapped inside with the young killer who had shot her husband before her eyes. I wanted the chance to mess with Daniel Boudreaux.

Boudreaux suddenly laughed into his megaphone — a high-pitched girlish giggle. Spooky as hell. A few people in the crowd of onlookers and ambulance-chasers laughed along with the boy. Nice to know you have friends out there.

"Well, it's about time, *Detective* Alex Cross. It's so nice that you can fit me into your busy schedule. Mrs. Johnson thinks so, too.

We're here waiting, waiting, waiting for you . . . so c'mon in the house. Let's have a party."

The boy was openly challenging me and my authority. He needed to be the one in charge. I was charting everything in my head, keeping track of his every move, but also the sequence. Paranoid schizophrenic was a possible diagnosis. Bipolar or conduct disorder was a better guess. *I needed to talk to him to find out the rest.*

Danny Boudreaux seemed coherent, anyway. He appeared to be following actions in real time. I wondered if he might be taking his Depakote again.

A voice close behind me said, "Alex, come over here, goddammit. I want to talk to you. Alex, *come here.*"

I turned around and faced the music. Sampson was scowling from ear to ear. "We don't need *another* hostage in there," he said in no uncertain terms. He was angry with me already. His eyes were dark beads, his brow deeply furrowed. "You didn't hear him raving before, through most of last night. The bad boy is real crazy. The boy is crazy as shit, Alex. All he wants to do is kill somebody else."

"I think I'll be all right with him," I said. "He's my type of boy. Gary Soneji, Casanova, Danny Boudreaux. Besides, I don't have a choice."

"You have a choice, Sugar. You just don't have any good sense."

I looked back at the house. Christine Johnson was in there with the killer. If I didn't go in, he'd kill her. He'd said so, and I believed him. What choice did that leave me? Besides, no good deed goes unpunished, right?

Chief Pittman signaled that I had the go-ahead from him. It was up to me. *Doctor-Detective Cross.*

I sucked in a deep breath and began to walk across the wet, springy front lawn to the house. The news photographers took a flurry of flashshots in the few seconds it took me to move to the front door. Suddenly, all the TV cameras were aimed at me.

I was definitely concerned about Danny Boudreaux. He was

incredibly dangerous right now. He'd been on a killing spree. Five indiscriminate murders within the last few weeks. Now he was cornered. Even worse, he had cornered himself.

My hand reached out for the front doorknob. I was feeling numb and a little out of it. My vision was tunneled. I focused on the whitewashed door and nothing else.

"It's open." A voice came from behind the door.

A boy's voice. A little raspy. Small and fragile without the megaphone to amplify it.

I pushed open the front door and finally saw the Truth School killer in all of his insane glory.

Danny Boudreaux wasn't much more than five three or four. He had thin, squinty eyes like a rodent's, large ears, a bad buzz haircut. He was an odd-looking boy, clearly an outcast, a freak. I sensed that other kids wouldn't like him much, that he was a loner, and had been for all of his life.

He had a Smith & Wesson semiautomatic aimed chest-high at me.

"Military school," he reminded me. "I'm an expert marksman, Detective Cross. I have no difficulty with human targets."

Chapter 99

MY HEART was clanging around inside the tight metal cage that was supposed to be my chest. The loud buzzing sound in my head was still there, like irritating static on a radio. I didn't feel much like a police hero. I felt scared. It was worse than usual. Maybe because the killer was thirteen years old.

Danny Boudreaux knew how to use the semiautomatic clenched in his hand, and sooner or later, he would. The only thing in the universe that mattered to me right then was to get that Smith & Wesson away from him.

The image before me commanded all my attention: a thin, pimply thirteen-year-old boy with a powerful, deadly handgun. A semiautomatic was pointed at my heart. Although Boudreaux's hand was steady enough, he appeared to be more mentally and physically out of it than I had thought. He was probably decompensating. His behavior was likely to become increasingly more bizarre. His instability was obvious and scary to confront. It was in his eyes. His eyes darted about like birds caught in a glass bubble.

He was weaving slightly as he stood in the foyer of the Johnson house. He waved the gun in small circles at me. He was wearing a strange sweatshirt with the printed message HAPPY, HAPPY. JOY, JOY.

His short hair was dripping wet with perspiration. His glasses were slightly fogged around the edges. Behind the glasses, his eyes were glazed and shiny-wet. He *looked* the part of the Truth School killer. I doubted that anyone had ever liked Danny Boudreaux too much. I didn't.

His wiry body suddenly snapped rigidly to attention. "Welcome on board, Detective Cross, *sir!*"

"Hello, Danny," I spoke to him in as low-key and non-threatening a way as I could. "You called, and now I'm here." *I'm the one who's going to take your ass down.*

He kept his distance. He was a jangle of raw nerves and incredible, pent-up anger. He was a puppet without a puppeteer. There was no way to predict how this was going to go from here.

He was almost definitely suffering a withdrawal from his prescription drugs. Danny Boudreaux had the whole package of symptoms: aggression, depression, psychosis, hyperactivity, behavioral deterioration.

A thirteen-year-old, stone-cold killer. How do I get the gun away from him?

Christine Johnson was standing in the darkened living room behind him. She didn't move. She looked very distant in the background and small, in spite of her height. She looked frightened, sad, tired.

To her right was an exquisitely carved fireplace that looked as if it had been scavenged from some big-city brownstone. I hadn't seen much of the living room before. I studied it closely now. I was looking for some kind of weapon. Anything to help us.

George Johnson lay on the off-white marble floor in the foyer. Christine or the boy had placed a red plaid blanket over the body. The slain lawyer looked as if he'd lain down to take a nap.

"Christine, are you okay?" I called across the room. She started to speak, then stopped herself.

"She's fine, man. She's mighty fine pudding. She's all right,"

Boudreaux snapped at me. He slurred his words, so that they sounded like "cheese alriii." "She's a-okay, all right. I'm the one who's losing it here. This is about me."

"I can understand how tired you are, Danny," I said to him. I suspected that he would be experiencing dizziness, impaired concentration, cottonmouth.

"Yeah. You got that right. What else do you have to say for yourself? Any more nuggets of wisdom about my delusional behavior?"

Wham! He suddenly kicked shut the front door behind us. More impulsive behavior. I had definitely joined the party. He was still very careful to keep his distance — he kept the semi-automatic always pointed at me.

"I can shoot this son of a bitch *real well*," he said, just in case I'd missed the point before. It reinforced my notion of his extreme paranoia, his agitation and nervousness.

He was overly concerned about how I viewed him, how competent I judged him to be. He had me confused with his real father. The policeman father who had deserted him and his mother. I'd just learned about the connection on the ride over, but it made sense. It tracked perfectly, actually.

I reminded myself that this nervous, skinny, pathetic boy was a murderer. It wasn't hard for me to hate such a fiend. Still, there was also something tragically sad about the boy. There was something so lonely and freakish about Daniel Boudreaux.

"I believe that you can shoot extremely well," I told him quietly. I knew it was what he wanted to hear.

I believe you.

I believe you are a stone-cold killer. I believe you are a young monster, and probably unredeemable.

How do I get your gun?

I believe I may have to kill you before you kill me or Christine Johnson.

Chapter 100

I LOOKED at the words HAPPY, HAPPY. JOY, JOY. I knew exactly where the saying on his sweatshirt came from.

Nickelodeon. Children's TV. Damon and Jannie loved it. In a way, so did I. Nickelodeon was about families, and it probably infuriated Danny Boudreaux.

He grinned at me! He had such a fiendish, madhouse look.

Then he spoke quietly, as I just had. He expertly mimicked my concern for him. His instincts were sharp and cruel. It scared me again. It also made me want to rush him and punch his lights out.

"You don't have to whisper. Nobody's sleeping in here. Well, nobody except George the Doorman."

He laughed, reveling in his crazy, creepy inappropriateness. Here was the real psychopathic deal. *Danny was a thrill killer in the flesh, even at thirteen.*

"Are you all right?" I asked Christine again.

"No. Not really," she whispered.

"*Shut the hell up!*" Boudreaux yelled at both of us. He pointed his gun at Christine, then back at me. "When I say something, *I mean it.*"

I realized I wasn't going to get the gun away from the boy. I had to try something else. He looked close to the breaking point, way too close.

I decided to make a move immediately.

I concentrated on the boy, trying to gauge his weaknesses. I watched him without seeming to watch.

I took a couple of slow, deliberate steps toward the living room window. An ancient African milking stool sat there. I glanced outside at the police lines staggered across the front lawn, keeping their distance. I could see riot shields and Plexiglas masks, battle dress uniforms, flak vests, guns everywhere. Jesus, what a scene. This mad boy had caused all this.

"Don't get any funny ideas," he told me from across the room.

I already had a funny idea, Dannyboy. I already made my move. It's done! Can you figure it out? Are you as smart as you think you are, creep?

"Why not?" I asked him. He didn't answer me. He was going to kill us. What more could he do?

There was a real good reason for me to be near the window. I was going to position myself and Christine Johnson on opposite sides of the living room.

I'd done it. I had already made the move.

Boudreaux didn't seem to notice.

"What do you think of me now?" he snarled. "How do I stack up against those assholes Jack and Jill? How about against the great Gary Soneji? You can tell me the truth. Won't hurt my feelings. Because I don't have any feelings."

"I'm going to tell you the truth," I said to him, "since that's what you want to hear. I haven't been impressed by any killers and I'm not impressed by you, either. Not in that way."

His mouth twisted and he snarled, "Yeah? Well, I'm not impressed by you, either, Dr. Hotshit Cross. Who's got the gun, though?"

Danny Boudreaux stared at me for a long, intense moment. His eyes looked crossed behind the lenses of his glasses. The pupils were pinpointed. He looked as if he were going to shoot me right then. My heart was racing. I looked across the room at Christine Johnson.

"I have to kill you. You know that," he said as if it made all the sense in the world. Suddenly, he was speaking in a bored voice. It was disconcerting as hell. "You and Christine have to go down."

He glanced around at her. His eyes were dark holes. "*Black bitch!* Sneaky, manipulative bitch, too. You dissed me bad at that stupid school of yours. How dare you disrespect me!" he flared again.

"That's not true," Christine Johnson said. She spoke right up. "I was trying to protect those kids out in the yard. It had nothing to do with you. I had no idea who you were. How could I?"

He stamped one black-booted foot hard. He was petulant, impatient, unforgiving. He *was* a mean little prick in every way.

"Don't tell me what the hell I know! You can't tell what I'm thinking! You can't get inside my head! Nobody can."

"Why do you think you have to kill anybody else?" I asked Boudreaux.

He flared at me again. Pointed his gun. "Don't fucking try to shrink-wrap me! Don't you dare."

"I wouldn't do that." I shook my head. "Nobody likes lies, or people trying to pull cheap tricks. I don't."

Suddenly, he swung the Smith & Wesson toward Christine.

"*I have to kill people* because . . . that's what I do." He laughed again, cackled, and wheezed like a fiend.

Christine Johnson sensed what was coming. She knew *something* had to be done before Danny Boudreaux exploded.

The boy turned to me again. He swiveled his hips and almost seemed to be preening. *He's watching himself act like this*, I realized. *He's loving this.*

"You've been trying to trick me," he said. "That's why the calm

Mr. Rogers voice. Backing off from me, so you're not so almighty big and threatening. I see right through you."

"You're right," I said, "but not completely right. I've been talking like this . . . *real softly* . . . to distract you from what I'm really doing. You blew your own game. *You just lost! You little chump. You weasly little son of a bitch.*"

Chapter 101

"YOU CAN'T SHOOT both of us," I told Danny Boudreaux.

I spoke in a clear, firm voice. At the same time, I angled my body sideways. Gave him less of a target.

I took another step toward my side of the large living room. I widened the distance between Christine Johnson and me.

"What the hell do you mean? What are you talking about, Cross? TALK TO ME, CROSS! I DEMAND IT!"

I didn't answer him. Let him figure it out. I knew that he would. He was a smart bad boy.

Daniel Boudreaux stared at me, then quickly back at Christine. He got the message. He finally saw the trap, subtle as it was.

His eyes bore deeply into my skull. He knew what I'd done. One of us would get to him if he shot at the other. He couldn't have his final blaze of glory.

"You dumb piece of shit," he growled at me. His voice was low and threatening. "You're the one who gets it first then!"

He raised the Smith & Wesson. I was staring down the barrel at him. "TALK TO ME, YOU BASTARD!"

"That's enough!" Christine shouted from the other side of

the room. She was unbelievable under the pressure, the circumstances. "You've killed enough," she said to Boudreaux.

Danny Boudreaux was starting to panic. Wild eyes stared out
from a head that seemed to be on a swivel. "No, I haven't killed
enough *fucking useless robots.* I'm just getting started!" His skin
was stretched tight against the bones of his face.

He swung the Smith & Wesson toward Christine. His arms
were stretched ramrod straight. His whole body was shaking and
canted to the left.

"*Danny!*" I yelled his name and started to move on him.

He hesitated for an instant. Then he jerked the gun and fired.
A deafening muzzle blast in close quarters.

He fired at Christine!

She tried to spin out of the way. I couldn't tell if she had.

I kept coming, then I was in the air.

Danny Boudreaux swung the semiautomatic back at me. His
eyes were filled with terror and intense hatred. His body shook
with rage, fear, desperation. Maybe he *could* get us both.

I moved a lot faster than he thought I could. I was inside the
radius of his arm and the outstretched gun.

I crashed into Danny Boudreaux as if he were a full-grown
man, an armed and dangerous one. I crushed him with a full
body-blow. I relished the contact.

Danny Boudreaux and I were down in a sprawling heap. We
were tangled up, a mass of flying arms and twitching, kicking
legs. The revolver went off again. I didn't feel any blinding pain
yet, but I tasted blood.

The boy screamed in his high-pitched wail. *He wailed!* I
wrenched the gun out of his hand. He tried to bite me, to rip into
my flesh. Then the boy growled.

He began to have a seizure, possibly from the drug withdrawal. A major surge of brain activity was being discharged in
his body. He was thrashing his arms and his legs. His pelvis thrust
forward as if he were dry-humping my leg.

His eyes rolled back, and his body suddenly went limp. Foam

spewed from his mouth. His arms and legs continued to flail and twitch. He might have lost consciousness for a second or two. He continued to drool, to make choking and gurgling sounds.

I flipped him on his side. His lips were dusky blue. His eyes finally rolled back into place. They started to blink rapidly. The seizure had ended as quickly as it had come. He lay limp on the floor, a pool of wild bad boy.

The police had heard the shots. They were all over the living room. Riot shotguns, drawn pistols. Lots of shouting and squawking radio-receivers. Christine Johnson went to her husband. So did two of the EMS medics.

The next time I looked, Christine was kneeling beside me. She didn't seem to be hurt. "Are you all right, Alex?" she asked in a hoarse whisper.

I was still holding down Danny Boudreaux. He seemed unaware of his surroundings. He was streaming with cold, oily sweat. The Sojourner Truth School killer now looked sad, lost, and unbearably confused. Thirteen years old. Five homicides. Maybe more.

"Grand mal?" Christine asked.

I nodded. "I think so. Maybe just too much excitement."

Danny Boudreaux was trying to say something, but I couldn't hear what it was. He sputtered, still drooling the bubbling white foam.

"What did you say? What is it?" I asked. My voice was hoarse and my throat hurt. I was shaking and covered with sweat myself.

He spoke in a tiny whisper, almost as if there were no one inside him anymore. "I'm afraid," he told me. "I don't know where I am. I'm always so afraid."

I nodded at the small, horrifying face looking up at me. "I know," I said to the young killer. "I know what you're feeling."

That was the scariest thing of all.

Chapter 102

THE DRAGONSLAYER lives, but how many lives do I have left? Why was I taking chances with my life? Physician, heal thyself.

I stayed at the Johnson house for more than an hour, until the Boudreaux boy and the body of George Johnson were taken away. There were questions I had to ask Christine Johnson for my report. Then I called home and spoke to Nana. I told her to please go to bed. I was safe and basically sound. For tonight, anyway.

"I love you, Alex," she whispered over the phone. Nana sounded almost as tired and beat-up as I was.

"I love you, too, old woman," I told her.

That night, miracle of miracles, she actually let me get in the last word.

The crowd of ambulance-chasers on Summer Street finally broke up. Even the most persistent reporters and photographers left. One of Christine Johnson's sisters had arrived to be with her in this terrible time. I hugged Christine hard before I left.

She was still trembling. She had suffered a horrible, unspeakable loss. We had both spent a night in hell. "I can't feel anything. Everything is so unreal," she told me. "I know this isn't a nightmare, and yet I keep thinking that it has to be one."

Sampson drove me home at one in the morning. My eyes felt lidless. My brain was still going at a million miles an hour, still buzzing loudly, still overheated.

What was our world coming to? Gary Soneji? Bundy? The Hillside Strangler? Koresh? McVeigh? On and on and on. Gandhi was asked once what he thought of Western civilization. He replied, "I think it could be a good idea."

I don't cry too much. I can't. The same is true for a lot of police officers I know. I wish I could cry sometimes, let it all out, release the fear and the venom, but it isn't that easy. Something has gotten blocked up inside.

I sat on the stairs inside our house. I had been on my way to my bedroom, but I hadn't made it. I was trying to cry, but I couldn't.

I thought about my wife, Maria, who was killed in a drive-by shooting a few years back. Maria and I had fit together beautifully. That wasn't just selective memory on my part. I knew how good love could be — I knew it was the best thing I'd ever done in my life — and yet here I was alone. I was taking chances with my life. I kept telling everybody that I was all right, but I wasn't.

I don't know how long I stayed there in the darkness with my thoughts. Maybe ten minutes, maybe it was much more than that. The house was quiet in a familiar, almost comfortable way, but I couldn't be soothed that night.

I listened to sounds that I had been hearing for years. I remembered being a small boy there, growing up with Nana, wondering what I would become someday. Now I knew the answer to that question. I was a multiple-homicide expert who got to work the biggest, nastiest cases. I was the dragonslayer.

I finally climbed the rest of the stairs and stopped in at Damon and Jannie's room. The two of them were fast asleep in the bedroom they share in our small house.

I love the way Damon and Jannie sleep, the trusting, innocent ways of my young son and daughter. I can watch them for long stretches, even on a howling-bad night like this one. I can't count how many times I have peeked in and just stood in the doorway. They keep me going, keep me from flying apart some nights.

They'd gone to sleep wearing funky, heart-shaped sunglasses like the ones the kids wear in the singing group called Innocence. It was cute as hell. Precious, too. I sat on the edge of Jannie's bed. I quietly took off my boots and carefully lay them on the floor without making any noise.

Then I stretched myself out across the bottom of both their beds. I listened to my bones crack. I wanted to be near my kids, to be with them, for all of us to be safe. It didn't seem too much to ask out of life, too much reward for the day I had just lived through.

I gently kissed the rubber-soled slipper-sock of Jannie's pajamas.

I lay my hand very lightly against Damon's cool bare leg.

I finally closed my eyes, and I tried to push the rushing scenes of murder and chaos out of my mind. I couldn't do it. The monsters were everywhere that night. They truly were all around me.

There are so goddamn many of them. Wave upon wave, it seems. Young and old, and everything in between. Where are these monsters coming from in America? What has created them?

Lying there alongside my two children, I finally was able to sleep somehow. For a few hours, I was able to forget the most horrifying thing of all, the reason for my extreme sorrow and upset.

I had heard the news before I left the Johnson house. President Thomas Byrnes had died early that morning.

Chapter 103

I WAS HOLDING and gently petting Rosie the cat. I had the kitchen door open and peered outside, squinted at Sampson.

He stood in a freezing-cold rain. He looked like a big, dark boulder in the teeming rainstorm, or maybe it was hail that he was weathering so stoically.

"The nightmare continues," he said to me. A simple declarative sentence. Devastating.

"Yeah, doesn't it, though? But maybe I don't care about it anymore."

"Uh-huh. And maybe this is the year the Bullets win the NBA championship, the Orioles win the World Series, and the raggedyass Redskins go to the Super Bowl. You *just never know.*"

A day had passed since the long night at the Johnson house, since the even longer morning in New York City. Not nearly enough time for any kind of healing, or even proper grieving. President Edward Mahoney had been sworn in the day before. It was necessary according to law, but it almost seemed indecent to me.

I had on dungarees and a white T-shirt. Bare feet on a cold linoleum floor. Steaming coffee mug in hand. I was convalescing nicely. I hadn't washed off my whiskers, as Jannie calls the act of shaving. I was almost feeling human again.

I hadn't asked Sampson in yet, either.

"Morning, Sugar," Sampson persisted. Then he rolled back his upper lip and showed off some teeth. His smile was brutally joyful. I finally had to smile back at my friend and nemesis.

It was a little past nine o'clock and I had just gotten up. This was late for me. It was shameful behavior by Nana's standards. I was still sleep-deprived, trauma-shocked, in danger of losing the rest of my mind, throwing up, *something shitty* and unexpected. But I was also much better. I *looked* good; I looked fine.

"Aren't you even going to say good morning?" Sampson asked, pretending to be hurt.

"Morning, John. I don't even want to know about it," I said to him. "Whatever it is that brings you here this cold and bleak morning."

"First intelligent thing I've heard out of your mouth in years," Sampson said, "but I'm afraid I don't believe it. You want to know everything. You need to know everything, Alex. That's why you read four newspapers every damn morning."

"I don't want to know, either," Nana contributed from behind me in the kitchen. She had been up for hours, of course. "I don't *need* to know. Shoo, fly. Go fry some ice. Take a long walk off a short dock, Johnnyboy."

"We got time for breakfast?" I finally asked him.

"Not really," he said, careful to keep his smile turned on, "but let's eat, anyway. Who could resist?"

"*He* invited you, *not me*," Nana warned from over by her hot stove.

She was kidding Sampson. She loves him as if he were her own son, as if he were my physically bigger brother. She made the two of us scrambled eggs, homemade sausage, home fries, toast. She knows how to cook and could easily feed the entire Washington Redskins team at training camp. That would be no problem for Nana.

Sampson waited until we had finished eating before he got back into it, whatever it was, whatever had happened now. His dark little secret. It may seem odd — but when your life is filled with homicides and other tragedies, you have to learn to take time for yourself. The homicides will still be there. The homicides are always there.

"Your Mister Grayer called me a little while ago," Sampson said as he poured his third cup of coffee. "He said to let you have a couple days off, that they could handle this. *Them*, like the great old horror flick that used to scare the hell out of us."

"*That*, what you just said, makes me suspicious and fearful right away. Handle what?" I asked.

I was finishing the last of half a loaf of cinnamon toast made from thick homemade bread. It was, honestly, quite seriously, a taste of heaven. Nana claims that she's been there, stolen several recipes. I tend to believe her. I've seen and tasted the proof of her tale.

Sampson glanced at his wristwatch, an ancient Bulova given to him by his father when he was fourteen.

"They're looking over Jill's office in the White House right about now. Then they're going to her apartment on Twenty-fourth Street. You want to go? As my guest? Got you a *guest* pass, just in case."

Of course I wanted to be there. I had to go. I needed to know everything about Jill, just as Sampson had said I did.

"You are the devil," Nana hissed at Sampson.

"Thank you, Nana." He beamed bright eyes and a thousand and one teeth. "High praise, indeed."

Chapter 104

WE DROVE to Sara Rosen's apartment in Sampson's slippery-quick black Nissan. Nana's hot breakfast had brought me back to the real world at least. I was feeling partially revived. Physically, if not emotionally.

I was already highly intrigued about visiting Jill's home. I wanted to see her office at the White House, too, but figured that could wait a day or two. *But her house. That was irresistible for the detective, and for the psychologist.*

Sara Rosen lived in a ten-story building on Twenty-fourth and K. The building had an officious front-desk "captain" who studied our police IDs and then reluctantly let us proceed. The lobby was cheery otherwise. Carpeted, lots of large potted plants. Not the kind of building where anyone would expect to find an assassin.

But Jill had lived right here, hadn't she?

Actually, the apartment fit the profile we had of Sara Rosen. She was the only child of an Army colonel and a high school English teacher. She had grown up in Aberdeen, Maryland, then gone to Hollins College in Virginia. She had majored in history and English, graduating with honors. She'd come to

Washington sixteen years ago, when she was twenty-one. She had never married, though she'd had several boyfriends over the years. Some of the staff at the White House press and communications offices called her "the sexy spinster."

Her apartment was on the fifth floor of the ten-story building. It was bright, with a view of an interior courtyard. The FBI was already at work inside. Chopin came softly from a stereo. It was a relaxed atmosphere, almost pleasant, devil-may-care. The case was, after all, *closed*.

Sampson and I spent the next few hours with the Feebie technicians who were searching the apartment for anything that might give the Bureau a clue about Sara Rosen.

Jill had lived right there.

Who the hell were you, Jill? How did this happen to you? What happened, Jill? Talk to us. You know you want to talk, lonely girl.

Her apartment was a one-bedroom with a small den, and we would examine every square inch of it. The woman who had lived here had helped to murder President Thomas Byrnes. The den had been used as an editing room for their film. The apartment had historical importance now. For as long as this building stood, people would point at it and say, *"That's where Jill lived."*

She had bought anonymous-looking furniture in a country-club style. They were middle-class trappings. A sofa and armchair made of brushed cotton twill. Local furniture store tags: Mastercraft Interiors, Colony House in Arlington. Cool, cold colors in every room. Lots of ivory-colored things at Jill's place. An ice-blue, patterned area rug. A pale, distressed pine armoire.

Several frames on the wall contained matted Christmas cards and letters from White House notables: the current press secretary, the chief of staff, even a brief note from Nancy Reagan. There were no pictures of any of the "enemies" mentioned to me by President Byrnes. *Sara Rosen was a secret starfucker, wasn't she? Had Jack been a star for her? Was Jack really Kevin Hawkins?*

Talk to us, Jill. I know you want to talk. Tell us what really happened. Give us a clue.

Sitting out on a small rolltop desk were mailings from the Heritage Foundation and the Cato Institute, both conservative organizations. There were several copies of *U.S. News & World Report, Southern Living, Gourmet.*

Also flyers about future poetry readings at Chapters on K Street, and Politics and Prose, bookstores in the Washington area. Was *Jill the poet?*

A poem had been cut from a book and taped to the wall above the desk.

> How dreary — to be — Somebody!
> How public — like a Frog —
> To tell one's name — the live-long June —
> To an admiring Bog!
>
> — Emily Dickinson

Emily Dickinson apparently had the same opinion of celebrities as Jack and Jill.

The walls of the den and bedroom were covered with books. The walls *were* bookcases. Fiction, nonfiction, poetry. High- and low-brow stuff. Jill the reader. Jill the loner. Jill the sexy spinster.

Who are you, Jill? Who are you, Sara Rosen?

There was even one bit of evidence that showed a sense of humor. A sign was framed in the front hallway: use an accordion, go to jail. That's the law.

Who are you, Sara-Jill?

Did anybody really care about you before now? Why did you help to commit this horrible crime? Was it worth it? To die like this, a lonely spinster? Who killed you, Jill? Was it Jack?

If I found one indisputable piece of truth, just one, all the rest would follow, and we would finally understand. I wanted to believe that it could go like that.

I looked through Jill's clothes closets. I found conservative business suits mostly in dark colors. Labels that told me Brooks Brothers and Ann Taylor. Low pumps, running shoes, casual flats. There were several sweatsuits for running and exercise.

Not many evening dresses for parties, for fun.

Who were you, Sara?

I searched for false walls, false bottoms, anywhere that she might have kept private notes, something that might help us to close this case forever, or open it wide.

C'mon, Sara, let us in on your secret life. Tell us who you really were.

What kept you going, Jill? Who were you, Sara? Sexy spinster? You want us to know. I know you do. You're still in this apartment. I can feel it. I can feel your loneliness everywhere I look.

You want us to know something. What is it, Sara? Give us one more rhyme. Just one.

Sampson came up behind me while I was standing at a bedroom window overlooking the courtyard. I was thinking about all the possibilities the case held.

"You got it solved yet? Got it all figured out, Sweets?"

"Not yet. There's something more, though. Give me another couple of days here."

Sampson groaned at the thought. And so did I. But I knew I would come back here. Sara Rosen had left something for us to remember her by. I was almost sure of it.

Jill the poet.

Chapter 105

MAYBE I WAS a glutton for crime and punishment, but I came back alone to her apartment very early the following morning. I was there by eight, long before anyone else. I wandered back and forth in the small apartment, nibbling from an open box of Nutri-Grain.

Something was still bothering me about the sexy spinster and her hideaway in Foggy Bottom. Detective's hunch. Psychologist's intuition.

For nearly an hour, I sat crouched at a window seat that looked out on K Street. I fixated on a bus shelter poster for a Calvin Klein perfume called Escape. The model in the poster looked unbearably sad and forlorn. *Like Jill?* Someone had written a thought balloon above the model's head. It read: "*Someone feed me, please.*"

What gave Sara Rosen sustenance? I wondered as I peered out into the D.C. ether. What was her secret? What drove her to the madness of celebrity stalking — or whatever she had been doing before she was killed in the Peninsula Hotel? She had been murdered in New York. What was her connection to Jack?

What was the whole story? What was the real story? What secret still hadn't been unlocked?

I started in on the massive collection of books that dominated every room in the apartment, even the kitchen. Sara had been a voracious reader. Mostly literature and history, nearly all of it American. Sara the intellectual; Sara the real smart cookie.

Diplomacy by Henry Kissinger. *Special Trust* by Robert McFarland. *Caveat* by Alexander Haig. *Kissinger* by Walter Isaacson. On and on and on. Fiction by Anne Tyler, Robertson Davies, Annie Proulx, but also Robert Ludlum and John Grisham. Poetry by Emily Dickinson, Sylvia Plath, Anne Sexton. A volume entitled *Woman Alone*.

I opened each book, then carefully shook it out. There were well over a thousand volumes in the apartment. Maybe a couple of thousand. Lots of books to look through.

There were handwritten pages of notes stuffed into some of the books. Jottings Sara had made. I read every loose scrap. The hours went by. Meals were skipped. I didn't much care.

Inside a biography of Napoleon and Josephine, Sara Rosen had written "N. considered high intelligence an aberration in women. Stroked J.'s breasts in public. Cur. But J. got her just deserts. Cunt."

Jill the poet. Jill the book lover. The mystery, the fantasy woman, the enigma. *The killer.*

There were several videotapes of movies in the den, and I began to open each of the containers.

Sara Rosen's film collection featured well-known romances, mystery thrillers, and romantic thrillers. *The Prince of Tides, No Way Out, Disclosure, The Godfather* trilogy, *Gone With the Wind, An Officer and a Gentleman.*

She also seemed to like older movies, especially noir mysteries: Raymond Chandler, James Cain, Hitchcock.

I opened every single cassette, row by row, every box. I thought it was important, especially with someone as orderly as Sara. If Sampson had been around, I wouldn't have heard the end of it. He would have called me crazier than Jack or Jill.

I opened a cassette box for Hitchcock's *Notorious*. I didn't remember ever seeing the film myself, but one of Hitchcock's favorite male leads, Cary Grant, was featured on the box cover.

I found an unmarked cassette inside the box. It didn't look like a movie. Curious, I popped the cassette into the VCR. It was the fourth or fifth unmarked cassette that I had viewed so far.

The film *wasn't Notorious.*

I found myself looking at footage of the murder of Senator Daniel Fitzpatrick.

This was apparently the uncut version, which ran considerably longer than the film that had been sent to CNN.

The extra footage was even more disturbing and graphic than what had been viewed on the TV news network. The fear in Senator Fitzpatrick's voice was terrible to hear. He begged the killers for his life, then he began to cry, to sob loudly. That part had been carefully edited from the CNN tape. It was too strong. It was brutal beyond belief. It put Jack and Jill in the worst possible light.

They were merciless killers. No pity, no passion, no humanity.

I jabbed at the PAUSE button. Jackpot! The next shot in the film had started tight on Senator Fitzpatrick, then pulled out to a wide angle, maybe wider than intended.

The tape showed Jack as he fired the second shot.

The killer wasn't Kevin Hawkins!

I suddenly wondered if Jill had left the tape here for someone to find. Had she suspected that she might be betrayed? Was this Jill's payback? I thought that maybe it was: *Jill had fucked Jack, straight from hell.*

I studied the frozen frame revealing the real Jack. He had short, sandy-blond hair. He was a handsome-looking man in his late thirties. There was no emotion on his face as he pulled the trigger.

"Jack," I whispered. "We've finally found you, Jack."

Chapter 106

THE FBI, Secret Service, and Washington police cooperated and worked closely together on a massive and important manhunt. They all badly wanted a piece of this one. It was the ultimate homicide case: a president had been murdered. The real killer was still out there. Jack was still alive; at least, I hoped that he was.

And he was!

Early on the morning of December 20, I watched Jack through a pair of binoculars. I couldn't take my eyes off the killer and mastermind.

I wanted to take him down. I wanted him for myself. We had to wait, though. This was Jay Grayer's plan. It was his day, his show, his plan of action.

Jack was just walking out of a three-story Colonial house. He went to a bright red Ford Bronco that sat in a circular driveway. By then, we knew who he was, where he lived, nearly everything about him. Now we understood a lot more about Jack and Jill. Our eyes had been opened very, very wide.

"There's Jack. There's our boy," Jay Grayer said to me.

"Doesn't look like a killer, does he?" I said. "But he got the job done. He did it. He's the executioner of all those people, including Jill."

Jack was herding along a small boy and a girl. Very cute kids. I knew that their names were Alix and Artie. Also coming along for the ride were the two family dogs: Shepherd and Wise Man, a ten-year-old black retriever and a frisky young collie.

Jack's kids.

Jack's dogs.

Jack's nice house in suburbia.

Jack and Jill came to The Hill . . . to kill the President. And then Jack murdered his partner and lover, Jill. He executed Sara Rosen in cold blood. Jack thought he got away with the murders, clear and free. Jack had an almost great plan. But now we had Jack in our sights. *I was watching Jack.* We all were.

He looked like the perfect suburban Washington dad in just about every way. He had on a navy hooded parka that was unzipped in spite of the cold weather. The open jacket exposed a blue plaid flannel shirt and stonewashed dungarees. He wore floppy, tannish brown Topsiders, gray woolen socks.

His hair was cut short, military-style. His hair was dark brown now. He was a ruggedly handsome man. Thirty-nine years old. The President's assassin. The stone-cold killer of several political enemies.

A conspirator.

A world-class traitor.

A real heartless bastard, too.

He is just about the perfect American killer, I thought as I watched him in command of his obedient troop of children and pets. He was a near-perfect assassin. He was a daddy, a husband, clean-cut as could be. He looked absolutely beyond suspicion. He even had alibis, though none of them would hold up because of the film footage of his shooting Senator Fitzpatrick. A Jackal for our age, for our country, for our naive and very dangerous way of life.

I wondered if he had watched the President's burial ceremony on TV, or maybe even attended it, as I had.

"He's such a devil-may-care fucker, isn't he?" Jay Grayer said. He was sitting beside me in the front seat of the unmarked car. I hadn't heard Jay Grayer curse much before today. He wanted to take down Jack real bad, real *hard*.

That's what we were going to do. This was going to be a famous morning for all of us.

It was all about to go down.

"Get ready to follow Jack," Grayer spoke into a handheld mike in our car. "You lose him, anybody, and you can *just keep going*. In whatever direction you're headed."

"We won't lose him. I don't think he'll even run," I said. "He's a homebody, our Jack. He's a daddy. He has roots in the community."

What a strange country we lived in. So many murderers. So many monsters. So many decent people for them to prey on.

"I think you're probably right, Alex. Spot on. I don't get it yet, I don't fully understand him, but I think you're right. We've got him nailed. Only what exactly do we have here? What makes Jack run? Why did he do it?"

"Money," I told him a theory I had about Jack. "Look for the money. It cuts through and simplifies all the other stuff. A little politics, a little cause, and a lot of money. Ideology and financial gain. Hard to beat in this venal day and age."

"You think so?"

"I think so. Yes. I'd bet a lot on it. He has some strongly held beliefs, and one of them is that he and his family deserve to live well. So, yes, I think money is a part of this. I think he's probably acquainted with some people with a lot of money and power, but not as much power as they would like to have."

The Bronco took off and we followed it at a comfortable distance. Jack was a careful driver of his valuable cargo. He must have been impressive to his kids, maybe even to the dogs, undoubtedly to his neighbors.

Jack the Jackal. I wondered if that was another of Sara Rosen's word games.

I wondered what Jill's very last thought was when her lover betrayed her in New York. Had she expected it? Had she known he would betray her? Was that why she left the cassette in her apartment?

Jay wanted to talk, maybe he needed to keep his mind busy right now. "He's taking them to the day school down yonder. His life is back to normal now. Nothing happened to change that. He just planned the murder and helped execute a president. That's all. No biggie. Life goes on."

"From what I can gather in his military records, he was a first-class soldier. He left the Army as a full colonel. Honorable discharge. Participated in Desert Storm," I said to Jay.

"Jack a war hero. I'm impressed as hell. I'm so goddamn impressed with this guy that I can't begin to tell you. Maybe I'll tell *him.*"

Jack *was* a war hero, *officially.*

Jack was a patriot, *unofficially.*

As we rode along, I remembered the inscription on the Tomb of the Unknown at Arlington National Cemetery. *Here rests in honored glory an American soldier known but to God.* Somehow, I thought that was how Jack probably thought about himself. *A soldier-hero known only to God.*

He probably believed he'd gotten away with several murders — *in a just war.*

Well, he hadn't. He was about to go down.

He dropped the two children off at the Bayard-Wellington School. It was a beautiful place: fieldstone walls and rolling, frost-slicked lawns; the sort of school I would have loved to send Damon and Jannie to; the kind of school where Christine Johnson ought to teach.

You could move out of D.C., you know, I told myself as I watched Jack kiss each of his children good-bye.

So why don't you? Why don't you take Damon and Jannie

away from Fifth Street? Why don't you do what this rotten piece of shit son of a bitch does for his kids?

Jay Grayer spoke into the hand mike again. "He's leaving the Bayard-Wellington School now. He's turning back onto the main road. *God, it's pretty out here in Jackville, isn't it?* We'll take him down at the stoplight up ahead! Just one imperative: *we take him alive!* We'll have four cars at the light with him. Four of us to get Jack. We take him alive."

"You have the right to remain silent," I said.

"What the hell are you saying?" Jay Grayer turned to me and asked.

"Just getting it out of the way. He doesn't have any rights. He's going down."

Grayer offered up a crooked smile. We both understood why. The good part was coming now. The only good part in this whole affair. "Famous stuff, huh? Here we go. Let's get this son of a bitch."

"Absolutely. I want to have a nice long talk with Jack, too." *I want to kick his ass from this stoplight, all the way back to Washington.*

I want to meet the *real* Jack.

Chapter 107

NOBODY had figured out the assassination plot until now. Not one of us had even been close. No one had been able to solve the mystery of Jack and Jill until it was too late. Maybe we could unravel the whole mess now. *A retrospective on Jack and Jill.*

We were less than a hundred yards away from capturing Jack. He was heading down a steep, rolling hill toward a stoplight.

It was a very picturesque scene. Long lens, like in expensively made movies. The light turned red and Jack stopped — a law-abiding citizen. Unconcerned about anything.

A free man.

Jay Grayer and I eased up right behind his trendy, off-road vehicle. I could read the sticker on the rear bumper of the Bronco: *D.A.R.E. to keep kids off drugs.*

Beartrap was the code for our operation. We had four mainline vehicles. Another half-dozen cars and two helicopters for backup. I didn't see how Jack could escape. I was thinking ahead to the massive ramifications of the assassin's capture, and the even more shocking surprise still to come.

This was going to get worse, much worse.

"We take him down on three," Jay Grayer said into his hand

mike. He was extremely cool now, the consummate professional, as he had been from the beginning. I liked working with
him enormously. He wasn't an egomaniac; he was just good at
his job.

"We take him *real easy*," I said.

The beartrap was sprung.

I was one of the six who jumped out of the intercept cars
stopped at the innocent-looking country-road light. It was an
honor.

There were two civilian cars waiting at the light as well. A gray
Honda and a Saab.

It must have looked like utter madness to them. That's because
it was, and much worse than it looked. The man in the Bronco
had killed the President. This was like arresting Lee Harvey
Oswald, Sirhan Sirhan, John Wilkes Booth. An ordinary stoplight
in northern Maryland.

I was there! I was glad I was there. I would have paid a huge
admission price to be there for this.

I got to the passenger door of his vehicle as a Secret Service
agent yanked open the driver's door. The two of us happened
to be the quickest on our feet. Or maybe we were the ones who
wanted Jack the most.

Jack turned toward me — and he got to look right into the
wide-eyed barrel of my Glock.

He got a real good look at death in an instant.

Execution-style!

Very professional!

"Don't move. Don't even breathe too hard. Don't move a
millimeter," I said to him. "I don't want to have an excuse. So
don't give me one."

He hadn't been expecting us. I could tell that by the shock
spread across his face. He thought he'd gotten away clean with
the murders. Thought he was home free.

Well, he had it all wrong for once.

Jack had finally made his first mistake.

"Secret Service. You're under arrest. You have the right to remain silent, and that's a real good idea!" one of the agents barked at Jack. The agent's face was bright red with anger, with outrage at this man who had murdered President Thomas Byrnes.

Jack looked at the Secret Service agent, and then back at me. He recognized me. He knew who I was. What else did he know?

At first he'd been startled, but now he became calm. It was astonishing to see the calmness and cool take hold. *He's calm as death,* I thought.

I shouldn't have been surprised. *This was the real Jack. This was the President's killer.*

"Very good," he finally said, commending us for doing a good job, for our professionalism. The son of a bitch nodded his approval. "I'm proud of you. You did your jobs extremely well." It made my blood boil, but I knew the order of the day: we take him real easy. The gentle beartrap.

He slowly got out of the spit-shined red vehicle. Both his hands were held up high. He offered no resistance; he didn't want to be shot.

Suddenly, one of the Secret Service agents sucker punched him. The agent threw a hard roundhouse right that connected with the killer's jaw. I couldn't believe he'd done it, but I was glad.

Jack's head snapped back and he dropped like a stone. Jack was smart. He stayed down. There was no provocation for the agent's punch, no excuse whatsoever — except that the freak sprawled on the ground had murdered the President in cold blood.

Jack shook his head and worked his jaw as he looked up at us from the pavement. "How much do you know?" he asked.

We didn't answer him. None of us said a goddamn word. It was our turn to play games. Now we had a few surprises for Jack.

Chapter 108

JACK WAS ONLY THE BEGINNING. We knew he was only part of the puzzle we were attempting to solve. We had decided to take him down first, but now came the second crucial stop.

As we rode back to his house on Oxford Street, I felt distant from the scene, almost as if I were watching myself in a dream. I remembered the few meetings I'd had with Thomas Byrnes. He'd told us all to have *no regrets,* but that advice didn't work out in the real world. The President was dead, and I would always feel partly responsible, even if I wasn't responsible at all.

I wasn't thinking only about the President's murder. There was thirteen-year-old Danny Boudreaux. I felt an unsettling connection between the two cases. I had from the very beginning. The murders and unprecedented violence were everywhere. It was as if a strange, crippling disease were spreading across much of the world, but especially right here in America. I had already witnessed too much of it. I didn't know how to make the nightmare stop. No one did.

It wasn't over.
We were finally at the beginning of the awful mystery.
This was where it had started.

At this house just coming into view.

Jay Grayer spoke into the car's hand mike. "Dr. Cross and I will go the front-door route. Everyone cover us like a blanket. No shooting. Not even return fire, if you can help it. Everybody clear on that?"

All the other agents were clear on the procedure and knew the stakes. Beartrap wasn't over yet.

Grayer pulled the black sedan up beside the front walk to the house. "You ready for one more shitstorm?" he asked me. "You okay with how this is going down, Alex?"

"I'm as okay as I'm going to be," I told him. "Thanks for keeping me in the loop. I needed to be here."

"We wouldn't even be here without you. Let's go do it."

The two of us got out of his unmarked car and hurried up the red-brick front walkway together. We matched each other, step for step.

This was where it had all started.

The big house, the whole street, seemed so innocent and appealing. A beautiful, white Colonial stood before us. The house had a big old porch supported by column pedestals. Children's bikes were neatly stacked on the porch. Everything out here was so neat. Was it all a disguise? Of course it was.

Jay Grayer rang the doorbell and it sounded like the "Avon calling" bell. *Jack and Jill came to The Hill. . . .* But Jack and Jill started right here, didn't it? In this very house.

The door was answered by a woman wearing a red plaid robe that looked as if it came straight out of the J. Crew catalog.

A grapevine wreath, one of those peculiar, decorative affairs that looks like Jesus' crown of thorns, was hung on the front door for the holidays. It had a big red bow tied around it.

Here is Jill, I was thinking.

Finally, the *real* Jill.

Chapter 109

"ALEX, JAY. My God, what is it? What's happened now? Don't tell me this is a social visit?"

Jeanne Sterling stood just inside the front door of her house. I could see a polished oak stairway glistening behind her. A formal dining room was visible through pocket doors, which were also polished oak. A tall stack of gift-wrapped Christmas presents lay piled near a desk and a six-foot-high standing mirror in the foyer.

Jill's house. The inspector general of the CIA. Clean Jeanne.

"What's happened? I just made some coffee. Please, come in." She sounded as if Jay Grayer and I were a couple of neighbors from just down the street. A social visit, right? She smiled and her prominent teeth made it look like a grimace.

What's happened? Has someone in the neighborhood been involved in a fender bender? I just made fresh coffee. Good as the stuff at Starbucks. Let's chat.

"Coffee sounds fine," Jay said, showing he could chat with the best of them.

We walked inside the house that she shared with her children and her husband. With *Jack.*

I noticed details — everything seemed important, telling, *evi-*

dence. The bright colors and exuberant style on the inside of the house said "American," but the accents communicated "world travel." French etchings. Flemish weavings. Chinese porcelain.

Jill the traveler. Jill the spymaster.

There's an old saying in classic mysteries, which I'd never felt made much sense — *cherchez la femme. Look for the woman.* I had my own catchphrase for solving many modern-day mysteries — *cherchez l'argent. Look for the money.*

I didn't believe that Jeanne Sterling and her husband had acted on their own. I didn't believe it any more than I had ever bought that Jack and Jill were celebrity stalkers. Aldrich Ames had supposedly received two and a half million for exposing a dozen American agents. How much had the Sterlings received for disposing of a troublesome United States president? A loose cannon who had gone against the system?

And who had given them the money? *Cherchez l'argent.* Maybe Jeanne would tell us if we twisted her arm a little, which I definitely planned to do.

Who would gain the most from the murder of President Thomas Byrnes? The vice president, now the president? Wall Street? Organized crime? The CIA? I would have to ask Jeanne about that. Maybe over steaming pewter mugs of coffee. Maybe that was what we could chat about.

She turned and led the way back to her kitchen. She was so calm and collected. I continued to notice the furnishings, the pristine decor, the neatness, even with three kids in the house. I thought that I knew how Jeanne and her husband could afford such a terrific house out here in Chevy Chase. *Cherchez l'argent.*

"There's been some kind of a break, hasn't there?" she said and turned to look at us. "You have me completely baffled as to what it could be. What's happened? Tell me." She rubbed her hands together gleefully. Quite an act. Quite an actress.

"There has been a break," I finally said. "We've found out some interesting things about Jack." We decided to take him down first. Now it's your turn.

"That's excellent news," Jeanne Sterling said. "Please, tell me everything. After all, Kevin Hawkins was one of ours."

We entered a large kitchen, which I remembered from my first visit there. The walls were covered with terra cotta tiles and expensive-looking wooden cabinets. Half a dozen windows looked out on a gazebo and a tennis court.

"We've arrested your husband, Brett, for the murder of the President," Jay Grayer told her in a cold, flat voice. "We have him in custody right now. We're here to arrest you."

"It's so *damn hard* to control every single detail, isn't it? One little slipup was all it took," I said to Jeanne. "Sara made a mistake. I think she fell in love with your husband. Did you know that? You must have known about Sara and Brett's affair?"

"Alex, what are you saying? *What are you saying,* Jay? Neither of you is making any sense."

"Oh, sure we are, Jeanne. Sara Rosen kept a dupe of the footage of Senator Fitzpatrick's murder at her apartment in D.C. Your husband is on the tape. She was in love with him, the poor spinster. Maybe you planned on that. You must have at least suspected it. We even have a partial fingerprint of his at Sara Rosen's apartment in Foggy Bottom. We'll probably find more now that we know what to look for."

Her look darkened, her eyes narrowed into slits. I sensed she might not have known everything about her husband's close "relationship" with Sara Rosen.

She knew about Sara, of course. In the last few days, we had discovered that Sara Rosen had been an Agency spy inside the White House. She had been the Agency's mole there for eight years. That was how Jack had found her, and knew she would be loyal. Sara Rosen had been the perfect Jill. Sara had believed in "the cause," at least as much as she was told about it. She was extremely right-wing. Thomas Byrnes wanted massive changes at the Pentagon and CIA. A powerful group felt the changes could destroy the country, *would* destroy the country. They had decided to destroy President Byrnes instead. Jack and Jill had been born.

Jay Grayer said, "This is going to be worse than Aldrich Ames, you know. Much, much worse."

Jeanne Sterling slowly nodded her head. "Yes, I suppose it will be. I suppose," she continued, her eyes trailing back and forth between Grayer and me, "that you're proud to be a part of the destruction of one of the few, *the very few,* advantages the United States holds over the rest of the world. Our intelligence network was second to none. It still is, in my opinion. The President was a foolish amateur who wanted to dismantle intelligence and the military. In the name of what? Populist change? What a mockery, what a sad, dangerous joke. Thomas Byrnes was a car salesman from Detroit! He had no business making the decisions he was entrusted with. Most presidents before him understood that. I don't care what you believe about us. My husband and I are patriots. Are we clear on that? *Are we clear, gentlemen?*"

Jay Grayer let her finish before he spoke again. "You and your husband are slimy traitors. You're both murderers. *Are we clear?* You're right about one thing, though. I am proud about bringing you down. I feel great about that. I really do, Jeanne."

There was a sudden flare of bright white light in the kitchen! A muzzle flash.

A deafening shot rang out in the most unexpected of places. Jay Grayer's body arched. He fell back against the kitchen counter, knocking over a row of tall wooden stools.

Jeanne Sterling had shot him point-blank. She had a gun hidden in her robe. She'd fired right through the pocket. Maybe she had seen us approaching the house. Or maybe she always had a gun nearby. She was Jill, after all.

Jeanne shifted her feet and turned the gun on me. I was already diving down behind the kitchen counter.

She fired the semiautomatic anyway.

Another deafening blast in the kitchen. A flash of light. Then *another* shot.

She kept firing as she backed from the kitchen. Then she ran. Her robe flew behind her like a cape.

I quickly moved to where Jay Grayer had gone down. He was wounded high in the chest, near the collarbone. His face was drained of color. Jay was conscious, though. "Just get her, Alex. Get her alive," he gasped. "Get them. They *know* everything."

I moved carefully but quickly inside the Sterling house. *Don't kill her. She knows the truth. We need to hear it from her just this once. She knows why the President was killed, and who ordered it. She knows!*

Suddenly, a Secret Service agent came rushing inside the front door. Another agent was close behind him.

Two more agents appeared from the direction of the kitchen. All of them had their guns drawn. Looks of shocked concern were on their faces.

"What the hell happened in here?" one of the agents shouted.

"Jeanne Sterling has a gun. We take her alive, anyway. We have to take her alive!"

I heard a noise in the direction of the front hallway. Actually, two noises. I understood what was happening, and my heart sank.

A car engine was being started.

An electric garage door was being raised.

Jill was getting away.

Chapter 110

MY CHEST was thundering, ready to explode, but my heart had gone icy cold.

Take her alive, no matter what! She's even more important than Jack.

The door to the garage was down a narrow hallway that led past a large sun room. The sun room was awash in blinding morning light. I sucked in a breath. Then I opened the garage door carefully, as if it might explode. It just might, I knew. Anything could happen now. This was the house of dirty tricks.

There was a dark, narrow corridor between the house and the garage. The passageway was about four feet long. I moved down it in a low crouch.

Another closed door was at the end.

Take her alive. That's the one imperative.

I yanked open the second door and jumped out into what I figured had to be the garage. It was.

Instantly, I heard three loud pops. I hit the concrete floor hard.

Gunshots!

Thunderous, scary noise in the confined space. No *thud* of a bullet to my chest or head, thank God.

I saw Jeanne Sterling leaning out of the window of her station wagon. She had a semiautomatic clutched in one hand. I pushed myself up again.

Take her alive! my brain screamed as I ducked out of sight.

I had seen something else in the car. She had her youngest daughter with her. Her three-year-old, Karon. She was using Karon as a shield. She knew we wouldn't shoot with the girl in the way. The little girl was screaming loudly. She was terrified. How could Jeanne Sterling do this to a child?

I crouched behind the oil tank in the darkened, cramped space. I was trying to think straight.

I shut my eyes for a beat. Half a second at most.

I drank in a huge breath of cold air and gasoline fumes. Tried to think in absolutely straight lines. I made a decision and hoped it was the right one.

When I came up again, I fired. I carefully aimed away from the little girl. But I fired.

I went down in the crouch again, hidden behind the dark tank. I knew I hadn't hit anybody.

My shot had only been a warning, a final one. Andrew Klauk had been right when we'd talked in the Sterlings' backyard. The CIA "ghost" was the one who told me all I needed to know right now — *the game is played with no rules.*

"Jeanne, put the goddamn gun down!" I called to her. "Your little girl is in danger."

No answer came back, just terrifying silence.

Jeanne Sterling would do whatever it took to get away. She had murdered a president, ordered it done, helped plan every step. Would Jeanne Sterling really sacrifice her own child, though? For what? For money? A cause she and her husband believed in? What cause could be worth the life of a president? Of your own child?

Take her alive. Even if she deserves to die here in this garage. Execution-style.

I popped up again. I fired a second shot into the car windshield — the driver's side, far right. Glass shattered all over the garage. Glass fragments sprayed against the ceiling, then rained back down again.

The noise was deafening in the closed space. Karon was sobbing and screeching.

I could see Jeanne Sterling through the mosaic of broken windshield glass. There was blood all over one side of her face. She looked startled and shocked. It's one thing to plan a murder, quite another to be shot at. To be wounded. To take a hit. To feel that deadly *thud* in your own body.

I took three fast steps toward the Volvo station wagon.

I grabbed the car door and yanked it open. I kept my head down low, close to my chest. My teeth were gritted so hard that they hurt.

I grabbed a full handful of Jeanne Sterling's blond hair. Then I hit her. I popped Jeanne with a full, hard shot. Same as her husband got. The right side of her face *crunched* as it met my fist.

Jeanne Sterling sagged over the steering wheel. She must have had a glass jaw. Jeanne was a killer, but not much of a prizefighter. She went out with the first good punch. We had her now. I had taken her down alive.

We finally had Jack and Jill.

Her little girl was crying in the front seat, but she wasn't hurt. Neither was the mother. I couldn't have done it any easier, any other way. *We had Jack, and now we had Jill. Maybe we would hear the truth.* No — we would hear the truth!

I grabbed the little girl and held her tight against me. I wanted to erase all this for her. I didn't want her to remember it. I kept repeating, "It's all right, it's all right. Everything is all right."

It wasn't, though. I doubted it ever would be again. Not for the Sterling children, not for my own kids. Not for any of us.

There are no rules anymore.

Chapter 111

THE NIGHT of the capture of Jeanne and Brett Sterling, the television networks were filled with the powerful, highly disturbing story. I did a brief interview with CNN, but mostly I declined the attention. I went home and stayed there.

President Edward Mahoney delivered a statement at nine. *Jack and Jill had wanted Edward Mahoney to be president,* I couldn't help thinking as I watched him address hundreds of millions of people around the world. Maybe he was involved with the shooting; maybe not. But someone had wanted him to be president instead of Thomas Byrnes, and Byrnes had distrusted Mahoney.

All I knew about Mahoney was that he and two Cuban partners had made a fortune in the cable business. Mahoney had then become a popular governor of Florida. I remembered that there had been a lot of money behind his campaign. *Look for the money.*

I watched the dramatic three-ring TV circus along with Nana and the kids. Damon and Janelle knew too much to be excluded from the big picture now. From their perspective, their daddy was a hero. I was someone to be proud of, and maybe even listen to and obey every now and again. But probably not.

Jannie and Rosie the cat cuddled with me on the couch as we watched the nonstop parade of news features on the assassination and the subsequent capture of the real Jack and Jill. Every time I appeared in a film sequence, Jannie gave me a kiss on the cheek. "You approve of your pop?" I asked her after one of her best, loudest smackers.

"Yes, very much so," Jannie told me. "I *love* seeing you on TV. So does Rosie. You're handsome, and you talk real nice. You're my *hee-ro*."

"What do you have to say, Damon?" I checked on his royal majesty's reaction to the strange goings-on.

Damon grinned ear to ear. He couldn't help himself. "Pretty good," he admitted. "I feel good inside."

"I hear you," I said to my young cub. "You want to give me a hug?"

He did, so I knew Damon was happy with me for the moment. That was important to me.

"Mater familias?" I asked for Nana's opinion last. She was propped up in her favorite armchair. She hugged herself tightly as she watched the traumatic news coverage with rapt attention and a snide commentary.

"Not familias enough lately," Nana offered a quick complaint. "Well, mostly I agree with Jannie and Damon. I don't see why the white Secret Service man is taking most of the credit, though. Seems to me that the President got shot on his watch."

"Maybe he got shot on all of our watches," I said to her.

Nana shrugged her deceptively frail-looking shoulders. "At any rate, as always, I am proud of you, Alex. Has nothing to do with the heroics, though. I'm proud of *you* because of you."

"Thank you," I told Nana. "Nobody can say anything nicer. Not to anybody."

"I know that," Nana got the last word in; then she finally grinned. "Why do you think I said it?"

I hadn't been home much during the past four weeks, and we were all hungry for one another's company. We were starved, in fact. I couldn't walk anywhere in the house without one of the kids firmly attached to an arm or leg.

Even Rosie the cat got into the act. She was definitely family now, and we were all glad she'd somehow found her way to our house.

I didn't mind any of it. Not one minute of the attention. I was starved myself. I had a quick regret that my wife, Maria, wasn't around to enjoy the special moment, but the rest was okay. Pretty good, actually. Our life was going to get back to normal again now. I vowed it would happen this time.

The next morning I was up to take Damon over to the Sojourner Truth School. The place was already bouncing back nicely. Innocence has a short memory. I stopped by Christine Johnson's office, but she wasn't back at work yet.

Nobody knew when she would return to the school, but they all missed her like a cure for the flu. So did I, so did I. There was something special about her. I hoped she was going to be all right.

I got home at quarter to nine that morning. The house on Fifth Street was incredibly quiet and peaceful. Kind of nice, actually. I put on Billie Holiday: The Legacy 1933–1958. One of my all-time favorites.

The phone rang about nine. The damn infernal phone.

It was Jay Grayer. I couldn't imagine why he would be calling me at home. I almost didn't want to hear the reason for his call.

"Alex, you have to come out to Lorton Prison," he said in an urgent-sounding voice. "Please come, right now."

Chapter 112

I BROKE every posted speed limit traveling out to the federal prison in Virginia. My head was spinning, threatening to come right off, to smash through the car windshield. As a homicide detective, you need to think that you're strong and that you can take just about anything that's dished out, but sooner or later you find out you really can't. Nobody can.

I had been to Lorton Prison a few times before. The kidnapper and mass killer Gary Soneji had been kept in maximum security there once upon a time.

I arrived about ten in the morning. It was a crisp, blue-skied morning. A few reporters were in the parking lot and on the side lawns when I arrived.

"What do you know, Detective Cross?" one of them asked.

"Beautiful morning," I said. "You can quote me. Feel free."

This was where the Sterlings were being held in custody, where the government had decided to keep them until their trial for the murder of Thomas Byrnes.

Alex, you have to come out to Lorton Prison. Please come, right now.

I met Jay Grayer on the fourth floor of the prison building.

Warden Marion Campbell was there, too. The two of them looked as pale as the institution's stucco walls.

"Oh, *goddamn*, Alex," Dr. Campbell groaned when he saw me approaching. The two of us went back. I took his hand and shook it firmly. "Let's go upstairs," he said.

More police and prison personnel were posted outside an examination room on the fifth floor. Grayer and I filed inside behind the warden and his closest aides. My heart was in my throat.

We had to wear blue surgical masks and clear plastic gloves for the occasion. We were having trouble breathing, even without the masks.

"Oh, *goddammit*," I muttered as we entered the room.

Jeanne and Brett Sterling were dead.

The two bodies were laid out on matching stainless steel tables. Both Sterlings were stripped naked. The overhead lighting was bright and harsh. The glare was overpowering.

The whole scene was beyond my powers of comprehension, beyond anyone's.

Jack and Jill were dead.

Jack and Jill had been murdered inside a federal prison.

"Goddammit. Goddamn them," I said into my surgical mask.

Brett Sterling was well-built and looked powerful even in death. I could imagine him as Sara Rosen's lover. I noticed that the bottoms of his feet were dirty. Probably walking barefoot in his cell all night. Pacing? Waiting for someone to come for him?

Who had gotten inside Lorton and done this? Was he murdered? What in the name of God had happened? How could it happen here?

Jeanne Sterling had pasty-white skin, and she wasn't in good physical shape. She looked much better in tailored gray and blue suits than in the nude.

Above her black pubic hair was a soft roll of paunch. Her legs were crisscrossed with varicose veins. She'd had a nosebleed either before she died or while she was dying.

Neither of the Sterlings seemed to have suffered much. Was

that a clue for us? They both had been found dead in their cells at the same 5:00 A.M. guard check.

They had died close to the same time. According to plan? Of course, according to plan. But whose plan was it?

Jack and Jill came to Lorton Prison . . . and what happened to them here? What the hell happened out here last night? . . . Who finally killed Jack and Jill?

"They both underwent extensive body searches when they were brought here," Warden Campbell said to Jay and me. "This *may* have been a joint suicide, but they had to have help, even for that. Someone got them the poison between six last night and early this morning. Somebody got inside their cells."

Dr. Marion Campbell looked directly at me. His eyes were bleary and wild and incredibly red-rimmed. "There was a small amount of skin and blood under her right index finger. *She fought someone.* Jeanne Sterling tried to fight back. She was murdered; at least, I think so. She didn't want to die, Alex."

I closed my eyes for a second or two. It didn't help. Everything was the same when I opened them again. Jeanne and Brett Sterling still lay naked and dead on the two stainless steel tables.

They had been executed. Professionally. Without passion. That was the eeriest part — it was almost as if Jack and Jill had been visited and murdered by Jack and Jill.

Had a "ghost" murdered Jeanne and Brett Sterling? I was afraid we would never know. We weren't supposed to know. We weren't important enough to know the truth.

Except maybe one tenet, one principle: *there are no rules.*

Not for some people, anyway.

Chapter 113

I ALWAYS WANT everything tied up nice and neat with a bright ribbon and bow on the package. I want to be the mastermind dragonslayer on every case. It just doesn't work out that way — probably wouldn't be any fun if it did.

I spent the next two and a half days at the Sterling house, working side by side with the Secret Service and FBI. Jay Grayer and Kyle Craig both came out to the house in Chevy Chase. I had an idea in the back of my head that maybe Jeanne Sterling had left us a clue to go on — something to get back at her murderers. Just in case. I figured that she was capable of something nasty and vengeful like that — *her last dirty trick!*

After two and a half days, we didn't find anything in the house. If there had been a clue, *then someone had gotten into the house first.* I didn't discount that possibility.

Kyle Craig and I talked out in the kitchen late the afternoon of the third day. We were both pretty well worn to the bone. We opened a couple of Brett Sterling's microbrewery ales and had a chat about life, death, and infinity.

"You ever hear of the notion — *too many logical suspects?*" I asked Kyle as we sipped our beers in the quiet of the Sterling kitchen.

"Not that specific language, but I can see how it applies here. We have scenarios that could implicate the CIA, the military, maybe big business, maybe even President Mahoney. History rarely moves in straight lines."

I nodded at Kyle's answer. As usual, he was a quick study. "*Thirty-five years* after the Kennedy assassination the *only* thing that's certain is that there was some kind of conspiracy," I said to him.

"No way to reconcile the physical evidence — ballistic and medical — with one shooter in Dallas," Kyle said.

"So there's the same goddamn problem — *too many logical suspects*. To this day, nobody can rule out the possible involvement of Lyndon Johnson, the Army, a CIA 'black op,' the Mafia, your outfit's old boss. There are such obvious parallels to what's happened here, Kyle. A possible coup d'état to eliminate a troublemaker in office — with a much friendlier replacement — *LBJ, and now Mahoney* — waiting in the wings. The CIA and the military were extremely angry at both JFK *and* Thomas Byrnes. The system fiercely resists change."

"Keep that in mind, Alex," Kyle said to me. "The system *fiercely* resists change, and also troublemakers."

I frowned, but nodded my head. "I have it in mind. Thanks for all your help."

Kyle reached out his hand and we shook. "Too many logical suspects," I said. "Is that part of the nasty, badass plot, too? Is that their idea for cover in daylight?

"It wouldn't surprise me if it was. Nothing surprises me anymore. I'm going home to see my kids," I finally said.

"I can't think of anything better to do," Kyle said and smiled and waved for me to go on and get out of there.

Chapter 114

I CAME HOME and played with the kids — tried to be there for them. I kept flashing on the face of Thomas Byrnes, though. Occasionally, I saw beautiful little Shanelle Green or Vernon Wheatley or even poor George Johnson, Christine's husband. I saw the corpses of Jeanne and Brett Sterling on those stainless steel gurneys at Lorton Prison.

I worked some hours at the soup kitchen at St. A's over the next few days. I'm "Mr. Peanut Butter Man" there. I ration out the PB&J, and occasionally a little pro bono advice for those more or less unfortunate than myself. I really enjoy the work. I get back even more than I give.

I couldn't concentrate on much of anything, though. I was there, but I wasn't really there. The concept of *no rules* was stuck like a fish bone in my throat. I was choking on it. There really were too many suspects to chase down and ultimately solve the murder of Thomas Byrnes. And there were limitations to how much a D.C. cop could do on such a case. *It's over now*, I tried to tell myself, *except the parts you will always carry with you.*

One night that week — late — I was out on the sun porch. I was scratching Rosie the cat's back and she was purring sweetly.

I was thinking about playing the piano, but I didn't do it. No Billie Smith, no Gershwin, no Oscar Peterson. The monsters, the furies, the demons were loose in my mind. They came in all shapes and sizes, all genders, but they were human monsters. This was Dante's *Divine Comedy,* all nine circles, and we were all living here together.

Finally, I began to play my piano. I played "Star Dust" and then "Body and Soul," and I was soon lost in the glorious sounds. I didn't think about a call I'd had earlier in the week. I had been suspended from the D.C. police force. It was a disciplinary action. I had struck out at my superior, Chief George Pittman.

Yes, I had. I was guilty as charged. So what? And now what?

I heard a knock at the porch door. Then a second rap.

I wasn't expecting company and didn't want any. I hoped it wasn't Sampson. It was too late for any visitors I needed to see that night.

I grabbed my gun. Reflex action. Force of habit. Terrifying habit when you stop to think about it — which I did.

I rose from the piano bench and went to see who was there. After all the bad things that had happened, I almost expected to see the killer Gary Soneji, come to finally get even or at least, to try his luck.

I opened the back door — and I found myself smiling. No, I actually glowed. A light went on, or went *back* on, inside my head. What a nice surprise. I felt much, much better in an instant.

It just happened that way. Pack up all my cares and woes.

"I couldn't sleep," Christine Johnson said to me. I recognized the line I had used once at her house.

I remembered Damon's line, *She's even tougher than you are, Daddy.*

"Hello, Christine. How are you? God, I'm glad it's you," I whispered.

"As opposed to?" she asked.

"Everyone else," I said.

I took Christine's hand in mine, and we went inside the house on Fifth Street.

Home.

Where there are still rules, and everybody is safe, and the dragonslayer is alive and well.

Chapter 115

IT REALLY DOESN'T END — the cruel, relentless nightmare, the roller-coaster ride from hell.

It was Christmas Eve and the stockings were hung from the chimney with care. Damon, Jannie, and I had almost finished decorating the tree — the final touch being long strings of popcorn and shiny red cranberries.

The damn telephone rang and I picked it up. Nat King Cole sang carols in the background. A fresh layer of snow glistened on the tiny patch of lawn outside.

"Hello," I said.

"Why hello. If it isn't Doctor/Detective Cross himself. What a neat treat."

I didn't have to ask who the caller was — I recognized the voice. The sound of it had been in my nightmares for a while — years.

"Long time, no talk," Gary Soneji said. "I've missed you, Doctor Cross. Have you missed me?"

Gary Soneji had kidnapped two young children in Washington a few years back, then he'd led us on an incredible search that lasted for months. Of all the murderers I'd known,

Soneji was the brightest. He had even fooled some of us into believing that he was a split personality. He'd escaped from prison twice.

"I've thought of you," I finally told him the truth, "often."

"Well, I just called to wish you and yours a happy and holy holiday season. I've been born again, you see."

I didn't say anything to Soneji. I waited. The kids had picked up that something was wrong about the phone call. They watched me, until I waved for them to finish up with the Christmas tree.

"Oh, there's one other thing, Doctor Cross," Soneji whispered after a long pause.

I knew there was something. "What is it, Gary? What's the one other thing?"

"*Are you enjoying her?* I just had to ask. I have to know. *Do you like her?*"

I held my breath. He knew about Christine, goddamn him!

"You see, I was the one who left little Rosie the cat for your family. Nice touch, don't you think? So whenever you see the little cutie, you just think — *Gary's in the house! Gary's real close!* I am, you know. Have a joyous and safe New Year. I'll be seeing you soon."

Gary Soneji hung up the phone with a gentle *click*.

And then so did I. I went back to the beautiful tree and Jannie and Damon and Nat King Cole.

Until next time.

The Midnight Club

James Patterson

Time after time, in an acclaimed series of runaway international No 1 bestsellers, James Patterson has delivered breathtaking rollercoaster thrills and incomparable page-turning readability. Now comes a mesmerising tale of non-stop action and suspense.

Nobody knows the underbelly of the city like New York cop John Stefanovitch. He's out to get Alexandre St-Germain, the most powerful member of the Midnight Club – a secret international society of ruthless crime czars, all of whom are 'respectable' businessmen. And Stef's the ideal man for the job – until he's levelled by a blast from St-Germain's shotgun and left for dead.

Now, Stef is back, wheelchair-bound, yet sworn to destroy St-Germain. With the help of a beautiful journalist and a Harlem cop, Stef is determined to crack the Midnight Club. And he's up against odds that are as unknown as they are deadly . . .

'It just might be his best ever.'   *USA Today*

'Guaranteed: you'll devour this yarn-burner in one sitting.'
New York Daily News

'A fast-moving narrative that never lets up. The villain is one of the most awful monsters I've encountered in recent fiction.'   campbell armstrong

'Sleek, fast, skilful and larger than life.'   *Los Angeles Times*

ISBN 0 00 649313 0

Along Came a Spider

James Patterson

The phenomenal international No 1 bestseller.

He had always wanted to be famous. When he kidnapped two well-known rich kids, it was headline news. Then one of them was found – dead – and the whole nation was in uproar.

For such a high-profile case, they needed the top people – Alex Cross, a black detective with a PhD in psychology, and Jezzie Flanagan, an ambitious young Secret Service agent – yet even they were no match for the killer. He had the unnerving ability to switch from blood-crazed madness to clear-eyed sanity in an instant. But was he the helpless victim of a multiple-personality disorder – or a brilliant, cold-blooded manipulator?

As the whole country watched his pursuers falling into his every trap, he knew he had made it – he was controlling the deadly game, and he still hadn't made his most devastating move . . .

'Brilliantly terrifying . . . so exciting that I had to stay up all night to finish it . . . packed with white-knuckle twists.'
Daily Mail

'An incredibly suspenseful read with a one-of-a-kind villain who is as terrifying as he is intriguing. One of the best thrillers of the year.'
CLIVE CUSSLER

'A first-rate thriller – fasten your seatbelts and keep the lights on!'
SIDNEY SHELDON

'Terror and suspense that grab the reader and won't let go. Just try running away from this one.'
ED MCBAIN

ISBN 0 00 647615 5

Black Market

James Patterson

From the author who would go on to create the superbly chilling international bestsellers *Along Came a Spider*, *Kiss the Girls*, *Jack and Jill*, *Hide and Seek*, *The Midnight Club* and *Cat and Mouse* comes an early work of astonishing pace and tension – a breathtaking novel of high finance, international terrorism and irresistible page-turning suspense.

The threat was absolute. At 5.05 p.m. Wall Street would be destroyed. No demands, no ransom, no negotiations. A multiple firebombing – orchestrated by a secret militia group – would wipe out the financial heart of America. Stop the world's financial system dead.

Faced with catastrophe on an unimaginable scale, Federal agent Archer Carroll and Wall Street lawyer Caitlin Dillon are pitched into a heart-stopping race against time, tracking the unknown enemy through a maze of intrigue, rumour and betrayal towards a truly shocking climax.

'The action is fast and furious.' *Wall Street Journal*

'A tough, twisting tale.' *New York Daily News*

'Among the best writers of crime stories ever.' *USA Today*

ISBN 0 00 649314 9

Kiss the Girls

James Patterson

HIS NEW NO 1 BESTSELLER

Along Came a Spider was one of the most talked-about thrillers for years – a phenomenal international No 1 bestseller. Now its memorable hero detective Alex Cross is back – thrust into a case he will never forget.

This time there isn't just one killer, there are two. One collects beautiful, intelligent women on college campuses on the east coast of the USA. The other is terrorising Los Angeles with a series of unspeakable murders. But the truly chilling news is that the two brilliant and elusive killers are communicating, cooperating, *competing*.

'As good as a thriller can get. With *Kiss the Girls*, Patterson joins the elite company of Thomas Harris.'
San Francisco Examiner

'This novel is hard to set aside. Pattterson's complex tale chills, enthrals and entertains the reader in a dazzling and unforgettable reading experience.'
Toronto Star

'James Patterson's *Kiss the Girls* is a ripsnorting, terrific read.'
USA Today

'Patterson hit the ball out of the park with his last go-round, the bestselling *Along Came a Spider; Kiss the Girls* is even better.'
Dallas Morning News

ISBN 0 00 649315 7

Hide and Seek

James Patterson

THE INTERNATIONAL BESTSELLER

First, there was the No 1 bestselling, page-turning *Along Came a Spider*. Next, the electrifying No 1 bestseller *Kiss the Girls*. Now, a breathtaking new novel of terror and suspense which proves, once again, that no one makes the pages turn faster than James Patterson.

Maggie Bradford is on trial for murder – in the celebrity trial of the decade. As one of the world's best-loved singer-songwriters, she seems to have it all. So how could she have murdered not just one, but two of her husbands?

Will Shepherd was Maggie's second husband. A magnificent athlete and film star, he was just as famous. But Will had dark, dangerous secrets that none of his fans could have imagined . . . that his own wife could never have dreamed of.

'James Patterson does everything but stick our finger in a light socket.'   *New York Times Book Review*

'It's interesting to note the point at which the word-of-mouth on a thriller writer becomes urgent recommendation. In Patterson's case, it began with *Along Came a Spider*. This latest will consolidate that esteem. *Hide and Seek* barrels along with an unforced drive. This well-paced novel could be the book that clinches Patterson's position.'
Publishing News

ISBN 0 00 649852 3